Phantom Baby

Phantom Baby © 2016 Sharon Love Cook

All rights reserved. Except for brief passages quoted in newspapers, magazines, radio and television reviews, no part of this book in any form by any means, mechanical or electronic, including photocopy and recording or information retrieval system, may be copied without written permission from the publisher.

This novel is entirely a work of fiction. Though it may contain references to products, places or people, living or dead, these references are merely to add realism to the product of the author's imagination. Any reference within this work to people living or dead is purely coincidental.

Published by Martin Brown Publishers, LLC
1138 South Webster Street
Kokomo, Indiana 46902
www.mbpubs.com

ISBN 13: 987-1-937070-72-4

Praise For This Author

Whether it's a newspaper office or an old-age home, the author manages to inject a convincing sense of reality into her imaginary settings.
--*Kirkus Review, December, 2016*

I'm willing to bet that even Sharon Love Cook's grocery lists would be fun to read. Cherie Jung, Editor, Over My Dead Body!
 --*The Mystery Magazine.*

If you read Janet Evanovich's Stephanie Plum books you want to read this.
--Bonajean McAneney, book reviewer, July 2016

Well written, good plot and my kind of humor throughout. Suzanne Young, author of the Edna Davies Mystery series
Like me, you'll find yourself laughing out loud
--Patricia Gligor, author of the Malone Mysteries

I feel I would be safe in saying that Ms. Cook is likened to a modern day Agatha Christie with her clever and bewitching plot; twists and turns and style of writing.
--Tillie Milwalki, book reviewer, November 2016

Also Published by This Author

The Granite Grove Mystery series:
A Nose for Hanky Panky
A Deadly Christmas Carol
Laugh 'til You Die

Biography:

Sharon Love Cook is the author of the Granite Cove Mysteries. A graduate of Bennington College's MFA Writing program, she's also an art school grad—Montserrat College of Art—and illustrated the Granite Cove Mystery book covers.

Cook grew up in Gloucester, Mass., America's oldest working seaport. Thus her novels have seaside settings, including Phantom Baby. Today she lives north of Boston in Beverly Farms, near the ocean, with husband Oliver, their rescued cats and ancient dog. Ms. Cook is VP of Friends of Beverly Animals.

If you enjoyed this book, please leave a review on Amazon.com. Good reviews are like gift-bearing relatives: always welcome. To contact the author, email her at cookie978@aol.com.

Phantom Baby

Sharon Love Cook

To my husband, Oliver

ONE

Iris woke in the middle of the night with the realization that Shannon was not at home. The heavy stillness of the house, coupled with a mother's instinct, convinced her. She reached across the bed and shook Frank, whose snoring abruptly stopped.

"Wha...? What is it?"

"Frank, Shannon's not home."

"So?"

"She's been out all night."

"What do you expect me to do?"

"Call the police."

He was quiet for so long she feared he'd fallen back to sleep. When he finally spoke, his voice was a growl. "It's three o'clock in the morning, Iris. I have to get up in a couple of hours. You wanna call the police, go ahead."

When his snoring resumed, she rolled onto her side and stared into the dark. Should she call? She pictured herself downstairs in the dark kitchen dialing the Harborvale Police, telling them that her seventeen-year-old daughter had not come home. Before long a cruiser would arrive, silent and ominous in the early light. The young cop—they were all young—would sit at the kitchen table taking notes. He would look at her with expressionless eyes as she talked about Shannon and "the troubles," as she'd come to think of them. For the first time she'd tell a stranger about the drinking, the school absenteeism, the staying out 'til all hours. If the cop appeared sympathetic, she'd cry. Talking about Shannon always did that.

The illuminated hands of the bedroom clock told her it was

3:15. Why couldn't she be like Frank, dead to the world while his only child was out doing God knows what? She listened to the rhythm of Frank's snoring until she could no longer stand it. She would have to get up, if only to pace the hall.

The floor was cold beneath her bare feet. She slowly approached Shannon's bedroom and stood outside, looking in through the open door. Moonlight created a dreamlike serenity. The white satin comforter and wooden bedposts gleamed. Pale curtains shimmered at the window like a bridal veil. She closed the door and headed for the stairs.

In the cold, dark kitchen she slipped her feet into worn canvas flats from a basket by the side door and stepped outside. The wind whipped at her hair. She pulled the cords of her bathrobe tighter and walked through wet grass bordering the driveway. Her car was unlocked. She climbed in and lowered the visor. The Jetta's keys fell into her lap.

She turned to glance through the rain streaked rear window. Where would she go to look for Shannon? As she gazed through the windshield, she saw a small triangular face peering in at her. She wiped the glass with her sleeve. It was Patticake, Shannon's cat. Iris got out of the car. The orange and white tabby flattened itself against her, its wet tail flicking her face. "Abandoned you, too?"

The cat purred its response. Iris carried Patticake into the house.

Upstairs, she stood before her bedroom window. Tender spring leaves, torn from their branches, lay flattened against the panes. When she finally climbed into bed, the sheets were cold. Frank had migrated to the opposite side, his snoring now a muted rumble. In the dark, she heard Patticake climbing up the mattress and settling at the end of the bed. Iris closed her eyes. A branch tapped an insistent message on the window pane. She drifted off to sleep.

"Ms. Camuso, I need an intake eval on a new student," Ms. Dutton, the assistant principal said. "You're seeing him this morning."

"When do you need it?" Iris had hoped to pass the woman's office undetected. Now she slowly approached her desk.

"Today, actually. He's been here two weeks." She flipped through a stack of folders and handed Iris a file with ROLAND T. SMEDLIE typed on a label.

"Why was he admitted so late in the year?"

Ms. Dutton squared the stack before answering. "The boy's history is complicated. You can read it later. Notes from past teachers and headmasters are all inside. According to test scores he's very bright. At fourteen, he should be in high school."

"Why isn't he?"

She shrugged. "His parents don't think he's mature enough. This is his fifth school in two years. The Smedlies are at wit's end."

"No doubt."

"Mr. Tomasillo seems to think you'll establish a rapport." Ms. Dutton opened her desk drawer and pulled out a brownie and tore at its plastic wrap.

Iris tucked the folder under her arm. "I'll do my best."

Bright light streamed from the single tall window in her office. The furniture was functional: a metal desk, two straight wooden chairs, a wastebasket. Stacked around the room's perimeter were huge cartons piled to the ceiling. Her office also served as the school's supply room. As a part-time school counselor, Iris had to accept the situation. At least she had her health insurance.

She took off her blazer. As always the room was stuffy. The old-fashioned iron radiator was still on. To make matters worse, the window was sealed shut from too many coats of paint over the years. She opened the new file. It was stuffed with test results and notes from pediatricians, psychologists, social workers, and Special Ed teachers. The diagnoses were as varied as the specialties: obsessive compulsive and attention deficit disorder, Asperger's syndrome; bipolar. Likewise the medications prescribed. Iris turned to the most recent entry, Ms. Dutton's. The assistant principal's script was childishly round. Her passage concluded with the summation: The family dysfunction continues.

A sharp rap on the door startled Iris. Ms. Dutton stood outside with a tall, husky young man. "Ms. Camuso, this is Roland Smedlie, our new student."

"Nice to meet you, Roland. Come in and have a seat."

"Don't forget that eval," she added, before rushing off.

Instead of taking a seat, the boy headed for the cartons lining the room. This gave Iris a chance to observe him. Roland was neatly dressed, a far cry from the average middle school student. Instead of sneakers, he wore polished loafers. His striped polo shirt was tucked into pressed khaki pants.

"Why don't we get started, Roland?"

He pointed to a carton. "See that toilet paper? It's flimsy. You have to use twice as much." She tapped the chair next to her. "Please sit. How do you know? Do you do the shopping in your family?"

He flopped into the chair. "I help Carl, the superintendent in my building. You know what he calls it?"

"Calls what?"

"Toilet paper."

"What does he call it?"

"Bum wad."

"Carl's got a sense of humor. What do you do to help him?"

"I unpack supplies, put stuff away. I tell him when we're running low. You know, inventory."

"That's a lot of responsibility for someone your age," she said. "I'd like to hear about it, but first let's get a little background." She attached a form to her clipboard. "You've been at Harborvale Middle School for almost two weeks, according to your file—"

"Feels like a month," he said, yanking his shirt out of his pants. "Oh man, it's hot in here."

"I know. I'm sorry. The window doesn't open."

"I'll bet Carl could open it."

"Carl?"

"You know, the superintendent."

"Yes. Well, it's unlikely Carl will show up here."

"He would if you gave him twenty bucks."

"For now we'll have to struggle along. Let me ask you a few questions." She glanced at his file. "You're in Ms. Whitback's homeroom. How is that going?"

"Do you know why the kids call her 'razorback?'"

"I wasn't even aware that they do," she lied. "Can you give me your general impression of your classes so far?"

"Sucks. I want to be tutored at home."

"Why is that?"

He shrugged. "Because everything's there-my TV, my computer, my games. Instead of sitting in school learning nothing, I could be home making money."

"You mean by helping Carl?"

"Not just Carl. I have other jobs."

"Can you tell me about them?"

He counted on his fingers. "I walk Mr. Demitri's corgi in the afternoon. Twice a week I take care of the Vargebedian's macaw. I clean the cage and vacuum birdseed off the rug. The last person's Gloria. I help her put her shoes on, stuff like that."

"Why can't Gloria put her shoes on?"

"She's having a hip operation. It's hard for her to do stuff."

"I take it Gloria's an older woman."

He shrugged. "I dunno."

"Do you have friends in your apartment building?"

"It's not an apartment, it's a condo. I'm friends with Carl."

"I mean your own age. What about your classmates?"

He wrinkled his nose. "Their parents won't let them come over. They say, 'no unsupervised play.' It's so lame."

"Any best friend?"

"Jasper."

"Where does he go to school?"

His loud braying laugh startled her. "Jasper's a corgi!"

She placed a finger to her lips. "Okay, let's move on." The cramped, overheated room had given her a headache. She got to her feet. "I'm going across the hall for some water. I'll be right back."

The teachers' washroom was empty. Iris ran cool water over her wrists and stared at the mirror. Her eyes looked washed out. She pressed a wet paper towel to her lids. Behind closed eyes she saw the words: The family dysfunction continues.

"Ms. Camuso, there you are!"

Iris spun around. Ms. Dutton stood in the doorway, blocking the light.

"I had a headache."

The woman's beady eyes bore into her. "I'm very disappointed. You know our policy. We never leave a child unattended."

"I'm right across the hall. The door's open if anything—"
. . .

"It's a safety issue. We never leave a child unsupervised for any length of time."

She shrugged. "I had to use the bathroom."

"In that case, bring the student to my office. He can wait there."

Ms. Dutton's office was on the opposite side of the building. Iris would lose control of her bladder before reaching the bathroom. "I'd better get back," Iris said, tossing the paper towel in the bin.

But instead of standing aside, Ms. Dutton moved closer. "I have something to tell you."

Iris felt a fluttering in her stomach. Was it about Shannon? Her daughter still hadn't returned home when Iris left for work that morning. "What is it?"

"When I went to your room just now, Roland had opened a carton containing items of . . . personal hygiene."

"Personal hygiene?"

The woman's face flushed. "Feminine products . . . tampons. I caught him putting one in his pocket."

"Did you tell him to put it back?"

"That's not the point."

"He's probably just curious. Roland's a teenager, after all."

"Who could create an unhealthy environment for the children."

Iris sighed. "You'd better take it up with the principal."

"Mr. Tomasillo is at a conference today, but I intend to."

Iris moved toward the door. "I'd better get back to Roland, don't you think?"

Mrs. Dutton moved aside. "When you're through, leave his file on my desk so I can document the incident. I'm afraid I'll have to mention your role, Ms. Camuso."

"Whatever you say . . ."

Late that afternoon, when Iris pulled into the driveway, her heart leaped. Parked in front of the garage was Derek's beat-up van. Normally, the sight would depress her. The boy was typical of Shannon's friends, totally unconcerned about creating a good impression. Today, Iris didn't care. Derek meant one thing, Shannon was home.

She squeezed the Jetta in next to his van and turned off the ignition. Derek lifted his chin in recognition.

Inside the kitchen, she heard hurried footsteps above. Instead of rushing upstairs, she forced herself to open the refrigerator and remove a carton of orange juice. As she poured a glass, she wished it were Chardonnay. Her nerves could use it. She drank the juice and rinsed out the glass. Then she headed up the stairs. Iris knocked once on Shannon's bedroom door.

"Come in."

She pushed the door open. Shannon stood in the center of the room, surrounded by chaos. Clothes were draped across the bed and bureau. Some lay tangled on the floor. She wore faded jeans and a plaid shirt tied at her waist. When she bent over, a band of smooth olive skin appeared above the waistband.

Iris watched her fill a duffel bag that she recognized from summer-camp days. She took a step into the room. "Shannon, your father and I have been worried sick. Where have you been?"

"With friends." She didn't look up.

"You're lucky the school didn't call. I won't lie, you know, and you can't graduate with unauthorized absences." When Shannon didn't respond, Iris pointed to the bag. "What are you doing with that?"

"Packing."

"I can see that. Where are you going?"

"To live with Amber."

"Amber! You mean Alyssa's sister? The one with the baby?"

"That's right. I'm babysitting while Amber's at work."

Iris struggled to keep her voice calm. "Shannon, I don't know what's going on, but don't be foolish. You've got less than two months to graduate from high school."

Instead of answering, Shannon tied the sleeves of a navy sweater around her narrow hips. Then she yanked the cords of the duffel bag and heaved it over her shoulder. With her free hand she removed the elastic band from her ponytail, releasing her long, dark hair. She faced her mother. "I'm not going back to school," she said, and headed for the door.

Iris moved to block her exit. "And I'm not letting you throw your life away."

Shannon's face was impassive. "I'm not staying here, Mom."

"Your father will call the police."

"He won't and you know it. Please move."

Iris clutched her arm. "Why are you doing this to me?" Shannon shook her hand away and walked past her. When she was midway down the stairs, Iris called out, "Please don't leave me!"

Shannon stopped to shift the duffle bag to her opposite shoulder. She looked up at her mother. "I'm pregnant, Mom. I'll work things out myself."

When the front door closed, Iris returned to the bedroom. She scooped up an armful of clothes, intending to put them away. Instead, she dropped everything in a heap and sank to the floor, her head resting against the bed. She felt so tired she didn't think she'd ever get up.

It was six when Frank arrived home. He walked into the dining room and stopped, staring at the table set with china and silver. "Don't tell me it's our anniversary."

"Frank Camuso, you know it's not." Iris lit white tapered candles. "I made a special dinner. Why don't you get washed up?"

"Fine by me. Where's Shannon?"

"We'll talk about that at dinner."

He nodded. "Okay. What smells so good?"

"Roast pork and your mother's stuffed sweet potatoes."

"Ma was the best cook in Harborvale," he said.

"And you never tire of telling me."

"Ask anybody in town. The night before a football game it was a tradition, Ma cooking dinner for the guys. Her lasagna won us the 1979 division."

"I apologize for being Irish and not Italian."

He grabbed her from behind, his arms around her waist. "Hey, you do fine for an Irish broad."

"Thanks a lot." She wriggled from his grip and moved to the kitchen. When she bent to open the oven door, he pressed himself against her. She stood. "Frank, I'm taking the roast out now."

"Shut off again," he said, "Story of my life." Nonetheless, he whistled as he climbed the stairs.

When Frank returned downstairs, dinner was on the table. He'd rolled up his sleeves, exposing the dark hair of his forearms. "We got any Cianti?"

"There's some white wine. . ."

"White's for wimps. How about getting me a beer while I carve?"

She went into the kitchen and poured his beer into a tall glass. "I used fresh ground nutmeg and chopped pecans for the sweet potatoes," she said. "Just like Mama."

They sat across from each other at the table. He gave her a sidelong glance. "Got something up your sleeve, babe?"

"What's wrong with wanting a nice dinner together?"

"Fine by me," he said, lifting his glass in salute.

They ate in silence until Frank reached for a second helping of pork. "Save room for dessert," Iris said. "It's strawberry mousse."

He patted his stomach. "You're fattening me up so you can

have me all to yourself."

"I thought I already did."

"It's a joke, babe," he said. "So, what's the occasion? You get promoted to full time at school?"

"I wouldn't call that a cause for celebration. Part-time is all I can handle right now."

He shrugged. "Wouldn't hurt if they gave you more hours. Goddamn school department takes enough of our taxes."

"I don't want to talk about work, Frank."

"Okay. You gonna tell me about Shannon?"

She took a sip of her wine. "She was here today."

"That so? Nice of her to visit."

"She packed her clothes and left."

He lowered his fork and stared at her. "Left where?"

"She's going to live with Amber."

Frank whistled. "The broad that got knocked up a couple years ago?"

"Amber's settled down. She's a single parent, working and raising her child."

"That broad's trouble, believe me."

"There's more, Frank."

"When Shannon's involved there's always more."

"She said she's pregnant."

When he resumed eating, she said, "Frank?"

"I heard you. Shannon's pregnant."

"Well, what do you think?"

He finished his beer. "I think it's pathetic, if you want to know the truth. I'm not surprised, considering the way she's been coming in at all hours like some tramp."

"Don't say that. Shannon's not a tramp. She's just . . . mixed-up right now."

"Fine, she's a mixed-up tramp."

"It's not funny, Frank."

He stared at her. "Do you hear me laughing?"

"No."

"And do you know why I'm not laughing?"

She shook her head, looking down at her plate.

"Because I'm exhausted, that's why. I'm on the road every day busting my ass just to pay the bills. Last month I lost another account. One of my best customers sold his boat, said he couldn't make a living fishing any more. He's not the only one, let me tell you. I've gotta hustle for new accounts. That means branching out all the way to New Bedford. That's a helluva drive from Harborvale, Iris. If that's not bad enough, Doc Moss says my blood pressure's too high. He wants me to take pills, ease up. What am I supposed to do? I can't afford to retire, that's for sure."

"Frank, don't get yourself all worked up . . ."

"Meanwhile, the princess uses this house as a goddamn hotel. She comes and goes as she damn pleases. How does she show her gratitude? She gets pregnant. Probably expects us to take care of her and the baby." He shoved his plate aside. "Tell me Iris, what the hell do you want me to say?"

"I don't expect you to have the answers, Frank. I just need to know that you and I are supporting each other, that we're a team."

He nodded. "Fine. We're a team."

"Because I've been thinking about the situation, how important it is that Shannon graduates from high school. I work in education. I see what happens when kids drop out. Sometimes they never return to school."

"Shannon's almost eighteen years old. If she doesn't know by now—'

"She's always spoken of going to college. Knowing Shan, she'd be embarrassed showing up at school pregnant. You can't blame her. If that's the case, she could get her GED. After the baby, she could take basic courses at the community college toward a Bachelor's—"

He held up a hand. "Wait a minute. You're saying Shannon should have this baby? This is a girl who can't take care of her cat, for chrissake."

"What's the alternative, Frank? Abortion?"

"It's safer than childbirth, if it's done early. We're not in the dark ages, Iris. Girls have them all the time."

She stared at him. "Frank, it's our grandchild you're talking about. What would your mother say if she could hear you?"

He reached for the bottle of wine, pouring it into his beer glass. "I'm forty-six years old in case you've forgotten. I'm not raising another kid. You're in la-la land for even thinking it."

Iris pressed her fingers to her lips. Things weren't going as planned. "Let's cross that bridge later. For now, Shannon needs time. She's too young to know the best course of action. She could end up making a huge mistake . . . "

Frank watched her. "In other words you're saying we should baby-sit until our daughter gets her shit together?"

"I'll raise the baby, Frank. You won't have to lift a finger."

"Uh-huh. What about your job?"

"I–I can take a leave of absence."

"That's fucking great!" He flung his napkin at the table and leaped to his feet. "I can kiss my retirement goodbye." With that, he charged out of the room.

"Frank, where are you going?"

Seconds later he appeared, red-faced and struggling to zipper his windbreaker. "I hadn't planned on going anywhere. I was looking forward to a quiet evening at home. Guess I was wrong again."

"Stay, Frank. I won't talk about it any more."

"Too late, Iris. You've ruined it."

"Where are you going?"

"To the Dirty Dinghy, if you want to know. People there don't sit around talking about family problems all night."

"I thought marriage was about sharing problems."

"I'm sick of problems. I want a life."

When the front door slammed, she got up and carried the dishes to the kitchen. After wrapping and putting away the leftovers, she dimmed the lights and returned to the dining room. She filled her glass with wine. As the candles burned, she sat in the darkened room. And she waited . . .

TWO

Early the next morning, Iris dreamed of Lily . . .
She and her sister were at Sandpiper Beach, building sand castles in front of the cottage her family had rented every summer. As they worked, they didn't notice the darkening sky, nor the eerie silence that descended upon the shore. Even the seagulls, huddled together, were silent.

When Iris finally glanced at the shoreline, she saw the ominous gray clouds stretched across the horizon. The ocean's surface was glassy. Silhouetted against the clouds, a massive wave rose. In all her summers at Sandpiper Beach Iris had never seen such a wave. She leaped to her feet and looked around to discover that she and Lily were alone. Her sister stopped digging in the sand. "What is it?" she asked, following Iris's gaze. Lily scrambled to her feet and grabbed her sister's hand.

Moments later, their parents appeared on the seawall, clutching the metal railing. They called to her: "Save Lily! Save Lily!" Their cries were blown away by the wind. Iris glanced further down the beach at the set of old wooden stairs against the wall. Could they make it in time? She turned back to the ocean. It was too late to run; the towering wave had reached the shallows. She and Lily would face it together.

She crouched behind her sister, wrapping her arms around her waist and fitting her knees behind Lily's. Above the roar of the wave she yelled for Lily to hold her breath. Seconds before the wave crashed over them, the sisters dived into the dark, churning wall of water . . .

Iris opened her eyes to the sound of running water. She sat

up, her heart thumping. The bathroom door was closed. Frank was taking a shower. She lay back when the door suddenly opened, and closed her eyes. He moved about the room, getting dressed.

Finally, when she heard his footsteps on the stairs, followed by the front door closing, she opened her eyes. Frank was gone, but his heavy cologne hung in the air. She threw back the covers. Her first appointment wasn't until eleven. She had time to visit Grace. Much had happened in the last twenty-four hours. She needed to talk to her friend.

In the kitchen, Patticake appeared and sat beside her bowl. Iris checked the pantry. All that remained in the Friskies bag was an inch or two of dried pellets. When she emptied it into Patticake's bowl, the cat gazed up at her, issuing a silent meow.

"I'll get more this afternoon, I promise," she said, remembering Frank's comment about Shannon's inability to care for her cat.

Harborvale's Main Street was busy that morning. The recent arrival of a Starbucks had invigorated the commercial district. Now merchants competed to lure the customers. Even Harborvale Hardware got into the act. After introducing a line of candles and potpourri they put up a sign, Nails 'n Things.

This didn't sit well with Josie, of Josie's Nail Salon. She filed suit, claiming the sign adversely affected her business by confusing potential customers. Judge Kuszko, however, ruled in favor of Harborvale Hardware. "If folks can't tell the difference between a hardware store and a nail salon, they shouldn't be out shopping."

Not all the merchants supported the downtown's gentrification. Mega Mug hung a sign in their window: Don't ask if we carry skones (sic). Some residents, fearing a rise in property values, wrote fiery letters to the Barnacle, the local newspaper. Others showed their allegiance with bumper stickers proclaiming, Keep Our Harbor Blue (collar). To one and all, the changing downtown was either a boon or a blight for Harborvale.

Now Iris parked across the street from Grace's store. For Your Thighs Only specialized in pantyhose, tights and silk stockings. Located on the fringes of the commercial district, it was situated between a vacuum cleaner repair shop and a senior citizens' clubhouse. Grace was in the back of her store unpacking a carton when Iris arrived. "I'll be right out," she called. "Take a look at the new jewelry."

Iris walked down the center aisle of the narrow shop. It had once belonged to a cobbler, and the smell of old leather and shoe wax hung in the air. One side of the store displayed stockings on pink plastic legs while the other was taken up by Grace's latest addition, a glass case filled with jewelry.

Iris peered at the array spread out on dark green velvet. The cluster of pins—owls, turtles and cats—reminded her of the white elephant table at the Lutheran Church fair.

"What are you looking at?" Grace asked from behind the counter.

"The pins. They remind me of my mother."

"I buy them for the older customers. They don't feel dressed without a big gold pin weighing them down." Grace slid open the door in an adjoining case. "What do you think of this?" She dangled a chunk of green glass on a silver chain.

"It's . . . big," Iris said, tapping her nail against the surface.

"It's sea glass. A woman in Biddeford, Maine makes it for me."

"How do you know it's really sea glass?"

"I have to take my supplier's word," Grace said, shrugging. "Even if it's broken beer bottles from Route One, my younger customers love the stuff. Guys come in and buy it for their girlfriends."

"How much is this one?"

Grace slipped her eyeglasses on to peer at the price tag. "It's one hundred twenty-two. On Newbury Street in Boston it'd go for at least three hundred."

Outside, a van pulled up with a screech of brakes. A set of mechanical stairs lowered to the sidewalk. Seconds later, a cluster of elderly passengers wielding canes and aluminum walkers alighted, assisted by the driver.

Iris turned to Grace. "Looks like we're not on Newbury Street."

Grace laughed. "You think I don't know that? Hell, I can barely afford this low-rent district." She put the necklace back inside the case. "By the way, what are you doing here? Don't tell me the teachers have another day off. Didn't they just have some kind of workshop?"

"I don't have to be in 'til later. I was hoping we could grab a cup of coffee at Mega Mug."

"I can do that," Grace said. "Let me put a sign on the door. If anyone drops by, they know where to find me."

Inside the coffee shop, Grace spotted the last empty booth. She charged across the room, passing a pair of women heading in that direction. Throwing herself into the booth, she grabbed a menu and proceeded to study it as the women stopped to glare.

Iris slipped in opposite Grace after giving the pair a nervous smile. "You just lost two potential customers," she whispered.

Grace studied the retreating pair. "Nah, they look like Hamilton village types. One's carrying a Coach bag. My clients shop at Target."

When the waitress arrived, they ordered coffee and for Grace, grilled English muffins with butter and jam. "None of those plastic jelly packets," she warned. "I want real jam." When their server left, she turned to Iris. "Have you lost weight? You look thinner."

"Maybe, I don't know."

"You don't know? If I lose an ounce, believe me, I know."

"I take after my dad. His side of the family tends to be lanky."

"Lanky is something I'll never be called," Grace said, frowning. "'Jiggly' is more like it."

After their order arrived, Grace asked, "Does this unexpected visit have anything to do with Frank?"

"Actually, it's about Shannon." Iris related the events of the past week.

Grace sat back in the booth. When Iris finished, she said,

"Do you think Derek is the baby's father?"

Iris shook her head. "Derek idolizes Shan, but he's a friend, someone who gives her rides to school or wherever she needs to go."

"Can't blame him. She's a beautiful girl. Do you think she'll tell you who's the father?"

"Maybe in time. Right now she's incommunicado, although I don't think she'll last long baby-sitting for Amber."

Grace sighed. "Seventeen's a crazy age."

"She'll be eighteen soon. At least now she'll need parental consent to get an abortion, and we'd never allow that." She reached inside her bag and removed a pastel pink business card. "I found this on her bureau."

Grace read aloud: "'A Woman's Issue: Nancy A. Proctor, MSW, Director.' Do you suppose it's a clinic?"

"I looked it up online. They don't give much information, just that they offer 'care and comfort for young women facing life decisions.' I think it's an adoption agency."

Grace handed back the card. "That's a hell of a decision for a young girl."

"As far as we're concerned, there's no decision," Iris said. "Shannon will have the baby. I'll help her raise it until she's on her feet."

"How does Frank feel about that?"

She stirred her coffee. "He'll come around."

As they walked back to the store, Grace said, "Let's get together this week, grab a burger and a beer at the Dirty Dinghy."

Iris shook her head. "That's Frank's hangout."

"He's there every night?"

"Not every night. Matter of fact, he'll be staying over in New Bedford Thursday night."

"Perfect. You need a night out, kiddo. Have some fun." Grace patted her back. "You're gonna be okay, hear me?"

Iris managed a smile. "I wish I were as confident."

After school, Iris stacked folders into a plastic milk crate in the trunk of her car. Mr. Tomasillo, the Middle School principal, appeared.

"Ms. Camuso, I want to ask about your session with our new student, Roland Smedlie." He stood close enough that she could smell his lime cologne.

"It went very well. He's a bright, curious young man."

"Do you foresee any difficulty?"

"You know his history. Roland dislikes structure. Basically, he wants to be at home, not at school."

"'To do his own thing,' as you say in this country." His smile revealed even white teeth. "I'm afraid his parents do not agree. They're older. Dr. Smedlie is head of radiology at Massachusetts General Hospital. Mrs. Smedlie is wardrobe curator at a local college. I've told them about your rapport with our students."

"Thank you, Mr. Tomasillo," she said. Although the principal's manner was formal, she felt at ease. The overhead trunk door created a cocoon around them that intensified his scent. She had an urge to press her face into his neck above the white collar and inhale the fresh, lime scent. Instead, she stepped back, keys in hand, to close the trunk.

She was almost home when she remembered the cat food. Patticake would be waiting. She decided to swing into the nearby Mighty Mart. The convenience store charged more, but she'd only buy enough for today.

After selecting a few items, Iris approached the counter, setting her shopping basket down. The stocky young woman at the cash register tossed aside the "Fangoria" magazine she'd been reading and said, "How you doin', Ms. Camuso? Still working at the middle school?"

The girl's heavy makeup didn't conceal the faint acne scars. Iris stared for a moment and said, "Shelley Ruberti?"

"Gotcha. You were my counselor 'bout ten years ago."

"That long?" Iris remembered a sullen, big-breasted girl that the boys teased, though not good-naturedly. Now Shelley wore a black t-shirt with Slayer emblazoned across her jutting chest.

"That's five fifty-five," she said, placing the cat food and milk in separate bags. "Yup, you set me on the right path, Ms. C."

"How is that?"

"Remember the boring stuff my teachers made me read, even though I had learning disabilities?"

Iris handed her a ten dollar bill. "I don't recall specific titles—"

"That's not important. What's important is your advice. You said for every chapter of the boring shit, 'scuse me, I should read a chapter of something I liked."

"Good. It worked?"

"It sure did. I discovered horror and science fiction. I'm so into it, I'm writing a screenplay." She handed Iris her change and slammed the register shut. Leaning against the counter, she said, "Wanna hear the plot?"

Iris hesitated. "If you give me the short version. I've got someone at home, waiting." It wasn't a lie; Patticake was waiting.

"I'll give you the pitch, the one I'm giving agents at the horror writers conference." Shelley boosted herself up onto the counter, her thighs straining the tight jeans. "The title is 'Alien Takeover,' and it opens in an old cemetery where one night, a big glowing rock crashes to earth. Over time it leaks a mysterious fluid. We see the stuff oozing into the ground where below lie the bodies of the people in their graves. The camera moves below the earth, showing the corpses in their coffins. As the fluid seeps into their graves, they begin to stir.

"I've written an awesome description of a corpse opening its eyes. Then the camera moves up, focusing on graves. The grass ripples. Soon fingers stick out of the earth. Eventually, four men corpses climb out of their graves, all covered with dirt and stuff. They head for a nearby pond to wash off. After that, they look pretty good, you know?

"Next, the four zombies show up in town. By this time they look like regular guys, only better looking. They're dressed old-fashioned and they act kinda awkward, but they manage to fit in. When anyone asks, they say they're from Ohio.

"It's not long before the newcomers are romancing the

towns' ladies." She flushed. "I wrote a couple of X-rated scenes that are crucial to the story. See, the living corpses–zombies– were transformed by the fluid that leaked from the rock. Now they're great-looking guys. So, their goal is to have sex with the town's women. It's their mission. The babies born of those unions are aliens from a dying planet, here to populate and take over Earth.

Shelly continued, "Before long, the newcomers are secretly killing off the men of the village with a bacteria that resembles a mysterious flu. The only ones who aren't affected are the kids. They're not fooled by the newcomers. They suspect something from the start. The kids band together to plan an escape before they're killed, too."

She scratched her cheek. "I'm not sure how it'll end. I was hoping to have the kids somehow blow up the aliens."

The store's entrance door swung open and a customer entered. Shelley slid off the counter. "So, Ms. Camuso, what do you think about my screenplay so far?"

"I think you've got a winner," Iris said. "Keep at it."

Iris scooped Patticake from the back steps. The cat's fur was warm from the sun. "Looks like I'm your new mother now," she said, unlocking the door.

The silence in the house was broken by the hum of the refrigerator. Years ago, when Iris had accepted the school counselor position, it was so she would be home when Shannon returned from school. Mother and daughter would sit at the kitchen table and talk over tea and cookies. When Shannon entered junior high, they still found time to be together. Iris assumed they would always be close, unlike her relationship with her own mother.

Thus, when Shannon began pulling away in high school, Iris figured it was temporary. She'd taken enough child development courses to know the symptoms. Yet when her daughter's separation showed no signs of letting up, Iris became impatient. "Can't you spare me a minute?" she'd ask.

Shannon would roll her eyes. "Do you mind? I just got home."

At work there was no one to confide in. The teachers were either recent college graduates, or older and hanging on until retirement. Iris got into the habit of calling Grace after Frank had gone up to bed. Sitting in the darkened kitchen with a glass of wine, she'd discuss the latest indignities, "Shannon's not speaking. Now she's communicating through notes. This morning's read, 'We're out of tofu.'"

"So," Grace said, "what did you do?"

"What else could I do? I bought tofu."

"Next time leave her a note," Grace said. "'Buy your own goddamn tofu.'"

Iris laughed. Grace had a way of cheering her up. "I wish I had the guts to do that."

"Just do it."

While she mixed a vodka and lime juice in the pantry, she heard Frank's car outside. She put the drink on a shelf and closed the cupboard door. Then she moved to the sink and ran water into the basin. When Frank opened the side door, she didn't turn around.

"I'm going to take a quick shower," he said, behind her. "Anything for dinner?"

She half turned. "There's kidney lamb chops in the fridge. They're ten dollars a pound."

"We're worth it," he said, briefly resting a hand on her shoulder.

Out of the corner of her eye she watched Frank climb the stairs. He looked different. He'd let his hair grow; it curled over his collar. His skin was tanned. Shannon had inherited Frank's olive coloring. In the summer the two got as dark as the Portuguese fishermen at the wharf. Iris, on the other hand, burned and peeled.

She washed lettuce in the sink as Frank showered upstairs, stopping occasionally to sip her drink. She was relieved that Frank's mood had improved. Maybe he was embarrassed by the way he'd stormed out the other night. Perhaps during dinner they could talk civilly about Shannon.

She waited for an opportunity to bring up the subject, but Frank surprised her. Five minutes into the meal, he asked, "Any word from our daughter?"

She shook her head. "I don't really expect any."

"Did you call Amber's place?"

"I left a message on her answering machine."

"What about the high school? Have they called?"

"I was planning to call Mr. Bullock to say Shan may not be returning this year." She took a sip of her wine. "If we want to take a stronger stance, we could take out a CHINS petition, as a last resort."

"What's that?"

"It stands for 'child in need of services.' When you file a CHINS, you're asking the Department of Youth Services to take over."

He stopped to consider this and shook his head. "By the time they do the paperwork she'll be eighteen. Waste of time."

"So what do we do?"

"For now? Nothing. Give Shannon more time at Amber's. After changing dirty diapers for a while, she'll be begging to come home."

"Okay." She smiled at him across the table. She and Frank didn't have a plan, but at least they were a united front.

Roland Smedlie was her first appointment the following morning. "Do you have a nickname?" Iris asked when he was seated. "Does anyone call you Rollie?"

"My parents don't like nicknames."

"I see. What classes interest you? And don't say none. Everyone has a special talent."

"When we lived in Boston, I took art classes. I liked drawing with pen and ink."

"Then you must enjoy Ms. Sweetzer, our art teacher."

He wrinkled his nose. "Nah, she makes us do team projects. I hate working with a bunch of dopey kids who can't even draw."

"It must be difficult to be the oldest student. "

"It feels like I'm in grade school."

"Yet I understand that high school isn't an option for you."

"My parents say there's drugs at the high school."

"And you didn't have a good experience at the private school?"

"I don't want to go to any school." He shifted in his chair. "I need to be home. Jasper must be walked at least twice a day. He goes to ty if you don't get him out in time."

"What about your other neighbor, the one who needs hip surgery?"

"Gloria needs help getting ready for her job. She plays piano at a fancy restaurant. And guess what? She used to be a magician's assistant in Las Vegas. I wish my parents would take me to Las Vegas this summer instead of Tanglewood."

"Maybe someday they will. Getting back to Gloria, you said you help with putting on her shoes. Anything else?"

He shrugged. "Sometimes zippers."

"Oh. Zippers."

On the ride home, Iris thought about the Department of Youth Services. Did she have the courage to call them? And if she did, was it retaliation against Shannon or an effort to protect her? Either way, she dreaded the thought of a caseworker nosing into their lives. She imagined a young woman in a trench coat, someone who used professional jargon. She would label the Camuso family "dysfunctional."

Later that afternoon, Iris called Grace's. When her friend answered, she said, "I'm nervous. I have to call Mr. Bullock, the principal at the high school, to tell him about Shannon."

"My God, is that fossil still there? Why don't you wait and see if Shannon comes back tomorrow?"

"Her teachers must be notified so that she gets an 'incomplete' rather than an 'F.'"

"Well if that's what you have to do--"

"I keep thinking about what my mother would say. She frowned on airing one's dirty laundry."

"My mother was the same. Her motto was, 'Die, but don't let the neighbors know it.' My motto is, 'Who the hell cares?'"

"I'm thinking if I call late enough I can leave a message on Mr. Bullock's voice mail."

"Why are you afraid to talk to him? You did everything a parent could do. You attended meetings with Shannon's teachers. You sent her to counseling. This is her problem. She's the one should deal with it."

"Thanks, Grace. I think I'll call him now." Iris hung up and punched in the number of the high school.

"Harborvale Regional High School."

"I'd like to speak to Mr. Bullock, please."

"Who is calling?"

"This is Iris Camuso—"

"Please hold."

An impatient-sounding voice said, "This is Raymond Bullock."

"Mr. Bullock, this is Ms. Camuso. I'm calling to notify you that my daughter Shannon may not be returning to school at this time."

"Shannon's already notified us, Ms. Camuso. She came in earlier to sign a release form."

"Really?" Iris sank into the nearest chair. Unfortunately, Patticake was occupying it. The cat howled in protest. "I'm sorry, sweetie," she said.

"What did you say?"

"I'd like to know what Shannon told you, please."

"I take it there's a communications breakdown between you."

"Mr. Bullock, what did my daughter say?"

"I'm sorry. That's all I'm prepared to mention. It's a privacy issue."

"Mr. Bullock, my daughter is a minor—"

"I'm aware of that, Ms. Camuso. And though I respect your parental role, I'm not comfortable discussing the issue until I have Shannon's permission. Now if you'll excuse me, I've said enough at this time. Good day, Ms. Camuso."

With that, the man hung up.

THREE

The late afternoon sun bathed the Harborvale Elder Housing Center in a warm golden light. Iris parked in the visitors' lot. After locking up, she followed the concrete path that circled the complex. On the way she passed a row of stunted trees and shrubs, battered by the offshore gales.

A red brick building housing the administration office stood in the center of the complex. The two-story structure was once an elementary school; her father had attended in the early 1930s. She pictured him running up the wide granite steps carrying a lunch pail. Fast forward to the present, the little boy is a white-haired man carrying a cane.

She entered the vestibule of her dad's building. An occupant of her dad's floor, a woman he called "the hermit," peered out. Iris waved to her, hoping to be let in. Her dad often didn't hear the buzzer. The woman inched closer to the entrance, watching Iris like a feral cat. Finally, she darted forward and yanked the door open.

"Thanks," Iris called to her retreating back. The neighbor fled to the mailroom, where she watched Iris from around the corner. Iris pressed the elevator button and waited. The lobby smelled of pork-fried rice. When the elevator door opened, she stepped inside, relieved to escape the hermit's scrutiny.

She stepped out on her father's floor to a cacophony of sound: TVs, radios and the whine of vacuum cleaners filled the corridor. Her dad's building housed many disabled residents, such as her father. A stroke victim, he performed many tasks one-handed, his affected left arm immobilized in a sling.

He answered the door. "Iris, it's you."

"Who were you expecting?" She kissed his stubbly cheek and moved inside to the living room.

"A gal from another building, Jeannette. I think she's after me."

"Is that why you look so tired?"

"I'm tired because I can't sleep. My leg's acting up. All night long it aches."

"Did you tell the nurse?" She went into his tiny kitchen. His coffee pot held two inches of murky-looking coffee. Iris emptied the dregs into the sink.

"What are you doing? I made that yesterday."

She rinsed out the pot. "What about the nurse?"

He pulled out a chair at the tiny kitchen table and sat. "Don't get me going on that one. She's supposed to be providing services, but all she does is sit on her can. I'd like to know what they pay her."

"Can't you ask her to look at your leg?"

"I already did. Saw the doctor, too"

"You didn't tell me. What did the doctor say?"

"First he tapped my leg with a little hammer. Then he said I should see a specialist."

"Are you going to? "

"By the time they set up the appointment I could be dead."

"Someone should take a look."

"That's all they do, look."

Iris poured fresh coffee into two mugs. She found a package of molasses cookies in the cupboard and placed three on a plate. At the table, her father poured cream and three spoonsful of sugar into his cup.

Iris bit into a cookie. "These are stale."

"They're good for dunking," he said, and demonstrated. As he lifted the sodden cookie to his mouth, it dropped onto his sling.

She rose. "I'll clean it off."

"Don't worry about it," he said. Iris moved to the sink. She rinsed out an ancient sponge and swiped at the stain. "You look like your mother now," he said. "She was always scrubbing something."

She stopped. "You think I'm obsessive-compulsive?"

"Your mother wasn't compulsive. She just liked to scrub."

"Well I don't." She proved it by tossing the sponge into the sink.

He shook his head. "I'm sorry I mentioned it. Sit and finish your coffee." He stared at her over his cup. "What's wrong? Is it Frank?"

She shook her head. "Frank's got a new account in Fall River. He's going there Thursday, staying overnight."

He whistled. "That's a hike. Must be a big account."

"He said it's a scalloper."

"In Frank's business, you've got to go where the money is."

"He says the money's in recreational boating, not marine supplies. The baby boomers are buying expensive boats. He wants to get in on it."

"Well Frank ought to know. The industry's taken such a beating, I'll never be able to make a living selling fish today." Iris moved to the counter and poured more coffee. "How's Shannon?" he asked, watching her. "I haven't seen her in weeks."

She turned her back. "I was going to tell you. Shannon moved out."

"What?" He turned in his chair. "What do you mean moved out? She's still in high school."

Iris returned to the table, setting her cup down. "She's pregnant, Dad."

"What?"

"I've thought of nothing else all week."

"That's a damn shame. I'm sorry to hear it. How's Frank taking it?"

"Okay, I guess. He doesn't like to talk about it."

"I suppose it's just as well, with his temper. Who's the baby's father?"

"I don't know. She doesn't confide in us. We may call the Department of Youth Services if she doesn't return on her own."

"You do what you have to do. What's wrong with kids today? Thank God you weren't like that . . . you and Lily."

She leaned toward him. "Lately I've been dreaming about Lily."

"Probably because you're worried about Shannon."

"Dad, do you ever have dreams about Lily?"

He was silent for a moment. "After she passed away, I thought I saw her everywhere. Once I pulled my truck over on Main Street. I thought I spotted her standing with a group at the bus stop. I must have looked strange. The people stared at me like I was crazy . . . ."

When it was time for Iris to go, her father hugged her. "Don't worry, you'll get through this."

She rested her cheek against his shoulder. "Sometimes I'm not so sure."

"Life's full of bad patches. After my stroke, I didn't think I'd live a normal life. Now I get around pretty good. Shan will come around, you'll see."

"Thanks, Dad. I'll call when I know more."

"You better."

That night when Frank got home, Iris told him about visiting her father. "He thinks it's okay if we call in youth services."

"Your old man's right for once," he said. "By the way, where's the newspaper?"

"In the TV room. One thing that troubles me, Frank, is the clients the DYS serves. Many are drug addicts with police records. We need to be absolutely sure before taking that step." He moved to the TV room where he picked up the newspaper and scanned the front page. Iris waited. When he didn't respond, she said, "Frank?"

He looked up. "What else are we supposed to do, sign her up for more counseling? She'll just blow it off. Calling the authorities is our only alternative."

"It's a major step—"

"Because we can't go on like this. I'm sick of working my ass off all day only to come home and fight about Shannon." His voice got louder. "Do you think she's losing sleep over us?"

She closed her eyes. Why did their conversations always end with Frank yelling? "I just need to know you support me on this."

Instead of answering, Frank grabbed the remote and clicked on the TV. He raised the volume. When she realized he wasn't going to discuss the issue, she left the room, slamming the door behind her. In the kitchen, she yanked open the freezer. What had she planned for dinner? She was too upset to think. She rummaged mindlessly among frozen plastic containers until her fingers were numb and stinging with cold.

The Dirty Dinghy was Harborvale's most photographed building. Situated on the wharf, it was quintessential New England with its cedar shingles bleached by the salt air. Inside, the walls were covered with driftwood; fishing nets containing wooden buoys hung from the ceiling.

The center of activity was the long wooden bar. Sebastian, the Dinghy's owner, known as "Busty," claimed it came from a Hong Kong brothel, although sometimes he said Trinidad. Whatever the case, the Dinghy was an authentic seamen's bar.

It was a far cry from the Regatta down the street. That bar attracted the trendy sailing crowd. The Regatta's tables were sealed in polyurethane. They offered a martini menu. In the parking lot, patrons' cars sported nautical flag decals.

Iris entered the Dinghy's side door and was immediately engulfed in an aroma of beer and fried fish. She glanced around and spotted Grace sitting at a tall wooden booth in the bar section. She crossed the room, dodging waitresses holding trays aloft. Slipping into the booth, she eyed Grace's tall, frothy green drink. "That looks delicious."

"A Margarita," Grace said, sipping from a straw. "Have one."

"I'll stick with white wine."

"Boring," Grace said, running a finger around the salted rim of the glass. "One of these nights you and I will have a pajama party. Not one of those girly events where women do their nails and eat chocolates. We will get drunk and make prank phone calls to every asshole in Harborvale."

Iris shook her head. "That's a lot of calls."

"Speaking of which, how's Frank?"

"He froze me out last night when I tried to talk about Shannon. He says he's sick and tired of coming home and arguing about her."

"It's not like you enjoy it. You're her parents. You have to deal with it."

"I know." Iris looked around. "Where's the waitress?"

The bartender, catching Iris's glance, leaned over the bar. Her breasts were like over-inflated pink balloons in the low-cut tank top. "What'll you have?" she called.

"Chardonnay," Iris said.

The bartender poured one-handed from a gallon jug. She pushed the glass across the bar, saying, "Come and get it."

"Charming," Iris muttered, sliding from the booth. When she returned with her drink, she said, "Have you ever seen such fake boobs? And those pants are so low, I wonder what's keeping them up."

Grace craned her neck to study the bartender. "I dunno. If I had her butt I'd wear low riders too. I'm destined to a lifetime of granny jeans."

"What are you talking about?" Iris said. "You're fit."

Grace shook her head. "I could exercise until they lowered me into the ground. I'd never have a decent butt. It's my family's DNA. We missed out on the nice ass gene."

"You look good," Iris said. "And besides, you're—"

Grace raised a hand. "Don't say it."

"Say what?"

"I'm big boned. I've been hearing that since fifth grade: 'Grace is a big-boned gal.' It makes me feel like Sasquatch."

Iris shook her head. "The word is statuesque, as in goddess."

"Thank you, ma'am. You know what?"

"What?"

"You're full of crap."

As they laughed, an elderly man at the bar turned and lifted his glass to them. Grace returned the gesture. "You see? Laugh and the world laughs with you."

"Cry, and you cry alone," Iris looked moodily into her glass.

"Hey, what happened? You look about to cry."

"I was just thinking there's not much laughter in my life right now," Iris said. "I feel like my family's breaking up. I can't count on anyone anymore." When Grace stood and slid out of the booth, Iris looked up. "Where are you going?"

"I am going to order two Margaritas. You are going to drink one."

Later, over fried scallops, Grace said, "I'm really surprised that Shannon's friend Amber has a kid. Wasn't she a beauty queen a few years back? I remember seeing her picture in the papers all the time."

"She was Tuna Tournament Queen one summer."

"Didn't she marry some guy with big bucks?"

"Rusty Spaglione, aka, Rusty Spags. He owned a string of party boats he called the Amber Fleet. At one time he was Frank's best customer."

"What happened to him?" Grace reached for Iris's untouched container of tartar sauce and scooped it on top of her remaining scallops.

"One night Rusty was coming back from a charter fishing trip with a group of guys onboard. One member of the party was Roger Kipper, our former superintendent of schools."

"Wasn't he the one that got caught peeking in the girls locker room?"

Iris nodded. "Mr. Kipper had a drinking problem. They didn't renew his contract. Anyway, they'd been out all day, drinking and fishing. Coming in, it was dark. Mr. Kipper fell overboard. No one saw a thing, although some thought he'd jumped."

"I remember," Grace said. "His body washed up on Sandpiper Beach a couple of days later. It put a damper on the senior citizens' annual cookout." She paused. "Didn't his daughter sue?"

Iris nodded. "Marge Kipper had a grudge against the town anyway for firing her dad over the locker room scandal. She needed to blame someone. She hired Vincent Tosi, who'd just opened a law practice here in Harborvale. Marge was one of his first clients. Vinny went after Rusty. He proved negligence. For one thing, the passengers on his boat weren't all wearing life jackets, including Mr. Kipper. Rusty was casual about regulations."

"He certainly paid for that," Grace said. "And Amber didn't exactly stand by her man, did she?"

"When they repossessed her Mercedes convertible, that was the last straw. She took the baby and fled. Last I heard, Rusty had moved to Sitka, Alaska."

What's Miss Amber doing now?" Grace asked.

"She's a receptionist at the Hemlock Point Yacht Club," Iris said, "where a few summer residents moor their boats."

"Knowing Amber's background, she's got her eye on some rich old captain. Are you going to call Shannon at Amber's?"

"Frank says we should wait. I want Shannon to know we can work things out as a family. After the baby's born, I could baby-sit while she gets her GED. "

Grace stirred her drink with her straw. "You could end up baby-sitting for a long time."

Iris shrugged. "It's my grandchild. I wouldn't mind."

"You're too cute to be a grandmother," Grace said.

"God works in mysterious ways."

When Iris got home that night, Patticake was huddled on the back steps. The cat rubbed against her legs as she unlocked the door. In the kitchen, Iris spooned Fancy Feast into a bowl and set it on the floor.

After hanging up her jacket, she went to the pantry. She made a vodka and cranberry juice and carried it upstairs. It was nice having the bedroom to herself. She put on her flannel nightgown and got into bed, setting the drink on the nightstand.

The room, having been closed all day, was stuffy. She got up to open the window, stepping over a pile spilling out from the bottom of Frank's closet. Frank always made a mess when he packed. With her slippered foot, she attempted to shove everything back inside, but the closet door wouldn't close.

She sank to her knees and peered inside the closet. Rubber boots, sneakers, sample PVC fishing gloves and socks lay in a tangle. Under the mess was Frank's tackle box. She dragged it out. The scarred metal relic had once belonged to Frank's father. She tossed the junk aside and opened the lid. The upper compartments held fishing lures, spools of twine and hooks. The now-tarnished silver flask she'd given to Frank on their tenth anniversary was nestled in its own compartment.

She attempted to open the lower compartment but something–an envelope—prevented it from opening. She located the long tweezers in the bathroom. Yanking on a corner, she managed to pull a small manila envelope from the box. She pried open the prongs of the clasp and shook out the contents. It was a photo. A woman in a metallic-gold bikini grinned at the camera. One hand gripped a fishing pole, the other a Sam Adams beer bottle. Her tanned and oiled breasts strained the material of her bathing suit. And though the copper-streaked hair was tucked inside a Red Sox baseball cap, Iris recognized the subject.

It was the bartender from the Dirty Dinghy.

FOUR

Her first counseling session the following morning was with Roland. "Did you do anything interesting this weekend?" Iris asked as he settled into the chair. He yawned. "My parents dragged me to the Boston Symphony."

"Your parents are music lovers?"

"Yeah. Sometimes they go to New York City. That's worse, 'cause we have to stay overnight at a hotel."

"Isn't it exciting, being in the big city?"

He gave her a withering look. "With your parents?" Before she could answer, he said, "Guess what, Ms. Camuso?"

"You tell me."

"I'm starting a new business."

"Doing what?"

He folded his arms across his chest. "Washing dogs. I got the idea a month ago, but had to wait for Carl to give me the okay."

"Carl, the superintendent of your building?"

"Uh huh. He said I could use the basement sinks if I give him half of what I make. I get to keep the tips."

"Well, I guess that's fair," she said, withholding what she really thought about the arrangement. "Do you spend much time with Carl . . . in the basement?"

He rolled his eyes. "Do you mean is he a perv? I'm not a baby, you know."

She laughed. "No, you're not. I have to ask. Part of my job description. Now about your new business, have you gotten any clients?"

"Not yet. I'm still putting up flyers. It's called the Clean Canine Club. I charge five bucks for a basic wash and dry. After ten visits, you get one free. Later, I'll offer extras, like conditioner and stuff."

"Roland, you're a born entrepreneur. What do your parents think?"

"I didn't tell them."

"Why not?"

"They won't like it. They'll say I'm supposed to be studying to get into prep school."

"What does Gloria think of your dog-washing business?"

"Haven't told her. She's got an appointment with a bone doctor this afternoon."

"Bone doctor?"

"For her hip, remember? She's having an operation."

A sharp rapping interrupted their conversation. Ms. Dutton peeked around the door. "Excuse me, Ms. Camuso. I wonder if you're free for Roland's IEP next Tuesday at ten?"

Iris pulled out her calendar and scanned the page. "That's fine."

"What's an IEP?" Roland asked after Ms. Dutton had gone.

"It stands for Individual Education Plan. All the teachers and professionals who are working with you have a meeting to give their input."

"Sounds boring," he said.

"They can be informative," she said, although she considered IEP's to be mental torture. The meetings tended to run on, each participant vying to appear more erudite than her colleagues.

Later, as Iris sipped coffee in the teachers lounge, Mr. Tomasillo entered. "Ah, Ms. Camuso, I hoped to find you here. You had a session with Roland this morning. How are things progressing?"

"He speaks freely with me, but he's not really enjoying his school experience."

He nodded, serious. "He's been neglecting his assignments.

His parents are speaking of sending the boy to a military school. They've tried everything. Of course I don't have to remind you this information is between the two of us."

"Of course." She paused, measuring her words. "I don't think Roland will react positively to that idea. He enjoys his freedom too much."

"Perhaps he has too much freedom. The Smedlies have arranged for a neighbor to keep her eye on him after school."

"This neighbor, the name's not Gloria, is it?"

He looked surprised. "Did Roland mention Gloria?"

"From time to time. He mentions other neighbors as well. Why do you ask?"

"The Smedlies have forbidden Roland to see her. They feel the relationship is not . . . wholesome." He laid a hand on her shoulder. "Let's say a prayer that the family finds resolution for these issues, shall we?"

"Right now?" She set her coffee cup on the table.

He smiled. "No, later, when you are alone. I sense you are a person of great compassion."

She felt the warmth of his hand through her thin sweater. "I'm just doing my job." She never felt uncomfortable with Mr. Tomasillo despite the fact he tended to stand too close. Perhaps his views regarding personal boundaries were more liberal.

Now his brown eyes looked into hers. "I've just learned that the district Social Services Coordinator plans to retire. I'd like to recommend you for the position, Ms. Camuso."

"You're nice to mention it, Mr. Tomasillo, but at the moment I have too much going on in my life."

"Please, call me Tomas."

"Tomas."

They gazed at each other until the door abruptly opened and a loud voice announced, "Someone said there's baklava in here." With that, Ms. Dutton charged into the room.

Mr. Tomasillo stepped away. "We were discussing Roland Smedlie."

The woman gave no sign of hearing as she rushed toward a large rectangular pan. Ripping back the foil cover, she exposed the honey-glazed confection. She grabbed a plastic knife and cut a large square. She bit into it, her hand cupped under her chin to catch the crumbs.

Mr. Tomasillo turned to Iris. "I must go. Think about that position I mentioned, will you?"

When the door closed behind him, Ms. Dutton stopped chewing long enough to ask, "What position is that?"

"The missionary position," Iris longed to say, but didn't; Ms. Dutton wasn't known for her sense of humor. "It's just a job opening in the district."

The woman carefully licked her fingers, staring at Iris. "Oh? Which opening is that?"

Iris tossed her cardboard cup into the wastebasket. "Not sure. You'll have to ask Mr. Tomasillo." She hurried from the room before Ms. Dutton could question her further.

That afternoon, she parked at a downtown gas station. She looked around before heading for the public phone hanging on the wall outside. It was one of the few left in town, a scarred and spray-painted relic from the past. She dropped two quarters into the slot and dialed the number she'd written on a slip of paper.

"Dirty Dinghy," a man said.

"I'd like to be connected to the bar, please."

She waited a long time before another man answered. "This is Lou."

Iris put her hand over the mouthpiece and lowered her voice. "This is Coral, the beauty supply representative. I'd like to speak to the bartender who was working last night. She ordered some things from my catalog that I learned are discontinued. I didn't get her name or phone number."

"Last night? That'd be Val . . . Valerie Moles. She won't be in 'til tomorrow. Give me your number. I'll have her call you back."

"Never mind. I'll come in and drop off the new catalog."

She hung up and returned to her car. The woman in the photo now had a name. Iris wondered how long Frank had known her. Was Valerie Moles a girlfriend? Why else would he keep a photo hidden in his tackle box? She pictured him sitting on the edge of the bed in his boxer shorts staring at the image of Valerie Moles. The thought made her nauseous.

She drove home along the scenic shore route, catching glimpses of the ocean. On impulse, she pulled into the tourists' viewing area, a small, unpaved lot. The only other vehicle was a bread delivery van. Its driver appeared to be dozing, his head thrust back on the seat.

Iris got out of the Jetta, dropping the keys into her sweater pocket. She scooted under the rope fence and made her way across the rocks until she came to the point. There she sat, her legs bared to the sun's rays. The tide was receding, exposing thick, wet seaweed that clung to the rocks. On the horizon, a tanker slowly made its way through the mist.

She breathed the salt air, feeling her tension receding. Being near the ocean put everything in perspective. She vowed not to let Frank's behavior poison her mood. It was nothing new, after all. Hadn't she known of his wandering eye when she married him? Nonetheless, she'd hoped that family life and the passing years would change him. So far it hadn't. Meanwhile, her fears, like buoys on a stormy sea, kept bobbing to the surface.

The first time she'd become aware of Frank's secret life was during their vacation at Sandpiper Beach. Once again they'd rented "Sundowner," a small white cottage with green shutters. In the tiny rented bungalow behind them lived Claudia, a single parent, and Travis, her son. Shannon became immediate friends with the boy, also six years old.

While the children splashed in the tidal pool, the two mothers got acquainted. Claudia, an attractive OR nurse, had been divorced for three years. She and Trav lived in Lee, in the western part of the state. She entertained Iris with outrageous stories about the doctors and nurses at her hospital. Iris warmed to Claudia's candor and lack of pretense.

Meanwhile, the other mothers at the beach drew their chairs into a tight circle. Although they greeted Iris, they ignored Claudia. She in turn laughed at their disapproving stares, calling them the "speckled hens." Of this group she said, "They don't like me because I'm a single parent, a reminder of what could happen to them."

"They don't like you because you look great in a bikini," Iris said, "and they secretly envy your independence."

Claudia stretched her long, tanned legs, wiggling her toes in the sand. "I earned my independence. I wouldn't trade it for anything."

On weekends, Frank arrived. He cooked burgers on the front porch, manning the grill in his colorful surfer jams, a beer can in one hand, a giant spatula in the other. Often Claudia and Travis joined them for an impromptu dinner. While the kids rode bikes up and down the boardwalk, the adults sat on the porch, drinking beer and wine. Frank and Claudia shared stories about growing up Italian.

"We used to have at least a dozen people for dinner every Sunday," Frank said. "For Thanksgiving, no less than thirty." When Iris groaned at that claim, he said, "Pardon my wife. She's an only child who doesn't understand big families."

"I'm not an only child," Iris said. "I had a younger sister."

"What happened to her?" Claudia asked.

"She died in childhood."

"You poor kid," Claudia said, reaching out to stroke her arm.

"That was long ago," Frank said. "Honey, wanna get the buns from the fridge?"

After dinner, Claudia carried a sleeping Travis back to their cottage. Iris and Frank remained on the porch. An August moon cast a silver path on the water.

"She's nice," Frank said.

"I'm really sorry they're leaving soon," Iris said. "It's been great for Shannon and me, having friends at the beach."

Before long a heat wave descended upon New England. Weather forecasters called it "triple H" weather—hot, hazy and humid. The beach filled up with day-trippers who trudged across the sand laden with gear like a desert caravan.

A weary Frank appeared Friday evening, lugging a cooler

filled with fresh swordfish. Iris invited Claudia and Travis to join them for dinner. They set up a table on the porch. While the kids played on the beach, the grown-ups drank Frank's homemade sangria.

Claudia, in faded cutoffs, sat on the porch railing swinging her legs back and forth. She gazed at the long stretch of beach and sighed. "I can't bear to think I'll be back at work in a few days, far removed from all this."

"All the more reason to enjoy every minute," Frank said, getting up to brush lemon and olive oil over the swordfish. "Have another sangria. I have a fresh batch in the fridge."

Claudia swallowed the remains of her drink. "Good thing our cottage is close. Trav will have to guide me home." She opened the screen door and went inside.

Iris, who was watching the children through binoculars, said, "I'm going down to speak to the kids. It looks like they've found a dead fish on the beach."

"Ah, leave them alone," Frank said, waving away the smoke. "Let them have fun."

"Frank, bacteria can be deadly," she said, kicking off her sandals. "I'll be right back."

However, she wasn't right back. First she had to convince the children that the flounder was dead and needed to be buried. Then she helped to dig a hole and wait as they recited prayers for the fish. When she finally returned to the cottage, the front porch was empty. The swordfish, nicely browned, lay on a platter.

While the children washed their hands and feet in the outside spigot, Iris went inside, letting the screen door slam behind her. She found Frank and Claudia in the kitchen. Frank was peering into the fridge while Claudia stood before the open cupboard. "I'm searching for a nice bowl for the potato salad," she said, glancing at Iris.

"You won't find any. All we have is plastic."

"Forget the bowl," Frank said, slamming the refrigerator door. "At the beach we rough it. Paper plates are fine." He carried a fresh pitcher of sangria to the porch. Iris noticed that Claudia's glass was empty, even though she'd come inside for more.

"I'll set the table," Claudia said. "I'm famished."

The next morning, when Iris and Shannon appeared on the beach, Claudia and Travis were already settled. As the children raced to the tidal pool, the mothers followed, dragging their beach chairs. "Frank sleeping in?" Claudia asked, unfolding her chair and stretching out. When she turned her face to the sun, Iris noticed she wore bronze lipstick that matched her tan.

"Uh huh, and when he gets up he'll dirty every pot in the kitchen just to fry one egg."

"At least he cooks," Claudia said. "My ex repeatedly asked me how to operate the stove, like he was a guest in the house."

"I guess I've gotten set in my ways this summer. Shan and I have our little routines. Because there's no dishwasher, we clean up right away. When Frank arrives, it's like a hurricane's hit. He piles clothes on the furniture, hangs his wet bathing suit on the kitchen chairs. He comes into the house with feet covered with sand, no matter how often I ask him to brush them off. " She sighed. "Don't get me wrong, I'm happy when Frank's here, it's just that—'

Claudia placed a warm hand on her arm. "Don't apologize for being the way you are. You're a neatnik and Frank is not. As for wanting your space, everyone needs time alone."

Iris stared at her friend. "I'm going to miss you, Claudia."

"The speckled hens will welcome you back," she joked.

"Sure," Iris said, "to talk about soccer and car pools."

"I'll miss you, too," Claudia said. "But we can e-mail each other. The town of Lee isn't exactly the end of the earth. Maybe you and Shan can come for a weekend to ski this winter."

"We'd love that."

The sun was directly overhead when Frank, lugging the cooler, descended the wooden steps to the beach. "Anyone ready for lunch?" he called out.

Shannon raced to him. "Daddy, can Travis eat with us?"

"He certainly can. There's peanut butter and marshmallow sandwiches for you guys and lobster salad for the grown-ups." He handed out plastic glasses. "We have Kool Aid for the kiddies, wine for the ladies, and beer for the chef."

Claudia accepted a plastic cup. "I really shouldn't. You've been so generous to us this summer while I haven't had you over once."

"No one's keeping score," Frank said. "Just for the record, what kind of cook are you?"

When his mother hesitated, Travis piped up, "She makes good hot dogs and Spaghetti-Os."

"That's not fair, Trav," she said, laughing. "We had chicken pie the other night."

"Frozen chicken pie."

She shrugged. "*Mea culpa.* I'm an Italian who can't cook. At least Travis shows no sign of rickets."

"It's okay, Mom," he said, resting his sandy head on her shoulder. "I love Spaghetti-Os and hot dogs."

"He's a good kid," Frank said, filling her glass. "You've done a great job."

Claudia blushed under her tan. "Thanks."

After lunch, Frank got to his feet. "I'm ready for a swim. Who's coming with me?"

Shannon scrambled to her feet. "I am, Daddy."

"Frank, wait," Iris said. "Shannon's getting too much sun. I want her to come inside for a nap."

"I don't want to take a nap," she whined. "I want to play with Travis."

Iris sighed. "In that case I'm getting the umbrella. You two can play under it."

Claudia got up, brushing sand from her thighs. "I'll help you."

"It's no problem," Iris said. "The umbrella's lightweight. You stay and swim, keep an eye on them."

She skipped over the hot sand and up the wooden stairs. The umbrella stood in a corner of the back porch. She carried it to the front yard, placing it on the ground. The afternoon sun bore down; she decided to grab a hat.

Inside the cool, darkened living room, she sank onto a wicker chair. She was grateful to be alone for a moment, out of the sun, away from the crowds. Frank's impromptu picnic had forced her to remain too long on the beach. Now the wine had given her a headache. She went into the bathroom for aspirin. The tip of her nose, seen in the medicine cabinet's mirror, looked like a ripe strawberry.

"Scottish coloring," her mother had proudly called it. Years ago, when vacationing at Sandpiper Beach, her mother had avoided the sun. While Iris, Lily, and their dad splashed in the surf, she sat on the front porch. In her wide-brimmed hat and flower-print dress, she'd looked like someone from another era.

Back in the living room, Iris stopped before the picture window. She picked up a pair of binoculars. Gazing through the lenses, the beach was a colorful kaleidoscope; umbrellas of every hue. She adjusted the focus and scanned the sand until she spotted Shannon and Travis playing in the knee-deep tidal pool.

She moved the lenses outward to the shoreline. The tide was low. After searching the few people standing at ocean's edge, she spotted Frank and Claudia standing waist deep in the water. Iris adjusted the focus, bringing them in closer. She saw Frank turn to Claudia and lift a strand of wet hair from her face. The two stared at each other . . .

Five months later, on a winter morning, Iris brought her car to Harborvale Auto Detailing. One of Frank's clients had given him a Christmas present—two gift certificates for auto detailing. After Frank's car had emerged looking shiny and new, Iris made an appointment for hers.

"It'll be ready at three o'clock, Mrs. Camuso," the shop manager said. "Will you need a ride home?"

"That would be nice."

"I'll get one of the guys to take you. By the way, I've got something for your husband. Wait a sec." He disappeared inside and returned with a crisp, white paper bag, stapled shut. "My guys were supposed to leave this in his trunk, but it got left out."

"What is it?" she asked, taking the bag.

"Just stuff we found inside the car. You know, gum, matches, coins. I tell my men to save everything 'cause you never know. Once we found a lottery ticket under a seat. Turns out it was worth $1,000. The car's owner almost kissed me."

"Thanks," she said. "I'll give it to him."

Back home, she emptied the bag's contents onto the bed. Out fell a quarter and two dimes, a half pack of breath mints, three cocktail napkins from the Dirty Dinghy, a dental pick, and a dried up tube of Blistex. She shook the bag again and a crumpled slip of paper fell out. Iris smoothed it out and peered at the faint print. It was a receipt from the Massachusetts Turnpike Authority. According to the printout, someone had paid a $1.25 toll at exit sixteen in Lee, Massachusetts on October 15, 1990.

Iris went down the hall to Frank's study. According to his desk calendar, Frank had attended a boat show at the Worcester Coliseum on that date. Iris remembered the circumstances surrounding the trip. The weather forecast had predicted snow for Sunday. She'd wanted him to return home Saturday night, but Frank had other ideas. "I'll be entertaining clients all day," he complained. "You don't want me drinking and driving on the Turnpike. I lose my license, there goes the business." In the end, Iris agreed that Frank should stay overnight.

That evening, as Frank read the newspaper in the TV room, she approached and handed him the receipt. "What is it?" he asked, squinting at the faint print.

"It's a receipt from the Mass Turnpike, dated October fifteen. Harborvale Auto Detailing found it in your car. As I recall, you were supposed to be at the boat show in Worcester on that day." She paused and added, "Lee's an hour away from Worcester."

He scratched his chin. "Right. Now I remember. I visited a client in Lenox, the town next to Lee."

"Frank, you sell marine supplies. Since when do you have customers in the Berkshire?"

"I told you about Jackie Burkhardt, the guy with a summer place at Lobster Cove? He's been searching for a Boston Whaler they don't make anymore."

"You never mentioned visiting Jackie when you got home. Lenox isn't exactly a stone's throw from Worcester."

"God's sake, Iris. Do I tell you every time I take a piss? It was no big deal. I met someone at the boat show who had the kind of boat Jackie wants. I decided to reach Jackie before someone else did. A lot of business you can't do over the phone. Selling that boat would bring in one helluva commission."

"Did he buy the boat?"

He shook his head. "The owner dragged his feet, pissed Jackie off. We're gonna wait 'til summer and look around."

"I see. I guess I was a little suspicious when I saw you were in the Berkshires. It's a coincidence, since Claudia lives in Lee."

"Who's Claudia?"

"Frank Camuso, don't tell me you've forgotten our neighbor at the beach."

"Oh, yeah, I remember. Nice broad. Kinda sloppy, though."

When he resumed reading his newspaper, Iris hesitated. Frank hadn't handed back the receipt. She wanted it for evidence, yet felt foolish asking. In the end, she decided not to make an issue of it. Nonetheless, she'd learned two things: that her husband was a skillful liar who couldn't be trusted.

When she got home, Frank was upstairs unpacking his suitcase. She sat on the bed and listened to his complaints about the New Bedford trip, how he'd been forced to conduct business from the Holiday Inn. "Some of the downtown bars are so tough I wouldn't go if the drinks were free."

She told him about her evening with Grace at the Dirty Dinghy.

"You went there?"

"For dinner. It was kind of fun."

Frank raised an eyebrow. "Babe, the Dinghy at night is no place for nice people."

"That doesn't stop you from going."

He shoved his empty suitcase under the bed. "I'm a guy, and I go there for business."

"The bartender was this trampy-looking woman with ridiculous implants."

"That so?" He gathered his dirty clothes and carried them to the bathroom laundry hamper.

"Do you know the one I'm talking about?" she called, watching him. "Her name is Val something."

He returned and without glancing her way, opened his closet door. "I'm not sure. They have a big turnover with staff."

She stared at his back, willing him to turn around, but he didn't.

Later that night, after Frank had gone out, claiming to be "meeting a client," Iris called Grace. "He left ten minutes ago. I asked him about the bartender. He says he doesn't know her."

"What did you expect him to say? Where's he going, by the way?"

"To the Dinghy. He's meeting a client from Portsmouth."

"What do you think?" Grace asked.

"I think he's got a date. I caught him staring at himself in the bathroom mirror. Do you know why I'm suspicious?"

"Why?"

"He told me to call him if I got worried. Yet he left his cell phone behind. He obviously doesn't want to be reached."

"Do you want to catch him?"

"What do you mean?"

"We could hide out at the Dirty Dinghy parking lot and play amateur sleuth."

"He'd spot my car."

"We'll take mine. He's not familiar with it."

"I don't think I'm ready for that."

"Suit yourself. I always say 'strike when the iron's hot.'"

Iris gripped the phone. "Okay. What time can you pick me up?"

FIVE

Iris sat with Patticake on her lap and waited for Grace in the darkened living room. She stroked the cat's fur and tried not to think about the upcoming mission and what it might uncover. Did she really want proof of Frank's cheating? If so, what would she do—file for divorce?

She remembered the stories of infidelity her friends had confided over the years. There was Maggie, a school counselor she's met at an education seminar. Over glasses of chardonnay at the hotel bar, Maggie told her story about catching her husband in the act. It had happened at the family's lakeside cabin in New Hampshire, in late fall. At the time, Maggie's husband was supposed to be attending a sales conference in Rhode Island. Based on a hunch, Maggie had driven to the lake.

"The lake houses were all shuttered up, the boats covered with tarps." When Maggie drove down the deserted road that circled the lake, she spotted her husband's Subaru and a green Volvo station wagon in the driveway of the family's three-bedroom cabin. Approaching stealthily on foot, Maggie noticed the cars' hoods were covered with leaves, as if they'd been there for a while. The Volvo, she noted, had a bumper sticker, ***See You in Church.***

"It was so quiet; my footsteps made loud crunching sounds on the pebble driveway." Maggie had stood outside, summoning the nerve to enter. What convinced her to proceed was the silence. "I started worrying that he was dead in there, a victim of some crazed prowler. When I finally entered the cabin and saw them in bed together, I wished they had been slaughtered."

According to Maggie, her husband was boffing a member

of their parish, a woman who read Scripture on Sunday. "It gave new meaning to the term lay reader," she said.

Now Grace's horn interrupted Iris's reverie. She shifted Patticake to a nearby chair and went outside. As she climbed into the Forester, Grace gave her the once-over. "A white sweater? You'd make a crappy detective."

Iris shrugged. "My jeans are black."

"The point is to not call attention to ourselves," Grace said, driving away from the house.

"Sorry. I'm not in the habit of snooping."

"It's okay. We'll park in the back of the lot where it's dark. By the way, did you tell Frank you were going out?"

"It wouldn't matter anyway. Lately Frank doesn't listen. I could tell him I was stripping at the Knights of Columbus and it wouldn't penetrate."

"Men are like that," Grace said. "When you're dating, they hang on your every word. I remember telling my Sven that I hated my middle name. He said it was 'adorable.' Yet after the wedding vows, he couldn't remember what it was."

"What *is* your middle name, by the way?"

"It's Agnes, and don't mention it again. My point is, after you've tied the knot, you have to shout to get their attention."

"I'll bet Valerie Moles has no trouble getting Frank to listen," Iris said.

Grace nodded. "Being in the proximity of big boobs seems to improve men's hearing."

The remark reminded Iris of an incident at Sandpiper Beach. She remembered looking out the cottage window and spotting Claudia leaning over her railing, watering the window boxes. Claudia's breasts were cascading from her bikini top. Had Iris been suspicious, she might have wondered why Claudia was taking an interest in flowers. Although tenants were encouraged to maintain the property, Claudia had shrugged. "I work my ass off all year long," she explained. "For the short time I'm here, I'm going to relax."

This memory kindled another—the time Iris had caught

Frank ogling their neighbor. It was late afternoon. Iris was curled up on the back porch with a book. The waning light made reading difficult; she rose to get her glasses inside. As she did, a screen door slammed and Claudia emerged from her cottage wearing a black bikini and carrying a watering can. Iris would have called to her, but Shannon and Frank were upstairs napping.

Iris entered the cottage, searching for her glasses. She remembered leaving them on the bedside table. She crept up the stairs, careful to not awaken her family. Shannon's door was closed. Across the hall, the door to the master bedroom was ajar. She peeked through the opening to see if Frank was asleep.

Not only was he awake, he was kneeling at the window, his nose pressed to the screen. Iris saw what captured his attention: Their neighbor was squatting on tanned haunches, watering a circle of zinnias. A trickle of sweat ran down her chest . . .

Now Grace drove into the Dirty Dingy's parking lot. "I'll circle while you see if Frank's car's here."

They drove past rows of vehicles until Iris said, "Over there, the Sebring convertible."

Grace flashed the high beams on the car. "Perfect. There's a space behind it."

"Don't get too close," Iris said, glancing around nervously. "I'd die if Frank caught us."

Grace continued to the second row behind the car. "This is okay. We're not directly behind him." She backed the Forester into the space and shut off the ignition. "Frank's not going to catch us. Chances are he'll be . . . preoccupied."

"But suppose he does?" Iris asked. "What's our excuse for being here?"

Grace drummed her fingers on the dashboard and thought. "I can say I'm making a delivery to a customer."

"Panty hose? At night?"

"For your information, I sometimes deliver to my older customers who are housebound. Don't be so paranoid. Frank's not going to interrogate us. Don't forget, he's the guilty party."

Grace moved the seat back and opened the window a crack.

For a moment they listened to the crickets and other night noises. At the same time their attention was focused ahead, on the bar's exit door. The light above it cast a sickly yellow glow over a nearby dumpster and some empty cartons piled around it.

"Nervous?" Grace whispered, breaking the silence.

"Uh huh."

"We don't have to go through with this, you know."

"It's best to know the truth," Iris said.

"The truth shall set you free."

"I don't want to wake up an old lady and realize I've thrown my life away."

Grace patted her shoulder. "Don't worry kid, you'll be gorgeous at eighty." She stopped and leaned forward. The rear door had opened. "Is that them?"

Iris stared at the emerging couple who had stopped to clumsily embrace, rocking unsteadily back and forth. She let out her breath. "No."

"If we do see Frank and this bimbo, you won't shriek or anything, will you?"

"Don't be silly," Iris said, although the thought made her heart race.

Grace produced a napkin and wiped moisture from the windshield. She stopped when the bar door opened again. A man in a baseball cap paused in the doorway to steady himself. Then he lurched across the parking lot to his car. He leaned against it while fumbling with his keys.

"Holy shit," Grace whispered. "He's going to drive. Give me my phone in the glove box. I'm reporting him."

Iris, her gaze fixated on the bar's exit, clamped a cold hand on Grace's wrist. "Look, there's Frank."

He stood in the open doorway, looking back into the bar. "He's alone." Iris exhaled slowly as Frank stepped forward. He stopped to withdraw a cigarette from his jacket pocket. A light flared, briefly illuminating his features.

"His periodontist told him to quit smoking," Iris whispered, peering at him. "He's having gum surgery."

Grace put a finger to her lips. "Shh."

Frank strolled across the lot, smoking and staring up at the sky. After a minute he flicked the cigarette away and turned to face the door. As if on cue it opened, emitting a blast of country music. A woman stood framed in the doorway. The yellow glare revealed a striped tank top and tight white jeans. Her copper-streaked hair tumbled to her shoulders.

"It's her," Iris hissed, clutching Grace's arm. "It's Valerie."

"She's kinda short," Grace whispered, "and that's four-inch heels she's wearing."

Hips jutting forward, Valerie strutted toward Frank. When she was a few yards away, she raised her arms over her head and shimmied, moving to the music from inside the bar.

"Oh, baby!" Frank called.

Valerie continued her dance, all the while moving closer to Frank. Finally she leaped into his arms, wrapping her legs around him, her fingers gripping his hair.

"I can't look," Iris moaned, closing her eyes.

"They're coming toward us," Grace said, her voice hoarse. "Get down." She ducked down, sliding her body forward onto the seat as Iris continued peering through the windshield.

Frank still carrying Valerie, reached the Sebring. There he hoisted her onto the hood. "Grace, look," Iris whispered. "She's sitting on the hood of Frank's car. He won't even let me rest my pocketbook there."

"Get down this minute," Grace pleaded, tugging at her sleeve.

But Iris continued watching through splayed fingers. When Frank hoisted himself onto the hood and covered Valerie's body with his own, Iris turned away. "Put the window down, she groaned. "I feel sick."

Grace stared at her in the darkness. "Are you nuts? I'd have to start the car. Kneel on the floor mat and rest your head on the seat. They'll leave soon."

Iris slid to the floor as she was told. She rested her cheek against the smooth upholstery while taking steadying breaths. She forced herself to think about something other than the scene outside. An image of Ms. Dutton's dimpled pink fingers ripping into a candy bar swam into view. She sighed. "Tell me when they stop."

Before Grace could respond, the sound of moaning reached them. Iris clamped a hand over her mouth. She pulled the Forester's door handle. Immediately the interior lights flooded the car.

"Oh shit," Grace muttered. She lowered her head, yanking the lapels of her trench coat to cover her face. In the process, her elbow hit the steering wheel resulting in a blast from the car's horn. The sound shattered the silence.

"Who the hell is that?" Valerie's voice was belligerent.

"Mother of God," Grace whispered, her voice muffled from inside her coat. "Stay down, for God's sake. Don't sit up."

Iris was stretched across the seat, her head hanging out the passenger door. She responded with a retching sound, followed by a splash of vomit on the pavement.

"That's disgusting," Valerie said.

"Want me to check, babe?" Frank said.

From inside the Forester, Grace whimpered.

"Forget it," Valerie said, easing out from under Frank. "I gotta go home anyway."

Through the opening in her coat, Grace watched the couple slide off the car's hood. For a moment, they stood motionless, their attention focused on the Forester. Then they turned and walked away.

"He's walking her to her car," Grace whispered. She reached for the ignition key. "Close the door. Throw up on the floor if you have to, but we're outta here." Immediately the Forester roared to life. Grace, her coat lapels still framing her face, looked like the Headless Horseman as she backed out of the space.

"Are they watching?" Iris asked from the floor.

Grace didn't answer. She squealed out of the parking lot, grimly clutching the steering wheel. When they reached the main road she said, "I think I peed my pants." She glanced at Iris, slumped on the floor. "We're safe now. You okay?"

"There's vomit on your door."

Grace rolled down her window. "All in a night's work."

The following day was warm for early spring. Iris's counseling room was stuffier than usual. An ancient desk fan in the corner circulated stale air. When Roland Smedley, her last appointment for the day arrived, he flopped into the chair, sweat beading his forehead.

"I've got a test for you," Iris said, "an interesting test. It measures your vocational strengths and skills."

He listlessly took the form from her and got to work. As he wrote, she organized her brief case. Inside a zippered compartment was the business card from A Women's Issue. She slipped it into her wallet, reminding herself to call the agency the following day if she hadn't heard from Shannon.

Soon Roland handed her the completed sheet. "That wasn't bad for a test."

"Now I put your answers into the computer. When the results are ready, they'll transfer to the printer."

"Ms. Camuso, can I go to the bathroom while you wait?"

She hesitated. "Fine, but I have to go with you."

"You mean inside the bathroom?"

She smiled. "I'll stand outside in the hall and wait."

"Why? Are you afraid I'll run away?"

"I'm sorry. It's Ms. Dutton's new rule"

"That's so lame," he said, getting to his feet. "Never mind. I'll look at the supplies instead."

While Roland examining the stacks of cartons, Iris typed in his answers. Before long the printer came to life with a clatter, spewing pages. "Come sit down, Roland," she said, scanning the pages. "Looking at these results. It appears you enjoy dealing with minutia."

He collapsed into his chair. "What's that?"

"It means you're detail-oriented. You're in a category with those who enjoy collecting and organizing."

"I've collected stuff for years," he said.

She glanced at him. "Is that so? You never mentioned it when we discussed hobbies. Come to think of it, I'm not surprised. Isn't your mother a curator?"

"She's wardrobe curator in the theater department at Lesley

College. She takes care of old costumes." He wrinkled his nose. "I don't like stuff like that."

"What do you like to collect?"

"I collect old tools used by undertakers."

"Undertakers?"

"You know, funeral directors. I've got hoses and funnels and something called a trocar. It's for sucking the guts out. You know what?"

"Uh, what?"

It's still used today."

"I'll take your word for it."

He sat up in his chair. "That's not the only stuff I collect. Someday I want to have my own shop and sell cool stuff. I've got a name for it, Roland's Retro Planet."

She nodded. "It might not appeal to mainstream shoppers, but you'll find your followers. They claim the Internet will eventually allow people to connect all over the world."

"That's what Gloria said. She's gonna lend me the money to get started after she gets paid from her lawsuit."

"What lawsuit is that?"

"She's suing the restaurant where she used to work. She fell down the steps going to the wine cellar. That's why she needs a hip operation."

"I hope she wins her case," Iris said.

"She will. The building inspector said the steps were old and rotted. Her lawyer managed to sneak in and take pictures of the steps before the restaurant's owner had them torn down"

"Is that so? Sounds like a smart lawyer. Do you know the name?"

"Dunno, but I can find out from Gloria."

"Would you, Roland? I might need someone . . . in the future."

Life progressed civilly though cheerlessly at the Camuso's. Iris ceased to confront Frank about Shannon. In fact, she ceased to approach him about anything. Although this was a relief to Frank, he was puzzled. He wasn't used to women ignoring him.

One night as Iris stood at the sink, he put his arms around her.

"You still mad at me?" he asked, nuzzling her neck.

"Whatever gave you that idea?" She continued scrubbing the dried bits of food from the cat's bowl.

"You've been quiet lately." He pressed his groin against her.

An image of Frank and Valerie lying atop the Sebring's hood flashed in her mind. "Why would that bother you, Frank?"

His hands moved to her breasts. "Because I wanna make love to you."

"Why the sudden interest?"

He abruptly released her and stepped back. "Forget it. I thought I'd ask if something's wrong."

She turned to face him. "Since when has it mattered? Every time I express my concerns you act like I'm tormenting you." She shrugged. "So I've stopped asking."

He held up his hands. "Have it your way, Iris. I was just trying to be a nice guy."

"Who felt it's his *duty* to inquire."

Frank, who'd walked away, stopped and pointed at her. "I don't know what your problem is, Iris, but you'd better get help."

She smirked. "The kind of help you're getting?"

He stared at her for a second before turning and stomping up the stairs. Seconds later the door to his office slammed shut.

Iris turned back to the sink. If she'd won a victory, there was no pleasure in it. Bitter words would surely drive Frank further into Valerie's arms. On the other hand, what did it matter? Why did she want to salvage their sham of a marriage? Yet she couldn't deny her conflicted feelings. The man she married had once greatly appreciated her. He used to gaze at her and ask, "How did a wharf rat like me end up with a classy broad like you?"

Thus Iris vacillated, entertaining thoughts of revenge along with scenes of martyrdom. In the latter, she pictured herself in a hospital bed, the victim of a rare bacterial disease. Outside her door, a doctor tells a haggard-looking Frank, "I'm afraid there's nothing more we can do for your wife."

Frank falls to his knees at her bedside. He takes her limp

hand. She opens her eyes and whispers, "I heard what the doctor said, Frank. Go home. Get some rest. You look tired."

He buries his face in the pillow, his voice muffled. "Iris, I have something to tell you. It's tearing me apart." He raises his head, tears dripping from his chin.

Her face goes soft, like Melanie on her deathbed in *"Gone With the Wind."* She says, "Hush, Frank, I know all about it."

He stares. "You know about—?"

Her eyes are luminous. "I know about Valerie Moles."

Frank's voice is anguished. "Mother of God, give me a chance to make it up to you."

She closes her eyes. "I'm afraid not, Frank. I'm afraid not . . ."

Ever since their night of spying at the Dirty Dinghy, she's gotten into the habit of calling Grace, her link to reality. Not surprisingly, they discussed Frank: "How can he expect me to be nice to him after I've seen him on top of Valerie Moles?"

"You're not making sense," Grace said. "Frank doesn't know you saw him."

"Not only that, Frank acts so normal, as if it never happened."

"Frank acts normal because, infidelity is normal behavior for him. It's like serial killers. After they're caught, everyone mentions how 'normal' they seemed. That's because killing is second nature to people like that."

"I guess on some level I've always known about Frank and didn't want to face it," Iris said.

"None so blind as those who will not see."

Her glimpse into Frank's double life had been unsettling. Memories once submerged flooded her thoughts. In the forefront was Claudia, her summer friend whose betrayal had hurt more than Frank's. She wondered if he'd approached Claudia first, or was the attraction a mutual madness?

Iris remembered the Saturday morning two days before Claudia left Sandpiper Beach to return home. Frank had appeared downstairs, freshly showered and wearing khakis and a polo shirt. His damp hair curled over his collar.

"Where are you going?" she asked.

"I saw a sign down at the landing. Someone's selling a Sea Fox outboard with twin engines. I'm gonna take a look. I know someone who'd be interested." He picked up his car keys from the coffee table. "I'll be back for lunch."

"You're driving?" The public landing was less than half a mile away.

"It's eighty-five degrees. You want me to show up all sweaty?"

After Frank left, Iris and Shannon headed down to the beach. "There's Travis," Shannon said, pointing across the sand. "He's got a baby-sitter."

"Really?" Sure enough, Travis was being watched over by Shelly, one of three red-head sisters who lived near the tennis court. The girls were much in demand by parents at Sandpiper Beach. "I would have watched Travis if his mother had to go someplace," Iris said. But Shannon had raced off to join her friend.

Later that afternoon, while Iris was hanging wet bathing suits on the porch railing, she spotted Claudia removing sheets from her clothesline. Iris crossed the lawn that separated their cottages. "Why did you hire a baby-sitter today? You know I'd easily have watched Travis."

Claudia continued removing the laundry. "I know Shannon naps in the afternoon. You'd never keep Travis quiet while she slept. It wouldn't be fair to you."

"Don't be silly," Iris said. "Well, I hope you had fun."

Claudia wrinkled her nose. "I wouldn't call it fun. You know how I've always wanted to buy a place here? Today I met with a realtor. We looked at a couple of cottages near the creek end. Nothing I could remotely afford."

"Summer's a bad time to look," Iris said. "Come back in the winter. You can stay with us." She felt sorry for Claudia, whose ex was often late with child support payments.

"With my finances, I can't afford a garage at Sandpiper Creek." With that, she picked up the laundry basket. As she bent over, the front of her gauzy cover-up opened, revealing a purple bruise the size of a quarter above her breast. She quickly adjusted the material.

Iris looked away. "I'd better check to see if Shannon's awake. Are you coming down later for a swim?"

"I think I'll lie down until the baby-sitter brings Travis back." She shrugged. "Gotta grab every minute of freedom." She flashed a smile and skipped up the steps and into the cottage.

When Iris returned, Frank was in the kitchen, flipping through the mail. He hadn't taken any action on the boat, he said. The owner wanted too much money. "Up close I could see it needed work." Nonetheless, he'd made a contact. The morning hadn't been a total loss.

"Shannon's still napping," she said, putting her arms around his neck. "Let's go upstairs."

He laughed and slipped out of her embrace. "Babe, look at me. I'm all sweaty. I gotta take a shower."

That night, after several glasses of Chianti, Frank slept. He snored so loudly, Iris was afraid he'd wake Shannon. When the time was right, she crept out of bed, clutching the tiny flashlight she'd hidden under her pillow. Kneeling on the floor, she lifted the sheet and ran the light over Frank's body, naked but for boxer shorts. While she was inspecting his back, he woke. "Iris, what in hell—?"

"Sorry." She flicked off the light. "I thought I felt a spider in the bed."

"That's stupid," he muttered and fell back asleep.

As Frank's snoring resumed, she lay awake, her thoughts churning. She hadn't spotted any incriminating marks, but that meant little; Frank was a cautious man. Despite his unblemished skin, the truth was as obvious as Claudia's silk panties hanging on the clothesline like a banner. Iris was convinced that Frank hadn't been checking out a twin-engine outboard that day. She was certain he'd been checking out the tanned twin breasts of their neighbor and her friend, Claudia.

SIX

The following morning, Iris again dreamed of Lily: The sisters were trudging barefoot across the sand carrying plastic pails. All the while, Lily complained that the dried seaweed hurt her feet. "I want my sandals," she said, dropping her pail and refusing to go any further.

Iris sighed. They were headed to the creek to catch the low-tide crabs. She'd wanted to go alone, but her mother had insisted she take Lily. Now she tried to reason with Lily: "You can't walk on the wet sand in sandals. They'll get ruined and Mom will blame me."

"I want my sandals."

Iris knew it was easier to give in than to argue with her sister. She removed the sandals from her pail. As she knelt to buckle them, Lily said in a voice filled with wonder, "Look at the wave."

Iris turned and saw an enormous wave, taller than the flagpole at the lifeguard's station. It teetered along while at the same time moved rapidly. She leaped to her feet. Someone called her name. Her mother stood at the sea wall, clutching a straw hat to her head. "Save Lily!" she shouted, her words blown by the wind.

Iris dragged the whimpering Lily to her feet. There was no time to outrun the wave. They would have to face it head on, diving under it. She stood behind her sister and hugged her, bending to Lily's height. "Close your eyes and hold your breath," she yelled in Lily's ear moments before the wave broke over them . . .

Iris continued to lie in bed, still affected by the dream's impact. She glanced around the room. She was alone. Frank must have left early. Lately he'd been getting up earlier as if possessed by a new vitality. Now she knew the reason for his vigor. The night before, he'd returned home before midnight. At least Iris had the satisfaction in knowing she'd spoiled Frank's plans for a romantic night with Valerie.

She glanced at the clock. There wasn't much time to get ready before Roland's IEP that morning. The thought of enduring an hour of self-satisfied, pontificating educators made her want to stay under the covers. Lately her life seemed awash in gloom.

At ten o'clock, Iris entered the conference room. She took one of the few remaining seats at the table, between Dr. Turley, the school psychologist and Ms. Dutton. Mr. Tomasillo sat at the head of the table. To his left was a middle-aged woman who wore a white silk blouse and a necklace of large copper beads. Her silver-streaked hair was so glossy, Iris suspected a wig.

Mr. Tomasillo started the meeting by introducing the woman, Lureen Smedlie, Roland's mother. Dr. Smedlie was detained at the hospital, Mr. Tomasillo said.

"I promised I'd tape the session," Ms. Smedlie said. She removed a small black cylinder, placing it in front of her.

Ms. Guskin, the Director of Special Education, spoke up: "Excuse me. No recording devices are allowed at IEPs."

"That is my fault," Mr. Tomasillo said quickly, "for not informing Ms. Smedlie." He turned to her. "Ms. Trowt, the school secretary, will take notes. A transcript will be mailed to you."

"When can I expect that?" Ms. Smedlie asked, frowning.

"As soon as I type it up," Ms. Trowt said from the end of the table. "Can't go any faster than that."

Mr. Tomasillo cleared his throat. "Let us go around the table and introduce ourselves, shall we? Please include a brief description of your function here at the school."

Ms. Guskin went first, launching into an account of the special education department's role in student learning. As she rambled on, Iris blotted her brow with a tissue. The room was hot. A standing fan in the corner whirred ineffectually.

The occupational therapist followed Ms. Guskin, detailing her work with Roland. She used terms such as "proprioception" and "spatial disabilities." Ms. Smedlie, taking notes, interrupted to ask questions. This resulted in more obscure terms. Appearing dissatisfied, Ms. Smedlie concluded with: "Standish Academy is equipped to deal with those issues."

Mr. Tomasillo glanced around the table: "For those who are not aware, Roland is on a wait list at Standish Academy, a boarding school."

"Isn't that a military school?" Iris asked, her voice sounding loud in the closed room.

Ms. Smedlie said, "Standish Academy students develop confidence and discipline through academics and team sports."

Iris nodded, aware that Ms. Dutton was staring at her. "I'm just wondering if it's the best alternative for Roland." She paused. "He hasn't shown much interest in sports." Or academics, she thought.

"The curriculum offers a variety of sports," Ms. Smedlie said, and added wryly, "including skateboarding." The group laughed heartily at this remark.

When the laughter died, Dr. Turley, the psychologist, launched into his spiel. Iris closed her eyes. Over the years she'd had numerous interactions with the man. It wasn't his air of self-importance that she found objectionable. It was his grooming, or lack of such. The graying mustache was often studded with crumbs and other detritus from lunch. It was difficult to hold a conversation without being distracted by food particles stuck in his bristly mustache.

Today Dr. Turley wore his conference outfit, a maroon polyester sports jacket and striped tie. As always, his droning voice induced a stupor. He should record tapes for insomniacs, Iris thought from behind closed lids. After several minutes of Dr. Turley's observations, even Ms. Smedlie stopped taking notes, her pen rolling from her hand as if giving up. Nonetheless, when he spoke of Roland's "refusal to interact with peers," Iris sat up straight.

"Excuse me, Dr. Turley—"

He peered at her over half-glasses. "Something to add, Ms. Camuso?"

"Yes. If Roland doesn't associate with his peers, as you put it, it's because he has no peers at the middle school. Roland is in early adolescence, a year or two older than his classmates. With this population, the age gap matters." She was aware of Ms. Dutton's beady eyes boring into her, yet she continued. "Not only that, Roland's interests lie outside those of mainstream students. He's inventive and idiosyncratic. In other words, he's unique."

Iris turned to Ms. Smedlie. "I wouldn't presume to tell you how to raise your child. But speaking as a school counselor who's worked with Roland, I believe he should be encouraged to follow his non-traditional path."

Ms. Dutton wasted no time in apologizing. "Ms. Camuso is a part-time employee and—"

Ms. Smedlie held up an authoritative hand to the woman. Turning to Iris, she said, "Roland has spoken favorably of you, Ms. Camuso." she said. "I appreciate and understand your point of view. However, Dr. Smedlie and I have arrived at our decision following consultations with Boston's best child development specialists.

"We assumed that Roland, our only child, would follow in his father's footsteps—college and then medical school. Although this may not be realistic, given our son's temperament, we feel that a structured environment will produce optimum results. Standish Academy also has a good record in turning around those less-than-enthusiastic students."

Iris felt all eyes upon her. "The final decision is yours."

When the meeting ended, Iris hurried to the main office to get the key to the women's bathroom. It was another of Ms. Dutton's safety precautions. "An unlocked door," the assistant principal claimed, "invites mischief."

She found an empty stall where she sat to pee, her eyes closed. She wondered if Mr. Tomasillo was upset with her for speaking up in Roland's defense. When the meeting had ended, he hadn't looked her way. Lately she and the principal had gotten into the habit of talking, and not only about the students. He had confided details about his personal life. His sister in Puerto Rico wanted to visit. He had encouraged her to come live with him. "You would like Aidita," he told Iris. "Like you, she has a caring soul."

Preoccupied with her thoughts, Iris forgot the bathroom key was attached to a ribbon around her wrist. Thus after flushing the toilet, she bent to lower the seat cover. The ribboned key slipped from her wrist into the toilet bowl. Quickly she plucked it out, shaking the dripping fabric.

She wrapped it in toilet paper, squeezing the moisture out. She would have to sneak it back to its hook in the office, hoping no one would notice her. However, when she opened the ladies' room door Ms. Dutton was waiting outside. Instead of a greeting, the assistant principal held out her hand, saying, "I'll return the key when I'm through."

"Oh." Iris glanced at the key, bundled in toilet paper. She unwrapped it and dropped it into the woman's hand.

"It's wet," Ms. Dutton said, staring at the offending key.

"That's right," Iris said. "I washed it. Just think of the germs that ribbon carried." Ms. Dutton's gaze went from the key to Iris. "Gotta run." Iris said, scurrying down the hall, the woman's eyes upon her.

"A Women's Issue," the voice on the phone said by way of greeting. "How may I help you?"

Iris glanced at the name on the card, although she'd committed it to memory. "I'd like to speak to the director, Nancy Proctor."

"And whom shall I say is calling?"

"Iris Camuso."

"One moment, please."

The soundtrack from "Cats" filled the silence as she waited, willing herself to breathe evenly. She had dragged her feet about calling the agency. Finally, after an impromptu visit to the Ship Ahoy apartments where Shannon was reportedly living, Iris realized it was time to act:

She was surprised when she was buzzed into the apartment building unannounced. Soon she was climbing the stairs to the second floor. The industrial carpeting in the hallway was worn but clean. The spackled walls were painted glossy beige. Apartment two-hundred-twenty-eight was on the side with a view of the parking lot; the other side had a view of the harbor.

She was again surprised to find the apartment door ajar. She approached and rapped lightly, at the same time easing the door open. The living room was dominated by a huge TV. Heavy maroon drapes hung over sliding doors that opened onto a small terrace.

A strawberry-blond toddler propped in a plastic kiddie chair in front of the TV turned to stare at Iris. In the kitchenette, Amber Spaglione paced, dragging the cord from a wall phone behind her. She wore a tight blue dress and high heels. Her long strawberry-blond hair was wrapped in large rollers. She stopped pacing to stare at Iris. "Oh hell, I thought you were the babysitter."

"I thought Shannon babysat."

Amber muttered something into the phone before hanging up. She crossed the room to the door. "Shannon used to babysit," she told Iris. "She said she'd stay at least six months. She stayed one."

"Do you know where she is?" Iris slipped her foot into the door to prevent Amber from closing it.

"No idea. Call that adoption agency—A Woman's Place, or whatever the hell it's called. They're paying for her apartment." She put a hand on the doorknob. "If you'll excuse me, I have to find out why my goddamn babysitter is late."

Iris removed her foot a second before the door slammed shut.

Now the director of A Women's Issue picked up the phone and said in in a clipped voice, "This is Nancy Proctor."

Iris introduced herself. "I'm Shannon's mother. I wonder if I could come in and speak with you."

A pause, followed by, "How's next Wednesday at three?"

Iris thanked her and hung up. Immediately she moved to the pantry and poured a glass of Cabernet, her hand trembling. She returned to the kitchen table and sat, going over her brief exchange with Ms. Proctor. She sighed. Finally, the wheels were in motion; she had an appointment with the director of the adoption agency. Grace, who'd been coaching Iris on assertiveness, would be proud. "Act confident," she had urged. "Otherwise she'll know how far she can push."

Iris looked out the rain-smeared window at the puddles in the driveway. She wasn't looking forward to visiting the adoption agency. She'd need more coaching to meet Nancy Proctor on her home turf. Something in the woman's voice filled her with dread.

Late that afternoon Iris stopped at Mighty Mart for cat food, milk, and juice. Sandy was at the counter talking with a heavy-set man in a well-tailored gray suit. Its sheen reminded Iris of a shark's skin.

"Ms. Camuso," Sandy called. "C'mere. I want you to meet somebody." Iris reluctantly approached. She didn't feel like meeting anyone. "This is my uncle Vince Tosi. He's a lawyer, one of the best."

Although the dark-haired man was on the stocky side, the well-made suit minimized his bulk. Vincent Tosi was attractive in a swarthy way. He offered his hand. "That's right, and I've got an office here in Harborvale."

"Your name is familiar," Iris said. Then she remembered Grace's story about Marge Kipper, the daughter of the former superintendent of schools who'd drowned on a party boat cruise. According to Grace, Attorney Vincent Tosi had gotten the family a handsome settlement.

"Nice to meet you," Iris said. "Where's your office?"

"I'm down the hall from the Chamber of Commerce." In a flash he produced a business card "Here you are, lovely lady. You never know when you'll need a lawyer."

She pocketed the card with a smile. "You're right, you never know."

The receptionist at A Women's Issue was on the phone when Iris entered. She stopped and gave Iris a glance. "Can I help you?" A velvet headband restrained the woman's wiry gray hair.

"Iris Camuso to see Ms. Proctor."

"Have a seat. I'll let her know."

The waiting area was homey, with overstuffed chairs and potted plants. The walls were decorated with framed posters of past Museum of Fine Arts exhibits. In the center of the room, a long wooden coffee table held an unruly stack of magazines.

Iris grabbed an issue of *Sailing* and moved to a chair in the farthest corner. Once seated, she studied the magazine's cover. Sailing was foreign to her. She didn't understand why people engaged in the activity. The only boats she'd knwown were the working kind, such as lobster boats. Of course there was Frank's boat, the *Lady Godiva,* with its big, noisy engine and built-in beer cooler, the boat was the polar opposite of the sleek sailing vessel on the magazine's cover. She glanced at the mailing label. The subscriber's name, Tad & Nancy Proctor, was legible but the address had been neatly blacked out. She wondered if Ms. Proctor did that, fearing clients stalking her.

The receptionist glanced her way. "Would you like a cup of tea?"

"No thanks. " What she wanted was a double-vodka and lime. She put the magazine aside and rummaged in her bag for lip gloss. As she was applying it, a door opened down the hall. Seconds later a slim, blond woman appeared.

"Ms. Camuso?"

Her hair was worn in a boyish cut. Her skin looked perpetually tanned, although weathered. She wore a fitted navy turtleneck over pale linen slacks and in her ears, pearl stud earrings. When Iris stood to shake the woman's hand, she was pleased to note she was a few inches taller than the director.

"Let's go into my office, shall we?" Ms. Proctor said.

Iris followed her down the hall to a sunny room with a view of the harbor. Framed photos adorned the walls—family pictures of Ms. Proctor at the tiller with a grinning, square-jawed man.

In another, twin blond girls commandeered a sailboat, their legs long and tanned in white shorts. Other photos depicted smiling, sailing families. All in all, there were more teeth displayed than at a Kennedy regatta.

"Let me lower the blinds." Ms. Proctor moved to the window. Like a veteran sailor, her movements were quick, efficient. The room dimmed, she took a seat behind an antique wooden desk and nodded to Iris. "I'm glad to meet you. Let's talk about Shannon, shall we?" She opened a folder on the desktop, giving Iris a tight smile. "I don't have to tell you your daughter is special."

"Thank you."

"She's very talented."

"That's why I was disappointed when she dropped out of school only weeks before graduation."

"That can happen with students when the public schools don't challenge them adequately," she said. "However, given the opportunity, those students do very well in college. I think that is Shannon's situation. She tested high in the sciences and math. That's a blessing, considering how it's needed for today's top careers."

"I'm glad to hear it," Iris said, though she wasn't surprised. Shannon, like Frank, had a knack for numbers. Both could add columns of figures in their heads. Iris, on the other hand, still drew clusters of tiny dots, a form of addition she'd invented as a child.

"We're very results oriented at A Women's Issue. We've encouraged Shannon to pursue the sciences when she's ready to move forward."

"What did Shannon say to that?" It felt as if they were discussing a stranger, this person presented to her.

"She's signed up for GED prep classes. Given Shannon's capabilities, they'll be easily mastered. My point is—and I think we're in agreement here—your daughter needs support and encouragement at this juncture."

"I'm pleased she's getting it," Iris said, shifting in her chair. "At the same time, I'm wondering what you, as a private adoption agency, expect of Shannon."

Ms. Proctor raised a hand. "I understand what you're saying, Ms. Camuso. You would be negligent if you didn't want to learn more about us. That's why I hope you and your husband come aboard and become involved."

Ms. Proctor reached into a drawer and removed a brochure, handing it to Iris. On the cover were two laughing children racing down a sloping lawn, a golden retriever in happy pursuit. An oversized white Colonial-style home loomed in the background. "We are unique here at A Women's Issue," Ms. Proctor said. "Our young women are the backbone of this agency, and we don't forget it. We offer housing, education, and training, along with ongoing support. We're a family here. We celebrate together. During the holidays, we have an enormous Christmas tree with presents from one end of the room to the other. Our doors remain open to our clients. As I said, we're a family."

Iris glanced up from the brochure. "You're referring to those who surrender their babies, right?"

She nodded. "Every child is placed in a loving home. Our adoptive parents are rigorously screened. They are professional people: doctors, lawyers, CEOs. Outstanding couples."

"I don't doubt they're worthy," Iris said, setting the brochure on the desk, "but you have to agree the best situation is for the baby to be with his biological family."

"Best for whom?" Before Iris could answer, she added, "I understand what you're saying. Every now and then one of our mothers decides to keep her baby and raise the child herself. She forfeits all we offer—an education, continued support, and an opportunity for a new life." She shook her head regretfully. "Needless to say, those young women face a rocky road."

"You're referring to girls who have no family support," Iris said. "That's not Shannon's situation. My husband and I feel strongly about this baby. After all, it's our grandchild."

"Ms. Camuso, don't you think we've dealt with this issue? Several of our clients have parents who've come forth with their reservations. It's only natural. Yet once they get to know us and meet the adoptive families, they realize their thinking wasn't centered on the baby's needs." She flipped through pages in a folder. "Not to chance the subject, but have you considered that the baby's father might become involved at some point?"

"The baby's father?"

She nodded at Iris. "The father of Shannon's child. The fact that he lives in Finland may not be a deterrent. His family could show an interest at any time."

"Finland?" Iris blinked, wondering for a moment if they were discussing the wrong case.

Ms. Proctor gave her a patient smile. "I'm talking about Mr. Mukkhonan."

Despite herself, Iris gasped at this bit of information. Eino Mukkhonan was a Finnish exchange student. He'd been a frequent visitor at their house last winter. Shannon claimed she'd been helping the good-looking young man with his English homework. Yet on the nights that Eino visited, the door to Shannon's bedroom—where they were inside ostensibly studying—had ended up being closed.

Iris and Frank had tried to make the young man feel welcome. However, Frank's attempts to talk football were met with blank looks. Things came to a head late one February night. Eino was still in the house despite Frank's hints. Finally, Frank's patience evaporated. He rapped on Shannon's door and when no one answered right away, he opened it. Through a cloud of marijuana smoke, he spotted the couple sprawled across the bed.

Eino raced from the room, his shirt clutched in one hand, his book bag in the other. The sound of his heavy boots pounding on the stairs reverberated through the house. Frank chased the boy out the door and into the snow. It was the last they saw of the young Finn.

Now she looked into Ms. Proctor's pale blue eyes. "Are you saying you'll notify the baby's father if we contest the adoption?"

The director closed the folder. "I make no implications, Ms. Camuso. I'm merely stating that the paternal family should be given the same opportunity as the maternal family. It's only fair, don't you think?"

"Then why not do it now?"

"Shannon does not want this."

"But—" Iris realized she'd get nowhere with Nancy Proctor, a shark who knew her territory. She got to her feet. "Nothing's changed, Ms. Proctor. I'm going on record to let you know our intentions regarding our grandchild."

Ms. Proctor stood. "This agency strives to make all parties happy, Ms. Camuso. Obviously there will be one or two we cannot reach."

"You make it sound as if I'm being difficult for not going along with your plans," Iris said. "I'll remind you that my daughter is still a minor."

"Who will soon become an adult. Shannon is a mature young woman. I applaud her for thinking of the baby's future, and I suggest you do the same." With that, she walked to the door and held it open.

Iris stood opposite the director. "Call me old fashioned, but I believe there's no substitute for family."

Ms. Proctor raised her eyebrows. "Even if the family is dysfunctional?"

Iris gasped. "Are you referring to us?"

She sighed. "Ms. Camuso, be honest. At this stage in your life, approaching middle age, why would you want to raise a baby? What is so lacking in your life that you'd even consider it?"

Iris felt the blood rush to her face. "That's a matter between my husband and myself. In the meantime, you'll hear from our lawyer."

"That's your right, of course. I might add that this agency retains the legal team of Fahnstock & Fairchild. Perhaps you've heard of them?"

Iris smirked. "I'm sure you can afford the best, Ms. Proctor. After all, newborns don't come cheap."

If the director responded to that remark, Iris didn't hear it. Any answer would have been drowned out by the slamming of the door.

SEVEN

Driving home from work, Iris felt empowered. It was a word she never used but suspected Ms. Proctor did. Ms. Proctor believed in empowering her young pregnant clients. And one can't reach her potential with a baby carriage in the hallway.

She was pleased that she'd been assertive with Frank. The role didn't come naturally to her. When dealing with Frank she'd often given in, conceding to his opinions; his wants and wishes. This time there was too much at stake—their grandchild. Despite Ms. Proctor's lofty ideals, babies were nothing but a commodity to her agency.

At home, she went straight to the pantry and poured herself a glass of wine. Drink in hand, she sat at the kitchen table and dialed Grace's number at the shop.

She answered, "For Your Thighs Only."

"I'm back."

"I've been thinking of you all afternoon," Grace said. "How'd it go with the dragon lady?" After Iris described the encounter, neglecting to mention the slammed door, Grace said, "Good. You let her know you can play hardball, too. It takes guts to stand up to a tough cookie like Nancy Proctor. I'm proud of you."

"I don't think Shannon will be proud. She'll hate me for meddling."

"What does it matter," Grace said, "she's already mad. Besides, you're Shannon's legal guardian until she turns eighteen. You have a right."

"It's ironic how things are coming together," Iris said. "I

was at Mighty Mart the other day. One of my former students works there. She introduced me to Vincent Tosi, the lawyer. He happens to be her uncle. I think it's a sign I'm on the right track." When Grace failed to answer, she said, "What's wrong?"

"I was thinking you're getting ahead of yourself. This is a baby we're talking about. Don't be impulsive. I've seen what happens to grandparents who raise their children's kids. There's a couple down the street from me, Jan and Fred. They got custody of their two grandchildren because the parents were on drugs. Instead of looking forward to their golden years, they're working full time to pay for daycare. When I walk by their door the kids are yelling and the TV's blaring. Jan and Fred are in their fifties but look seventy."

"Well, I'm talking about one baby, and we don't see it as a burden."

"We?"

"Frank and I."

"Frank? Honey, are you forgetting that little scene in the Dinghy parking lot? He certainly wasn't acting like grandfather material. You've got stars in your eyes that blind you to the truth."

"I do not have stars in my eyes. I'm very level-headed."

"How about before you married Frank? You said your dad warned you. At the time Frank was running around with a married woman."

"*Rumored* to be running around with a married woman," Iris replied, although she suspected it was true . . .

"That guy can't keep it in his pants," her dad had said, his remark shocking her. Not the statement itself, but the fact he'd utter such a crude expression. As for its veracity, her father was in a position to know. His fish distribution business was based at the wharf; he heard the gossip.

Yet if his words were meant to warn her, they had the opposite effect. One glimpse of a tanned and shirtless Frank aboard his powerboat, Lothario, and she was hooked like a bluefin tuna. After the wedding she'd urged Frank to change the boat's name, feeling it inappropriate for a married man. He'd refused, citing the old seamen's superstition, "Change a boat's name and soon you'll be crab bait."

Frank had entered her life during a period of turmoil. As a result, he became a savior figure. She had attended a state college in western Massachusetts, majoring in education. Midway through her student teaching she faced the truth: She wasn't cut out to be a teacher. She wanted to befriend her students, not teach them. She'd only chosen the major because her mother had taught grade school for thirty years.

The realization had created anxiety and she didn't know what to do. Meanwhile, she felt like a fraud in the classroom. Did the children sense her heart wasn't in it? One day when it was too cold to go out, she had them sit in a circle. They talked about their hopes for the future. In a way, she was trying to prevent them from making the same mistake she had made by blindly following in her mother's footsteps.

Iris had considered the activity a success, but Ms. Grande, her supervisor, thought otherwise. "Are you training to be an educator or a therapist?" she asked. The question remained in Iris's mind. The woman's query had planted a seed.

Her classroom work continued to suffer as she went through the motions. During the midyear review, Ms. Grande gave Iris a "poor" in disciplinary skills. In order to successfully complete her student teaching, she would have to show improvement.

More and more Iris felt trapped inside the classroom. She gazed out the window at Mount Greylock, the iconic behemoth that loomed over the town, blocking the sunlight. The mountain made her feel claustrophobic. She swore it moved in closer at night while she slept. Having grown up on the coast, she longed for the wide-open sea.

At night Iris lay in her dormitory bed, her mind churning. Finally, she took her roommate's advice and visited the student wellness clinic. There she met Dr. Whitback, a psychiatrist with a long, wispy beard and morose expression. The antidepressants he prescribed energized her to an alarming degree. Not able to sleep anyway, she found herself doing laundry at one in the morning. She continued this dreary routine until her prospective teaching career came to a crashing halt. It was Mount Greylock, ironically, that finally set her free.

The intervention came one gray afternoon as the class worked on a geology project. Iris was in charge, Ms. Grande having migrated to another room. She surveyed the class. Under the fluorescent lights the children's faces looked pinched and colorless. As they dutifully identified samples of rock from a handout, Iris stood at the window. She looked out at the snow-capped mountain and said, "When the weather gets warm, perhaps we can have a picnic on Mount Greylock."

The comment had a surprising affect. The students looked at each other and cheered. A couple of the more rambunctious pupils leaped to their feet and chanted, *"Pic-nic! Pic-nic! Pic-nic!"* Others stomped their feet and chanted.

Iris rushed to the front of the class, waving her hands to silence them. Caught up in the moment, the children ignored her. They egged each other on. Two students climbed up on their chairs and chanted loudly, "Pic-nic! Pic-nic! Pic-nic!"

Iris rushed from one side of the room to the other, a finger pressed to her lips, trying to quiet them before another teacher heard the commotion. They didn't stop until a grim-faced Ms. Grande burst into the room shouting, "Sit down this minute!"

When the room was silent, she turned to Iris. "Ms. Quirk, please join me outside the classroom." Before exiting, the teacher glared at the students and said, "If I hear a sound, you will lose recess privileges for the rest of the month."

Iris followed her to the corridor. There Ms. Grande demanded an explanation. In a halting voice, Iris repeated her remark to the classroom and added, "It was only a suggestion."

Ms. Grande sighed. "I realize you are new to teaching. However, your failure to consider the consequences of your remark is inexcusable. It makes me wonder if you have the maturity to be in charge of a classroom." She peered at Iris with eyes as cold as the frost etching the windows. "Frankly, I don't have confidence in your ability."

Her supervisor's summation had a curious affect upon Iris. On the one hand, it made her ashamed for her perceived inadequacy. On the other hand, it released her. She would no longer have to participate in the travesty of student teaching.

That night Iris left two voice messages, one for the school principal and for Ms. Grande. She apologized, while informing them of her departure. After that she packed her bags. She spent the rest of the night saying goodbye to her dorm mates.

The following morning she drove the Mass Turnpike across the state. When she reached Harborvale, the ice had melted from her car's hood. The temperature was a balmy forty-four degrees. She immediately headed for the wharf. She hadn't told her dad she was dropping out of college; she wanted to break the news in person.

Few people were hanging out at the waterfront that time of year. Her dad's truck was not in its usual spot. She pulled up in front of Clancy's Boat Yard and went inside. Rows of boats hung suspended in wooden cradles inside the cavernous space. From somewhere came the sound of paint scraping. She headed in that direction and came upon Frank.

Wearing a paint-spattered tee shirt and jeans, he was on his knees scraping the hull of his boat, Lothario. Iris excused herself and asked if he'd seen Chester Quirk.

"Chet? Saw him earlier. He's probably on a delivery." When she introduced herself, he stood, wiped his hands on a cloth and shook her hand. Holding her hand longer than necessary, he said, "Chet never mentioned a beautiful daughter. Guess I don't blame him."

After dinner that night, Iris and her dad worked out a plan. She would take the rest of the semester off. Come summer, she'd take courses in Boston. In the fall, she'd return to school, having changed her major from Education to Psychology. In the meantime, she'd help her dad with the business. "I can use an extra pair of hands," he admitted.

Early mornings they loaded the truck, filling coolers with fresh haddock, shrimp and scallops. They made deliveries to local markets and restaurants. After two hours of lugging fish from the truck bed, Iris's shoulders and arms ached. In the evening she soaked her sore muscles in the bathtub, scrubbing fish scales from her nails. After a month of hauling fish, she was strong enough to handle the deliveries by herself.

From time to time she spotted Frank, who waved but kept his distance. After she'd become a regular on the waterfront, he approached one morning. She was alone, loading the truck. After watching her for a moment, he said, "Is that thing comfortable?"

"What thing?" she asked. He indicated her heavy rubber apron that fell to the tops of her boots.

She shrugged. "It keeps the fish scales off my clothes."

He stood back and looked her over, his glance impersonal. "What are you, a size eight? Ten?"

"Something like that," she said, blushing. "Listen, I don't mind wearing this. The only people who see me are the guys in the kitchen. They don't even look when I come in."

"That's a pity," he said before walking away.

One week later, as she was hosing down the truck bed, Frank appeared. He had a package wrapped in brown paper tucked under his arm. "I got something for you."

She climbed down off the truck and watched him unroll the package. It was a sea green apron with pale blue trim. "This is made of sail cloth, a new color. The trim and ties are PVC." He held it up against her, his fingertips lightly resting on her shoulders. "The length's good. Want to try it on?"

"Yeah, sure." She took off her gloves and untied the heavy rubber apron, letting everything fall at her feet. Then she slipped into the new apron, turning so he could tie it in the back. "It's so much lighter than the other one," she said. "It's pretty, too. Who made it?"

"One of my clients is a sail maker. He stitched it using my design. More women are getting into fishing. They don't want to wear men's gear." He stood back and looked her over. "I'd like to take your picture in it. My bookkeeper says I should have a catalog to display the stock."

"I'm afraid I wouldn't show it off to best advantage," Iris felt her cheeks flush

He moved behind her to untie the apron and stood so close

she felt his breath on her neck. "You'd look good in a cod barrel."

Before long, her summer classes started. Three times a week she commuted into Boston on the train. Then she walked from North Station up to Beacon Hill and Suffolk University. She was rattled by city traffic. Aggressive Boston drivers materialized every time she stepped off the curb to cross the street.

One day, a student in her Abnormal Psychology class invited her to lunch. Scott Lester and she had become "class buddies." He called from time to time, verifying their assignments, but mostly to talk. Scott liked to joke about their professor, a pale, studious man whom he called "the Mole."

Scott was five years older than Iris. He was at Suffolk finishing up his degree after dropping out of college a few years earlier. "Too much hearty partying," he'd explained. Iris wasn't surprised by his invitation; she'd sensed his interest. In any case, lunch in the city sounded like fun, providing it didn't cost her more than fifteen dollars.

They walked to a nearby parking garage where Scott kept his car. Iris repressed a gasp when he unlocked a white BMW convertible. They drove out of the garage, Scott maneuvering the narrow maze of streets that made up Beacon Hill.

Soon they reached the Copley Place garage. They walked the short distance to Newbury Street. Iris noticed the stylish crowd carrying shopping bags from expensive shops lining the fashionable street. She became apprehensive. "I'm afraid we're out of my league, Scott. Can't we get a burger someplace?"

Laughing, Scott took her elbow and guided her across the street to Le Precipice, a tiny French restaurant. Inside the dim interior the tables were draped with white linen. On each sat a spotted orchid. The maitre 'd, who greeted Scott warmly, seated them. "I didn't bring enough money," Iris whispered, leaning toward Scott. "I might not pay you back right away."

"Don't be silly," Scott said. "You're my guest." He settled his lanky frame onto the delicate-looking gilded chair and nodded to a waiter. Speaking in French, he pointed to the wine menu and ordered a bottle.

Iris stared at him. "I'm speechless."

"What do you mean?"

"All this time I thought you were like me, another student schlepping into the city. Now I find out you're a bon vivant who orders in French."

"Nope. I'm a commuter just like you."

"From where?"

"Wellesley Hills."

"Pretty chi-chi town, not to mention your car."

He shrugged. "My parents got it for me when they heard I was going back to school. They're rejoicing that I'll finally graduate and move out." At that moment the white-jacketed waiter arrived with their wine. After Scott approved it, the waiter poured Iris a glass. Scott raised his in a toast. "To your career. What do you want to be, anyway?"

"I know it sounds corny, but I'd like to go into counseling and help kids."

"It's not corny at all. You'd be great at it."

"How do you know?" She took a sip of her wine. It was musky yet velvet-smooth. She'd never tasted anything like it.

"Because you enjoy our class," he said, responding to her question. "You're always raising your hand, asking the mole questions."

She laughed, no longer feeling out of place in the elegant restaurant. "Doesn't the subject interest you?"

"Not really. It's an elective for me. I just want to pass and finally graduate."

"What then?"

"Then I'll go into the family business and officially be on the payroll." He poured more wine into their glasses.

"I'm in the family business too," she said brightly, "delivering fish. What's your family's business?"

He grinned. "Ready for this? It's toilets."

"Toilets?" She spoke so loudly, nearby diners turned and frowned.

"Not just toilets," he said, "sinks and faucets. It's upscale commercial. Our motto is *Lester Lasts*."

She nodded. "The world needs good toilets."

"That's a better motto." He clinked his glass against hers.

Eventually, they ordered lunch. On the advice of their waiter, they chose Coquille St. Jacques. This was accompanied by a bottle of white wine. After a creme brulee dessert with cognac, they left the restaurant. Iris clutched Scott's arm for support. She was surprised to discover the sun was low in the sky. The afternoon shoppers were gone, replaced by people dressed for the evening. The pace of the city had picked up and Iris, befuddled by booze, had no idea what time it was. She feared the five fifteen commuter train had long deserted the station.

Scott put a steadying arm around her as they crossed the busy street. The alcohol hadn't appeared to affect him. He guided her through the dim parking garage to his car. Seated inside, she fumbled with her seat belt. He reached across her to help. When she looked up, he kissed her.

One morning Iris sat in the passenger seat of her dad's truck. He was inside the Marine Building settling an account. It was a mild spring day, the sky absent of clouds. She alighted from the truck and strolled to the edge of the pier. At the railing she slipped off her sneakers and rolled her jeans to her knees. She lowered herself onto the sun-warmed wooden planks, her bare legs dangling over the edge. She closed her eyes, turning her face to the sun. The long dark winter was a distant memory.

Before long she heard the *put-put-put* of an outboard motor. She opened her eyes and spotted the bow of the Lothario coming around the point. Soon Frank appeared behind the wheel of the motorboat. He was shirtless, his tanned chest reflecting the sun. When he reached the pier, he cut the engine and looked up at her, shielding his eyes. "Hi."

"Hi."

"Want to take a ride to Thatcher Island?"

"Where's that?"

"Where'd you grow up, in Iowa?"

She laughed. "I'm a newcomer to the seafaring life."

"You'll catch on," he said. "For the record, Thatcher Island is in Rockport. It's beautiful now, before the day-trippers arrive."

"I promised to help my Dad today. "

He nodded. "My loss."

He revved the engine and reversed, turning in a wide circle. When he reached the end of the pier, he opened it up full throttle and roared away, the water churning in a white-capped frenzy. The sound was so loud she didn't hear her father arrive and stand behind her at the rail. They watched in silence. When it was quiet, her father said, "What did *he* want?"

She looked up in surprise and scrambled to her feet. "Nothing much. We talked about his boat." The lie came automatically. "Don't you like him?" For some reason she couldn't say Frank's name.

"No, and he knows it."

"Why don't you like him?" Her tone was mild.

"I liked his old man, Frank senior. The son's different. He's a hot head, impatient with the old ways."

"Maybe that's what this place needs—new ways."

"You could be right about that, but Frank Junior's not the one to change them. He's out for himself. Not only that, he likes the ladies too much. One of these days it'll land him in trouble."

"I don't know anything about that," Iris said. "He made me feel welcome when I arrived here. Everyone else ignored me." She didn't mention the new apron.

"Give him a wide berth, Iris. Listen to your old man. Don't get involved with Frank Camuso."

"Don't be silly," she said, feeling that she was already involved.

Her plan to tell Frank about her visit to A Women's Issue evaporated the minute he walked in the door, an ice pack pressed to his cheek. "I forgot," she said. "You had gum surgery this afternoon." He nodded and opened the freezer door. After tossing the pack inside, he opened the refrigerator door and removed a can of Budweiser. "Did Dr. Shanley give you a prescription for pain pills?" When he nodded again, she asked, "Is it okay to drink while taking them?"

"I didn't ask, for chrissake." He yanked off the beer tab. "If you knew what I've been through this afternoon you wouldn't ask dumb-ass questions. They stuck me with four Novocain injections, one in the roof of my goddamn mouth." He grimaced. "Now he says I need more areas done. Hell with that."

"Do you think you can eat something? I made a meat loaf."

"I'm not hungry. I'm gonna watch a little TV and go to bed." He held the can to his cheek. "I've got to keep it iced or I'll swell up."

Alone in the kitchen, Iris poured herself a glass of wine. She sat at the table and stared out the window. A faint crescent of moon appeared in the darkening sky. Tomorrow she would talk to Frank about her visit to Ms. Proctor . . .

"Roland, are you falling asleep?"

The boy's eyes were closed, his head resting on his forearm. Together they'd been working on a homework assignment—writing an essay about grandparents. It hadn't interested him. "I hardly remember my grandparents," he complained. "They died when I was a little kid."

"Where did they live? Do you remember visiting them?" Iris asked.

"In South Carolina, a place called Lagoon Villas. It was cool because it had alligators lying on the banks of the lagoon."

"That sounds like an interesting place."

"It was, but it sucked because they didn't let me go outside alone."

"I can see their point," she said, smiling.

"It's too hot in here," he said, looking around. "Why can't we talk outside?"

"It's an excellent idea, Roland, but I'm afraid it's against school rules."

She had approached Mr. Tomasillo about conducting the counseling sessions on the wooden bench in the school yard. To make her point, she'd cited the Greek scholars' outdoor classrooms. Mr. Tomasillo thought it a good idea and agreed to clear it with the superintendent. Things looked promising until Ms.

Dutton intervened; any breach of regulations got her attention. She cited liability issues, the possibility of Roland running away once outside, or tripping on the concrete.

"I'm sorry to disappoint you," Mr. Tomasillo had said. It was the end of the day. He'd spotted Iris near the first floor stairwell.

"At least you're willing to try new ideas."

"What is that expression—I think 'out of the box?'" He flashed his even white teeth.

"You do, Mr. Tomasillo, and it's 'outside the box.'"

He placed his hand on her arm. "Please, call me Tomas."

She nodded. "By the way, have you heard anything from Roland's parents?"

"I heard from Mrs. Smedley. The boy has been accepted to Standish Academy. She and Dr. Smedley believe structure and discipline are what is best at this stage."

Iris shook her head. "Roland is *not* military school material. Anyone meeting him would realize that." She pictured the boy in an ill-fitting uniform lumbering across a leafy quad.

"Maybe not, but I have to respect the parents' decision." When he gazed into her eyes she was reminded of her neighbor's black Lab whose soulful eyes were the color of melted chocolate. "As we must, Ms. Camuso," he added.

"I'll try," she said, holding his gaze. For a moment, staring into the principal's eyes, she forgot all about the Smedleys.

Now she watched the boy's face, untroubled in sleep. No doubt he hadn't been told about Standish Academy. She gently shook him. "Roland, it's time for your next class." He blinked and looked around the room. "You fell asleep," she said. "What time did you get to bed last night?"

He yawned. "Midnight."

"That's too late. Were you watching TV?"

"Nah." He glanced at her. "I was out."

"Out?"

"Promise you won't tell?"

"That depends on what you say. I'm obligated to reveal information if it concerns a student's endangerment." Her prim tone was reminiscent of Ms. Dutton's.

"I snuck out last night and went to the hospital."

"What? Why did you do that?"

"To visit Gloria. She had hip surgery, remember?"

"Did your parents find out?"

"My parents drink a lot of wine at night," he said with a shrug. "They snore like a couple of rhinos."

"How did you get to the hospital?"

"Carl gave me a ride."

"That wasn't very responsible of Carl."

"I told him I was visiting a classmate who's having a heart transplant."

"It's dangerous for a young boy out at night. How did you get back?"

"Gloria gave me money for a cab."

"Didn't you worry that your parents would discover you missing?" She remembered Shannon's rebellious period, the empty bed, the open window. Children were oblivious to a parent's terror.

"I fixed my bed by bunching up a pile of clothes under the covers. Then I stuffed my Dracula wig to make it look like my head on the pillow." He grinned, pleased with himself.

She held up her hand. "I've heard enough. I won't say anything today, but you've got to promise you won't go out alone at night again."

"I promise." He stretched his arms over his head. "I can visit Gloria after school." He pulled a gold hoop with keys attached from his pocket. "I'm taking care of her condo, getting the mail and watering the plants while she's in rehab."

"Gloria must trust you."

He pocketed the keys. "She says I'm all she's got."

Late that afternoon, Iris sat at the kitchen table reading a Miss Marple mystery. She liked the elderly sleuth's cozy village of St. Mary Meade. Its residents were respectful of each other, even those they were plotting to kill.

She stopped to look at the rain coming down steadily, filling the potholes in the driveway. Last fall, Frank had planned to have the driveway repaved. Then he had a fight with the paving company. It wasn't the first time he'd clashed with tradesmen.

"They think I'm an idiot," he told Iris. "The guy quotes me a price and we agree. The first day, before they even start working, he says, 'Sorry, it looks like we gotta level an area we didn't notice before.' Then he goes, 'You don't want water collecting on your new driveway.' Then he adds, 'And by the way, Mr. Camuso, that'll be another two-hundred.' I said to him, 'Do I look like I fell off a goddamn turnip truck?'"

Iris deliberated making a phone call that could change the course of her life. She reached for her pocketbook and removed the business card, studying the black letters on white stock: **Vincent Alfred Tosi, Attorney at Law**. At the same time, she didn't notice when Patticake leaped onto the table until the cat nudged the card with her nose.

"Are you telling me to make the call?'" she asked. The cat rubbed its face up and down against the card, as though nodding. "Okay, I'll do it." She reached for the wall phone and dialed the number.

A woman answered. "Law office, Vincent Tosi."

"Yes, I'd like to make an appointment with Mr. Tosi."

"Are you a new client?"

"I am."

"What's the nature of your visit?"

The question surprised her. Somehow it seemed indelicate. "It concerns a possible adoption," she said, lowering her voice although she was alone in the house.

"How's tomorrow at four?"

Iris accepted, giving her name and phone number. After hanging up, she moved to the pantry. The situation called for a drink. She was finally taking action, moving forward as Grace had instructed, one foot in front of the other—baby steps. Yet at the same time, it felt like a giant leap into the void.

EIGHT

Vincent Tosi's law office was located in one of the older buildings in the harbor area. The two-story structure housed a diverse group of businesses. The first floor was occupied by a physical therapy clinic, a marine art gallery, and a graphic design studio. Vincent shared the second floor with the Harborvale Chamber of Commerce at one end and Silva's Plumbing & Heating at the other.

Iris climbed the steps to the office and found the door ajar. A reception desk near the entrance was empty. Its surface was cluttered with multiple photos of children. On the desk blotter sat an opened bottle of red nail polish.

"Hello?" Iris called.

A door opened and Vincent appeared, his sleeves rolled up, his tie loosened. "Ms. Camuso, how you doing?" He beckoned to her. "My secretary's here mornings. Afternoons she studies massage at the community college. She's applying for her license. You're not looking for a legal secretary position, are you?"

She shook her head. "You wouldn't want my typing, Mr. Tosi."

"Nobody's perfect." He motioned her into his office, where a glass-topped desk was piled high with files. Two wooden captains chairs sat opposite the desk. Framed photos of Vincent and local politicians decorated the walls. When Iris was seated, he said, "My niece Sandy thinks you're pretty cool."

"She's a nice girl with a great imagination."

"She's a good kid. Never got involved with drugs, like some of her generation."

"You're a good role model, Mr. Tosi."

He held up a hand. "Call me Vinny. I'm in my early forties, but people think I'm older. That's a good quality for a lawyer, maturity." He grabbed a yellow legal pad and tore off the top sheet, tossing it in the wastebasket. He picked up a pen, saying, "Suppose you tell me why you're here."

She felt the familiar resistance. "Well, it's about my daughter, Shannon."

"Beautiful girl. Takes after her mother." When she blushed, he said, "Don't mind me, it's my Italian blood. You know how it is, you're married to one."

"Do you know Frank?"

"There aren't many people in this town I don't know. Frank's made a name for himself in marine supplies. You know the state of the fishing industry. If you don't diversify, you're dead." Before she could respond, he said, "Let's start with Shannon's date of birth."

After the formalities were out of the way, Iris got around to recent events—Shannon's pregnancy and Iris's visit to A Women's Issue. As she spoke, Vincent took notes. When she was through, he paused. "You say Shannon will be eighteen in another month?"

"Uh huh."

"Hmm. Anything we file, by the time the court takes a look at it Shannon will be legally an adult. You won't have a leg to stand on."

"I can't believe there's nothing I can do as a parent."

"I didn't say there was nothing. You could file a CHINS petition—children in need of services. Some parents go that route when the kid becomes what the court deems 'incorrigible.' They used to call it wayward."

"Shannon doesn't fit that category . . ."

He looked at her. "You said she's run away from home?"

"In a matter of speaking. She's living somewhere, courtesy of A Women's Issue. We don't know the actual address."

"Listen to me, Ms. Camuso. You have an option to give the Department of Social Services jurisdiction over your child. They'll decide what action to take. She could be put in foster care or a group home. Is there a chance she'll return home on her own?"

"I don't think she'll come home, especially now when she learns I've been interfering." She reached for a tissue and dabbed at her eyes. "I've learned to live with that. Now I'm hoping to adopt her baby."

"What about Frank? He wants the baby too?"

"He's expressed . . . resistance."

"But he'll go along with it?"

"I don't see why not." Her voice trailed off.

He tore the pages of notes from the pad and shoved them into a folder. Then he sat back in his chair. "I'll tell you what I'm gonna do. I'll call this Nancy Proctor and feel her out, get an idea how firm their policy is. In the meantime, we can use the CHINS as leverage. I know how these private agencies operate. They want to keep a low profile, avoid controversy."

"I hope you can make some headway with Ms. Proctor. We're not on the best of terms."

"You leave that to me," he said, getting to his feet. "Lemme show you something." He led her to the opposite wall where a bright yellow sign hung. Under the silhouette of a snarling dog were the words: ***These Premises Protected by a Pit Bull***.

He tapped the sign. "Gift from a client who called me a pit bull. Once I sink my teeth into a case, I don't give up."

She looked at the dog's fierce stance. "You'll need it when dealing with Nancy Proctor."

"Ms. Camuso, I grew up on the Harborvale wharf. People like her don't scare me."

The following week, Iris, accompanied by Grace, visited the Harborvale Department of Social Services. Grace drove to the downtown location, parking the Forester in a lot enclosed by a rusted chain link fence. Iris stared at the aging four-story building. "My dentist had an office here. I remember walking over from the high school."

"He's probably still here," Grace said. "It looks like the kind of place where you move in and you don't move out."

"He passed away. His receptionist found him dead in the elevator one morning."

Grace shook her head. "Didn't even get a chance to enjoy

his retirement."

They got out and walked to the building's entrance. Inside the lobby, Grace's glance took in the pea-soup-green walls and speckled linoleum. "This place is a time capsule," she said. "Why are government agencies housed in such depressing surroundings?"

"It's like that expression, 'Abandon hope all ye who enter.'" Iris pressed the elevator button. "By the way, thanks for coming with me. I hope you're not losing too many sales at the shop."

"Nah, this time of day the only customers are the old ladies. They buy a pair of support stockings they'll wear five years."

They boarded the elevator. It shuddered to a stop at the third floor. The doors opened on a hallway lit by fluorescent ceiling lights. The passageway was so narrow they were forced to walk single file. On the way, they passed the local office of the Sex Offender Registry Board. Grace stopped and stared at the rows of photos posted on the glass doors.

"Come on," Iris said. "I want to get this over with."

"I'll join you in a second," Grace said. "I want to check out these mug shots, make sure I'm not dating one of these guys."

"Don't be long." Iris continued on to the DYS office, where a white-haired clerk stood behind the counter. "I'd like to fill out a CHINS petition," she told the woman, glancing around to make sure she wasn't overheard.

"You a resident of Harborvale?" The clerk peered at her.

"I am."

"I'll need to see some identification—a driver's license."

After approving Iris's license, the clerk turned to a long shelf stacked with pastel forms. She selected a half dozen sheets and said, "Fill out the pink, the green and the yellow. The rest you can take home, learn about our policies."

Iris brought the forms to a nearby table piled with tattered magazines. After clearing a space, she got to work filling out the forms. After a few minutes Grace returned, taking the seat next to her. "Did you recognize anyone?" Iris asked without looking up.

"One looks just like the guy that sang at my Aunt Florence's funeral." she said. "We invited him to the reception afterwards."

She peered over Iris's shoulder. "How are you doing?"

"Almost through." Minutes later Iris collected the forms and handed them to the clerk. She told the woman, "I'd like to point out that my daughter will be eighteen soon. I'd appreciate a timely response."

"First come, first served," the elderly clerk said. "Maybe you didn't hear the governor cut our budget by twenty percent. We lost two social workers. Now we're down to three, one part-time. In the meantime, the number of foster homes has shrunk. People won't take in kids with police records, and today they all got records." She shook her head. "What're you gonna do."

"I understand," Iris said. "I just wanted to call it to your attention. Time's running out."

"I hear you," the woman said, turning away. "Someone will be in touch, though I can't say when that'll be."

As they waited for the elevator, Grace put an arm around her. "I'm proud of you."

"I'm glad someone is. This won't go over well at A Women's Issue."

"You wouldn't have to take such drastic measures if that snooty agency wasn't holding Shannon hostage."

"I'm curious to know how much they get for a healthy newborn," Iris said.

"A fortune: My nephew and his wife tried to adopt from a private agency a couple of years ago. They couldn't afford the thirty thousand dollar price."

"I could always refinance the house."

"Don't even think of it," Grace said. "That baby is your grandchild. You have legal rights." They boarded the elevator. "Besides, Frank would have a cow."

As they drove through the downtown, Grace asked, "Want to stop at Mega Mug for coffee?"

"Thanks, but I was planning to visit my dad. I haven't seen him for two weeks."

"Say hello to the old dear for me," Grace said. "And let me know what Frank says about today's visit."

"I don't think I'll mention it tonight. Maybe later."

"Why not?" She glanced at Iris. "Is Frank aware that you

know about his new bimbo?"

"You say 'new bimbo' like he has a string of them."

"And you sound like you're excusing him," Grace said.

"I'm waiting for the right time. Frank's having gum surgery now. He's in pain. The timing's bad." Before Grace could respond, she added, "I don't want to rush into something I'm not prepared to deal with."

Grace pulled up in front of her shop where Iris's car was parked. "Kiddo, the longer you put it off, the harder it'll be to confront him."

Iris opened the car door. "Don't say anything more. I'll deal with it."

As she approached Harborvale Senior Housing, Iris spotted her dad limping along on the sidewalk, a plastic shopping bag dangling from his arm. She pulled to the curb and beeped the horn. He slowly lowered himself to look inside the car.

"Get in," she shouted, because he was hard of hearing.

He sank into the front seat with a loud sigh. "Thank God. Didn't think my leg would make it all the way."

"It's good you make an effort to walk."

"I didn't feel like taking the van to the supermarket, so I went to Mighty Mart, those crooks. I paid two dollars more for the same laxative I get at CVS."

"Why didn't you ride in the council's van?"

"I only go on those trips when I'm out of everything. A bunch of biddies go along. They don't stop talking."

She drove around the circular driveway. The flag in the center was at half-mast. "Who passed away?" she asked.

"I have no idea," he grumbled. "They always ask me to donate for flowers—people I don't even know."

Iris arrived first at his door. "Just push it open," he said, behind her.

"Dad, it's unlocked?"

"I've got nothing to steal."

Inside, the smell of bacon grease and stale laundry hung in the air. Iris moved to the tiny kitchen. Coffee grounds peppered the counter piled with dirty dishes. "Hasn't the housekeeper visited lately?" she asked.

He hung up his jacket on a wooden coat rack. "Not this week. She's got problems at home."

Iris moved the laundry basket off the sofa and onto the floor. "Aren't they supposed to send a replacement?"

"She didn't tell them she wasn't coming in. She says they'll fire her if she calls in sick again."

She sighed. "It sounds like this woman's taking advantage of you."

He removed two mugs from the kitchen cupboard. "I feel sorry for her, a single mother. Her son's giving her trouble. "

Iris filled the mugs with coffee and put them inside the microwave oven. "Don't give her any money, Dad. You're a pushover for a sob story."

"What money? All I got is my pension and Social Security. I couldn't afford to keep a bird."

Iris brought the heated mugs to the table. "I didn't know you wanted a bird."

"I wouldn't mind one of those canaries," he said. "My aunt Mildred had one years ago. That bird would sing rain or shine, like it didn't have a care in the world."

"How come you never got one?" She poured cream into his coffee.

"Your mother wouldn't put up with the mess. I used to have a dog, Sparky, when I was courting her. He was just a mutt, but what a smart dog."

"Really? What happened to him?"

"Before we got married, I gave him to one of my Navy buddies. His family had a farm in Ohio."

She sat at the table. "You never told me that. Why did you give him up?"

He shrugged. "You know how your mother was. She'd never have a dog in the house—too messy."

They were silent for a moment. "Did you regret it?" she finally asked.

He glanced at her. "I'm still talking about it fifty years later. What do you think?"

She shook her head. "Sorry. By the way, are you socializing more?"

He nodded. "I went to Bingo in the community center."

"That's nice. Was it fun?"

He snorted. "About twenty women and two men."

"I thought you'd like those odds."

"I would if the women were under eighty."

"Dad, you're almost that age yourself."

"I can wait," he said. "Why all the questions? Is something wrong?"

"What makes you think something's wrong?"

"I've known you for forty years. I know when something's wrong."

Briefly, she told him about visiting the lawyer, Vincent Tosi. "The thing is, I want to adopt the baby."

He raised his eyebrows. "I can't image Frank's wild about the idea."

"Why does everyone mention Frank? I'll be doing all the work."

He sighed. "It's a funny world we live in; rules changing every day. I'm glad we raised you in different times. You never gave us any worries."

It was true. Until she met Frank, Iris hadn't created a ripple. After Lily's death, she'd worked hard at being good. But no matter how many school awards she won, no matter how helpful she was around the house, it never filled the hole her sister had left.

After Lily's passing, her mother took a leave from her teaching position. She retired to her bedroom. After school, Iris would knock on her door. If her mother responded, she'd enter. In the darkened room, Iris told stories—funny incidents that had happened at school, many of which she made up.

Sometimes she'd be in the middle of a story when her mother would interrupt. She would ask Iris to repeat her account of that terrible day when her sister died, when Iris found Lily red-faced and gasping for breath in the tall grass. Iris would fall into a stony silence as her mother prodded her, saying, "Why didn't you run to the nearest house, Iris? Why?"

Iris had no answer. In fact, she'd often asked herself the same question.

NINE

After her school day was over, Iris headed for Mighty Mart; she was out of Patticake's cat food. Although the convenience store charged fifty cents more per can than the supermarket, she'd gladly pay it. She wasn't up to facing the crowds at the big, impersonal store.

All day she had experienced what the faculty called the "end-of-year-blues." It struck in mid-May, a widespread ennui among the staff. While they dragged their exhausted bodies through the lengthening days, the students, conversely, experienced a rebirth. Their attention span was that of the butterflies flitting past the open windows. Their hormones as well mirrored nature's awakening.

Thus the teachers sought respite in the faculty lounge where coffee and cake awaited. The custodian's wife, a cake decorator at Price Busters, often donated cakes that went unclaimed. That morning's offering was an orange and green sheet cake. Written in blue icing were the words *Arnie, We Will Miss You.*

Now Iris picked up a plastic knife, debating whether to cut into the cake. The garish colors, the thick, sugary frosting, were unappealing, particularly so early in the day.

Mrs. Trowt watched her from across the table. Finally, she said, "Don't tell me *you're* on a diet."

"No," Iris replied, irritated at being watched. "I was just wondering why Arnie didn't get his cake."

"Someone ordered it for his retirement party," Mrs. Trowt said, her voice animated, "but the poor fella had a heart attack and died the night before."

"That's criminal," Iris said, putting the knife down.

Mrs. Trowt sighed. "Just goes to show, doesn't it?"

"It sure does," Iris agreed, at the same time wondering what it showed—that it's bad luck to hold a retirement party? "I'm not hungry anyway."

As she poured a cup of coffee, the door burst open and Ms. Dutton rushed in, red-faced. Crescents of perspiration stained the underarms of her ruffled pink blouse. She headed for the table. Grabbing the knife, she plunged it into the gooey cake. The heavy slice sagged under the weight of the flimsy paper plate.

"Mmm, chocolate," she murmured, her eyes closed as she chewed.

Iris finished her coffee and tossed her cup into the barrel. "That's it for me. I've got a student coming."

"If it's Roland Smedlie, don't mention Standish Academy," Ms. Dutton said, licking her fingers.

"I don't intend to."

Roland dropped his backpack on the floor and flopped into the chair with a groan. His forehead was beaded with sweat.

"How have you been?" Iris asked.

"Tired."

When he didn't offer more, she asked, "Tired from doing what?"

"Dog washing and helping Carl with inventory."

"What about your friend Gloria? How did the operation go?"

He brightened. "She's in rehab for a week. You know what's cool? Her new hip is made of titanium, the toughest metal in the world. When she goes to the airport, it'll set off the metal detectors. She has to carry a card from her doctor, explaining."

"That's interesting. Did you visit her in rehab?"

"She said to wait 'til she gets home. But last night I watched TV at her condo. I laid on her bed and ate popcorn."

He grinned at the memory.

"Did your parents know you were there?"

"Nah, they were asleep."

Iris drove into the Mighty Mart lot and parked. When she entered the store, Sandy didn't look up. Iris made a beeline for the pet food section. She dropped a half-dozen cans into her shopping basket and headed for the check-out aisle. Sandy was still draped across the counter, reading a magazine while loudly munching sour cream potato chips.

She yawned and tossed the magazine aside to ring up Iris's purchases. "You're here every time I come in," Iris said. "Don't you have a day off?"

"I'm saving to go to Montreal this summer. It's a film festival, a week of horror movies from around the world."

"That sounds like fun."

"Directors George Romero and Wes Craven, the 'Halloween' guy, will be there. I'm hoping someone will read my screenplay."

"How's that coming along?"

"Right now it's two-thirds finished." She glanced at Iris. "Remember how I said the undead newcomers have sex with the towns' women, and their babies are born aliens? And while that's going on, the newcomers are killing off the towns' men, leaving only the kids?"

"Yes, I remember," Iris said.

"Well I'm stuck." She stopped and frowned. "I got a plot problem. The towns' kids join forces, you know? What I can't figure out is how they're gonna wipe out the alien population." She shrugged. "They're little kids. What can they do against this super alien race?"

"I can see where that might be a problem."

"That's six fifty-eight," Sandy said, handing her a weighted plastic bag. "Yeah, it's a problem. I'd like something dramatic, like an explosion. But how many kids would know how to blow people up?"

"You're right," Iris said, "it's not realistic." She gave her a ten-dollar bill.

After handing Iris her change, Sandy slammed the register shut and leaned against the counter. "I thought about a virus or something like that, but it's been done a hundred times.

I'm bumming. I want to discuss it with my online horror writers group, maybe post sections, but I've held back. Someone could rip off my story. You never know."

"You're smart to wait." Iris pondered the girl's dilemma. "It seems to me you need a device that arises naturally among the children."

"What do you mean?"

"Suppose one of the kids is a budding scientist. You could show him in science class, taking part in experiments. To banish the aliens, he might concoct something out of common household ingredients, something that would prove lethal to the aliens."

Sandy stared at her, transfixed. "Oh my God. One of the kids is a math nerd. I could make him a science nerd instead."

"Good."

"Why didn't I think of that?" Sandy reached across the counter and gave Iris a crushing hug. "Thank you, Ms. Camuso. You're awesome."

Iris felt pleased. "When you write the new scenes, it would help if you know something about basic chemistry."

Sandy rolled her eyes. "Man, are you serious? You know how I was in school. I took math for dummies. I was happy to get a 'D.' Forget chemistry."

"Is there someone at home you can ask?"

She laughed. "At my home?"

"I'm sorry I can't help you there," Iris said. "How about your customers?"

Sandy scratched her head, her mouth twisted in thought. "Wait. Do you know Dr. Fung, the retired chemistry teacher?"

"Sure." Dr. Fung had given Iris a C- in his class. Like Sandy, she'd been grateful just to pass.

"He lives at Harborvale Senior Housing, down the street. He comes in about once a week and asks me questions, like which TV dinners or ice cream is the best. I'll bet he could tell me about basic stuff at home that can cause an explosion."

"You might first explain why you need the information," Iris said.

Sandy nodded. "Gotcha. I don't want him thinking I'm some kind of terrorist."

"I think you're on the right track," Iris said, turning away. "Don't be afraid to reach out for help."

Sandy pointed a finger. "When this screenplay becomes a movie, you're getting creative credit."

"Fair enough."

At home, Iris opened a can of Fancy Feast Liver Pate. Patticake hunkered down over her dish, eating noisily. The cat had filled out nicely since Iris had taken over her care.

After hanging up her jacket, she went upstairs. She stretched out on her comforter and listened to her phone messages. The first was from the oil company, seeking a date to service the burner. The second was from Ms. Proctor. She said, "Ms. Camuso, could you call me as soon as you get in?" Iris sat up. It wasn't a request, it was a command.

She closed her eyes and lay back down. After a minute she played the message again. It filled her with dread.

She went downstairs. The kitchen clock told her it was four twenty. Not too late to call Ms. Proctor nor too early for a drink. She mixed vodka and lime juice and carried her drink to the table. Before dialing the number of the adoption agency, she called Grace at her shop.

After five rings the answering machine picked up and Grace's voice announced, "You've reached For Your Thighs Only, specializing in hosiery and selective jewelry. Please drop in to see our new line of sea glass earrings and while you're at it, enter our Hot Legs contest. In the meantime, leave your name, number, and a brief message. *Ciao*"

Hot Legs contest? What was that all about? Iris left a message: "Grace, it's me. I just wanted to touch base before I make a phone call. I'll talk to you later."

She hung up, feeling silly. What did she expect Grace to do, hold her hand while she called Ms. Proctor?

She sipped her drink. Perhaps she was being too negative. Maybe Ms. Proctor wanted to discuss Iris's adopting the baby. Maybe Vincent Tosi had gotten her to cooperate. Vincent claimed to not be intimidated by the likes of Nancy Proctor.

The clock's hands moved closer to five. If she didn't call soon it would be too late. Then she would fret about it all night. She took a final gulp of her drink and remembered Grace's instructions: "Don't apologize and don't make excuses."

She set her empty glass on the table and dialed the agency's number.

The following afternoon Iris left her office, her arms laden with folders. As she pushed open the building's side door, Mr. Tomasillo appeared. He held the door open wide, and bowed in a ceremonious manner. "Thank you," she said, embarrassed but pleased. The principal treated their every encounter as an event.

"I hope you are not going to waste such a lovely day," he said, standing next to her. She noticed that his tie matched his coffee-colored eyes.

"It is lovely," she said, looking around. Almost overnight the bare branches had sprouted the frilly lace that heralds new leaves. "I think today calls for a ride to the shore." She nodded at him, seeking agreement.

He looked around quickly. "That would be pleasant, Ms. Camuso, but I have an important conference this afternoon."

His nervous smile indicated he'd misunderstood. Should she explain that she wasn't issuing an invitation? What could she say without sounding awkward? Finally, she muttered a hasty, "I'd better get going," and scurried to her car, feeling his eyes upon her.

She took the shore road, the Jetta's windows lowered. When she reached the ocean, she spotted the seagulls overhead, lazily circling the rocks. The May afternoon was that rarity, sunny yet breezy; perfect for strolling the beach.

Before long she pulled into the parking lot of the Sandpiper Beach Motor Inn. At that time of year the motel had few guests. They wouldn't object to her parking in the lot. She locked her handbag in the car's trunk. Pocketing the keys, she headed toward the beach.

Standing on the boardwalk, she surveyed the mile-long beach. An offshore breeze ruffled the ocean's surface, creating choppy whitecaps. Small mounds of seaweed dotted the sand. A few people in windbreakers walked briskly on the hard-packed sand near the water's edge. Two dogs, forbidden during the summer, raced up and down, barking in a frenzy of delight.

Iris descended the rickety wooden steps to the beach, stopping at the bottom to slip off her shoes. The warm sand massaged her bare feet. She took a deep breath of ocean air and began walking, swinging her arms wide.

When she reached the hard sand, her eyes were drawn to the boardwalk and the long row of shuttered cottages stretching along its length. Many were traditional gray-shingled dwellings. Interspersed among them, rising high above the rooflines like grotesque mushrooms, were the newer "McCottages."

These oversized newcomers had every gewgaw known to contemporary builders, including wraparound porches, multiple decks, and sliding glass doors. Instead of the tall eel grass native to the area, they perched on manicured lawns. Needless to say, the new cottages belonged to newcomers. Not content to live a rustic beachside life, they demanded all the "conveniences" of home.

Soon Iris came upon Sandy Toes, the cottage her parents had rented years ago. She remembered the smell of mildew and sleeping on beds whose rusted springs chirped like a chorus of crickets. Likewise, the sinks and toilet were streaked with rust. The wiring, too, was primitive; the family couldn't use the stove and toaster simultaneously without blowing a fuse.

Yet these shortcomings mattered little to the two Quirk sisters who spent their days on the beach, riding the waves on their inflated tubes. When the tide went out, they built castles made of mud. Their mother, meanwhile, sat bundled on the porch, out of the sun, doing her needlepoint.

Further along the sand, Iris spotted the white clapboard cottage with faded blue shutters called "Laughing Water." She noted the recent update: a second-floor deck with sliding glass doors outside the master bedroom. Frank would have loved that, she thought. She pictured him standing high above the crowds, observing the masses sprawled on the beach.

Hidden from her view was the cottage behind Laughing Water. "The Barnacle" was the tiny bungalow that Claudia and Travis had rented. Yet though it wasn't visible from the beach, Iris remembered every detail, such as the green wooden rocking chair on the porch, the sagging rattan sofa inside, the miniscule bathroom with its lavender toilet seat.

How many years had passed since that summer? Ten? Iris often wondered if she hadn't found the evidence in Frank's car—the Mass Turnpike receipt—would she and Claudia still be friends? Would they have met during the winter for the "girls' night out," as planned? Claudia had failed to reply to her inquiry. Now Iris knew why. Few women can maintain a friendship having bedded that friend's husband.

Iris had been tormented by images of the pair. She pictured them at one of the motels at the creek end of the beach. While Sandpiper Beach was family-friendly, everything changed when you crossed the creek's wooden bridge. On the opposite side, the ice cream stands and miniature golf sites gave way to gambling bars, tattoo parlors, and a strip of cheap motels.

Iris imagined Frank and Claudia in one of those rooms. She pictured a torn window shade drawn against the afternoon sun. Claudia, her skin dark against white sheets, lay stretched on the bed while Frank hovered over her, sweat dripping on her glistening breasts. "Frank." Claudia said hoarsely, pulling him to her—

Now Iris stopped and said aloud, "That's enough." She squeezed her eyes shut, yet the image remained. In a moment, Claudia's face morphed into Valerie Moles's. Iris began walking, hugging herself. The sea breeze had developed a cutting edge.

She turned and headed back, walking into the wind, the salt spray stinging her eyes. She broke into a trot. Her feet were cold and wet, yet she had to put distance between herself and the two cottages. Once a place of carefree summer memories, Sandpiper Beach had become a dark stain, thanks to Frank's selfishness.

TEN

The offshore wind that had chilled the citizenry all week eventually ran out of force. In its wake was a balmy breeze. Harborvale residents were quick to take advantage of it. Open convertibles cruised Main Street while mothers in tank tops pushed baby carriages to the park; there every bench was occupied.

Downtown at the end of Main Street, the front door of For Your Thighs Only was propped open. As Iris approached, she heard Grace talking loudly, "You can always bring it back if it doesn't match."

A thin, reedy voice answered, "In that case, I'll take it."

"Lovely," Grace said. Looking up, she spotted Iris at the door. "Come in."

"Don't rush." Iris stepped inside and moved down the center aisle, peering at the jewelry glittering under tiny overhead lights. More sea glass items had been added to the array including a pair of earrings. The blue glass was dull from years of exposure to the ocean's waves and the churning sand.

After Grace saw her elderly customer to the door, she turned to Iris, saying, "She'll be back tomorrow to return it."

"Who will?"

"Florence, the lady I just waited on. She comes in every week and spends an hour deciding what she wants. The next day she's back, saying the same thing: 'It doesn't go with my wardrobe.' I tell her fine, pick something else. The next day she returns that."

"You're very patient with her."

"My grandmother was like that," Grace said. "She lived

through the Depression and was afraid to spend a cent. When she finally bought something, she'd torture herself, debating whether she needed it. Her towels were threadbare. She saved bits of soap to mold into a new bar. Maybe that's why I humor Florence."

"Or maybe it's because you're a softy," Iris said.

"Look who's talking. By the way, what are you doing here? Aren't you supposed to be in school?"

"Students' conferences. I don't have to be there until after lunch." She turned back to the case. "I thought I'd buy a sea glass necklace to go with the tan I intend to get this summer."

"A tan? So you can compete with the bronze bimbo bartender?"

"Please. Let's not mention her."

"In that case, maybe you want to impress your principal, Tomacito what's-his-name."

She laughed. "It's Tomasillo. Tomas Tomasillo." She told Grace about the misunderstanding they'd had. "Apparently he thought I was inviting him to visit the beach."

"What's wrong with him thinking you've got the hots for him? "

"I don't." She blushed. "Where did you get that idea?"

"I saw him watching you at that school auction you dragged me to. Not only that, I think you're sweet on him, as Grams used to say."

"What makes you think that?"

"Because right now your face is redder than a baboon's butt."

"That's a lovely analogy, comparing my face to a monkey's butt." Iris hesitated. "Well, if you must know, Mr. Tomasillo is very attentive, and right now that's appealing."

"Maybe you're attracted to him."

"Who knows," she said, turning her gaze to the jewelry case. "Or maybe it's because of Frank's indifference. Perhaps I'm looking for self affirmation."

"Quit the self-therapy," Grace said. "Life's simpler than that. It's because it's springtime and you're horny. Is Tomas married?"

"No, he's single. He's very courtly. It's old-fashioned, but it makes me feel good." She shook her head. "I don't want to have this conversation. Lately I'm not sure of anything, I'm so confused."

"I guess you haven't spoken to Frank about the bimbo."

"Not yet. The timing's wrong."

"I don't mean to come down hard on you, honey. You're going through a lot. But I think you should examine your motives in not discussing the issue with Frank. You're playing it safe."

"You think I'm afraid to face the facts?"

"Let's call it denial," Grace said. "Many marriages are built on denial. But if you want my opinion, I think you're merely being practical."

"What are you talking about?"

"You're eager to adopt Shannon's baby. In order to do that, you've got to look good to A Women's Issue. That means you and Frank present a solid front—the happy, wholesome couple."

Iris mulled over Grace's remarks. "You've got a point. But you're right; I've been putting off confronting Frank. Anyone would think I was afraid of him."

"It's normal for wives to stick their heads in the sand," Grace said. "I didn't want to confront my ex when I suspected he had someone else. Why rock the boat? It turns out I was right. Sven was having an affair, but his lover was a he, not a she. I wished it had been another woman. At least I'd have known how to compete."

Iris glanced at her watch; it was time to go. Before heading for the door she asked, "By the way, what's the hot legs contest you mention in your phone greeting?"

"It's generating excitement. I've got contestants ages eighteen to eighty. They're all anonymous. I photograph their legs and give each photo a number. Next time you're here, take a look at the bulletin board in the back."

"What's the prize?"

"A month of pantyhose, a free pair every week. You want to enter? I'll get my trusty Polaroid."

Iris shook her head. "My legs are too pale this time of year."

"Your legs are fabulous. Listen, this contest is causing quite a stir. *The Barnacle* is sending a reporter to do a story. It'll be great for business."

"Who's going to be the judge?" Iris asked.

"I was thinking of asking the guys at the fire station."

Iris nodded. "I'm sure they wouldn't mind."

"Next time you come in, I'll take your picture. Seriously, I could use some younger legs to spice up the board."

"I'd have to go tanning first."

"Believe in yourself," Grace said. "Don't hide your light under a barrel."

"Maybe that's why my legs are so white."

Grace ignored the humor. "I'm being honest with you. Start taking yourself seriously."

Iris nodded. "Thanks, coach."

After leaving Grace's shop, Iris decided to visit the fish store. She would buy haddock and make chowder for dinner. Frank loved fish chowder.

She walked down lower Main Street. Near the end, she turned into a long, narrow cobblestone alley between two abandoned brick buildings. As she reflected upon her conversation with Grace, she paid little attention to her surroundings. Soon a rustle at her feet caused her to glance down. A large, shaggy wharf rat scurried past her and ducked into a jagged hole in the building.

Iris broke into a run and continued until she reached the end of the alley. There she leaned against the building, her heart thumping. When her breathing returned to normal, she joined the pedestrians on the waterfront walkway.

Go Fish was in the middle of a line of small shops facing the harbor. She climbed the worn granite steps. Inside the shop, she studied the day's catch chalked on a blackboard. When it was her turn, she asked for a pound of haddock. The clerk scooped crushed ice into the foil-lined bag. The fish would remain chilled in her car's trunk while she was at school.

After seeing her last student for the day, Iris hurried to the parking lot. She needed time to prepare the chowder. She would use Frank's mother's recipe. According to her son, Lena Camuso made the best haddock chowder in Harborvale. On her way home Iris stopped at the liquor store for beer and wine.

The dinner would set the stage for the talk Iris hoped to have. When Frank was feeling mellow, she'd tell him how alienated she'd been feeling. Perhaps it would lead to an open discussion. The stress over Shannon's pregnancy and estrangement, coupled with Frank's struggle as a marine supplier in a downsized industry, had contributed to what she considered his midlife crisis.

Because despite their problems, she still loved Frank. From the moment she met him, he'd gotten into her blood. As a result, she hadn't been fair to Scott Lester, her Suffolk University boyfriend. Had she met Scott earlier, before she set eyes on Frank, maybe things would have been different . . .

After a succession of lunches and late night phone conversations, Scott invited her to dinner at his house to, "meet the fossils and tie on the feedbag," as he put it.

Although Iris was flattered, she was reluctant. Meeting the parents was a significant step in a relationship. What was holding her back, she wondered. Scott was witty, wealthy, and handsome. She liked his easy-going nature. Most girls would be thrilled to be dating Scott, who was what her mother's generation called a "catch."

More importantly, Scott liked her and wasn't afraid to show it. In class, she'd catch him gazing at her. Yet despite Scott's sterling qualities, she couldn't stop thinking about Frank, whose behavior puzzled her. When Iris first met him, Frank had been eager to please her. Hadn't he given her that custom-made apron?

Yet not long after that, things changed. When Iris passed Frank in his truck he waved, yet never slowed to talk. What had caused the sudden change in attitude? After dwelling upon the situation, she arrived at a conclusion—her dad had warned Frank away.

Phantom Baby

The night Iris arrived at the Lester's home, she sat in her car and stared. Ahead was a stately brick mansion with a four-car garage converted from a former stable. Glossy ivy climbed over the dark-red bricks. Leaded windows glowed in the waning light. Although she assumed Scott's family was comfortable, she didn't realize how comfortable. Yet the clues had been there: Scott's familiarity with wine, his late-model BMW, the Wellesley Hills address. Add the fact that although Scott didn't have a job, he had plenty of spending money.

He'd typically downplayed his status, making light of the family business. Bathroom fixtures to Iris meant soap dishes and toilet paper holders. Yet one afternoon, lunching at the Copley Fairmont, she discovered how grand Lester Fixtures was. Scott had casually mentioned that the plumbing fixtures in the hotel's bathrooms were his family's design.

"You mean your family made them?" she asked.

"They're made at a factory in East Boston."

"Does the ladies' room have Lester Fixtures?"

He laughed. "I'm not stepping in there to find out."

Iris, who'd had three large glasses of Beaujolais, decided to see for herself. Minutes later she was inside a bathroom stall on hands and knees examining the base of the toilet, as Scott had instructed. Embossed on an oval disk was the company name and the slogan, *Lester Lasts.*

Now Iris approached the black lacquered front door. An unsmiling uniformed maid answered. She led her down a long corridor to a room where tall palladium windows overlooked a putting green. The Lester family trio sat in opposite corners of the formal room. Wendy Lester, her silver hair worn in a neat bob, was straight out of *Town & Country* in a peach linen dress and pearls. Warren Lester—"Wags" to his friends—wore summer WASP attire, a Madras jacket and tie. Scott also wore a jacket and tie.

Iris glanced down at her sundress, more appropriate for a clambake than dinner in Wellesley Hills.

After the introductions, Mrs. Lester poured each a small glass of sherry. Following a discussion about the budding trees outside the window, the group adjourned to the dining room. There the silent maid waited to serve them dinner.

Iris stole glances at a subdued Scott, checking what silverware he used. He winked at her across the table. Dinner conversation was like the cocktail conversation—sparse. At one point Warren Lester asked his son: "Did you sign up for tennis lessons at the club?" Scott merely nodded. To Iris, he seemed to be functioning on autopilot.

During the main course of salmon, new potatoes and spring peas, the room lapsed into silence. The only sound was the muted clink of silverware. Iris felt her shoulder muscles tighten. She wished the maid would serve wine, but none was forthcoming. The sherry aperitif appeared to be the extent of the alcoholic offering. This despite what Iris had heard about WASPs' enthusiastic drinking. Obviously the senior Lesters were cut from a sterner mold.

When the silence got too oppressive, Iris finally spoke, "This salmon is excellent."

"Thank you," Mrs. Lester said, her voice a whisper.

"Glad you enjoy it," her husband added, nodding briefly.

This small exchange encouraged Iris. "If there's one thing I know, it's fish."

Wendy Lester raised her eyebrows at this, prompting Iris to launch into an account of her job. Talking too loudly, she babbled on about unloading and delivering seafood to local restaurants. As she continued, Mrs. Lester's tanned, lined face looked stricken, as if she'd swallowed a fish bone.

"That sounds like a demanding job," Mr. Lester said when Iris finished. "I wish Scott would take a page from your book."

"He's still in school, dear," Mrs. Lester murmured.

"Thanks, Mother," Scott said, winking at Iris across the table.

Now Iris pulled into her driveway. When she parked, Patticake jumped onto the hood of her car. Iris got out and scratched the cat's arched back. "I'm happy someone's here to greet me," she said, picking the cat up and carrying her into the house. She climbed the stairs to her bedroom. The light on the answering machine flashed. Iris stretched out on the bed and played the messages.

The first was from Fatima, Frank's sister in California. She knew about Frank's gum surgery and cooed into the phone, urging her "little brother" to be brave. "If I wasn't on another coast, I'd be with you at the dentist's. You could sit on my lap, like you used to do at the barber's, remember Frankie?"

Iris thought it would require a very large dental chair to accommodate Fatima's bulk.

After listening to the rest of the messages, Iris got up and slipped into a pair of jeans. It was time to make the chowder. In the kitchen, she peeled and cut up red potatoes. Then she chopped sweet onion and celery stalks. From the refrigerator, she got two slices of bacon. Frank's mother, a traditionalist, had used salt pork. But few markets still carried that product, so Iris substituted the bacon.

After the bacon was crisp, she poured off the fat, leaving a little in the pan to cook the onion and celery. When they were soft, she added the potatoes and enough water to cover. As it simmered she added seasonings: salt, fresh ground pepper, thyme and tarragon, a bay leaf, and a splash of Worcestershire sauce.

When the potatoes were almost tender, she added the fish, a can of evaporated milk and water. While the pot came to a boil, she snipped fresh parsley and chives. Into the mix they went, along with the crumbled bacon.

Patticake, drawn by the smell, watched Iris stir the chowder with a wooden spoon. As the pot simmered, Iris began making corn muffins. When they were in the oven, she headed into the dining room. There she removed her grandmother's Wedgewood bowls from the sideboard, along with the good wine and water glasses.

Finally, she set the table. When she was through, she stood back and admired how the silver and glassware gleamed in the candlelight. It was a perfect setting.

When he arrived home, Frank peered into the dining room, his brow creased. "Don't tell me we're having company."

"I thought we'd have dinner together, just the two of us."

"I'm not hungry. I had the fish stew for lunch at the Dinghy." He patted his belly. "I think I got a couple bad mussels."

"I made haddock chowder and corn muffins," Iris protested, "your favorites. Why don't you get washed up and see how you feel."

He shrugged and headed up the stairs. She was placing the corn muffins in a basket when Frank returned and took his place at the table.

"How's your mouth?" she asked.

"I can't chew on the right side. It's still sore." He stuck a finger into his mouth and gingerly felt the area.

"I'll get you a cold beer." She went into the kitchen and returned with a bottle of Sam Adams, pouring the contents into his glass. Sitting opposite him, she raised her wine glass. "To your good health."

He drank, glancing suspiciously around the table. "You gonna tell me what's up?"

"What do you mean?"

"Candles, china . . . What's the occasion?"

"I thought we could have a nice evening, just the two of us. Shannon may be gone, but we still have a life together."

"Fine by me," he said, stirring his chowder. They ate in companionable silence until Frank spoke. "Speaking of Shannon, she called me at my office."

"Really? Shannon never calls me."

"Wanna know why she called?"

Iris poured more wine into her glass and drank. "Sure. Why?"

"She told me about your visit to the adoption agency and the Department of Youth Services. She's worried you'll spoil things for her at the agency." He stopped to take a big swallow of beer. "And I don't blame her."

Iris shrugged. "I don't trust that agency, nor its director. If they kick Shannon out, she can come home where she belongs."

"Sure, bring the baby home and we'll raise it. One big happy family."

"Listen to me, Frank. That agency will get thousands for

Shannon's baby. Our grandchild is just a commodity to them. Once the baby's legally adopted, we'll never get it back. But if we claim our rights now, as Shannon's guardians, we have a chance. I know because I've seen a lawyer."

He stared at her. "You've seen a lawyer?"

"You can't go up against these people alone."

"What lawyer?"

"Vincent Tosi, he's a—"

"He's an asshole is what he is."

"Vincent Tosi is a well-regarded attorney. He's handled some important cases."

"Vincent Tosi will handle anything if the money's upfront. What's with you, Iris?"

"What do you mean?"

"You don't listen. I told you I no more want a baby in this house than a herd of buffalo."

"Don't raise your voice, Frank. Finish your chowder before it gets cold."

"And while we're on the subject, have you priced colleges lately?"

"What's that got to do with it?"

"You're always talking about Shannon's education. Have you put any money toward it?"

"I've put a little aside. I expect she'll get student loans."

"Shannon says the agency will pay for her education. We're talking private colleges, Iris, at least thirty thousand a year. Where would we get that kind of money?"

"Shannon can go to a state college. Lisa Varjebedian, the girl down the street, got a degree in business from Salem State. She's only twenty-nine and already owns two spas in New Hampshire."

He shook his head. "This agency is the best thing that's happened to Shannon. They're paying her rent, her health insurance. They'll cover college tuition. When the baby's born she'll have a nest egg to fall back on." He pointed a finger at her. "My advice to you? Butt out."

She stared down at her bowl. "What about us, Frank? That

child is a part of us. It's our blood. Don't we have rights too?"

He rubbed his eyes. "You forget it's Shannon's decision. She's not a child, you know. When I talked to her, she sounded sensible. She's doing what's best for her *and* the baby."

"She may feels that way now, but she'll regret it later."

He shrugged. "That's a chance she'll have to take. Right now Shannon's looking at the future, and it doesn't involve being a welfare mother."

"Shannon won't have to go on welfare. I'll raise the baby. We'll convert the TV room into a nursery, put in acoustic tiles so you'll never know the baby's there."

He drummed his fingers on the table. "You're not listening, Iris. This is some ritzy agency. It deals with doctors, lawyers, CEOs, the cream of the crop. The kid'll go to private schools, learn to play tennis." He looked at her with narrowed eyes. "But that won't happen if you keep interfering and spoiling things."

The withering look in Frank's eyes reminded her of Ms. Proctor's contemptuous stare. She got to her feet. "Spoiling everything am I, Frank? Stay right there."

She raced up the stairs to the bedroom. Under the folded scarves in her top dresser drawer lay the photo. Clutching it to her, she flew back down the stairs, her feet barely skimming the steps.

She strode into the dining room table and stopped opposite Frank. "I'll show you who's spoiling everything," she said, her voice breaking. "What about this?" She flung the photo at him, but instead of landing on the table, it fell into his bowl. Valerie Moles floated on a sea of chowder, grinning up at them.

"Where did you get that?" His voice was quiet.

"What does it matter?"

"You've been snooping."

"That's beside the point. You're a hypocrite, Frank. You pretend to care about your daughter's welfare when all you care about is your sex life."

He pushed back his chair and got to his feet. "I've tried to be understanding, Iris, but you've got serious problems that I can't fix. All I know is I've had enough." He left the room. Soon she heard his measured footsteps on the stairs

Iris lowered herself onto the chair and listened to Frank upstairs opening and slamming drawers. After a while she got up and moved to the bottom of the stairs. "Frank, what are you doing?" she called.

When there was no response, she sat on the bottom step to wait. Minutes later he appeared above her, carrying his zippered gym bag. "Where are you going?" she asked. Silently, he descended the stairs and stopped at the hall closet. There he removed his leather jacket. "Please tell me where you're going, Frank."

He struggled into it. "Why don't you snoop around, find out for yourself?"

"Are you going to see her?"

"What I do is my business."

"It's always your business. Frank's happiness always comes first. Family issues? Just pack a bag and go." She got to her feet, gripping the bannister. "You know what, Frank? I'm tired of being second place in your life. Go run to your whore. Go and live with her, for all I care."

Without turning, he opened the front door and shut it firmly behind him. Iris held her breath, listening to the silence. Then she sprang to the door and flung it open. Frank was getting into his car when she yelled, "Don't come back! Do you hear me, Frank? Don't come back!"

She slammed the door and returned to the stairs, where she sat huddled on the bottom step. Patticake warily climbed onto her lap. "Oh kitty," she whispered, stroking the cat's fur with trembling fingers, *"What have I done?"*

ELEVEN

The next morning, Iris dreamed of Lily: The two sisters were playing in the sand using plastic figures from their dollhouse. Iris was first to see the wave. Earlier she'd been puzzled by the tide receding from the shore, as if sucked up by a giant vacuum cleaner. Now she realized they were the only people left on the beach. Engrossed in play, the sisters hadn't noticed the towering wave moving in.

Iris looked up at their cottage. Their mother stood on the porch, shouting and waving a towel to get their attention. Iris glanced at the wooden stairs leading to the boardwalk; they would never reach them in time. Their bodies would be swept up by the wave and tossed against the concrete seawall. They had no choice but to face the tower of water.

She wrapped her arms around Lily's waist and fitted her knees behind her sister's. "Close your eyes and hold your breath," she shouted in Lily's ear. For a long moment the two stood as one, braced for the onslaught—

Iris sat up in bed, her heart pounding. The dream was over, but she'd awakened to another nightmare—Frank's side of the bed was untouched. He hadn't come home last night. The terrible fight, her shouting, all came back to her. She felt ashamed for having lost control. The dinner she'd planned so carefully had ended disastrously.

She pushed the blankets away and struggled to a sitting position. Her mouth was as dry as sand. She remembered finishing the bottle of wine and starting on another.

Rain drummed on the roof. Although Iris rarely missed work, she decided to call in sick. When Frank returned, she needed to be at home. She reached for the phone and dialed.

"Harborvale Memorial School."

Iris groaned upon hearing Ms. Dutton's voice. She'd hoped to reach Mrs. Trowt, the school secretary. Ms. Dutton obviously came in very early; perhaps she slept at the school. "This is Iris Camuso. I'm afraid I won't be in today . . . I have the flu."

"I wish I'd known earlier," Ms. Dutton said.

"I wasn't sick earlier."

Ms. Dutton sighed into the phone. "Why don't you give me the names of the students you're seeing today? I'll contact them during homeroom."

"Well, my file is downstairs—-"

"I'll wait."

Iris put the phone down and descended the stairs in her nightgown, swearing with each step. Upon reaching the kitchen, she realized her tote bag was in her car. Damn that Dutton, she thought, grabbing a jacket from the hall closet.

The wind whipped the aluminum storm door from her hands. When she got it closed, she raced to her car. Rain pelted her face as she fumbled with her keys. Finally she opened the car door and grabbed the tote bag from the back seat. She returned to the kitchen, her nightgown clinging to her wet legs. Setting the bag on the kitchen table, she pawed through the files with numb fingers. Eventually she found the schedule. Rainwater dripped off her as she picked up the kitchen phone and said, "Ms. Dutton, I have the list."

As she recited each student's name, Ms. Dutton asked for the spelling. When Iris was through, the woman said, "I'm obligated to inform Mr. Tomasillo that these sessions were canceled."

"I doubt he'll consider it a problem. I intend to make them up."

"I'm only following school policy, Ms. Camuso."

By the end of the week, when Frank hadn't returned, Iris met with Grace at Mega Mug. They huddled in an end booth as Iris talked about the latest crisis. "Right now I don't know what to do, contact a private investigator or a lawyer."

"You should have called a lawyer the minute Frank walked out on you," Grace said, taking a bite of her BLT sandwich. She'd wrapped one-half in plastic, intending to take it home, though invariably she ended up eating both halves including some of Iris's.

"Frank didn't *walk out.* He left because I told him to in anger. Naturally he'll come back."

"Staying away for four days with no word? Frank's sending a message, loud and clear. That's no way to treat a spouse."

Iris stirred her coffee. "I wasn't exactly loving when I told him not to come back."

"That's crap. He's using it as an excuse to stay away. Everyone says things they don't mean when they're mad."

"I know, I know." She closed her eyes. "This is a nightmare."

"Hang in there, honey. By the way, have you visited the bank recently? Frank could be cleaning out your joint account. He's had plenty of time."

She stared at Grace. "He wouldn't do that."

"Husbands and wives do stuff like that all the time. Ask your lawyer. My ex was the last person in the world I thought capable of such a devious act. He'd felt so guilty about leaving me, he even cried. But after Sven was gone, it was another story. How quickly he forgot. One day I got a notice saying our account was overdrawn. I raced to the bank and sure enough, the account was empty. *Zero dinero.* Sven had taken everything.

"When I finally got hold of him, he cried and apologized. He said the boyfriend needed an emergency hair transplant because he's in the public eye and—"

"Was he an actor, this boyfriend?" Iris asked.

"An airline steward. He'd developed *alopecia areata,* the hair loss disease. Sven said it was from stress. It was like he blamed me for causing the stress. I told Sven, 'I don't give a rat's ass. Tell lover boy to wear the pilot's cap.' Then I warned him, 'Put that money back or I'm calling the police.'"

"Did he put it back?"

Grace shook her head. "There was nothing I could do about

it because both our names were on the account. That's why I'm telling you before it's too late. When a midlife married guy moves in with a new babe, the money goes like a fart in a hurricane."

"Frank hasn't moved in with her."

Grace unwrapped the other half of her sandwich and bit into it. "How do you know?"

"The other night I drove by the Ship Ahoy apartments. His car was there until midnight. An hour later it was gone. That tells me he's probably staying at a local motel."

"How'd you know Valerie lives at the Ship Ahoy?"

"I called the bar pretending to be the cosmetics salesperson. I said I was driving around Harborvale searching for Valerie's place and couldn't find it. They told me."

Grace put her sandwich down and stared. "You were outside Valerie Moles's apartment at one in the morning? Iris, that's stalking."

"It's not stalking, it's documenting. My lawyer needs to know this information."

"Isn't the Ship Ahoy the place where Shannon lived with that beauty queen?"

"Yeah, with Amber. Good thing Shannon moved out. She'd be mortified knowing her father's girlfriend lived practically next door." Iris shook her head. "And Frank used to care about his reputation"

"How's he hurting his reputation?"

"What are you talking about? He's involved with that bimbo."

"I know a lot of guys—meatheads, of course—who'd envy Frank."

"But she's a tramp! She's got fake hair, fake boobs—"

Grace shrugged. "Men love tramps."

"This time Frank's gone off the deep end. I don't know if I can ever forgive him."

"Right now I'm more worried about you." Grace ate the last morsel of her sandwich. "You're obviously not getting any sleep if you're driving around spying at all hours. You're also drinking too much." Although Iris protested, she continued, "I hear it in your voice when we talk at night. You can't fool me, kid. Drinking alone's a bad habit. And you're not eating. You haven't touched your tuna melt." She glanced down at the evidence.

"I'm not hungry," Iris said. "I'm too upset to eat."

"In that case, I'll take it. No sense throwing it away." Grace smoothed the foil from her BLT and wrapped up the untouched sandwich. "My advice? Call your lawyer as soon as you get home."

Iris sighed. "I don't know. It's still too early."

Roland was her first student the following morning. As always, the boy sank into his chair with a huge yawn, dropping his book bag with a thud. "So, Roland," Iris asked, "what are your thoughts about the school year ending?"

"I'm crying my eyes out." He peered at her. "Hey, have you been crying?"

"What makes you say that?"

"I dunno. Your eyes are red, like my mom's were the time my grandmother was in the hospital."

"It's allergies. Tell me, did your grandmother get better?"

"Nah, she died, finally.

"Why do you say 'finally?"

"Mom kept getting phone calls that my grandmother was dying. She had to take a plane and rush to Ohio. Then my grandmother got better. But as soon as Mom got home, another call came saying Grams was dying again."

"That must have been hard on your mother."

"Yeah, then one night I heard Mom say, if she doesn't go the next time, I'm pulling the plug."

While Iris may have fooled Roland with her swollen eyes, she couldn't fool her dad. That afternoon they sat at his kitchen table eating the grilled cheese sandwiches Iris had made on his electric skillet. As she poured tea from a pot, he looked up at her. "How's Frank? Still at home?"

She set the pot down. "Did one of your neighbors say something?"

"Are you kidding? Half the people in this building think

George Bush is still President, and they're the bright ones."

"Then how did you—?"

"Let's just say I know my daughter and I know men like Frank."

Men like Frank. Her husband's essence captured in three words. Her dad had been wise to Frank from the beginning. And in the beginning, when he realized Iris was falling for him, he tried talking sense into her. Unfortunately, it was too late. Iris had already slept with Frank; all bets were off.

Following dinner at the Lester's, Iris invited Scott to Harborvale. She planned to take him out for fried clams. To her amazement, Scott had reached the age of twenty-six without having sampled the local delicacy.

When she introduced him to her dad, he pumped Scott's hand, his smile beaming his approval. Later, heading to Essex for clams, she suggested a ride around the harbor. Her suggestion was twofold: She wanted to show Scott where she worked and at the same time, she hoped Frank spotted them in the classy convertible.

After drinks and seafood at Periwinkle's, Iris suggested taking the waterfront route back. When they crossed the Harborvale Bridge, she pointed out the Dirty Dinghy below, on the waterfront. Live music poured from the bar's open windows. "Do you like country music?" she asked.

"I like whatever you like," Scott said, reaching for her hand.

"Except for fried clams."

He laughed. "Those will take time. You want to stop for a drink?"

"Why not."

As always on a weekend night, the bar was packed. They had to settle for a booth in the back of the room. After they ordered drinks, Iris headed for the ladies' room. Inside, she found an unoccupied mirror where she applied lipstick. A woman at the adjacent sink waved a can of hair spray over her hair, covering Iris in a fine mist.

Before heading back to Scott, Iris glanced over at the

crowded bar. People stood three deep, shouting orders to the harried bartenders. In the midst of the throng she spotted Frank. His arm was draped around a woman perched on a barstool. She wore pink cowboy boots and white satin shorts.

As if on cue, Frank turned and looked at Iris. Emboldened by alcohol she held his gaze. The hot, noisy bar with its crowds vanished as she stared into Frank's eyes. She lost all track of time. She might have stood there all night, their eyes locked, if Frank's date hadn't swung her chair around to face him.

When she joined Scott in the booth, the blood roared in her ears. She tossed down the last of her drink and jumped up. "C'mon, let's dance."

He glanced at the crowded dance floor. "There's no room."

But she was out of the booth, pulling him to his feet. "Just one dance."

They moved into the crowd, carving out a space on the tiny floor. She danced, her arms over her head, her hips swinging to the honky tonk beat. She moved with an abandon she'd never experienced before. All the while she imagined Frank's eyes upon her.

Too soon the music ended and they headed back to their booth. Fresh drinks were waiting. Again, Iris gulped hers. "Watch it," Scott said, laughing. "Your old man won't like me carrying you in the door."

She kissed his cheek. "I'm going to the ladies'. Be right back."

"Don't be long," he said, winking.

Once inside, she moved to a sink and stared at herself in the mirror. Her cheeks were flushed, her eyes glittering. She smiled dreamily at her reflection. It was the best Saturday night she'd had in a long time.

She left the bathroom and this time avoided looking over at the bar. As she made her way back to the booth, she spotted Frank from the corner of her eye. He quickly closed the distance between them, reaching out to grab her arm. Over the noise of the crowd he spoke into her ear. "One o'clock tonight. Meet me at the end of your road, off Birch Hill." He released her and moved away. She stared at his retreating back, amazed by the encounter and at the same time, not surprised.

When she slid into the booth, Scott put an arm around her. She pulled away and asked, "What time's it?"

He held up his watch. "Twelve-ten. Why?"

"My dad likes me back around midnight." She shrugged, apologetic. "He says he can't sleep until I'm home."

"I was hoping we could take a walk on the beach." Scott put an arm around her. "You got me in the mood on the dance floor."

"I'd like to, but I don't want to worry Dad."

"That's what I love about you," he said. "You don't have a selfish bone in your body." When he kissed her, she hoped Frank was watching. At the same time, she felt guilty for using Scott in that way. Nonetheless, her guilt was overpowered by a rising sense of anticipation. It was as if her whole life had been leading to the upcoming rendezvous with Frank, and nothing, *nothing*, would stop her . . .

After the grilled cheese sandwiches were eaten, it was time for Iris to go. She gathered her things and leaned down to kiss her dad's cheek. "Wait," he said, getting to his feet. He put his good arm around her in a hug. "My little girl, things will work out, just you wait." Her eyes filled with tears and he handed her a hanky from his breast pocket. "Here, it's clean."

She wiped her eyes. "Thanks. I must look a mess."

"You look beautiful, like your Grandmother Quirk"

"You used to say Lily looked like Gramma Quirk."

"Well, you've grown to look like her. You've got her blue eyes."

"I still dream about Lily, Dad. Do you dream about her?"

"I don't have to," he said, patting his pocket. "She's here in my heart."

Iris nodded. Even after so many years she still felt awkward discussing her dead sister. She wondered how much time would pass before she'd feel comfortable. More importantly, would she ever learn the answer to her question: Did her dad hold her responsible for Lily's death?

That night, lying alone in the dark, Iris listened to the trees creaking in the wind. Fearful thoughts supressed during the day emerged. What if Frank didn't come back? How long could she continue living in the house before she'd have to sell?

She sat up and turned on the bedside lamp. Tomorrow she would speak to Mr. Tomasillo about the job he'd mentioned. She hadn't been interested at the time. She had felt secure, married to Frank. She grabbed a note pad from the bedside table and scribbled a message to herself. Writing made her feel in control. As she wrote, her stomach growled. She'd eaten little that day. Maybe some toast and juice would help. She got out of bed.

In the cold kitchen she poured orange juice and dropped a slice of bread into the toaster. As she waited, Patticake padded in and stared up at her. "You hungry, too?" Iris switched on the pantry light. On the shelf above the cat food was a bottle of Russian vodka. She stared at the silver label. A little in her juice would stop her thoughts from spinning and help her to sleep. It was important she be rested when she spoke to the principal tomorrow.

She unscrewed the cap and poured a splash into her glass. Then she opened the cat food. She set Patticake's dish on the floor, saying, "Are you gonna leave me like everyone else?"

She buttered the toast and carried the plate and her drink to the table. The vodka soon worked its magic, easing the knot in her stomach. It helped her to view her situation objectively. Things seemed frightening because of their unfamiliarity, she decided. Outside of the occasional overnight when he'd been away on business, she'd never been separated from Frank. She realized how dependent she'd become. An unhealthy dependence, she thought, sipping the vodka-laced juice. Moreover, she'd given Frank too much power over her. He was the puppeteer, controlling her strings. She hadn't noticed his manipulations until recently. Now she saw how Frank had called the shots even when their romance was new:

After showing great interest in Iris, Frank's retreat was baffling. She feared her dad had spoken to him. In the meantime, when Iris learned that Frank's sister Fatima worked at a tourism booth downtown, she decided to pay her a visit. She thought up an excuse—cousins were visiting from Worcester and Iris needed tourist information.

"This is our latest publication," Fatima said, handing Iris a brochure titled, ***Harborvale: First for Family Fun!***

"Thanks," Iris said, taking the new brochures. Before turning away, she said casually, "By the way, I know your brother."

"Frankie?" Fatima tapped plum-colored nails on the counter. "All the girls know Frankie."

Iris felt her cheeks flush. "Oh, I suppose you're right." She turned away.

Perhaps Fatima recognized the disappointment in her tone. She called out, "Hey, what's your name?"

She turned. "Iris, Iris Quirk."

Fatima tossed her long, curly hair. "Never met anyone by that name. I'll be sure to remember." To Iris's retreating back she called, "Have fun with your cousins."

Having waited in vain for Frank, she decided to make the first move. She sent him a note, thanking him for the apron. Inside the card she wrote, *Since you won't accept payment, let me buy you a drink.* Originally she'd written "coffee," but discarded that note. A drink sounded more sophisticated.

Before dropping the card in the mailbox, she experienced a moment of fear. Was the note an act of desperation? Had Frank warped her judgment? Despite her misgivings, she proceeded. She had little choice. It was as if Frank had turned on a switch inside her and she was powerless to shut it off.

When the days went by with no response from Frank, she became certain her father had spoken to him. It was the only explanation that made sense. She knew Frank was interested. That was her state of mind that summer and it affected her work. One day the cook at the Red Skiff called to complain. He'd ordered small bay scallops and Iris had delivered large. Her dad had taken the irate call. "You make careless mistakes like that, it'll cost me their business," he told her. "Pay attention."

Her relationship with Scott also deteriorated. He wanted to go away for an overnight in Portland. Admittedly, it sounded glamorous—ferrying to an island in Casco Bay and staying at an old seacoast inn. "Away from the mainland, you won't have a care in the world," Scott promised.

Iris was torn. She was attracted to Scott and didn't want to lose him. Yet she wasn't ready to go away overnight. That was a big step. She had to get Frank out of her system before she slept with Scott.

"How about if I get two rooms?" he asked, sensing her trepidation. "Would that make you feel better?"

She felt ashamed. Scott thought her reluctance stemmed from modesty. "I can't leave my dad right now," she told him. Even to her ears the excuse sounded lame.

One afternoon when he dropped her off at North Station, he said without looking her way, "Give me a call when you make up your mind." He roared away in his white BMW without a backward glance.

That night, Iris moped around the house feeling sorry for herself. Not long ago she'd had the interest of two men. Now it appeared she had none. The proof was obvious; she was alone on a Friday night.

She put the kettle on for tea. As she waited for it to heat, she heard snoring coming from her dad's bedroom. He was always in bed by nine o'clock, giving her time alone to relax.

She switched on a standing lamp in the living room and leafed through the magazines on the coffee table, finally choosing *Yankee*. With a cup of tea at her elbow, she stretched out on the sofa to read. As she turned the pages, a cluster of toenail clippings fell from inside the magazine onto her chest. She stared at the gnarled yellow bits and rolled off the sofa with a loud shriek.

Seconds later her father appeared in the doorway. He wore a t-shirt and rumpled boxer shorts. "What's wrong?" His eyes darted around the room.

She pointed to the clippings scattered on the sofa. "You cut your toenails and left them inside the magazine for me to find."

He blinked at her. "Is that why you screamed?"

"Dad, can't you throw them in the wastebasket? Why leave them in a magazine?"

He scratched his head. "You woke me up because of toenails? What's bothering you, Iris?"

"Nothing's bothering me." Tears filled her eyes. "Just stop meddling in my life."

"What are you talking about?"

"I'm talking about whatever you said to Frank Camuso that's made him avoid me."

"I have no idea what you're talking about."

Looking at his confused expression, she knew he was telling the truth. "It's just that he used to be so friendly, and now he avoids me."

"If that's the case, consider yourself lucky." Her father turned and left the room.

TWELVE

"Hey, Ms. Camuso, are you sleeping?"

Roland's voice jolted her awake. She'd dozed off, her chin resting in her palm—for how long? It was the heat. The cast iron radiator in the corner remained on even though the days were warm. "I wasn't sleeping, Roland," she told him. "I was resting my eyes."

"You were snoring, too."

She glanced at his grinning face. What if Ms. Dutton had caught her? "It's the change in the weather that makes me tired. By the way, do you have your Family of Origin project to work on?"

"First I have to take it home and ask my parents questions, like where my grandparents were born, stuff like that."

She rubbed her eyes. "Do you see much of your grandparents?"

"Nah, they're dead."

"Oh, that's too bad."

"It's because my parents were old when I was born."

It occurred to her that with school getting out in a week she may never see Roland again. She decided to broach the topic. "Have you finalized your school plans for next year?"

He shrugged. "My parents signed me up for a military school, a place called Stanford. Something like that."

"Do you mean Standish?"

"Yeah, that's it, Standish Academy." He looked at her. "Did you know they were doing that?"

"I might have heard something," she admitted.

"Why didn't you tell me? You're supposed to be my counselor."

"I wasn't at liberty to discuss it, not until your parents talked to you first. How do you feel about it?"

He yawned. "It doesn't matter. They can sign me up for Concord State Prison, for all I care."

"What does that mean?"

"My parents don't listen to me. I have to make my own plans."

"What kind of plans?"

He looked away. "Gloria's gonna help me. She's the only one who listens."

After Roland left, Iris deliberated on whether to document his comment. If she did, Ms. Dutton would no doubt get Dr. Turley involved. He would overreact, likely bringing Gloria to the attention of the authorities. An innocent woman's reputation would be ruined by overzealous school officials. Not only that, Iris had no proof Roland planned a getaway. Most likely it was typical adolescent bravado. And finally, wasn't the poor kid under enough pressure already?

For those reasons, she decided to speak to Mr. Tomasillo privately. She would allude to Roland's remarks at the time she discussed the district job opening. When the day was over and the school empty, they could talk uninterrupted.

After making notes on the day's sessions, she locked her door and headed for Mr. Tomasillo's office, her footsteps loud in the empty corridor. When she reached the main office, she found the door closed, the lights out. Had everyone gone home? She tried the door. It swung open. The reception desk was empty, an old gray cardigan hanging from the back of Ms. Trowt's chair. The secretary's computer was hidden under a tan plastic cover.

Perhaps Mr. Tomasillo was inside, working late. She crossed the room and rapped lightly on his door. Immediately, an adjacent door swung open and Ms. Dutton peered out. "I . . . I'm here to see Mr. Tomasillo," Iris managed to say.

"He's at a conference in Haverhill. I'm acting principal while Mr. Tomasillo's away. Whatever you have to say, you can say to me." With that, she opened her office door wide.

Iris got a glimpse of a glazed cinnamon bun the size of a CD on the desk. "Thanks anyway," she said, backing up. " I'll stop by tomorrow."

"Tomorrow Mr. Tomasillo will be busy with graduation rehearsals. I'll be dealing with employee issues." Ms. Dutton advanced closer. "What's the purpose of your visit?"

Iris, impaled by the woman's beady eyes, backed up until she banged into a metal wastebasket. It tipped over, spilling its contents on the floor. "Oh, sorry." She dropped to her knees, grateful for the diversion, and began tossing everything back into the barrel. "It's so dark in here, I didn't see it." She glanced at the assistant principal's feet, inches away. They were small and wide, stuffed into velvet slippers with embroidered flowers. "There," Iris said, righting the wastebasket and placing it between them. She leaped up and glanced at her watch. "Oops, gotta go," she said, turning away.

"Ms. Camuso!" It was a command.

"Sorry, I'm late!" Iris scurried to the door and flung it open. She raced down the hall so fast she almost lost a shoe. At the end of the corridor, she glanced back. Ms. Dutton's troll-like figure stood silhouetted in the dim hallway. Even from that distance Iris felt the woman's eyes boring into her.

Wednesday afternoon found Iris in the law office of Vincent Tosi. She discussed the situation prior to Frank's desertion and as she spoke, the lawyer scribbled notes on a yellow lined pad. She hadn't referred to Frank's departure as a *desertion*; that was Vincent's term. She ended by telling him about the photo of Valerie Moles and how it had resulted in Frank's departure.

"Do you have the photo?"

She reached into her bag and removed the chowder-stained picture, handing it to him. He whistled and said, "She's a bartender?"

"That's not very professional."

He looked pained. "C'mon, Ms. C., you know I'm joking."

"Lately I've had little sense of humor."

"Considering what you've been through, you're entitled.

But if you want my professional opinion, you're a very attractive woman."

"You're kind, Mr. Tosi."

"It's Vincent, and I'm not being kind. It's the truth." He glanced at his notes. "I think I've got enough information right now. Although Frank hasn't declared his intent, you need to protect your assets."

"We're not talking divorce, are we?"

"It's one partner protecting her assets due to the fact her spouse is behaving unreasonably."

"What do I do now?"

"First I'll need a retainer. Twelve hundred is standard. You can send it to my office. As soon as I get your check, I'll write Frank a letter of notification saying I'm representing you. He'll want to contact his lawyer."

"Frank doesn't have a lawyer."

He grinned. "He will. Now you said you have joint credit cards and bank accounts?"

"That's right."

"When I file a Complaint for Divorce, your husband will be served a summons. There's an automatic restraining order on the marital assets."

"Restraining order?"

"It's basic protection. Otherwise Frank's liable to dissipate your assets, and we don't want that." He tore the pages from the legal pad and shoved them into a folder. "Along with the divorce summons, I file an *ex parte* motion requesting the judge put a restraining order against Frank."

"Ex-what?"

"It's Latin for 'without notice to the other party.'"

She rubbed her forehead. "Vincent, this legal talk is making my head spin. I didn't come here for a divorce. I just want to know my rights."

He looked at her. "You're saying you don't want to upset Frank?"

"I just want everything to be civilized. I don't want to burn any bridges."

He rolled his eyes. "You want to be nice while your husband is shacked up with another woman and having no contact with his family."

"He's not technically living with her." During Iris's nightly surveillance of apartment number two-hundred-twenty at Ship Ahoy Village, she'd gathered more information. For instance, Frank usually left the premises at midnight. "And after all, he's only been gone three weeks."

"So what's your plan, sit back and wait for Frank to get tired of Valerie?" He glanced again at the photo lying on the desk. "Not bloody likely. If you want my opinion, this babe looks like high maintenance. She'll deplete your account like a drunken sailor."

Iris felt that Vincent was practicing a form of tough love. Nonetheless, his warning rang true. If she dragged her feet, she could be left penniless, unable to adopt Shannon's baby and unable to afford legal help. She had reached a crossroads and had two choices: Either wait for Frank to come to his senses, or take action to protect herself. The former didn't seem likely.

She got to her feet. "All right, Vincent, do what you have to do."

He stood. "You're doing the right thing, Ms. C.. Do you know what a client called me after I got his divorce?"

"Pit bull?"

"No, this was another client. He called me the 'trash man.' That's because he walked away with everything: the cars, the house, the pension. Everything including the goddamn trash barrels."

"I don't want everything. I just want my fair share."

"Sweetheart, when it comes to divorce, ain't no such thing as fair."

After Iris got home, she called Grace at her shop and described her visit with the lawyer. "I feel like I'm on a runaway train and can't get off. Vincent's proceeding with a legal separation. He says it's the only way to protect my assets. At the same time I can't help thinking, what if Frank's ready to come home?

When he finds out I've retained a lawyer, he'll never come back then. Frank hates lawyers."

Grace chuckled. "Of course he does. Frank's accustomed to laying down the law himself."

"But he's always looked out for me. He helps with my car insurance, my registration . . . things like that."

"He's not looking out for you if he's boffing that bartender." She paused. "By the way, you're not still stalking them, are you?"

"No," she lied. "And it's not stalking, it's gathering evidence for my case."

"Whatever you call it, Iris, just stop. That kind of behavior destroys a woman's self-esteem."

"What's left of it," Iris said.

Despite her promise to Grace, Iris parked outside the Ship Ahoy units that night at eleven o'clock. Her eyes swept the rows of cars, taking note that Frank's Sebring was in lot number two-hundred twenty. Parked next to it was Valerie's low-slung white Miata with the license plate TOOHOT.

Iris circled the lot and finally eased into the space numbered three-hundred-thirty, which she'd come to think of as hers. It was always empty, it's adjoining space occupied by a beige Taurus. She speculated about the Taurus's owner, picturing an older woman, divorced or widowed and living alone. She would seldom leave the complex except to visit the doctor's office or occasionally, the senior center. A lonely soul, someone observing life from the fringes.

After shutting off the ignition, Iris rested her head against the seat. She was tired. Since Frank's departure, she'd hardly slept. Tonight's surveillance would be brief, she promised herself. She'd leave after an hour whether she saw activity or not. Usually there was nothing to see; Valerie Moles kept her curtains closed.

One night, however, Iris was rewarded. The sliding glass door opened and Valerie appeared on the balcony in a short, white belted robe. She leaned over the railing to flick a cigarette into the bushes below. Iris was convinced Valerie wore nothing under the robe.

She had noted the time on her pad. Documentation was important, and she didn't care if Grace thought the practice demeaning. Iris had to watch the love nest. When she forced herself to stay home, she couldn't contain her restlessness. She was tormented with images of Frank and Valerie. Here in the parking lot, Iris was in control. She was the observer and they her subjects.

The car's interior grew warm. She shrugged off her jacket, turning her attention to the dimly lit terrace on the second floor. It was hard to focus; her eyelids kept drooping. Soon her head sagged forward. The notepad dropped from her lap.

She slept.

A sharp rapping on the window woke her. A dark silhouette stood outside. Iris gasped. Was it Frank or Valerie? She stared, her heart racing.

"Mrs. Camuso, lower the window!" The woman's voice was loud.

Iris pressed the button to lower the window a few inches. "Who is it?" Her voice was a whisper.

"It's me, Amber. Shannon's friend. Are you okay?"

"Amber, you scared me." She lowered the window all the way and glanced at the clock. She'd been asleep for an hour. She looked around the parking lot. Frank's car was gone. "What are you doing out here?"

"I'm getting back from a date, "Amber said, resting her forearms on the window. The young woman reeked of alcohol and perfume. Her breasts, in the low-cut dress, were ghostly white in the moonlight. "What are *you* doing?"

"I . . . I dropped a friend off," Iris said. "I must have been awfully tired. I think I dozed for a few minutes."

Amber giggled. "Is the friend named Frank?"

Iris's face flushed. "I'd better get on home."

"Don't worry, Mrs. Camuso, I won't tell anyone. I heard you kicked him out." She reached inside and placed a cool hand on Iris's cheek. "Take my advice and forget him. Men are assholes, you know what I mean?"

Iris nodded. "I'll remember that. Nice talking to you, Amber." She turned on the ignition and shifted into reverse, forcing Amber to step back. She swayed in her high heels.

"Remember, I won't tell," she called, her voice ringing out.

Iris gave a brief wave and wheeled out of the parking lot. When she reached the on ramp to the highway, she realized her headlights were off.

Two days later Iris made sure that Mr. Tomasillo was in his office and Ms. Dutton was otherwise engaged before visiting the principal. Ms. Trowt buzzed his office, saying, "Ms. Camuso here to see you."

Immediately he appeared at his door, beckoning her in. The office was surprisingly sumptuous, containing a wooden desk as sleek as a Steinway piano. Adjacent was a standing lamp with a flowered silk shade. Two chairs facing the desk were covered in brocade. The walls, however, contained only a framed diploma from Northeastern University and next to that, a studio portrait in a heavy gilded frame. The subject was a heavyset young woman with rosy cheeks and dark curly hair held back with frilly white ribbons.

"My sister Aidita," he said, noting her gaze. "She is a gifted early-childhood educator." He shrugged. "Unfortunately, there are few teaching jobs in Puerto Rico. I'm hoping Aidita will join me here in the States."

"Good luck," Iris said, studying the portrait. The girl had a pugnacious look.

"Time will tell," he said. "Excuse me, Ms. Camuso, are you feeling well? You look pale."

She smiled. Makeup couldn't conceal the effects of her late night surveillance. "I'm getting over a touch of flu."

He nodded. "It is this time of year, when the students become so . . . ramshackle."

"I think you mean 'rambunctious,' Mr. Tomasillo."

He laughed. "You are right, and please call me Tomas." He gestured for her to sit. "But you did not come here to correct my poor English, though a visit from you is sunshine on a rainy day."

"You're very kind. No, I'm interested in the job you mentioned, as social services coordinator."

He made a sad face. "Unfortunately, it has been filled. Mr. Bullock's daughter-in-law applied. I'm sorry. Had I known you were interested, I would have spoken up."

"It's my fault for not acting sooner," she said.

"We must bite while the iron is hot, yes?"

She nodded, too discouraged to correct him.

"Perhaps I am selfish for thinking so, but I am happy you will remain at the middle school. By the way, has Roland Smedlie said anything to you about Standish Academy?"

She hesitated, not knowing how much to divulge. "I don't think he's accepted the idea yet. I suppose he'll adjust in time."

"He must. The Smedlies plan to travel. Dr. Smedlie was invited to lecture in Germany. While they are away, Roland will be at the military academy." He hesitated. "Apparently the boy has been associating with people the Smedlies do not consider good roller models."

"Role models," she corrected. "Are you referring to a woman named Gloria?"

He nodded. "The Smedlies are concerned because the boy spends time with this person rather than with others his own age."

She sighed. "Fourteen is a tough age. If you want my opinion, military school is not an appropriate choice for someone with Roland's temperament."

He smiled and tapped his desktop. "Perhaps he will turn out to be a war hero like your General Patton."

She got to her feet. "Knowing Roland, I doubt that very much." She'd decided to not mention the boy's vague remarks about running away. The poor kid didn't need any more aggravation.

THIRTEEN

Almost a week passed before Iris returned Ms. Proctor's call. She hadn't been avoiding the woman, she told herself; she'd simply had a lot on her plate. Thus when she arrived home to discover another message from Ms. Proctor, she felt the familiar sense of dread.

After two glasses of Chianti, Iris dialed the agency, her hand clenched around the phone. She was put through to Ms. Proctor who got right down to business: "It's very unfortunate, Ms. Camuso, this action you've taken. A woman from the Department of Social Services recently appeared at Shannon's door demanding to be let in."

"I had no choice," Iris said. "If Shannon hadn't shut us out, we wouldn't be forced to seek outside help."

"In view of the fact the D.S.S. is harassing one of our clients, our lawyers are now involved."

"Why don't we handle this privately?" Iris said. "I've mentioned how we want to be the adopting parents. Not only that, we're prepared to pay whatever your agency normally receives."

The woman sighed into the phone. "You haven't been hearing my message, Ms. Camuso. Shannon decides what is best for the baby. She has made her decision and I'm sorry that it doesn't include you."

"How can Shannon decide? She's a child herself."

"She's a mature young woman. For some reason you can't accept your daughter as an individual who knows her own mind. In the meantime, I hate seeing her go through this ordeal. In my book, that is abuse."

"What about the abuse I'm going through?" Iris jumped to

her feet. "I've lost my daughter to your agency and now I'm losing my grandchild to strangers. That's my idea of abuse, Ms. Proctor."

After a pause the woman spoke, her voice resigned. "I've tried to be understanding, Ms. Camuso. I've been patient. But this latest development indicates you're not capable of listening to reason."

"Excuse me," Iris said. "You are unreasonable. Your agency breaks up families, manipulates their lives. You pretend it's for the sake of the children when in fact it's about money. By the way, how much will you get for Shannon's baby—thirty or forty thousand? We can match that." Iris dug her nails into her palm as she waited for the woman's reply. It never came. Ms. Proctor had hung up the phone.

Iris sank back into the chair. Her talk with Ms. Proctor had gone badly. It was like her discussions with Frank; things started out civilly yet quickly went downhill. She wondered if Ms. Proctor was right—was she being unreasonable?

She felt the familiar stirrings of guilt and remorse. Before they deteriorated into despair, she reached for the phone and called Grace.

"Let me get this straight," Grace said after Iris's briefing. "Proctor's mad because you called the D.S.S. on Shannon? You're her mother, for chrissake. That's your right. None of this would be necessary if Shannon hadn't behaved like a prima donna."

"That's what I thought," Iris said. "Then Proctor hung up on me."

"That bitch. Why'd she do that?"

"I hinted that the agency was only interested in money."

"That might be a bit harsh. Nonprofits get touchy about things like that."

"I realize that. I had a couple glasses of Chianti before I called. Proctor always sounds so self-righteous. It gets to me."

"Yeah, but she holds the cards. Proctor's in the driver's seat, like it or not. You've got to make nice with her. And while we're on the subject, you shouldn't be calling when you've been drinking—"

"It wasn't serious drinking, two glasses of Chianti."

"Honey, you sought my advice and I'm telling you. Booze messes with your judgment. You don't want Proctor thinking you're a lush on top of everything else."

"What do you mean 'everything else?'"

"Shannon's probably filled her head with all sorts of stories. You know how teenage girls exaggerate, especially when there's a sympathetic ear."

"I won't call her again. I was simply returning her call. Now that's out of the way, I have to call Frank."

"Frank!"

"He's been gone a month. The quarterly tax bill came the other day and I don't know what to do with it. Frank always handled the finances. Plus I'm thinking of canceling our cable. I can't go forward until I know his plans."

"Sweetheart, do yourself a favor. Ask your lawyer before you call Frank."

She sighed. "I already did."

"I gather he didn't think it was a great idea."

"Uh-huh. But I can't remain in limbo. If this is the end of our marriage, I want to hear it from Frank. Valerie Moles has him brainwashed. He's not using his head."

"No," Grace said, "he's using another part of his anatomy."

"Listen, let's not talk about Frank right now. I get a gnawing in my stomach when I do." She took a sip of wine. "So tell me, do you have a winner for the hot legs contest at your shop?"

"It's still undecided until I find a judge. When the mayor found out that the firefighters were judging, he nixed that idea. He claims it's 'not appropriate' for the department's image. Now I'm looking for another judge, preferably someone known in the community."

"Hmm, why not ask Vincent Tosi?"

"The lawyer? Would he consider it undignified?"

"Are you kidding? He'd put it on his resume."

"Okay, I'll call him. If you don't mind, I'll say you recommended him."

"Fine. I have to go now. Patticake's crying to be let out."

"Let's get together next week. Come over for dinner. I'll cook my specialty, blue cheese burgers, on the grill. If it's warm enough, we can sit outside at the picnic table."

"I'd like that. I spend too much time here, waiting for Frank to show up."

"Good. No matter how lonely you feel, resist the urge to call Frank. Listen to your lawyer, he knows best."

"You're right again," Iris said with a sigh. "It was a moment of weakness but I'm over it. I have no intention of calling Frank."

Ten minutes later she called Frank.

The following day Iris pulled into a parking space near Mighty Mart's entrance door. Sandy was leaning against the building, smoking a cigarette. "Taking a break?" Iris asked, getting out of her car.

"Yeah. Things are slow." She flipped the butt into the air. "I ain't complaining."

"How's the screenplay coming along?"

At the mention of her screenplay, Sandy's face lit up. "It's coming along awesome. Dr. Fung, the chemistry teacher, took the script home. He's looking over the science stuff and making some great suggestions. For instance, you know how the fluid oozes out of the UFO after it crashes in the cemetery?" Iris didn't know but nodded anyway. "Dr. Fung said make the color a muddy green instead of blue—more realistic. He also figured out my biggest problem, finding ordinary household chemicals to combat the aliens. Dr. Fung said baking soda and vinegar. I tried it out soon as I got home." She grinned. "That shit foams up big time, pardon my French."

"It sounds like Dr. Fung's getting into the spirit of things."

Sandy nodded. "He comes in when I'm working nights. Fewer interruptions."

"Uh huh. I'm glad he's able to provide authenticity."

"Absolutely. If I'd known Dr. Fung was such a cool dude, I would of taken chemistry in high school. I didn't think I could handle the college track. I ended up at the tech, studying cosmetology."

"How'd that turn out?" Iris asked.

Sandy pulled out a pack of Marlboro Lites wedged in the pocket of her jeans. "It sucked. My first job was at Green Pastures Nursing Home where they had their own salon for the residents. Me and another stylist did perms all day for blue-haired ladies. The chemicals would knock you out. After a month I started wheezing. My hands broke out in eczema."

"Sounds awful."

She took a deep drag of her cigarette, turning her head to expel the smoke. "After Green Pastures, I got a job at Fusionista. You know, the salon at the mall, the one that's got neon mannequins?"

Again Iris didn't know, "Was that better?"

"Worse. I went from working on eighty-year-old fossils to eighteen-year-old bitches. They tipped better than the old ladies, but I couldn't take their attitudes. Finally I decided I'd rather scrub toilets at Fenway Park than try to please a bunch of women."

You're young," Iris said. "You'll find your niche someday."

"If I sell this script, I'm hauling ass and moving to southern California."

At home, Iris listened to two new messages. The first was from Grace, following up her dinner invitation. "I'm buying the food after work, so no excuses. Be here tomorrow around six."

The second message from Vincent Tosi concerned a document he wanted her to fill out. "All the information can be found by looking at your '99 tax forms."

She wondered where she'd find those forms—in Frank's study, perhaps? According to Vincent, Iris had to get her papers in order ASAP. At her last visit to his office, he'd suggested she change the locks. "Why? Frank's not going to break in," she said, scoffing at the idea. "He'd ask me if he needed anything."

Vincent rolled his eyes. "Ms. Camuso, are you familiar with the children's tale, 'Babes in the Woods?'"

"I used to read that to Shannon."

"Then you know what happened to those trusting kids?"

She shook her head. "I forget."

"They get eaten by a wolf. You know why? Because they were trusting."

She had decided not to tell Vincent about her phone call to Frank. Vincent hadn't been receptive to the idea when she suggested it. In fact, he'd gone into a tirade: "If you want me to represent you, Ms. C., you gotta do what I say. That means no contact with the other party. If Frank needs something, tell him to get in touch with me, your lawyer."

She knew, however, that if Frank were to call Vincent it would be to threaten him. Yet Vincent's warning hadn't stopped her from calling Frank. Now she wished she hadn't. Their conversation hadn't resolved anything. In fact, it left her more agitated than ever:

"According to my lawyer, I'm not supposed to be talking to you," Frank said. "And I wouldn't need a lawyer if you hadn't hired that dirtbag, Vinnie Tosi."

"I needed legal advice, Frank. I hadn't heard from you in weeks. A man walks out after twenty years of marriage—"

"Nineteen years, Iris. And I was planning to call you, but now I can't. You screwed things up good this time."

"Don't shift the blame on me, Frank. You're the one having the affair. You're the one that walked out."

He sighed. "I'm not having an affair and for what it's worth, I'm sorry. I didn't mean to hurt you, but I had to go. If I stayed I'd be dead now."

"Frank Camuso, what are you talking about?"

"I'm talking about saving my life."

"How was your life in danger?"

"How? For openers, let me tell you what Dr. Schanley, the periodontal surgeon said when I asked what's causing my gum problems. You know what he told me?"

"What?"

"Stress. It's all stress, and that got my attention. That's how my old man died at fifty-one years of age. Saturday morning he's at the North End getting a haircut, like he's done for twenty years. He had the same barber, Dino, every time.

"But this time after he gets outta the barber chair and reaches for his wallet, *bam!* down he goes. He was dead when he hit the floor. Never knew what hit him. At least his last day was a good one."

"You forget your father had a heart condition," she said.

"And I'm a prime candidate. I told you Doc Moss wants me to start taking blood pressure pills. I tell you no way am I gonna end up dead on a barber shop floor. That's why I had to get out. The stress was killing me."

"Frank, we all have stress, but we deal with it. We can do things to help, like go to counseling. We can communicate more with each other."

His laugh was harsh. "What did counseling do for Shannon? Basically, Iris, you and I have come to a crossroads. We want different things from life. You want to spend the next twenty years changing diapers and chasing a kid around. I want to move to the Keys, buy a boat and start a little charter business. I don't want to sell marine supplies until I drop."

"We can still do those things, Frank."

"While dragging a kid like a ball and chain?"

"Is that how you see our grandchild, Frank, a ball and chain?

He exhaled loudly. "You wanna know how I see the kid? Seriously?"

"I do."

"Whenever I think of Shannon's unborn baby, all I see is that pimple-face weasel, Derek."

She sucked in her breath. "Derek is not the baby's father. Whoever told you that?"

"No one had to tell me. His shitbox van was in our driveway every day, for chrissake. The kid practically lived at our house."

"It's not Derek, it's Eino. Eino is the baby's father."

"Who the hell is Eino?"

"Calm down, Frank. Eino Mukkhonan was the Finnish exchange student. Don't you remember chasing him out into the snow that night?"

"Holy shit. I should have pounded the little bastard. Didn't

I say they weren't studying in her room? But no, you said it was good for Shannon to be 'exposed to other cultures.'"

"You did, Frank. I gave them the benefit of the doubt and I was wrong. But if you recall, Eino was not only good-looking, he was smart. Finns score very high in the sciences."

"Good for them. Shannon could be carrying Donald Trump's baby, it doesn't change a thing. I'm not spending the rest of my life paying for her mistakes. What if she gets knocked up again? We can start a goddamn nursery."

"Frank, you even admitted that Shannon's turning her life around."

"Yeah, thanks to that Proctor broad. I hope you're not screwing things up over there."

"I don't care to discuss it on the phone," she said. "Can we get together and talk?"

"I'm sick of talking, Iris. Not only that, I'm not supposed to have contact with you. My lawyer calls the shots now. He charges two hundred bucks an hour. Pretty soon I'll be broke, sleeping in my car. I hope that makes you happy."

Before she could respond, Frank hung up.

"Take the cucumber salad out, will you?" Grace stood at her kitchen counter, tossing a bowl of cole slaw.

"You don't think it'll go bad outside?" Iris removed the plastic covered bowl from the refrigerator and grabbed a serving spoon.

"Nah. Too early in the season to worry about salmonella."

Iris carried her drink in one hand and the salad bowl in the other. She followed Grace outside. The wooden picnic table under the big pine tree was set with straw place mats, colored glasses and flowered napkins. A pot of African daisies sat in the center flanked by candles inside hurricane globes.

Iris peeked inside a styrofoam cooler. "You made red bliss potato salad. All this food for just the two of us. I feel hungry for the first time in weeks." She pulled out the wooden bench and sat. "Sven might not miss your cuddling, but I'll bet he misses your cooking."

Grace, pouring glasses of sangria from a plastic pitcher, stopped to consider the remark. "Living in the city, he eats out about every night—upscale joints, too."

Iris took a big swallow of her drink. "When did he tell you that?"

"He came to the shop the other day looking for a gift for his boss. He bought some gorgeous black lace stockings with garters."

"Isn't that kind of personal?"

Grace shrugged. "Maybe for a straight man. A gay man can get away with buying lingerie. They also know what makes women feel feminine."

"It sounds like Sven is a shrewd player."

"He's good at reading people. That's why he's done so well in public relations."

"What was it like, seeing him again?"

Grace sighed. "When he stood in the doorway of the shop, the sun shining on his golden locks, I fell in love all over again."

"Really? I'm sorry—for your sake."

"Yeah, he looked great. He's tanned, toned, and his hair's highlighted. He and the boyfriend had just spent a long weekend on St. Croix. Sonny's with the airlines, so they can fly anywhere for zip."

"That's the boyfriend's name, Sonny?"

Grace nodded. "Apparently his mother loved the musical duo, Sonny and Cher."

"It's hard to believe we're talking about the same Sven," Iris said, "although I never knew him well. I remember meeting him at the library's Nutcracker party. He was a teacher then. He wore argyle vests and bow ties. He always looked stern. I was a bit intimidated. "

"That's when he was teaching drama to high schoolers. He hated it."

"Why was that?"

"He claimed it was because the school department stifled him. The only plays they approved were the old standbys about Joan of Arc and Paul Revere. They even rejected *'The Glass Me-*

nagerie,' because it dealt with mental illness." Grace stopped to sip her drink. "I felt bad that Sven was depressed. For Christmas I gave him tickets to fly down to Florida and see his mother during school break."

"That was nice of you," Iris said.

"It was worth it, or so I thought. When he got back he was like another person, happy and upbeat. Later I found out why. He'd met Sonny-the-steward on that flight. As a result, Sven spent two days with his mom in St. Pete's and five with Sonny in Miami." She rattled the ice in her glass. "Now the happy couple live on Boston's Back Bay with a view of the Charles River."

"I wish I hadn't asked you," Iris said, nodding.

Grace moved to put the patties on the grill. "Things happen for the best. Sven would have come out eventually. Today we're like old friends."

"I could never be friends with Frank if he left me, permanently, I mean."

"I never thought I'd speak to Sven after what he put me through. For a long time, I plotted acts of vengeance." She smacked a burger with the spatula. "I'll definitely never speak to my former mother-in-law. Do you know what the old cow said when Sven told her he was leaving me?"

"What?"

"She said, 'I told you never to marry a woman whose pant size is bigger than yours.' She's a modern day Confucius."

"Just be thankful it's history," Iris said. "I'm living my nightmare. I can't forget the image of Frank and that bimbo having drinks on the deck at the Ship Ahoy. Not a care in the world, those two."

Grace turned and frowned. "How do you know that?"

Iris looked down into her glass. "I mean, I imagine they're doing that. All the apartments have decks." She swallowed the rest of her drink.

Grace continued to stare. "You're still stalking them, aren't you?"

Iris rose to pour more sangria. "Will you stop calling it that? A stalker is someone crazy, someone obsessed. I'm taking notes, doing surveillance for my case."

Grace shook her head. "Stop before it gets out of hand."

"Don't be ridiculous. I have."

Iris couldn't admit the truth—it had gotten out of hand. If stalking could be considered an addiction, she had progressed to another level. Not content to merely sit in the parking lot waiting for a glimpse of the lovers, she had gone inside the building. There she had done the unthinkable: She had gone face-to-face with Valerie Moles.

During the long hours in the parking lot, Iris had pictured the interior of apartment number two-hundred twenty. She imagined a big-screen TV on one wall. On another, a seascape, done in lurid colors. The drapes were velvet burgundy with tassels. The carpet would be plush wall to wall. Finally, the *piece de resistance* would be an oversized submarine of a sofa covered in crushed imitation leather.

Was it any wonder she had to see it for herself?

FOURTEEN

The four buildings that made up the Ship Ahoy apartment complex were named after local islands: Baker, Ten Pound, Thatcher, and Misery. Valerie Moles's building was—appropriately—Misery.

On that afternoon Iris drove to the building's rear lot. As she cruised along, she spotted a Zap! Exterminator van backing into a service space. She quickly parked and followed the jump-suited bug tech as he was buzzed into the lobby. Wasting no time, she boarded an elevator for the second floor.

When she alighted on the second floor, she paused. In the glass enclosing a hallway fire extinguisher, she checked her image. The curly gray wig and black-framed glasses were perfect for her role as middle-age dog groomer. Her outfit of a below-the-knee brown corduroy skirt and blazer the color of wet mushrooms completed the disguise. She nodded in approval.

Her confidence didn't leave her when she knocked on the door of two-hundred twenty. The minute it swung open, she launched into her pitch. "Good afternoon, ma'am. I've got some exciting specials today for you and your lucky pup."

"What?" Valerie Moles, in a short terry robe, stared at her. "Are you the upholstery cleaning service?"

"Good heavens, no. I'm with Downtown Doggie. We offer walking, grooming, and day care services for your pet."

"How'd you get in here?" She leaned out, looking up and down the hallway. "Solicitors aren't allowed in this building."

"I was seeing a client on the first floor," Iris explained, talking rapidly. "A Yorkie who needed a conditioning treatment." She touched Valerie's arm. "We only charge an extra fifteen dollars for at-home procedures. Didn't you get the promotionals I mailed you?"

"Listen, you've got the wrong apartment. I don't have a dog." She grabbed the doorknob and pulled it toward her.

Iris grabbed it as well. She squinted at the number on the door. "Oh silly me, I wanted the third floor. Looks like I need new glasses. Don't laugh, but I thought I spotted a dog over there on your floor."

As she had hoped, Valerie turned, allowing Iris a better view of the apartment. "See? No dog," she said with a wave of her hand. "It's a rug."

"Quite realistic looking," Iris said, her eyes taking in every detail of the lair.

"It should. It's a rare Bengal tiger."

"Is that so? Must be warm on chilly nights."

"It's good for snuggling," she said with a wink. She gripped the doorknob. "Now if you'll excuse me—"

Iris quickly handed her a flyer. "This explains our services, in the event you and your husband get a dog."

"I'm divorced," Valerie said, "and my boyfriend's allergic."

"Is he now?" Iris said, leaning toward her. "Since when?"

But Valerie had firmly shut the door.

Iris briefly leaned against the wall. Her body trembled as she walked to the service stairs at the end of the corridor. She was confident she'd aroused no suspicion. At the same time, she knew that lingering was risky. It was a basic rule of surveillance: Go in and out quickly and while you're inside, do nothing to attract attention.

Outside, she crossed the parking lot and stood on the sidewalk. Her car was parked across the road. Before crossing, she glanced up at the building she'd just visited. Her eyes were automatically drawn to the second floor window she knew so well. At that moment the curtains moved and a flash of white appeared. Was she being watched? Clutching her folder, Iris stepped off the curb into the street.

With an ear-splitting screech of brakes, a black Mustang convertible skidded to a stop, inches away from her. Sitting behind the wheel was Amber Spaglione, in mirrored sunglasses. Strapped into a kiddie seat next to her was her toddler, also in sunglasses. Mother and daughter wore their red-gold hair in ponytails. "Lady, are you frickin' blind?" Amber yelled.

Iris, unnerved by the near-collision, dropped the folder. She watched in dismay as her flyers scattered to the wind. Her head down, she scurried across the street. On the other side, she glanced around. Had Amber recognized her? Most likely not; she'd roared off without a backward glance.

Iris reached the Jetta and unlocked the trunk with trembling hands. She took off the wig and glasses, stuffing them inside a tote which she tossed back into the trunk. Then she lowered herself into the driver's seat. She waited until her breathing slowed before leaving the lot.

She'd had a close call. She'd almost given herself away and gotten run over in the process. She desperately needed to talk to Grace. However, Grace would accuse her of stalking. Iris hated that word. It conjured up a driven, tormented soul. She, on the other hand, saw herself as someone cool, shrewd, and canny. While stalkers acted with desperation, she planned her forays with stealth and imagination.

Soon she merged with traffic on the main road. Although she'd gotten away with her charade, she wouldn't push her luck. The encounter with Amber Spaglione was a warning. In any event, she had satisfied her curiosity; she'd finally glimpsed the love nest. It had looked as she'd imagined, like something out of a tacky romance novel.

On the highway, she accelerated, putting the windows down. The wind whipped at her hair. She turned the radio on. When she found a song she liked, she sang along. She hadn't felt so alive in years.

The outdoor picnic came to an end when the black flies descended like seagulls at a clambake. Iris and Grace scooped up the plates and bowls and fled into the house. "Just pile everything on the counter," Grace said. "I'll do the dishes later."

"I'm not leaving you with this mess," Iris announced. She

grabbed a plate and vigorously scraped the contents into the trash bin. Instead of landing inside, the mess fell onto her shoes. She looked around to see if Grace had noticed. She had.

"I told you I'd do the dishes later," Grace said. "C'mon, I'll give you a ride home."

"What are you talking about? My car's outside."

"You can't start it without keys." Grace stood with hands on hips, watching her.

Iris grabbed her pocketbook from a kitchen chair and searched inside. "Where's my car keys?"

"I hid them."

Iris carefully replaced her bag and asked, "Why did you do that?"

"Because I don't want you driving. Now let's go."

Iris attempted a smile. "Just because I dumped potato salad on my shoes?"

"You've had too much sangria and I can't in good conscience let you drive. Simple as that."

"I had just as much as you." Grace looked at her with raised eyebrows. Iris knew her friend had witnessed her augmenting her drinks. She felt her cheeks flush. "You're the host," she said with a shrug, and headed for the bathroom.

She ran water over her hands while staring into the mirror. Her eyes were lackluster. Frank's desertion was evident in her face. She had a desperate look.

Grace didn't understand what she was going through, first losing a daughter and then a husband. If a drink now and then helped to steady her, she saw no reason to deprive herself. Vodka was more acceptable than the Valium her mother had relied upon. Iris wouldn't fall into the trap of addiction. She had to stay strong.

Grace dropped her off at home with a promise to return in the morning. "I can get a cab," Iris said, but Grace wouldn't hear it. She waited while Iris unlocked the side door. Then, with a toot of her horn, she drove away.

Inside the kitchen, Iris refilled Patticake's bowl. The silence in the house felt heavy. She fixed a vodka and lime juice, adding a teaspoon of sugar to offset the tartness. Carrying the drink up the stairs, she was joined by Patticake. The cat, beset with arthritis, navigated the steps slowly. Iris scooped her up with her free arm and continued.

She placed her drink on the bedside table, atop a copy of *Smart Women, Dumb Choices.* Nearby, the answering machine flashed. She kicked off her shoes and stretched out across the smooth cotton comforter. With her drink in one hand, she pressed the machine's play button.

The first message was from Mr. Tomasillo, who spoke in his formal principal's voice. He said he was soon leaving for Puerto Rico; her contract for the school year was in the mail. If Iris had any questions, she was to contact Ms. Dutton.

"No way, Jose!" she hooted. A startled Patticake jumped off the bed.

The next message, recorded at eight forty-five, was from Frank. He growled from the speaker, "Iris, I'm gonna say this once, so you better listen. Some goon from the sheriff's office served me papers today. You better tell that grease ball clown Vinnie Tosi he'd better remember who he's messing with. I've got friends in this town. Tell him he picked the wrong guy—"

The message abruptly ended. She rolled off the bed, her heart pounding, and replayed the message. Even with the volume turned low, Frank's words and tone were scary. She stabbed at the delete button with her finger.

She sat before the phone. It was almost ten. Was it too late to call Vincent? Perhaps she would call his office. As she sat biting her nails, she remembered her mother's instructions regarding phone etiquette, "Never call before nine in the morning and after nine at night."

On the other hand, her mother hadn't had a threatening bully for a husband. Iris punched in Vincent's number. The lawyer's voice on his recorded message was smooth as melted butterscotch: "You've reached the law offices of Vincent Tosi. At the moment, I'm either in court or with a client. Please leave a brief message with your name and number."

At the pause, her words came in a rush: "Vincent, it's Iris

Camuso. I just got a disturbing phone call from Frank. Please get back to me soon as you get this."

She hung up and looked around the room. Where was her drink? Then she remembered she'd finished it. She skipped down the stairs and fixed another lime and vodka, her hands trembling. Calm down, she told herself. Frank wants to intimidate; she was playing right into his hands. She clutched her drink and climbed the stairs. Before she reached the top, the phone rang. She grabbed the railing to steady herself.

In the bedroom she rushed to the phone and picked it up. Yes?"

"It's me, Vincent."

"Vincent? Thank God." She sank onto the mattress.

"I was checking my calls before going to bed. What's up?"

Iris told him about Frank's message. "He was so . . . angry."

Vincent chuckled. "Damn right. Frankie got a divorce summons. We're not playing by his rules anymore."

"He sounded threatening. It scared me."

"Bully tactics. Ignore him. I'm used to dealing with guys like Frank."

"If he calls back, I won't answer the phone."

"Good girl. Can you forward his message to me?"

"I erased it."

"You erased it? Jesus, Mary and Joseph, that's evidence." He sighed. "Okay, can you remember his words?"

"I think so." She repeated Frank's message, leaving out the "greaseball clown," to spare Vincent's feelings.

"Good," he said. "I wrote it down. Next time, don't erase anything. Any remarks like that you save."

Later when she crawled into bed, sleep eluded her. Frank's menacing voice echoed in her mind. He sounded like he hated me, she thought. The possibility of their getting back together seemed truly remote. Not only that, if Frank did return, could she forgive him?

The next day Iris cleared out her files. Normally the Harborvale Middle School allied health staff— counselors, speech and physical therapists—left their records at school. Iris, however, didn't like the idea of Ms. Dutton poking through her files. Thus she packed up everything to take home. She worked quietly and finally slipped out the side door without being detected.

The afternoon stretched before her; she headed for Main Street, in no hurry to go home. With no job to fill her days and no family to care for, she would be at loose ends.

She considered her situation as she inched along in downtown traffic, noting at the same time the new stores. Another gift shop selling tourist trinkets—seagull mobiles and rhinestone flip-flops—had opened. At the same time, many of the old standbys—the stationery shop, the children's shoe store—had vanished.

Thus she was happy to note that Harborvale Jewelry was still in business. Almost twenty years ago on a day much like today, she and Frank had visited the store to buy her engagement ring. Four months earlier, she'd been out with Scott Lester at the Dirty Dinghy when Frank had taken her aside and whispered in her ear . . .

Scott reluctantly drove her home that night, parking in the driveway. He turned off the radio and pulled her to him. "Wait," she said.

"What is it?" He kissed her neck.

She turned, staring at the house. "I see a light in my dad's bedroom. He gets worried if I'm not in by midnight."

"When he looks out the window, he'll see you're home," Scott said, his voice muffled.

"I don't want him going downstairs in the dark. He might fall." She pulled away, avoiding his eyes. "Do you mind if we cut it short tonight?"

Scott shrugged. Without looking at her, he started the car. She grabbed her purse from the floor. At the same time guilt prevented her from leaving. Yet she didn't hesitate long. With a whispered "Bye," Iris got out of the car. She waited for Scott to leave, hoping he'd peel out of the driveway and roar off, angrily fishtailing down the street. Instead, he quietly backed the car out. Without a glance in her direction, Scott Lester drove away.

Inside the house, she raced up the dark stairs to pause outside her father's bedroom door. Satisfied that he was asleep, she tiptoed to her room and turned on a small table lamp. She stood before the mirror and smoothed back her hair. Her cheeks were flushed. She undid the top buttons of her blouse and spritzed Elizabeth Arden cologne on her breasts. Finally, she grabbed a sweater and tied it around her hips. The clock in the living room said twelve fifty-five when she gently closed the front door behind her.

The moon illuminated the neighbors' rooftops. She moved swiftly down the street, keeping in the shadows of the maple trees. When she reached the end of the road, she spotted Frank's truck slowly approaching from Birch Hill. She stood at the curb and wondered why the sight of a beat-up pickup truck should make her heart race.

The truck came to a stop. Frank leaned across the seat to open the passenger door. Iris hoisted herself up onto the seat, glancing shyly at Frank. "I hope you like Chianti," he said, handing her a paper bag twisted at the top. "There's cups on the floor. I'll let you do the honors." He let out the clutch; they lurched forward and drove away.

She poured, holding a plastic cup between her knees. "Where are we going?"

"Someplace special."

She handed him his drink, feeling a tingle when their fingers touched. Leaning back against the seat, she sipped the Chianti. It was bitter, a far cry from the wines she'd enjoyed in the French restaurant.

As they drove through darkened streets, Frank was silent, intent on the road. They were in the back shore area, a section of town with few houses and no streetlights. He slowed and turned into a lane densely bordered with shrubbery. They bumped along on an unpaved dirt road, Iris holding her drink with both hands.

Soon they came to a circular clearing surrounded by trees. Moonlight filtered through the overhead branches. In the headlights' glare, Iris spotted a narrow path cutting through the thicket. At the end of the path was a stretch of silver sand and beyond that, dark water. "Is that the beach?" Her voice was a whisper.

"Uh huh." He shut off the engine. All was silent.

She looked around. They were alone in an alien place. "Won't the police come and kick us out?"

He laughed. "This is where the cops go when they want to get away."

She turned to him. "Really? How do you know?"

He winked. "I've got friends in the right places." He grabbed the wine bottle and a pack of Winstons from the dashboard. "Take the rest of the cups, okay?" He hopped out and moved to the truck bed. Through the window she watched him reach in and remove a blanket. Seconds later he stood outside her door. "Ready?"

She slid off the seat, glancing around at the shadowy landscape. "You're sure it's okay to be here?"

"You don't have to whisper. Are you scared?"

At the moment, she didn't know what scared her more, being alone with Frank or the eerie surroundings. "It's just that I've never been here before. It's kind of creepy."

He gestured toward the path. "At the end is a private beach with a nice flat rock to spread out the blanket. We can drink a little wine, smoke a little weed, look at the stars. The water's nice and calm. If you promise not to peek, we can go for a swim."

She smiled at him in the darkness, yet remained anxious. "We won't be out too long, will we?"

Instead of replying, he kissed her and said, "You're safe with me."

She followed as he led her down the narrow path, stopping at times to hold the prickly brambles aside so she could pass. Before long they came to a moonlit stretch of beach bordered by large rocks. Pinpoints of light from faraway ships twinkled on the horizon. The only sound was the gentle lapping of waves on the shore.

Together they spread the blanket on the flat rock. They sipped wine and talked. A soft breeze blew off the ocean. Later they floated on the dark sea, holding hands and looking up at the stars.

Now Iris glanced at the diamond ring on her finger. A perfect cut, the sales clerk had claimed. Iris wondered what it would be worth today, should she need to sell. On impulse, she made a left turn and drove into the store's parking lot.

Little had changed inside Harborvale Jewelry during the past decades. Iris recognized the clerk who'd waited on them years ago. The woman's hair was now dyed a metallic gold. Pouches under her eyes gave her a mournful look. "Looking for something in particular?" she asked.

Iris held out her ring hand. "We bought this here years ago. I wonder if you'd appraise it for me."

The woman approached, fingering a magnifying disk worn around her neck. Without pausing, she took Iris's hand and peered at the diamond for several seconds. She looked up at Iris. . "You're thinking of selling?"

"I'm not sure."

"Let me show it to Mrs. Bird and see what she says."

"Mrs. Bird's still here?" The store's owner had sold Iris her high school class ring twenty-five years earlier. Even then she'd appeared elderly to Iris's youthful eyes.

The woman chuckled. "She comes in a couple days a week. Mr. Bird passed away ten years ago. Want to give me the ring?"

Iris glanced at the ID tag pinned to her sweater: Judith Bangs, Store Manager. "I'd appreciate that." She twisted the ring from her finger.

Judith Bangs moved to the back of the store and slipped inside a door marked Office. Iris caught a glimpse of the brightly lit interior. A tiny, bird-like woman with wispy hair sat behind an old-fashioned metal desk.

Iris roamed the aisles, stopping before a display of pewter bracelets. They looked antique, with dark embedded stones. A sign identified them as *Scottish Agates, said to Bring the Wearer Good Luck*. Iris slipped one on her wrist. It looked like an heirloom, the pewter having the patina of age. Rust-colored stones glowed dully. She turned her wrist, admiring the bracelet.

From the rear of the store the office door opened. The manager joined Iris, handing her a folded slip of paper. "Here's our appraisal figure." She pressed the ring into Iris's hand. "Let me know if you'd like to have it reset into something more contemporary. Sometimes that's all you need, a new look."

Or a new husband, Iris thought. Before she could respond, the bell over the entrance door jingled. Two teenage girls in tight jeans and tank tops entered. "Are you girls looking for anything in particular?" Judith Bangs's voice held no hint of welcome. When the newcomers replied in the negative, Judith turned back to Iris. "Got to watch them every minute," she muttered, and moved away to follow the girls.

Iris slipped her ring back on. She called out her thanks at the door. Outside, she headed for the parking lot. When she was seated in her car, she unfolded the slip of paper. Written in a spidery script was the appraisal amount—three thousand, five hundred dollars.

She rejoined the traffic on Main Street. As she crawled along, she rolled back the sleeve of her jersey. In the light, the polished stones of the Scottish bracelet glittered. Perhaps its claim to bring good luck would come true. She smiled, feeling lucky already.

Back at home she fixed herself a drink, first breaking the seal on the bottle of Finlandia vodka. She'd stopped at the liquor store to reward herself. After all, she'd be coming into money if she sold her ring. And why not sell? It was a constant reminder of Frank's betrayal.

She carried the drink to her bedroom where Patticake slept on the pillow. Iris sank onto the mattress and glanced at the answering machine's pulsing red light. She sipped her drink, debating whether to listen to the message. What if it was Frank, leaving another threat? When she'd finished her drink, she pressed the "play" button.

An urgent voice said, "Ms. Camuso, this is admissions at Harborvale Hospital. Your husband Francis was brought in fifteen minutes ago. Please come directly to Emergency as soon as you get this message—"

FIFTEEN

Iris gave her name to the woman behind the desk at Harborvale Hospital Emergency Services. "You called about my husband, Francis Camuso. Can you tell me why he's here?"

"First we need his insurance information. His card wasn't on him, so if you could just stop by registration— "

"Please, tell me why he's here. I need to see him."

"I'll call for an escort, but you must stop by registration before you leave." She frowned and picked up the desk phone. "I need an escort for emergency to intensive care." After hanging up, she said, "Have a seat. Someone will be down to get you."

"Excuse me, did you say intensive care?"

"That's right. Someone will take you there."

Iris put a hand on the desk to steady herself. "No one on the phone said anything about intensive care."

The woman tapped her clipboard. "That's another department. I'm going by what it says here, Francis Camuso, Intensive Care."

"Do you know why he was brought in?"

"I can't give out that information. Have a seat. It'll only be a few minutes."

Iris looked around the waiting room. Overhead fluorescent lights cast hash shadows on the faces of those sitting slumped on orange plastic chairs. They gazed out the window at the parking lot, drinking from Styrofoam coffee cups.

Iris took a seat and glanced nervously around. She wanted to tell someone her husband was in intensive care where very sick people ended up. Was it his heart? She remembered their earlier conversation, his fears about a heart attack. She hadn't taken him seriously. What if he didn't survive?

She got to her feet and went to a window. Where was Grace? Iris had phoned her immediately after getting the hospital's message. She'd also left a message for Shannon with the adoption agency.

Now a rumpled-looking young man with a plastic ID card around his neck stood in the doorway. After checking his clipboard, he called out, "Camuso."

She jumped up. "That's me."

He motioned her to the elevator. As they stood silently waiting, the ER's double entrance doors opened. Grace rushed in.

"Got here as soon as I heard," she said, wrapping Iris in a hug. At that moment the elevator arrived. The three stepped inside. The escort pressed the button for the fourth floor.

"I'm scared," Iris whispered to Grace. "We're going to the ICU." Grace nodded and squeezed her hand as the elevator made its slow ascent. Iris said, "What's that buzzing sound?"

Grace nodded at the escort who leaned against the wall, his eyes shut. Thin wires ran from his ears to the pocket of his flannel shirt where an MP3 player bulged. The music seeping out sounded like a swarm of angry bees.

The elevator stopped with a jolt. The escort led them down a stark white corridor. On the way, they passed a door whose sign said Meditation Chapel. Two doors further down they stopped. "This is it," the young man said, "the ICU." Before they could thank him, he'd ambled away, the angry bees still buzzing in his ears.

They entered a brightly lit room. A gray-haired nurse sat behind a desk flanked by rolling carts, one holding a row of blue vinyl binders, the other jars of cotton balls and gauze pads. Spaced around the periphery were curtained cubicles.

Although Iris had always imagined the ICU as a noisy hub of activity, here all was quiet. She approached the desk and introduced herself. Then she added, "Is it okay if my friend stays with me?"

The nurse glanced at Grace. "We prefer family members only, but I'll overlook it tonight, since you just arrived." She got to her feet. "Let me take you to him."

As they followed, Iris gripped the sleeve of Grace's jacket. Together they passed a cubicle whose open curtain revealed an elderly woman. Her skeletal frame barely made an impression under the bed sheets. The nurse stopped at the adjoining cubicle and yanked the curtains open.

Inside, Frank lay prone, a clear plastic mask covering his nose and mouth. Moisture inside the mask blurred his features. The nurse moved to the head of the bed and lifted the mask away from his face. It made a wet, sucking sound. When she wiped his nose and gaping mouth, Iris gasped. The nurse adjusted the sheet covering him. As she did they saw, attached to his shaved chest, five round white tabs the size of sand dollars. Each was connected to a wire that led to a squat black box on a nearby table.

"Why is he so . . . gray?" Iris asked, her voice a whisper.

"When he came in he was cyanotic," the nurse said, making adjustments to the IV cord.

"Cyanotic?"

"He was blue."

At this, Grace put an arm around Iris who stared at Frank's face and said, "Can he hear me?"

"On some level he might," the nurse said, tidying up the bedside clutter.

"I want to talk to him," Iris said, "alone, if you don't mind."

"I'll be outside," Grace whispered, squeezing her hand.

"There's a visiting room down the hall," the nurse told Grace. "Take a left. You can get coffee and soft drinks." Before leaving, the nurse closed the cubicle's curtains.

Iris sat on a wooden chair next to the bed. She touched Frank's cold hand and said, "Frank, it's me, Iris. Can you hear me?" She stared at his eyelids, expecting them to flutter. "When you come home, I'll fix up the den for you. It's nice there in the afternoon with the sun coming in. We'll put a bed in there. You can watch TV while you recuperate."

She waited, hearing only the rhythmic hiss and wheeze of the ventilator. As she got to her feet, the nurse appeared. "Dr. Kram just called. He'll meet with your family in the visitors' room down the hall."

"Who's Dr. Kram?"

"Your husband's admitting physician. He'll answer the family's questions."

"There's no family," Iris said. "So far it's just me."

"I believe there are others waiting. Why don't you go there now. He'll be right along."

The visitors' room was near the end of the corridor. When Iris opened the door, she got a jolt. Valerie Moles, wearing a pink terry jumpsuit, sat at the far end of the room. She looked up briefly when Iris entered and returned to her magazine.

Iris sat next to Grace. "What's she doing here?" She stared at her nemesis. Under the room's fluorescent lights, Valerie's tan looked more orange than bronze.

"Be cool," Grace whispered.

While Iris stewed, the door opened. Nancy Proctor entered, her arm wrapped protectively around a pregnant Shannon.

"Shannon!" Iris leaped to her feet. She stopped, seeing her daughter's startled face.

"One moment, please," Nancy Proctor said. She guided Shannon to a chair. Valerie Moles stared curiously at the newcomers. When Shannon was seated, Nancy removed her tan trench coat and draped it on a chair. "This young woman is not feeling well tonight," she announced to the room. "After we hear from the doctor, I'm taking her home."

Iris stared at Shannon, willing her to look in her direction. An uncomfortable silence fell over the room. Iris debated what to say until the door abruptly swung open. A short, trim man with graying sideburns entered. He wore a tie and an immaculate white lab coat. "I'm Doctor Kram," he said, his gaze settling on Valerie Moles. "Are you Mrs. Camuso?"

"I'm the patient's fiancee," she said.

"Fiancee!" Iris jumped to her feet. "Excuse me, Dr. Kram, I'm Mrs. Camuso. The patient is my husband." She indicated Shannon. "And she is our daughter."

Nancy Proctor smiled. "Doctor Kram, I need to get this young lady home as soon as possible."

"And you are?" he asked.

"I'm Nancy Proctor, Executive Director of A Women's Issue."

He nodded approvingly. "I've heard good things about your agency." Turning to Valerie Moles, he asked, "Were you the one who called for help tonight?"

"Yeah."

He glanced at his clipboard. "According to the admitting notes, you said the patient's breathing and color alarmed you."

"It didn't look right or sound right."

He nodded and glanced at the assembled. "Let me give you a quick rundown. What we've pieced together is that the patient had a severe reaction tonight after ingesting a combination of alcohol, narcotics, and sleeping pills."

"Narcotics?" Iris stared at him.

"That's right, Ms. Camuso. According to his chart, your husband was taking Percocet, prescribed by his periodontist. According to Ms. Moles's earlier remarks, he'd taken more than the recommended dosage. This was in addition to several cocktails he'd consumed earlier. Additionally, he took a prescription sleeping pill before bedtime.

"The combination affected his CNS—central nervous system—in that it slowed and repressed ventilation. At some point Ms. Moles called nine-one-one.

"For the time being, Mr. Camuso is stabilized on a respirator. Hopefully, he'll soon breathe on his own. At some point we'll insert a feeding tube."

"Doctor Kram, are you saying my husband's in a coma?"

"His responses are poor at the moment," the doctor said.

"When do you think he'll come out of it?" Iris asked.

"We'll know more tomorrow after he's been evaluated by neurology."

"Do you think his brain will be . . . damaged?" Iris asked.

He pursed his lips. "Your husband had a lot of medication in his system. Not only that, his BAL—blood alcohol level—was high." He tucked the clipboard under his arm. "Let's see what tomorrow brings."

Iris pointed at Valerie Moles. "If anything happens to my husband, she's responsible."

Nancy Proctor leaned forward. "Ms. Camuso, this is not the time and place for—"

"Mind your own business," Iris said. "You're not a family member. You shouldn't even be here."

"Stop it," Shannon said, awkwardly getting to her feet. "I'm sick of the fighting."

Ms. Proctor grabbed her coat and addressed Dr. Kram. "There's nothing we can do here, doctor. I'm sure you'll agree this young lady should be resting at home."

Grace also got to her feet. "Excuse me, Ms. Proctor, this is an appropriate place for Shannon to be. Her father's life hangs in the balance. She belongs with family."

"Shannon," Iris said, "Grace is right. The ICU nurse said your dad was cyanotic when they admitted him."

"What's that mean?" Valerie Moles asked, looking up.

"It means he was blue," Grace said.

"I told him it's a bad idea mixing booze and pills," Valerie said, "but you can't tell Frank anything."

"Don't talk to her," Iris hissed at Grace.

Nancy Proctor turned to Shannon and asked, "What do you want, dear? Would you like to remain here?"

Shannon looked at the floor. "I want to go home with you."

Valerie Moles stood and tossed her magazine on the adjacent chair. "I think I'll go, too. Nothing I can do here. I'll check in the morning." She bent to tie her sneaker. As she did, the thin material of her jumpsuit stretched across her buttocks like an over-inflated balloon.

Dr. Kram, transfixed at the sight, said, "You won't get any information from the front desk." Without taking his eyes from her posterior, he pulled a card from his pocket. "Here's my cell number." He handed it to her.

Iris waited for him to offer her a card but none was forthcoming.

The group found themselves sharing an elevator, the mood tense as they descended to the ground floor. When the doors parted, all went their separate ways: Ms. Proctor and Shannon to the ladies' room, Valerie Moles to the main exit, and Iris and Grace to the ER parking lot. "Help me find my car," Iris said. "I don't even remember parking it."

"I'll give you a ride home if you're too upset to drive," Grace said.

"I'm all right. I'm glad you were with me. Otherwise I wouldn't have had the courage to confront Nancy Proctor and Valerie Moles." She reached for a tissue in her pocket. "Did you see how Shannon looked at me? It's like she hates me."

"No, but I saw how Dr. Kram looked at Valerie's butt."

"I've lost my daughter to Nancy Proctor." She wiped the tears that ran down her cheeks.

"No you haven't," Grace said. "It's temporary. Right now Proctor knows how to make herself indispensable. She's played this role before."

But Iris wasn't listening. "I lose my daughter and my grandchild. If that's not bad enough, my husband's in a coma."

Grace put an arm around her. "Come on. I see your car up ahead." After Iris unlocked the door, Grace said, "I want you to go home and make some hot, sweet tea. When Frank recovers you've gotta be strong to help with his rehab. Valerie Moles certainly won't lift a finger."

Iris gasped. "Oh dear, I forgot to call Frank's sister, Fatima." She glanced at the clock on the dashboard. "It's seven o'clock, California time. What should I tell her?"

"Tell her what Dr. Kram said, that Frank is stabilized."

She pressed her fingers to her lips. "I feel so responsible."

"You! What did you do?"

"After being served with the divorce papers, Frank left a message on my machine. He was furious. He always drinks too much when he's mad."

"That's Frank's way of dealing with things," Grace said. "Getting a lawyer is what any self-respecting wife would do. If anyone should feel guilty, it's that bimbo. She didn't call nine-one-one until Frank was blue. Why was that, her nail polish wasn't dry?"

Iris looked away. "It was awful seeing Frank in that condition. My sister Lily was blue when I found her. We were riding bikes, going up a hill. I was in front. Near the top, I turned to look around. Lily wasn't there. I thought maybe she'd given up and gone home. Lily wasn't strong. She was always small for her age. I was going to continue up the hill when I saw it—a pink sneaker sticking out of the tall grass that bordered the road. I dropped my bike and ran to her—"

Grace patted her back. "Don't think about that tonight, sweetie. You've had a rough day."

She nodded. "I'm probably in a state of shock."

"Try to be more like Valerie," Grace said. "That girl looks out for number one. You can be sure she won't lose any beauty sleep tonight."

Iris nodded. "The funny thing is, I'm not mad at Frank anymore. Not after seeing him hooked up to those machines. If he comes out of this, it could be a fresh start for us."

The following morning Iris returned to the ICU. Inside Frank's cubicle, an Asian woman in a white lab coat was seated at the end of his bed. Using a pencil, she methodically poked the soles of his feet with the point. After each jab, she made a notation on a chart. Iris watched silently until the woman turned and asked, "Are you the patient's wife?" When Iris nodded, she said, "I'm Dr. Chew from Neurology."

"Hi," Iris said. "Has there been any change?"

"None that I can determine."

Iris paused. "Do you expect any change?"

Dr. Chew turned back to her work. "Your husband's ventilation was severely compromised. A respirator is breathing for him now. At the moment, his tactile responses appear nonexistent."

Iris mulled over the doctor's words. Inside the cubicle, the only sound was the hiss of the respirator that was breathing for Frank. Finally she spoke, "I guess you're saying it doesn't look promising."

The diminutive doctor rose, her clipboard clutched to her

chest. She patted Iris's arm before leaving. "Life promises no guarantees, Ms. Camuso. All we have is hope."

Now Iris dragged the chair closer to the bed. She leaned over Frank and said, "Hi, it's me, Iris. On the ride over here I was thinking how nice the TV room would look with some yellow flowered curtains and a matching bedspread. How does that sound?"

She stared at Frank's darkened eyelids, willing them to open. As she waited, she became aware of loud voices accompanied by heavy footsteps outside the cubicle. She moved to the entrance and peeked out. Three heavyset people were crowding into the enclosure of the old lady next door. The last to enter was a middle-age woman. She stood at the entrance and addressed the group, "Listen to me. I told the function manager we'd show up after the cemetery. I said I didn't know how many would be with us. We just want a simple reception—friends and family."

"You talking about the VFW hall?" a man said from inside. "They charge double for the room when you supply your own beer and wine."

The woman answered, "Oh really, Nick? What do you care? You're not paying for it."

His response was loud. "I told you I'd pay my share soon's I get the child support check to Linda."

"Oh yeah? That's what you said about Elisha's graduation party, and look what happened. Ma got stuck with the bill."

A woman inside the cubicle said,"Will you two knock it off. The lawyer said it all comes out of the funeral expenses."

When the bickering continued, Iris decided to go for coffee in the cafeteria. As she was closing the flap behind her, a woman in a sequined sweater peeked out of the noisy cubicle. "Honey, if you're going, could we borrow your chair?"

"Go ahead," Iris said. She got a glimpse inside. The three visitors towered over the diminished figure in the bed. Despite the noise they made the patient was asleep. And though she looked barely alive, Iris noticed she was breathing on her own.

On her way to the elevator, Iris stopped outside the meditation chapel. The door was open. She stepped inside the empty room. Four short wooden benches faced an altar where a framed picture of a white dove sat propped. Behind the makeshift altar a stained glass window cast a warm, rosy glow over the room.

She moved to the front bench and sat. Immediately she was engulfed in soft music issuing from hidden speakers. It was like the New Age tapes her Yoga teacher had played during class. Iris closed her eyes. She tried to remember the prayers she'd learned in Sunday school. She had been a regular at St. Anthony's Church. After her mother died, she'd accompanied her dad to early Mass. Following her marriage, she'd urged Frank to join her but he begged off. "Sunday's the only day I can sleep," he protested, burrowing under the covers and reaching for her. Before long Iris had switched to the later Mass. Eventually, she stopped attending altogether.

Now she gazed at the white dove and wondered how to compose a prayer. Sister Florene had instructed the class not to request specifics. "Don't ask Jesus for a dog," the nun instructed. "Ask instead for the strength to carry out His will."

Iris wondered if it was God's will that Frank recover. Just in case Sister Florene was wrong, she whispered, "Lord, please let Frank awaken from his coma. And when he does, let him have no memory of Valerie Moles."

She leaned back. The chapel was warm and peaceful, the hushed music relaxing. She dreaded a return to the sterile ICU with its harsh lights. She closed her eyes and dozed.

She awoke abruptly to the sounds of shouting amid the pounding of feet in the corridor. A mechanical voice repeated a message about a "code." It was like a TV medical drama, she thought, listening to the noise outside. They were heading toward the ICU. The old lady in the cubicle next to Frank's, she thought, and wondered if the family members had witnessed the ordeal.

She got up and peeked out at the corridor. A last-minute doctor scurried inside the ICU, his white coat flapping. She decided to go home; she would come back tonight.

She stayed in the chapel a few minutes longer and then reluctantly left. As she waited at the elevator, the ICU door opened. A half dozen medical personnel, their masks hanging loose around their faces, silently exited the room and filed past her to the stairs.

Behind them were the family members of the elderly lady. With stricken faces they approached the elevator. The one Iris had pegged as the mother to the two middle-age siblings held a handkerchief to her mouth. Whatever they had witnessed inside had silenced them.

Iris contemplated taking the stairs, not wanting to intrude on their privacy. As she debated, the elevator door opened and she followed the group inside. The woman who'd ask to borrow Iris's chair broke the silence. Holding out a hand, she said, "Jesus, look at me. I'm shaking."

"I'm going across the street for a drink," a man in jeans and a flannel shirt said. He removed his baseball cap to wipe his forehead. "Anyone care to join me."

Iris realized they didn't recognize her from the neighboring cubicle. "I'm sorry," she said. "I heard the commotion in the hall. Did your loved one pass away?"

"No," the woman in the sequin sweater said. "It was the guy in the enclosure next to her." She placed a hand on her broad chest. "Oh my God, I need a drink."

When the elevator doors opened, Iris ran out, heading for the stairs at the end of the hall. She raced up to the third floor. There she flung open the ICU door and spotted Dr. Kram at the reception desk. He was leaning over, writing in a blue plastic binder. From the doorway, Iris read the name on the spine: CAMUSO, FRANCES B.

She rushed across the room, but Dr. Kram intercepted her. "Ms. Camuso, your husband had a CVA. He expired ten minutes ago. We did everything to save him." He spoke loudly and deliberately.

She stared at him. "CVA?"

"Cardio vascular accident. Call it a stroke. It's not unusual for coma patients."

"It's best you weren't here," the nurse said, emerging from the cubicle. "A code can be disturbing for families."

"Can I see him?" Iris asked.

"You can visit for a minute until someone comes for him." The nurse turned away. "Just let me tidy up." She returned to Frank's cubicle, yanking the curtains behind her.

Dr. Kram resumed writing. As he wrote, he said, "I wonder if you'd consent to an autopsy. We learn a lot by studying a CVA's effect on the brain."

Fortunately Iris was spared a response when the nurse opened the curtains. "You'll have a few minutes to pay your respects, Ms. Camuso." She stepped aside to let Iris enter.

The cubicle's bright overhead lights were now off. The space was eerily silent without the beeping of the monitor and whoosh of the respirator. Iris's eyes traveled around before finally setting on her husband's body.

He lay flat, a white sheet pulled to his bare shoulders. The plastic mask was gone; without it, Frank's face looked empty. Iris moved to his side. She gripped the cotton sheet, twisting it in her hands. "Frank," she whispered, "I had such wonderful plans for us."

SIXTEEN

When Iris emerged from the cubicle, the nurse handed her a white paper bag bearing the hospital's logo and the words, *Harborvale Hospital, we're here for you!*

"Go to Patient Accounts on the first floor," she said. "They will release your husband's effects. Do you have identification with you?" Iris nodded. She took the empty bag and thanked the nurse.

In a daze she boarded the elevator, pressing the button for the first floor. When the doors opened, she found herself on an unfamiliar floor. Instead of beige tiles and sand-colored walls, a luxurious room lay before her. The polished wood floor stretched forever. Instead of hospital-issue plastic chairs, the furniture was upholstered. Large tropical plants were scattered throughout the spacious room.

She wondered if she'd arrived at a hotel until she spotted a sign indicating it was the hospital's newly renovated lobby. Had she somehow passed the office? Confused, she stepped off the elevator. At the same time, a loud, familiar laugh rang out. Iris glanced around. Across the room, Roland Smedlie was sprawled on a brocade sofa. A silver-blond woman in a wheelchair sat nearby.

"Ms. Camuso!" he called, and hurried toward her.

"Roland, I thought I recognized your voice." Iris spontaneously hugged the boy. She noted how he'd grown taller since school had ended. "What are you doing here?"

"I'm visiting Gloria. She had a hip operation but she's going home soon." He tugged at her hand. "C'mon and meet her."

"This isn't a good time—"

"I've told her all about you."

"Well, just for a minute."

Roland led her across the room. To Gloria, he said, "This is Ms. Camuso. You know, my counselor from school."

The woman in the wheelchair held out her hand. "I've heard so much about you. Forgive me for not getting up." Her voice had a hint of southern accent. The older woman was dignified looking and attractive. Her eyes were large and blue, like a doll's. Her red silk robe was a contrast to her pale skin and silver hair worn in an upsweep.

Iris sat onto the sofa next to Roland and asked Gloria, "How did the surgery go?"

"I'm told very well. Now's the tough part—rehab. Thanks to my assistant here"— she leaned over to pat Roland's knee— "I'm going to be well taken care of."

"Don't tell anyone you saw me here," Roland said. "I'm supposed to be at computer camp downtown."

This made Gloria laugh. "He's incorrigible, isn't he?"

"That he is," Iris said, pleased to see Roland looking happy.

"How come you're at the hospital?" he asked her.

For a brief instant, Iris had forgotten. Now the past hour came rushing back. She waited several moments and managed to say, "It's my husband. He was sick and . . . and now he's gone."

Gloria released the brake on her wheelchair and eased it forward. She took Iris's hand. "I'm so sorry."

"Thank you." Iris glanced at a wall clock. "It's hard to believe it happened an hour ago. I must still be in shock. Sitting here with you, for a moment I forgot."

Gloria nodded, still holding her hand. "It's the mind's protective response."

"I have no idea what to do. There are people I have to call—"

"Go home and rest," Gloria said. "When you're feeling stronger, ask your spirit guide for help."

"Spirit guide?" Iris glanced at her.

"Our spirit guides are all around us, if we'd stop to notice. Often they take the form of animals. If you sincerely ask for help, your spirit guide will appear. Maybe not at that moment, but sometime in the future."

"I'll remember that," Iris said. At the same time she wondered if Gloria practiced witchcraft. Perhaps that was why the Smedlies didn't want Roland associating with her. "I'd better get back," Iris said, getting to her feet. Roland stood and shook her hand. She told him, "Enjoy the rest of your summer."

"Bye, Ms. Camuso."

Gloria held out her hand and looked into her eyes. "You're stronger than you know," she said.

"I hope you're right, Iris said, her voice breaking. She hurriedly crossed the lobby, her footsteps echoing on the wooden floor.

Back home, the house was steeped in the stillness of early twilight. It was as if nothing had changed, Iris thought. She made herself a drink and headed up the stairs. In the bedroom, she set her glass on the night table and kicked off her shoes. She stacked her pillows against the headboard and finally crawled under the comforter. Leaning back, she let out a long sigh.

She was too exhausted to make phone calls. Earlier she'd called Grace and after that, Shannon. Struggling to get the words out, she had left a message with the agency. No doubt Nancy Proctor would break the news. The woman had usurped Iris's role. Seeing the two of them at the hospital, they were more like mother and daughter.

She sipped her drink. First thing tomorrow she'd call her sister-in-law. Fatima wouldn't like the delay, but after all, Iris was a grief-stricken widow. She reached for her notepad on the night table and quickly scribbled a list:

1. Call Fatima and Dad.
2. Visit funeral parlor, write obituary.
3. Contact church, speak to priest.

When she set the notepad down, she felt better. She would take care of the details tomorrow. She reached for the lamp switch. At the same time she noticed the answering machine's flashing light. Maybe it was Shannon calling. Iris rolled onto her side and pressed the "play" button. Instead of her daughter's tearful voice, it was Vincent Tosi's booming baritone:

"Ms. Camuso, I've been away, and just got back today. You know that threatening message you got from Frank on Friday? Well, guess what—I got one too. Mine came a few hours after yours. Sounds like Frankie had had a few. He threatened me.

"I'm thinking of taking out a criminal complaint. In any event, it strengthens our case. Next time you're in, I'll play it for you." He chuckled. "It's a keeper."

Iris leaned over and shut off the answering machine. She got back into bed and turned out the light. In the dark she sipped her drink and gazed out the window. The moon was full tonight. Its face—cool, white, indifferent—stared down at her.

Somehow Iris got through the next few days. She pulled herself together to greet the visitors who poured into Limone's Funeral Home for the evening wake. Earlier she had stood up to her sister in law's insistence on holding afternoon *and* evening visiting hours.

"I can't do it, "Iris told Fatima over the phone. "I can't make conversation for two hours in the afternoon and then do it all over again at night."

"But what about the aunties?" Fatima asked exasperatedly. "They'll expect an afternoon wake. Old people don't like going out at night."

"Tell them we'll tape it. I've got too many things to do. By the way, do you know the priest at St. Anthony's?"

" Father Gladioli? Didn't you meet him at Crystal Lafata's confirmation?" When Iris didn't respond, Fatima said, "Don't tell me you didn't attend. That was an important ceremony for the family."

"Do you know Father Gladioli?" Iris asked, trying to sound patient.

"Of course I know him. Before Ma passed, he was at the hospital every day giving her Holy Communion. Father Gladioli's a doll."

"I might ask him about holding a simple service at the funeral home," Iris said.

Fatima gasped. "Instead of a Mass at the church? You can't do that. The aunties would have a stroke. Besides, Frank would want a Mass at his church."

"But he never went to church."

"That has nothing to do with it. Every Catholic has a funeral Mass."

"In that case, will you discuss it with Father Gladioli, since you know him so well?"

"I don't mind at all," Fatima said. "And by the way, do you mind if I stay at Janice's when I'm home? The last time I came back, she thought I was avoiding her. Not only that, Aunt Bernie's not doing so good. She's gotta be way in her eighties. Janice says I'm the only person who makes her laugh."

Hearing that Fatima wouldn't be staying at her house was the first positive news Iris had heard. After hanging up she moved to the next person on the list of people to call, her father. "Dad, I've got bad news."

"I know all about it, dear. Betty-Ann, my friend on the second floor, told me. She volunteers at the hospital gift shop. She saw Frank's name on the 'expired' list. Do you want me to come over? I don't mind taking a cab."

"Thanks, Dad, but I've got a lot to do. I'm picking up Fatima at the airport and still waiting to hear from Shannon. I have to plan for a reception. Right now I'm just going through the motions."

"Don't try to do it all yourself. Let Frank's sister help. She likes to take charge."

That's what I'm afraid of," she said.

Driving back from Logan Airport, Iris gave Fatima an update. "It will be the three of us walking behind the casket—you, me, and Shannon. The rest will follow."

"Did Shannon agree to that?" Fatima asked.

Iris glanced at her sister in law. "What do you mean?"

"I'm talking about the situation between you two. Frankie, God rest his soul, told me about it."

"He did? What did he say?"

"Watch the road. He said you two weren't speaking. Let me talk to Shannon. She's always been straight with me."

"You'll never get near her. The director of the adoption agency keeps Shannon on a short leash."

"Yeah, Frankie told me about that, too." She hesitated. "He also mentioned you wanted to adopt Shannon's baby. I said, 'Iris should take a couple Xanax and chill out.' Take her on vacation, I told him." She gasped and covered her face. "Mother of God, that was the last time I talked to my brother." She dug into her voluminous bag and pulled out a wad of tissues.

Iris waited for Fatima's sobs to subside before she said, "Remember, that baby is Frank's grandchild."

Fatima sniffed. "Oh, Shannon's a beautiful girl. She'll meet the right guy someday and have a family. But you gotta think of your future. Raising a kid, you'll ruin your chances of meeting someone." Before Iris could protest, Fatima clamped a hand on her shoulder. "You had the best guy in the world, but trust me, you'll move on. After my divorce I said to my friends, 'That's it.' I vowed to never walk down the aisle again."

Iris waited for Fatima to continue. When she didn't, she asked, "What are you saying, you're getting married?"

"I'm in love again."

"Someone new?" Iris asked. She rarely spoke to her sister in law in California. Fatima usually called Frank, who half-listened and thus never passed on news.

"Someone who was a customer at my dog spa." Now Fatima launched into a tale of her current boyfriend. "Alan was a client even though I have a policy of not dating customers. My spa has an excellent reputation and I want to keep it that way. But this was different. Alan and Louise moved to Santa Rosa from New Jersey after he sold his plumbing supply company. Louise was his bookkeeper.

"They started bringing Dimples, their Maltese, in for weekly grooming sessions. Alan dropped him off and Louise picked him up. Before long I noticed Louise wasn't coming in to pick Dimples up. I didn't think too much about it. I knew she took classes at the senior center; I figured that's what she's doing.

"One afternoon I happened to be in the reception area when Alan comes in. I asked him how he was and he got all choked up. He said Louise was in the hospital with cancer.

"Well, you know me, Iris. My heart rules my head. I told Alan to leave Dimples behind for a while. We were going across the street to Mario's for a glass of wine. When he begged off, I said, 'Listen Mr. Kobroski, your wife is sick. You've gotta stay strong for her.'" Fatima smiled, remembering. "The guy was a basket case. Someone had to take charge. I'm like Ma in that respect."

"That's what Frank used to say," Iris added. She didn't mention Frank's actual words, that his sister Fatima was a ball buster. "Finish your story," Iris said. "What happened to the Kobroskis?"

"What happened was, Alan enrolled Dimples in our doggy daycare. It made sense, him spending every day at the hospital. The poor dog shouldn't be alone all day. Then, at the end of the day, I drove Dimples back. Alan had given me a key to their house. It was gorgeous but needed attention. He'd been living there alone while Lousie was in the hospital. You know how guys are. What I did was set him up with the Brazilians who clean my condo.

"When I looked in his fridge, it was full of Chinese take-out containers. I got in touch with a local caterer that delivers homemade soups and casseroles. Alan loved their Moroccan pulled chicken—"

"When did you start calling him Alan?"

"Huh? I guess it was from being in his house and helping out. He said I'd become like family."

"When did you start dating?"

"We never thought of it as dating. It was a natural outgrowth of the friendship. I think it was one night I dropped off some stuffed shells. Alan goes, 'You're always doing for me. At least let me buy you dinner.' We went out to some local place where he cried buckets. Then I suggested we stop at an all-night store so he could buy Louise some flowers for his visit the next day."

Iris pictured Fatima helping the hapless husband buy flowers. Her next question was bold, yet at the same time she didn't think Fatima would mind. "Do you think you'll get married?"

Fatima slapped her playfully. "Get outta here. His wife's only been gone six months. Right now we're playing it by ear. We've both been through a lot, Alan losing a wife and me a brother. We need time to heal. I was thinking a cruise on the Gulf of Mexico. I'm trying to talk Alan into it. He's a little set in his ways."

"Any luck?" Iris asked.

Fatima winked. "I'm working on it."

It was a cool spring night. The line of mourners at Limone's Funeral Home snaked out the door. Inside the receiving room, Iris and Fatima stood next to a gleaming casket shrouded in flowers. Frank's body lay inside, his head and shoulders visible. Even in the muted light of the funeral home, his skin was an unnatural orange-bronze.

Seated on a row of wooden chairs were the three elderly "aunties," surrounded by their adult children and their spouses. The adults got up periodically to monitor the children who, after the novelty of being in a funeral home had worn off, had grown restless. This was particularly true of cousin Janice's twins, Justin and Joey, who were rumored to be smoking marijuana in the parking lot.

Earlier in the evening, Shannon, arriving with Nancy Proctor, had taken her place in line with Iris and Fatima. After twenty minutes she complained of back pain and left to join her mentor. Ms. Proctor, in a black silk pantsuit and pearls, had sat in a small front parlor, typing on a laptop computer.

Watching the door, Iris spotted Grace in the foyer. "Excuse me," she said to Fatima, "my friend has arrived." She made her way through the crowd and embraced Grace.

"How're you doing?" Grace asked, looking around.

Iris told her about Shannon's defection. "She can't be away from that woman's side for a minute."

"Hell with her," Grace said. "How are things going with

your sister in law?"

"Mercifully, she's staying with Janice. Fatima's the ringleader for the Camuso family. Everyone takes their cues from her."

Grace looked across the room. "You'd better get back in line, kiddo. The ringleader is waving to you."

Iris sighed. "Will you tell her I'll be right back? I haven't been to the bathroom all night."

She was grateful to find herself alone in the ladies room. The past few days she'd been surrounded by people offering condolences. She found herself hearing and saying the same words, over and over.

Now she paused at the door to adjust her panty hose. Voices carried from outside—someone said her name. She moved closer to the louvered door. Through the slats, she could make out two women standing outside. Their heads were together and they spoke in subdued voices. "You didn't know he walked out on her? There was a girlfriend, a bartender . . . Dirty Dinghy—"

Iris flung the door open wide, surprising the pair. She confronted her colleagues, Mrs. Trowt, the school secretary, and Ms. Dutton, assistant principal. "Don't let me interrupt your conversation. I couldn't help overhearing my name."

Although Ms. Dutton's face turned pink, she didn't appear at all flustered. Mrs. Trowt muttered something about her bladder and scurried past Iris into the ladies room. Ms. Dutton squared her shoulders and said, "I'm here representing Mr. Tomasillo, who's out of the country."

"I don't think Mr. Tomasillo would like his assistant principal gossiping about an employee, especially one whose husband is dead in the next room."

"You need to rest," Ms. Dutton said, "and I must find my coat."

"I'm not an object of pity," Iris said to her retreating back. When Ms. Dutton continued on to the coatroom, Iris loudly repeated her remark. Those standing nearby fell silent and turned to stare.

At that moment Nancy Proctor appeared in a doorway, a

look of professional concern on her face. "Ms. Camuso, can I call someone to take you home?"

"I think you've done enough," Iris said loudly.

Those around her pretended to look away as they simultaneously drew closer. Fatima's booming voice broke the tension. "What's going on?" She pushed her way through the crowd like a tugboat in a busy harbor until she came to Iris's side. "My sister in law's had a tough day," she announced, clamping a hand on Iris's shoulder. "She needs to go home."

"Don't talk like I'm crazy," Iris hissed at her. "They came here to gossip about me."

Fatima put an arm around her. "You know what Frankie would say to that? He'd say, 'Don't get your bowels in an uproar.'"

The crowd, relieved yet disappointed that the crisis had passed, chuckled. As they drifted away, Fatima gripped her arm, pulling her close. "What was that all about?"

"They ridiculed me. I'm not an object of pity."

Fatima sighed. "No one pities you, Iris. Now get yourself home. We've got a big day tomorrow."

At the closing of the funeral Mass, Iris and Fatima walked behind Father Gladioli and four altar boys, trailing the casket down the center aisle of St. Anthony's Church. Behind them were the three loudly weeping Camuso aunts, the cousins and their spouses and children. Bringing up the rear was Shannon, aided by Ms. Proctor.

The entourage passed long wooden pews filled with tearful mourners. Iris kept her eyes ahead, focusing on the priest's tall gold and white brocade hat. Next to her Fatima, a black mantilla covering her face, sobbed loudly.

Upon reaching the door, the procession stopped while the pallbearers, Frank's high school football team mates, maneuvered the church steps. Iris averted her gaze in the sun's sudden glare. At the same time she spotted Gloria and Roland in the back of the church, Gloria in a wheelchair. She wore dark glasses and a white suit. Roland, looking grown-up in a navy blazer, leaned against the back wall. As the procession resumed, Iris nodded to the pair. Gloria bowed her head as if bestowing a benediction.

One hour later, at the Knights of Columbus Hall, Fatima, Iris, and Janice talked in the kitchen. Actually, it was Fatima who talked while the two women listened. "Remember to call the engravers before the end of the week," Fatima instructed. "If you want your name on Frank's stone, do it soon. Today they'll charge you three bucks a letter. You wait and soon it'll be four."

"I don't know," Iris said, taking a sip of her vodka and tonic. "It seems so grim, my name on a tombstone while I'm still alive."

Fatima rolled her eyes. "It's not called a tombstone any more. I'm just trying to save you a few bucks by doing it early."

"Every time I visit Frank's grave I'll see my name, my birth date and a space waiting to be filled in. It's depressing."

"Listen, honey, you're the one who asked me to handle the stone. I'm just saying what they told me. Now's also the time if you want a special saying engraved. Frankie had a couple of favorite expressions you might consider—"

"Don't get your bowels in an uproar?" she asked.

Fatima frowned. "There you go, carrying a grudge. I had to say something last night to break the tension. I thought you were going to lose it in front of everyone."

"I've forgotten the matter already," Iris said, reluctant to discuss the previous evening. "By the way, what expression do you have in mind?"

"Remember how he used to say, 'A day without Chianti is like a day without love?'"

Iris nodded. "Actually, it was 'a day without sex.' You know what? I prefer just Frank's name and the dates. If I decide to include my name, I'll get in touch with the engravers next week."

Janice, who was sipping rum and Coke from a tall plastic cup, said, "Maybe Iris has another reason for not wanting her name on the stone."

"What's that?" Fatima asked.

Janice shrugged. "Maybe she'll meet another guy someday

and get married."

Fatima shrugged. "Maybe, but he won't be as fabulous as my baby brother."

Janice glanced around. "Just between us girls, if something ever happened to Artie, I'd hit the clubs and find a guy who's ten, fifteen years younger."

"Sure, Janice," Fatima said. "You're boffing this guy upstairs while Aunt Bernie's downstairs yelling for her spaghetti." Janice laughed, spraying rum and coke. Fatima stepped back, blotting the front of her dress with a napkin. "Chrissake, take it easy on the rum. Why don't you go see if the aunties want another sherry before the kitchen starts putting the food out." Fatima watched Janice scurry away. "She's not the brightest bulb, but she's been good to Aunt Bernie, who's a pain in the butt if you ask me."

"I saw Janice say something to Nancy Proctor in church," Iris said. "It looked like a confrontation."

"A minor confrontation. She told that skinny bitch that our section was reserved for family. Imagine that woman trying to sit with us, like she and Shannon are joined at the hip." Fatima shook her head. "You know what? After a couple of these Manhattans I'm gonna tell that broad what I think of her." Fatima glanced around the room. "Is she here?"

"I doubt if Ms. Proctor would step foot in a Knights of Columbus hall."

"Yeah," Fatima said. "She'd be scared someone might steal her designer handbag." She rattled the ice in her glass. "If it was *my* kid she'd latched onto, I'd kick her skinny butt."

The fact that Fatima had no children—preferring to lavish her affection upon a pair of pugs—didn't stop her from commenting on child-rearing. Iris responded with, "It's not been easy dealing with the woman."

Fatima patted her shoulder. "Poor Iris, everyone picking on you."

When the bar finally closed and the leftover food wrapped and distributed among the relatives, the mourners collected their coats. The children, who'd chased each other around the room while breaking all the black and white balloons in the process, began to yawn. The older generation, having consumed their share of lasagna and tiramisu, were nodding off in the wooden chairs lining the walls. Fatima herded everyone to the parking lot. The three aunts, laden with leftovers, were driven home by a none-too-sober Janice.

Iris, who'd left her car in the church parking lot, rode with Grace. Her goodbye to Fatima was short, having overheard her sister-in-law telling Grace to make sure Iris was "okay" to drive home.

"Frank's sister's not so bad," Grace said as they drove out of the lot. "I like her can-do attitude."

Iris sighed. "She's a know it all. Frank used to call her a steamroller."

"She must miss Frank, the way she was crying in church." Grace said.

Iris nodded. "Italians are like that, crying one minute, laughing the next."

Grace chuckled. "That sounds like a healthy way to live, if you ask me."

"Frank never let things bother him. Not a guilty bone in his body."

Grace, sensing Iris's glum mood, attempted to change the subject. "Do you remember your first date with Frank?"

"Of course I do."

"Where'd you go?"

Iris thought of the clandestine night at the moonlit beach. Although it was their first time together, it couldn't be considered an actual date. Her father was opposed to Frank; they had to sneak around. As a result, she and Frank rarely went anywhere outside of the beach, where they drank beer and Chianti under the stars.

"Once I asked to borrow Dad's truck, saying I was meeting friends at the movie theater. I met Frank instead. Afterward, he reached into the cooler in his truck bed and handed me the biggest, most gorgeous bouquet of flowers I'd ever seen."

"How'd you explain them to your dad?" Grace asked.

"When I got home, Dad was already in bed. I snuck the bouquet into my room and hid them in the closet." She shrugged. "What else could I do? Dad was stubborn about Frank."

When the flowers began to wither, she tried preserving them, pressing the blossoms between sheets of waxed paper. She found, entangled in the leaves, a thin satin ribbon. Embossed in gilt letters was the name *SS Nina Rosa.* The next day she asked her dad: "Does a ship named Nina Rosa mean anything to you?"

"It sure does," he said. "The Nina Rosa capsized in a storm, eight men lost."

"When was that?"

"Let's see, it was 1974. I know because they recently had a memorial service at the pier. After the ceremony, the dead men's grandchildren threw flowers off the pier, into the water." He shook his head. "Not a dry eye in the crowd after witnessing that."

Iris nodded. She thought of mentioning her suspicions to Frank, who would nonetheless be offended. In the end she said nothing. At the same time, she stopped trying to preserve the flowers.

SEVENTEEN

"Ms. Camuso, this is Judith Bangs, manager of Harborvale Jewelry," said the voice on the phone. Iris remembered visiting the store and the woman suggesting she get her diamond reset. Business must be slow if the store manager had to chase down customers. "This isn't a good time, Ms. Bangs. Perhaps later in the summer."

"Ms. Camuso, it's about the Scottish bracelet."

"Scottish bracelet? Iris's head ached from the night before. She'd only intended to have a nightcap or two, an after-dinner drink to settle her nerves and help her sleep. "I think you've got me confused with someone else."

"I don't think so," Ms. Bangs said. "Our security camera captured you perfectly."

Then Iris remembered the rust-colored stones in the pewter setting, the bracelet she'd walked out wearing. A wave of heat infused her face. "Ms. Bangs?"

"I'm still here."

"I'm sorry. That was a mistake. I—I'm afraid I forgot all about it. I meant to return the bracelet. Imagine my surprise when I got home and discovered I was still wearing it." She attempted a laugh. "Let me bring the money in today—right now if you're there. The bracelet's in the glove compartment." The latter was the only true statement she'd made.

Judith Bangs hesitated. "Normally with a theft I turn the security tapes over to the police. However, in your case I'll make an exception. I saw your husband's obituary in the paper." She paused. "But I have two requirements. The first is payment in the amount of two-hundred twenty-two, the price of the bracelet plus tax. Do you agree, Ms. Camuso?"

"Of course. What's the second requirement?"

"You'll find out when you come in."

Dr. Laurence Spinney's office at the Harborvale Medical Building was on the hospital grounds inside a three-story building dating back to the 1950s. Iris had visited the psychiatrist before, during the height of Shannon's rebellion. At the time, he'd prescribed Valium, which made her fuzzy-headed.

Now, one year later, she sat opposite Dr. Spinney. The psychiatrist's wiry gray hair was freshly clipped, sporting two half-moons of pink around his ears. He wore a tweed sport coat and navy tie with a fading insignia. He sat with his legs crossed, revealing hairy white shins.

"How are you feeling?" he asked.

"Fine, I guess, considering my husband was recently buried."

"I'm sorry to hear that." He glanced at the clipboard perched on his knee. "You said you have symptoms. What are you experiencing?"

"Insomnia. Nervousness. I suppose that's common for recent widows."

"It is, during the adjustment period. Is that why you're here?"

She decided to tell him outright. "Actually, you might say I'm here against my will. You see, it's part of my . . . retribution." She told Dr. Spinney about accidentally taking the bracelet from the store and then returning it. She didn't mention that the store manager had called the matter to her attention. She said she'd paid in full but had to comply with the manager's requirement that she go for counseling.

"And how will the store manager know you're complying?" he asked, looking vaguely amused.

"I have to bring in a confirmation from you."

He cracked a rare smile. "Well, it is an unusual request."

"It's ridiculous, if you ask me. It was an honest mistake. I'd been under a lot of stress, losing my husband like that."

"Why do you think you took the bracelet?"

"I didn't intend to take it. I tried it on and got distracted. Then I forgot all about it. As a matter of fact, I put it in the glove compartment, intending to return it the next time I was downtown." She shifted in her chair. "It's not like I have a compulsion or anything."

"If you refused the manager's offer, would she turn the tapes over to the police?"

"Maybe. She's an odd one."

"Have you taken items before, deliberately or mistakenly?"

"I may have when I was a kid. Children go through such a phase."

"Did you?"

She nodded, remembering the period after Lily died when she'd stolen items of little value: a dish towel from the neighbor's clothes line, a cream cheese-and-olive sandwich from her teacher's desk, a Red Sox cap from the church's lost and found box, a pack of gum palmed at the cash register. Along with the guilt, she'd felt a thrill.

"How's your mood been?" Dr. Spinney asked, looking at her over his glasses.

She shrugged. "What you'd expect of someone in my situation."

"And that is?"

"Periods of depression and little energy . . . insomnia."

He glanced at the clipboard. "What about alcohol use? That was an issue when you first saw me."

"I was experiencing a crisis at the time and drinking more than usual."

"And now?"

His pale blue eyes impaled her. She turned to gaze out the window. "I have a lot of stress. My only child won't speak to me nor let me adopt her baby. My husband, before he unexpectedly died, was living with another woman. Now, outside of the cat, I'm all alone." She attempted a smile. "Other than that, everything's fine."

He took a prescription pad from his jacket pocket. "I can help with the short term issues, such as insomnia." He scribbled on the pad. "We can also try a course of antidepressants." He finished writing and tore off two sheets, handing them to her. "Let's talk more next week, shall we?"

Iris shrugged. "I have no choice."

Back at home, she studied the plastic vial of antidepressants she'd had filled at the pharmacy. A warning on the label, in bold print, instructed not to combine with alcohol. She stood at the kitchen sink and poured a glass of water. Then she shook out a gray and white and a blue capsule and swallowed them.

Although it was late afternoon, she felt as tired as if it were midnight. She dragged herself up the stairs where she sank onto her bed. After dozing for a while, she pressed the button on the answering machine. The first message was from Fatima: "Hi honey. I just wanna tell you, if you call on my cell phone you won't reach me. Alan and I are going on a cruise to the Gulf of Mexico, where service will be interrupted. Just leave a message and I'll get it eventually. Love ya, sweetheart. Bye for now."

The next message was from Tomas Tomasillo. He apologized for not attending Frank's funeral. He'd been away but was back from Puerto Rico with his sister Aidita. "I would like her to meet you." He ended with a promise to call at a later date.

Iris canceled the messages and fell back onto the pillows. She didn't want to see or talk to anyone. She felt empty, drained of energy and emotion. All she wanted was to sleep, hours and hours of blessed relief.

She pulled the curtains shut. As she plumped the pillows, a sound startled her. Was it Patticake? She stood still and listened. It was a baby's cry, thin and plaintive. The sound came from her closet. She crossed the room and opened the door to peer inside the shadowy depths. The cries continued, growing more faint.

When they ceased, she wiped a tear from her cheek and whispered, "Don't be afraid. I'll find you."

Two weeks later Iris dropped an envelope containing Dr. Spinney's invoice—confirmation of therapy—on Judith Bangs's desk. The woman wasn't in sight at Harborvale Jewelry and Iris hustled out, hoping to escape undetected. Alas she was almost at the front door when the manager called out, "Iris, wait!"

Iris slowly turned to face her. "I'm in a hurry," she said. "I've got an appointment."

"Want some coffee?" Judith asked.

"No, thanks. I just wanted to drop off the invoice. I left it on your desk. I don't understand why I can't mail it."

Judith rested an elbow on the glass counter. "I prefer that you stop in so we can touch base."

"I've seen Dr. Spinney twice already. I'll continue for two months, as we agreed."

"Once you begin to unburden yourself, you'll want to continue. Therapy made a world of difference in my life."

Iris wasn't going to encourage the woman by asking how therapy had helped. She would complete her end of the bargain and be done with it. "Look Judith, we agreed to eight sessions. Whether I continue or not is my business."

"One of these days you'll thank me, Iris."

"Do you blackmail everyone who forgets to pay for merchandise in this store?"

Her smile was bland. "Only those I consider worth saving. I feel a sense of responsibility toward you."

"Why is that?"

She approached, taking Iris's hand and tapping the diamond ring with a long red nail. "When you came in here twenty years ago with your fiancé, I knew who he was."

"You knew Frank?"

She nodded. "Not personally. He'd dated my niece, a lovely young girl, naive and trusting. Unfortunately, Frank led her on." She looked at Iris. "He used her."

Iris pulled her hand away. "That was a long time ago. I know nothing about it."

"You're right. It's water under the bridge. Sarah eventually got over him. I'm just thankful she didn't get pregnant. Nonetheless, I regretted not speaking up when you came in here with him. You seemed sweet and sincere, like my niece."

"Just because my late husband had a failed relationship isn't proof of anything. We were married for twenty years."

"I don't have to know the couples personally," Judith said. "When they come in to look at rings I sense how things will go for them. The best couples are committed, like two peas in a pod. In your case, I wanted to take you aside and tell you to run and not look back."

"Oh? And what stopped you?" Iris asked, smirking.

"If I'd done that and lost a sale, the Birds would have let me go." Judith shrugged. "Diamond rings are expensive."

"And now that you're running the store you're free to interfere?"

"You call it interfering," she said, unperturbed. "I call it saving someone from a lifetime of misery."

When Iris arrived home, she discovered a shiny black Buick parked in her driveway. At that moment Tomas Tomasillo emerged from the car. She parked the Jetta alongside him and got out. "Tomas, how nice to see you." They approached each other awkwardly and shook hands. Although it was warm, the principal wore a shirt and tie.

"It is good to see you again," he said. "I am sorry for your loss. You got my card of sympathy?"

"Yes, that was very nice." She glanced at the front seat of his car; someone was sitting in the passenger seat.

He caught her glance. "My sister Aidita and I are on our way for ice cream. We hoped you would join us." Before she could offer an excuse, he took her arm and led her around the Buick to the opposite door. A stocky young woman with dark curly hair observed them glumly from behind the passenger window. He rapped on the glass, saying loudly, "Put the window down, Aidita." He turned to Iris. "My sister is shy."

Silently Aidita lowered the window, her eyes fixed on her brother.

"This is Ms. Camuso, the school adjustment counselor," Tomas said. When the girl gave no response, he continued, "She wishes to join us for ice cream."

"Oh, I can't." Iris stepped back. At the same time, he opened the rear door.

"Please," he said, his voice low. "It is good for Aidita to meet professional women—roller models."

"Role models," she corrected. "I'll go with you, but just a short while." She slid across the back seat. "I've got much to do at home."

Inside the car, the air conditioner was noisily operating at full blast. Iris shivered and said, "Nice to meet you, Aidita," to the back of the girl's head. Up close, her hair was a cascade of gelled curls. When Aidita didn't respond, Iris wondered if she was hearing impaired.

Tomas slid behind the wheel and turned to his sister. In rapid-fire Spanish, he uttered what sounded like a directive, to which Aidita nodded. He turned the ignition key and glanced at Iris in the rear view mirror. "Are you hungry for ice cream?"

"Sure am," she said, wishing she'd brought a sweater to combat the frigid air. "But if you'd prefer a cocktail, there's a cafe nearby called the Patio."

"My sister does not drink alcohol," he said, apologetically. "Perhaps another time we will go there." He backed the car the length of the driveway.

"I'd rather have ice cream anyway," Iris said, lying.

No one spoke during the ten-minute ride to Dairy Depot. When they arrived, Tomas insisted upon getting their order while they stayed behind in the car. "To give you a chance to talk," he said. "Aidita is eager to learn about your work with students."

He took their order. Iris was surprised to hear Aidita speak, saying, "fudge ripple." He alighted from the car; they watched him approach a window and stand in line. With the air conditioner now off, the silence inside the car was oppressive. Finally Iris spoke, "I understand you're interested in early childhood education."

After several seconds, the girl said, "Yes."

"Do you have an interview lined up?"

"My brother is taking me next week," she said, still staring straight ahead.

"That's nice you have a brother who helps you."

"Tomas is good to our family."

"He's a good principal at our school," Iris said.

"My father prays he will return to Puerto Rico some day and take over the family business."

"What is the family business," Iris said to the back of Aidita's head.

"We make sisal rugs," she said. "It is like straw, only stronger."

"That's . . . interesting," Iris said.

"Our great-grandfather started the company with one handmade loom. Today we have six looms and five employees. We ship our rugs to stores in the United States."

"That's impressive."

"My father worries that Tomas will meet a woman who will trap him, and he will not return home."

Iris considered her response. "Your brother is a sensible man. Your father shouldn't worry."

"I have seen the women here. They dress like prostitutes."

Fortunately, Tomas arrived with their ice cream. He got behind the wheel and handed them their cones. "Did you have a nice conversation?"

"Lovely," Iris said.

That summer, Harborvale experienced record-high temperatures. The excessive humidity curtailed Iris's activities, not that she was doing much of anything. Outside of sessions with Dr. Spinney, cookouts at Grace's, and the occasional ice cream outing with Tomas and Aidita, she stayed home.

When it got too hot in the house, she removed the sofa cushions and lined them up on the floor. Here she stretched out, reading and sipping vodka and lemonade. Nearby, a standing fan circulated the muggy air.

Her life was reduced to the basics. During the day, she wore a thin cotton shift that substituted as a nightgown. She used disposable paper plates and plastic utensils. When she ran out of cat food and microwave dinners, she visited Mighty Mart convenience store.

When Sandy rang up Iris's purchases, the girl failed to notice that her former counselor had alcohol on her breath in the middle of the day. Sandy was too involved with her screenplay, and gave Iris updates on her progress

"Guess what, Ms. C? I'm going to a three-day horror movie festival in Montreal. They'll show dozens of films with directors from all over the world. I'm hoping to make a few contacts there."

"Good for you," Iris said. "Are you going alone?"

"No, David's coming with me. He's renting a car, which means I don't have to take a bus."

"David?"

"You know, Dr. Fung. We're good friends now. He's like co-author of my script 'though he doesn't want credit. Dr. Fung might be old, but he's a cool dude."

"So you're driving up there together?"

"Uh huh. We're staying at a motel nearby." Sandy double bagged Iris's frozen dinners and handed her the sack. "Separate rooms, of course."

"Does your mother know you're going together?"

She laughed. "Ms. C., I'm twenty-five years old and I outweigh David by about forty pounds."

Iris felt tears filling her eyes. "I'm happy for you, Sandy. Follow your own path, okay?"

Sandy gave her a thumbs-up. "Right on, Ms. C."

For the next few days the town of Harborvale was blanketed in hot, humid weather. This gave Iris an excuse to stay home, although the outside world continued to intervene. After three phone calls from her dad, she called him back. He asked if she would take him to the cemetery; he wanted to tidy up Lily's gravesite, something he'd failed to do all summer. Iris thought the request timely. She would visit Frank's final resting place, something she'd been avoiding.

When she rapped on her father's door, it swung open. He sat at the tiny kitchen table, a mug of coffee and a half-eaten donut before him. "Dad, your door was unlocked," she called out, stepping inside.

"So what? I've got nothing worth stealing."

She crossed the room. "Do you mind if I shut off the TV?"

"What? Go ahead. I wasn't watching anyway. I can't make out what's on the screen half the time."

She sighed, not wanting to get into another discussion about his television. "I've told you before," she said, "you won't get good reception until you get cable. If you had cable, you could see dozens of programs."

"Dozens! What do I want with dozens?"

"You don't have to watch them all."

"All I watch is the news, the Bruins, and the Red Sox. It's a waste of time because the picture's lousy. I should have gotten a Magnavox."

"They don't make them anymore." She dropped onto the sofa, tired of the subject. When he stood up, she said, "You've got stains on the front of that shirt."

"We're visiting the cemetery. No one cares how I look there."

Shady Rest was one of the oldest cemeteries on Boston's North Shore. Ancient trees dating back to the days of the early sea captains shaded the weather-beaten gravestones. Nearby was a newer section, laid out like a grid.

Iris followed the dirt road that wove through the cemetery. She stopped when her dad pointed out the Quirk family plot. He got out and opened the trunk. His tools were kept inside a plastic bucket: a trowel, clippers, a brush, and a hand rake.

Together they made their way over the uneven terrain, stopping before Lily's grave. The speckled-granite stone was engraved with the words, **Lily Alice Quirk, 1980 -1985**. Under that were the words: *Although we wanted you here, God needed you in heaven.*

Years ago, when Iris used to accompany her mother to the cemetery, people sometimes stopped and read the words aloud. Invariably they commented on their poignancy. Her mother would tell the story of Lily's congenital heart defect, how the family had been unaware of its existence. She concluded with,

"A hole in her heart the size of a pea. We had no idea."

By that time Iris had slipped away, unnoticed. She wandered over to the Italian section of the cemetery; there the gravestones were fascinating. Each had a small oval portrait the size of an egg set in the stone. She liked to study the faces of the deceased, searching for clues in their expressions as to whether they knew what lay in store for them.

Now her father lowered himself onto the grass in front of Lily's stone. One by one he removed his gardening tools from the pail. "This place is a mess," he said, looking around. "Look how the grass is overgrown. I don't know why we pay these people."

Iris watched him for a while. Then she stood. "Dad, why don't you continue here, I'm going over there." She indicated the Italian section where the Camuso family lay. "I won't be long."

He nodded, understanding. "Take your time, dear."

She turned, grateful she hadn't had to say the words, "Frank's grave." She couldn't bring herself to even speak his name, his passing still too raw. Dr. Spinney had said she'd adjust in time. "That's what life is," he said, "a series of adjustments."

The sun beat down as Iris followed the dusty, meandering path. She spotted Frank's gravesite by the still-green sod surrounding it and stopped a dozen feet away. The polished stone, made of rose quartz, was impressive. Chiseled into the surface were the words: Francis Alberto Camuso, 1970 - 2016. Other stones nearby represented family members lying in eternal rest.

She took a newspaper from her tote bag and spread it on the ground. She sat, grateful that the Camuso family plot was situated under leafy maple trees. She hugged her knees and leaned against the nearby stone of Caspar and Bernadetta Camuso, Frank's grandparents. She turned her head to gaze at Frank's stone. How strange that her husband was lying under the ground she sat upon. How very peculiar that Frank, a man who never hesitated to express his opinion, was now silenced.

The days following his passing, she'd expected to hear something. She'd read of people who claimed they'd heard a loved one speak—an utterance in an empty room. Iris had expected this of Frank, although in his case it would be an admonition such as, "Chrissake, Iris!" Hearing Frank's voice would have been unnerving, although not as unnerving as his silence.

Now she glanced around, making sure she was alone. When she felt certain, she said, "Frank, it's me. I don't know if you can hear, but I have something to tell you." She paused, choosing her words. "You're going to think I'm crazy, but I want you to be the first to know. You see, Shannon's baby—our grandchild—is trying to contact me. I heard the cries last week and no, I wasn't imagining it. It was a baby, crying.

"This indicates to me the child is due any day now. Do you know what this means? Already we have a bond, the baby and I. It's blood calling to blood. It tells me I'm meant to adopt this infant." She wiped the tear that trickled down her cheek. "I know what you're thinking, Frank. You think I'm crazy." She smiled. "Okay, it sounds crazy. But I know what I heard, and those cries were as real as my voice right now."

She stopped, suddenly tired. The drowsy late-summer afternoon heat enveloped her in a warm cocoon. She lowered herself until the soft grass cushioned her head. Through half-closed lids she watched a bumblebee moving among the flowers. Before long its buzzing lulled her to sleep . . .

Iris woke when a shadow fell across her face. She opened her eyes. Directly above, a seagull sat on a branch of a maple tree, its head cocked, observing her. She sat up and waved an arm, saying, "Shoo," but the bird didn't budge.

The gull had unusual markings. A cap of dark feathers dipped over its right eye, resembling a rakish curl. Also unique was the bold manner in which the bird regarded her, its head tilted as if amused.

Turning away from the gull's scrutiny, Iris got to her feet. She spotted her father slowly approaching on the path. Abruptly the bird flew from the tree with a loud flapping of wings and rustling of leaves. Her dad shielded his eyes, watching the bird swooping in the air. "Never seen a seagull this far inland," he said.

"It startled me," Iris said. "I looked up and there it was on the branch above me."

"He's a big one, all right," he said.

The gull settled in a nearby tree where it continued to watch them.

"Maybe he thinks we've got food," Iris said.

"He's hanging around for some reason," her dad said.

They headed back to the car, Iris carrying the pail, his arm around her. "When you visit a loved one's grave, it's hard in the beginning," he said. "Over time, it's a comfort."

"I'll admit I was apprehensive," she said, "but it wasn't so bad." She had felt comfortable talking to Frank. In fact, she'd never addressed him so confidently. "I'd like to come back soon."

After dropping her dad off, Iris stopped at the Liquor Mart. She was in the mood to celebrate. The baby's cries and the seagull's visit were somehow tied. She thought the bird represented the spirit guide that Gloria had mentioned.

Thus she treated herself to a bottle of Grande Marnier. The pricey liqueur was the perfect late-evening drink—soothing yet strong enough to induce slumber. Ever since Frank had walked out of the house her sleep had been troubled.

At home she listened to her messages. The first was from Grace, sounding exasperated, "Have you gone underground? Let's get together before you go back to school. Give me a call. Tonight."

Iris sipped her drink and considered telling Grace about the events of the past few days, the baby's cries; the seagull's presence at the cemetery. Then she imagined her friend's blunt response and decided to keep the latest developments to herself.

The next message caused her to gasp:

"Ms. Camuso, it's Nancy Proctor. I just want to let you know that Shannon had a seven-pound baby boy at four fifteen this afternoon. A bit early, but both are doing well. She had a difficult labor and will be resting for several days. Please leave any messages at the office: 978 531-4030. We'll be sure to convey them. Flowers and cards can also be sent here. Thank you."

Iris skipped down the steps to the kitchen. There she poured liqueur into her glass, spilling it on the counter. As she took a large swallow, her glance fell on the vial of antidepressants on the shelf above the sink. Had she taken her dose this morning? She couldn't remember, so she shook two into her palm and washed them down with the Grande Marnier.

She carried her drink into the TV room and sat in Frank's recliner. She clicked on the TV but was unable to focus, Ms. Proctor's words running through her head. She rose and returned to the pantry to pour another drink. This she carried up the stairs, clutching the railing.

At the top, she spotted Patticake exiting the room that had been Frank's office. It was now the site of the cat's litter box. Iris guiltily realized she hadn't changed the litter lately. "I'm sorry, kitty," she said, avoiding the cat's gaze. "I'll clean it now."

Moonlight illuminated the room; she didn't need a lamp. She knelt beside the litter box, shifting and scooping the contents into a plastic bag. As she worked, her attention was drawn to the juniper outside the window. Although the night was calm, its branches shook. Iris wondered if a raccoon—or another cat—were in the tree. She'd heard a pitter-patter on the roof the past couple of nights.

She raised herself up, balancing on her knees to peer out. As she did, the boughs began to shake. She leaned forward, staring into the shadowy branches that trembled and cracked under the weight of a nocturnal intruder. She spotted a flash of white and remembered the seagull in the tree that afternoon.

Excited by this, Iris leaned closer. Her knees banged the litter box, causing her to lose her balance. Her outstretched hands clutched air as her head hit the edge of the window sill. Blood spurted from her forehead as she fell, sprawling, into the darkness.

EIGHTEEN

"Ooh, white roses. That means he's in love with you," Barbara announced to Iris. She was perched on the edge of her bed at the Laurence Suggs Mental Health Center. Iris sat on the opposite bed, holding the dozen roses wrapped in green florist's paper.

"Don't be silly," Iris told her. "They're from my boss, the school principal. He's aware I'm having . . . difficulties." She set the flowers in a vase on the Formica-topped bureau between their twin beds.

"Maybe so, but he's still in love with you." Barbara stood and stretched. Her baggy madras Capri pants rose to reveal knobby red kneecaps.

"We've been roommates for four days," Iris said, "and you think you know everything about me."

"I've got psychic abilities. My great-grandmother was a witch in Ireland." She leaned over until her nose touched the flower tops. "I'm picking up vibrations." She closed her eyes. "This admirer of yours is a mellow soul, but very strong-willed."

"You know all this from sniffing flowers?" Iris asked.

"From their vibrations. Anything you touch retains your vibration, even rocks."

"I'll have to remember that," Iris said. She stretched out on her bed and turned to the wall, hoping Barbara would get the hint. With all the meetings, lectures, and therapy sessions, there was little time to relax at the Suggs Center.

But Barbara was slow to pick up on subtleties. "I was training to be a medium until my drinking got in the way. Drunks make lousy psychics, you know." She looked at Iris, curled up on the bed. "I sense you've got psychic potential too."

"Uh huh," Iris mumbled. She knew she had psychic potential. After all, she'd heard the baby's cries; she'd recognized the seagull's mission. Yet she knew better than to talk about such things, and certainly not to the gabby Barbara.

When Iris thought about the recent events, it was as though they'd happened to someone else. Everything was hazy. According to Dr. Spinney, that was the result of mixing alcohol and antidepressants. Yet certain moments were etched in her mind, such as Fatima leaning over the coffin to straighten Frank's tie; the children at the K of C reception racing around the room trailing black crepe ribbons; the layer of flowers tossed on Frank's coffin before it was lowered into the ground.

Following her arrival at the ER, Iris had been examined, evaluated, and admitted. Suggs was a locked unit on the fifth floor of Harborvale Hospital. She was given a schedule of groups she was required to attend. She'd glanced at the list and wailed to Barbara, her new roommate, "What are they trying to do, cure us, or bore us to death? Five groups a day? Is this a joke?"

Barbara, sitting cross-legged on the opposite bed, said, "And that doesn't include the sessions with your shrink and alcohol counselor. Your ass is gonna be as flat as a tortilla when you get out of here."

"It's ridiculous," Iris said. "I'm here for therapy to help with my grief." She glanced at the sheet. "Look at this group, Family Issues. I'm a counselor. I don't need this." She got to her feet. "I'm going to get this straightened out."

List in hand, Iris had approached the nurses' station, a circular white desk that resembled a giant plastic marshmallow. Roberta Muldoon was on duty. While most of the nurses wore jeans, Roberta Muldoon, RN, wore a starched white uniform. She listened impassively as Iris complained about her schedule. "They've also signed me up for Alcoholics Anonymous meetings. I understand the public is allowed in for these."

The nurse continued writing in a patient's chart. "They meet in the hospital cafeteria."

"Ms. Muldoon," Iris said, glancing around, "I may have

used alcohol to cope with recent tragedies, but I'm no alcoholic. I'm a counselor myself. I'd certainly know."

"Ms. Camuso, you signed yourself in for seventy-two hours. Should you want to leave after that, you may. In the meantime, why don't you relax and get to know us. You'll be surprised how much you can learn here."

Iris nodded, too weary to argue. For the next three days she'd be held captive at the hospital's mental health unit whether she liked it or not. She walked back to her room, mulling over the situation. She would keep an open mind. Perhaps she'd learn something useful during her stay at the clinic.

When she returned to her room, Barbara had unpacked her suitcase. Iris stared at the neatly folded clothes in the lower drawer of the bureau they shared. "I borrowed a whisk broom to give your things a good brushing," Barbara said. "They were loaded with cat hair."

"I've got a long-haired cat," Iris said.

"Who's caring for it while you're here?"

"Grace, my best friend. She brought me here, though I don't remember much."

"You walked in like 'Night of the Living Dead,'" Barbara said, chuckling. "By the way, I hope you don't mind me unpacking your stuff. Some folks don't like it."

Iris lowered herself onto the bed. The Valium and Xanax she'd been given, a precaution in the event of alcoholic seizures, had caught up with her. She sank onto the bed, telling her roommate, "I've cared for people my whole life. If you want to look after me, be my guest."

For the next few days, Iris fell into the rhythm of life on the ward. She ate her meals in the community dining room, attended groups and lectures, and saw her psychiatrist and substance abuse counselor twice a week. After the third day, upon Nurse Muldoon's suggestion, she replaced the hospital issue nightgown with clothing from home.

The groups were interesting, albeit similar. Nonetheless, the group she'd thought she'd enjoy was one she'd come to dread. Caring & Sharing was a women's group for those with "addictive behaviors." It was led by Meredith, an Expressive Therapy grad student doing an internship. Although Meredith was the leader, the group was actually ruled by Yvonne, a sixty-year-old chronic alcoholic.

At her first group meeting, Iris told the assembled how she happened to arrive at the Suggs Center. Yvonne immediately spoke up, asking in a raspy voice, "You claim you hardly ever got drunk before your husband died, right?"

Iris felt her face flush. "Maybe a couple of times I'd have to think twice about driving home, but—"

"But that's bullshit."

"Excuse me?" Iris felt everyone's eyes upon her.

"Lemme get this straight," Yvonne said, leaning far back in her chair. "You say you were a goody-goody wife and mother until your old man croaked. So overnight you became an alcoholic?"

"I never said I was an alcoholic."

"Oh, you came to the hospital by accident?"

Iris glanced around. The other members of the group stared fixedly at the rug. She sat up. "I'm here because I failed to deal with issues in my life. When I found myself in crisis, I made the mistake of combining antidepressants and alcohol."

Yvonne smirked. "Well, doesn't that sound pretty. Did you learn that from one of your textbooks?"

Meredith leaned forward. "Yvonne, let's remember this is a caring and sharing group. We support, not confront, each other."

"Maybe so," Yvonne said, "but if someone's in denial, I'm doing them a favor by speaking up." She jerked a thumb at Iris. "This broad's in denial."

Meredith moved forward to perch at the edge of her seat. "Ladies, this is a good time to talk about the onion." She looked around the circle. "Are you all familiar with the onion?"

"Screw the onion," Yvonne muttered.

Meredith ignored this. "Focus on what I'm saying, will you. What you learn in your journey to recovery will result in how you view yourself when you leave here. Now, imagine an onion"— she cupped her hands—"and its many layers. As you grow in recovery, you shed layer upon layer until you finally reach your core." She looked at each woman in the circle. "The core is the essence of what makes you special. And as long as you continue growing, you'll shed layers."

Yvonne, who considered herself fully peeled, spoke. "I'm sorry for being hard on a newcomer. But when I hear a load of bullshit, what do I do, ignore it?"

"You remember that we're all at different stages in our journey," Meredith said. "Some folks have farther to go."

Iris preferred a support group called, simply, Trust. Led by Fern, a Unitarian minister with a long, gray braid hanging down her back, its members were older. Thus after Dorothea confided long-term feelings of jealousy for her younger sister, Fern turned to Iris. "You're looking reflective. Do you have something you'd like to add to the topic of jealousy?"

"Not really." She shook her head a little too vigorously.

"In the past, you shared how your husband had moved in with another woman. I imagine this event would stir powerful feelings."

"Technically, my husband hadn't moved in," Iris explained. "He was staying at a Holiday Inn while spending time at her apartment. I used to see his car parked there on those occasions when I drove by."

"How did you feel," Fern asked quietly, "seeing his car parked outside this woman's apartment?"

Iris was silent for a moment. "At the time, I was more frightened than jealous. I'd never lived alone and didn't know what would happen to me. Would I be forced to sell the house if he didn't come back? What about paying the taxes? You could say I relied too much on Frank."

"Did you ever feel secure in his love?" Fern asked.

"I thought so, but it seems I was wrong."

Under the hurt and anger was the nagging thought that she'd expected too much of Frank. She'd wanted him to be not just a husband, but a fairy tale prince with a prince's sterling qualities. Her vision of the perfect mate was formed, nay hardwired, in a darkened movie theater many years ago . . .

It was a matinee showing of "Snow White" at the old Harborvale Cinema. Nine-year-old Iris had attended with her mother.

When the handsome prince lifted the glass dome to kiss the unconscious Snow White, Iris had melted. At the movie's end the couple rode away, Snow White perched astride the prince's stallion, he walking beside her. They followed a flower-strewn path to a distant castle veiled in mist. As the music swelled, the narrator announced that the couple "lived happily ever after."

In the car on the ride home, she'd been silent, unwilling to break the spell. In bed that night, she replayed in her mind the moment when the prince's lips touched the sleeping Snow White's. She knew what she'd witnessed—true love—and she would settle for nothing less.

Four years later she accompanied her father to the wharf early one June morning. While he tended to business inside the Seafood Exchange building, Iris waited inside the truck, eating an ice cream cone. When the cab got too warm, she got out and walked the short distance to the pier.

There she leaned over the railing and watched a fishing boat below empty its load of whiting. Seagulls hovered over the boat like fruit flies on blackened bananas. Amid the noise and activity, a young man stood on the upper deck, leaning on a shovel. He watched the fish funnel through a chute into a trough below. A river of silver fish poured through the chute. When some fell outside, he shoveled them back in.

The young man, who looked to be about eighteen, was shirtless in denim cut-offs, a red bandana around his neck. From time to time he swiped at the dark curls clinging to his forehead. When the deck was temporarily cleared of fish, he resume leaning on the shovel. Sunlight glinted on his tanned, muscled arms and shoulders.

Iris had forgotten the ice cream cone in her hand. She remembered it when drops spattered the boy's shoulders. When he glanced up, she scooted out of sight. She raced to the truck, ice cream running over her hand.

The young man was Frank. Had he spotted the skinny young

girl, he wouldn't have given her a second thought. Iris, on the other hand, remembered him. Although they didn't meet until seven years later, Frank's image was imprinted on her brain.

"You've got a visitor," Nurse Muldoon informed Iris as she left the conference room following Family Issues group.

"Thanks," she said, turning to the reception area. No doubt it was Grace, delivering her mail. She hoped it wasn't her dad, who wanted to visit with his neighbor Betty-Ann, who had a car. "You wouldn't like it here," Iris told him. "Some of the patients are unpredictable."

It wasn't a lie, although outbursts were rare. Eighty-one year-old Florence, awaiting placement at an Alzheimer's facility, was a common offender. She would sneak up on unsuspecting visitors and whack them with a rolled up magazine, demanding they get "out of her house."

But her dad wasn't discouraged. "Don't forget I'm a Navy vet," he said, "and Betty-Ann used to do the hair at Limone's Funeral Home." He'd concluded with, "We've seen plenty."

When she arrived at the reception area, she found Tomas Tomasillo sitting on the visitors' bench. He wore gray trousers and a yellow sport shirt and he carried a bouquet of purple iris.

"Tomas," she said, admiring the flowers, "they're beautiful."

"The lady at the shop told me they were iris. I told her they are as lovely as my friend, Iris." He looked around. "Is there someplace where we can talk?"

Nurse Muldoon suddenly appeared. "Let me find a vase," she said, taking the flowers. "Why don't you visit in the dayroom. It's quiet now."

Iris led him to the large room where they sat at a wooden table scarred with cigarette burns from the days when patients smoked indoors. The only person in the room was Sylvia, an older woman with alcoholic dementia. She sat in the corner working on a jigsaw puzzle. During lucid moments Sylvia told stories about her days as a "crackerjack" legal secretary in nineteen-fifties Boston. Although she could recite the name of every lawyer at the old Milk Street law firm, she couldn't remember the name of her husband.

Tomas reached across the table to touch Iris's hair. "I like this style."

"Straight as a poker? I have no choice. They don't allow curling irons in here."

"Did you get my roses?"

She blushed, remembering what Barbara had said about the flowers' meaning. "I meant to write and thank you. Being in here, you forget things like that."

He reached across the table and squeezed her hand. "I care nothing for thanks. I just want you to get well."

She leaned forward. "Does the staff know why I didn't return to school in the fall?"

He shrugged. "It is your business, not theirs. They miss you. Ms. Dutton got everyone to sign a card she will send."

Iris was afraid of that. If her colleagues hadn't heard about her stay at the funny farm, Ms. Dutton was sure to let them know. "By the way, have you heard anything about Roland?"

He nodded. "The Smedlies took him to Standish Academy in New Hampshire two weeks ago. Apparently his roommate is a soccer player from Argentina. They are hoping he will be a roller model for their son."

The report was so discouraging Iris didn't bother correcting Tomas. "Military school is the wrong environment for someone with Roland's sensitivities. I'm sure the Smedlies will find out soon enough."

"Time will tell." He patted her hand. "My sister Aidita sends her love. She misses you."

"That's nice. Has she had any luck finding a job?"

"She has another interview with the Tot Spot. Aidita loves the little ones."

"I'm sure it's mutual," Iris said, stifling a yawn. She'd forgotten how calming it was being with Tomas Tomasillo—better than Valium. Now she felt like drifting off to sleep.

"I must not tire you," he said, getting to his feet. "Take as much time as you need to get well."

"I've used up my bereavement and also my sick days," Iris

said. "What will the superintendent say?"

"I will speak to Dr. Klamkin if it becomes necessary. I don't think it will. I have heard through the grape leaves that he is considering a position in New Jersey. If that is so, Dr. Klamkin has much on his mind."

"What about my substitute?"

"Dwight Snelson, a nice young man who Ms. Dutton is mentoring."

"I can imagine," she said, standing. "I'm sorry Tomas, that I can't give you a definite date when I'll be back."

"Whenever you feel well enough, that is the date."

"You've been awfully good to me, "she said, and felt doubly guilty. The truth was, she couldn't imagine going back to her job. She had no stomach for the devious Ms. Dutton, nor the gossiping faculty. All she wanted was to sit home and watch old movies on TV. She'd grown accustomed to life on the ward, where interactions with fellow patients didn't require tricky social skills. Here no one engaged in small talk. Patients spoke honestly, albeit bluntly.

Additionally, the thought of going back to her house, with Frank's clothes in the closet and Shannon's empty bedroom, was depressing. When her discharge date arrived, she would consider a halfway house. She pictured life inside such a place. It would be populated with soft-spoken women who shared popcorn in a cozy parlor before bedtime. They would recite inspirational messages to one another. Such a life would be like "Little Women," one of her favorite books.

The next day, Iris had her weekly appointment with Dr. Spinney, who kept a small office at the Suggs Center.

She waited in the narrow reception room, gazing at the doctor's tarnished sailing trophies inside a glass case. Likewise, the office walls were hung with sailing photos of Dr. Spinney and a tanned, wiry-haired woman with a toothy smile like Katherine Hepburn's. If this was Mrs. Spinney, her face was as suncreased as Nancy Proctor's.

After telling Dr. Spinney about her progress, Iris broached the subject of transferring to a halfway house when her stay ended. "I'm not ready to go back home," she stated.

"Are you talking about a sober house?" he asked.

"I don't care if it's sober or a social drinker," she said. "I'm flexible."

Dr. Spinney didn't smile at her joke. "It would be a waste of our time to recommend further rehab if you're not prepared to embrace sobriety."

"Isn't there a halfway house for women like me?"

"What is a 'women like me'?"

She shifted in her chair. "You know, those who are overwhelmed with life and need a respite."

"I'm afraid insurance companies demand a diagnosis. Otherwise we couldn't have admitted you."

"What was my diagnosis?"

He glanced at her file. "Alcoholism with anxiety and mood depressive issues."

"I don't like the sound of that," she said. "I don't normally drink a lot. I told you I was self-medicating due to a life crisis."

"Ms. Camuso, according to the intake notes, you were found lying unconscious in kitty litter. You had a high blood alcohol level."

"I fell *across* the kitty litter receptacle, not in it."

"What do you have against a recovery house? You'd meet others in early sobriety. At the same time, you'd continue to go to work."

She picked at her nails. "It sounds dreary, everyone hugging and holding hands, saying the Serenity Prayer at the drop of a hat."

He scribbled a note in her file. "I'll have the social worker talk to you. Maybe you two could visit a couple of places in the area." He gave her a tight-lipped smile. "Don't say no until you've checked them out."

"No harm in looking," Iris said, to placate Dr. Spinney. She didn't want to live in a house with rules and regulations. She wanted a place where she felt safe until she felt whole. She was reminded of the framed sampler that hung in her grandmother's bedroom. The words, embroidered on faded linen read, *Let me live in a house by the side of the road and be a friend to man.* That's what she wanted, to be a friend to man . . . from a distance.

Later that afternoon Grace visited. She carried a bulging tote bag. On the top was a chocolate muffin from Mega Mug. They sat at a corner table in the day room. The late afternoon sun cast a golden light on the walls. Iris peeked inside the bag. "That's a lot of mail for one week."

"It's mostly catalogs," Grace said. "But there's something official looking from Lighthouse Insurance. "

"I'll get to that," Iris said, breaking the muffin in two and handing half to Grace. "How's Patticake? Are you leaving the garage door open for her?"

"She comes in with no coaxing. I think she's lonely. I was thinking of taking her home with me while you're here."

"I won't be here much longer. Besides, I'd worry about her in the woods behind your house."

"Are you kidding? She'd have a ball in those woods. It's a kitty's paradise."

"Maybe years ago," Iris said. "Today the woods are full of predators."

"When we were growing up, cats and dogs ran free. Today, parents won't even let their kids go to the mailbox alone."

"They fear abductors," Iris said, "lurking around every corner."

"What a difference when we were young," Grace said. "One summer, my best friend and I had a battered old rowboat we launched at the creek. We had one oar and bubble gum stuck in the cracks. We paddled to Salt Island, bailing like crazy with Dixie cups." She smiled at the memory. "I'm glad we grew up when we did. It's a wimpy world today."

Iris licked chocolate crumbs from her fingers. "Before I forget, did you hear anything unusual while you were at my house? Anything upstairs?"

"Unusual? Like what?"

"Oh, I don't know . . . a baby crying?"

Grace blinked. "A what?"

"If I tell you, promise you won't say a word to Dr. Spinney?"

"What kind of friend do you think I am? Besides, I wouldn't tell that old coot if his coat was on fire."

"Okay, then keep an open mind." Iris took a sip of her coffee and told Grace about hearing the baby's cries emanating from her closet.

When she was through, Grace asked, "You heard it just that once?"

"Three times. To me, it's one of those unexplained phenomena, like the statues of the Holy Mother that shed tears. I can't offer a logical explanation. All I know is, I hear a baby crying and I'm positive it's Shannon's baby, trying to reach me. It's blood calling to blood." When Grace continued to stare, Iris said, "Okay, you think I'm nuts. Why shouldn't you? After all, I'm on the nut ward."

Grace reached for her hand. "Honey, I don't think you're nuts. I think you've experienced some rough situations. First Shannon and then Frank—"

Iris yanked her hand away and jumped to her feet. The tote bag fell over, spilling its contents on the floor. "Forget I mentioned it," she said. "Now where's that letter from Lighthouse Insurance?"

Grace knelt and pawed through the pile, finally locating the envelope. She handed it to Iris, saying, "Don't be mad. At least get your hearing checked. You might have that condition where people hear sounds, like ticking clocks and music." As Iris ripped into the letter, Grace continued, "At least mention it to your doctor. Maybe he could prescribe something."

"I'm taking so many pills I get up early just to swallow them all. I don't care if you don't believe me because I know what I heard."

"What you think you heard," Grace said quietly.

Iris didn't respond. Her attention was focused on the letter that she gripped with both hands. When she finished, she let it drop to the floor. She sank onto her chair, her head sagging forward.

"What is it? Grace picked up the letter.

"They said they're not honoring Frank's policy. They claim his death was a suicide. I was counting on that money for the custody suit. Now I'll lose the baby like I've lost everyone else." She covered her face with her hands.

Grace read the contents and returned the letter to the envelope. She sat watching her friend. Then she leaned forward and said, "You listen to me, Iris Camuso. You're going to fight that insurance company's decision. Frank was the last person in the world who'd commit suicide. Anyone who knew him knows that. Now as soon as I leave, you call your lawyer. You tell him you're going to fight those bastards because you're entitled to that money. Do you hear me?"

Iris raised a tear-stained face. "I don't have the strength," she wailed. "I can't even face going back to work. You don't understand. I'm all empty inside."

"What about the baby, the custody battle? Won't you fight for him?"

Iris stared at Grace, who handed her a napkin. She wiped her eyes and blew her nose. "I'll call Vincent in the morning."

NINETEEN

Vincent Tosi rubbed his hands together as he contemplated the upcoming trial against Lighthouse Insurance Company. "Ms. Camuso, it's perfect."

Iris eyed him warily. "What do you mean 'perfect?'"

"Just picture this scenario. The widow, just out of the hospital, sitting huddled at the plaintiff's table. Next to her is the fatherless daughter. Meanwhile, at the defense table, a couple of slick Boston lawyers representing one of the biggest insurance companies in the Northeast. It's classic David and Goliath, could be a movie script."

"What if Valerie Moles refuses to appear as a witness?"

"You mean what if she blows off a summons?"

Iris nodded.

"She can't do that. You receive a summons and you don't show up, they put out a warrant for your arrest."

She chewed a fingernail. "Will there be a jury?'

"That's right. In a civil case you have a jury of twelve. It'll be heard at the superior courthouse, right here in Harborvale. Ever been in there?"

"I was once at the district court."

"The young lady who does the trial scheduling is an old girlfriend. I'll have her move the date up so we won't have to wait."

"I don't mind waiting," Iris said. "I need lots of time to prepare myself."

"By the way, is your dad still at elderly housing?"

She stared at him. "You're not thinking of asking my father to testify."

"Why not? Chet's got his marbles. I was talking to him at the post office the other day. The fact he's a disabled veteran will earn us sympathy."

"Vincent, I don't want my dad at the trial. He'd be embarrassed, hearing details about Frank and Valerie Moles."

His smile was patient. "Ms. C., your dad was in the Navy. You think he's never heard such talk?" When she didn't reply, he said, "Tell me honestly. Did he like Frank?"

She shook her head.

"I figured. The jury will love a nice old guy protecting his daughter—"

"You're going too fast," she said. "I've only been out of the hospital a month."

"Just remember that the jury is made up of ordinary citizens like you and your dad. They'll hear, through witness testimony, what you've been through. They'll discover that while Frank loved his family, he was no saint. He was a big-hearted guy with a passion for life. But was he suicidal? Gimme a break."

When she nodded glumly, he stood. "Go home and rest. First thing tomorrow I'm writing Lighthouse Insurance to notify them we're filing suit. Leave everything to me."

She gave him a wan smile. "Thanks, Vincent. I may not show it, but I'm glad you're committed to my case."

He spread his arms wide. "Are you kidding? Something like this is why I went to law school."

Her dad smacked his palm on the table when she told him about the trial. "If you're going to be there, I'm going to be there." They were having a late lunch at Mega Mug and aside from two uniformed meter maids at the counter, they had the place to themselves. Iris picked at her tuna melt while her dad dug into his beef stew.

"It could get embarrassing," she said, "especially the details of Frank's affair. I keep thinking what Mom would say. You know how she frowned on airing one's dirty laundry."

He nodded. "When she was pregnant with you she kept it a secret 'til she couldn't hide it any longer."

"Is that true?"

"I guess she didn't like folks knowing what we'd been up to." He blushed and changed the subject. "Vinnie Tosi, huh? I can't believe that guy's a lawyer."

"Why? Vincent works hard."

"You got that part right. I remember one summer when he was a high school kid working at the wharf. They put him in with a bunch of older Finnish guys, unloading fish. When they'd stop for mug-up, Vincent kept right on working. I think he was trying to prove he was as strong, or stronger, than the old timers.

"It was hot that day. Before long, Vincent fainted dead away—sunstroke. He was as white as a cod's belly." He chuckled at the memory. "They had to put a hose on him."

"That proves he doesn't give up easily. Not only that, Vincent makes me feel like we're a team, we're in this together."

He covered her hand with his. "That's how I feel. I'm going to be there every minute if I have to ride a bicycle to the courthouse."

"Thanks, Dad." She pulled a napkin from the dispenser and blotted her eyes. "Look at me, crying in public."

He smiled. "You'll be the talk of the town."

"I already am," she said. "I certainly will be once the trial starts. I hope it doesn't appear in the newspaper."

"You can't stop people from talking. When you reach my age, you don't care what they think." He wiped gravy from the front of his flannel shirt. "Since we're downtown, do you mind taking me to Nelson's? I'll need a new shirt for the trial."

"Vincent wants us to look like ordinary citizens," she said. "Nothing classy."

He slurped the dregs of his coffee, set down his cup and burped. "No chance of that."

Later that week, Iris accompanied Tomas to Essex for clams. Aidita was at home, he apologized, working on a project for her Tiny Tots class.

"I'm happy she found a job she likes," Iris said. She herself was happy to be free of the girl's disapproving face.

They carried their clam plates to a picnic table under the

trees. Red and gold leaves had drifted down, a reminder that autumn was around the corner. As Iris told Tomas about the upcoming trial, he reached around his Styrofoam cup of clam broth to take her hand. "I will pray for a successful outcome in court."

"Pray hard," she said.

When she arrived home, the phone was ringing. She navigated the shadowy kitchen to answer it. Vincent Tosi's loud voice announced, "I got a letter from Lighthouse Insurance. They offered a settlement."

Iris gripped the phone. "What's their offer?"

"Thirty thousand."

"That's not much for a hundred-thousand dollar policy."

"No," he admitted, "but to be honest, I expected less. This tells me they're nervous. They know we've got a good case. Think it over and decide if you want to accept it."

"Wait, Vincent." Her mind whirled. If she refused their offer and proceeded with a trial, the jury could find in the insurance company's favor. This would leave her with nothing. Yet if she accepted the settlement, it wouldn't be enough for a custody suit, not to mention raising a baby. "It's not enough," she finally said.

Vincent sighed. "I was hoping you'd say that. We've got a solid case here. I'll tell Lighthouse Insurance they can stick their offer up the old wahzoo. By the way, what's your dad's shirt size?"

"He's already bought a new shirt. He won't buy another."

"He doesn't need to buy anything. I go to the Lutheran thrift shop and pick out clothes." He chuckled. "You can call me the costume director."

"What about Valerie Moles?" she asked. "Will she be wearing the Lutherans' cast-offs?"

"Uh-uh. That babe's got a wardrobe that'll put Victoria's Secret to shame."

"While I, the mousey little wife, sit wearing orthopedic shoes?"

"Ms. C., that's not the point. I want every man in that courtroom to look at Valerie and think no way would a guy kill himself. They'll get the message."

She sighed. "I understand it's what you have to do."

"A trial is like a stage production. Everyone has a role to play."

She closed her eyes; her head ached. The upcoming trial was like a runaway train and she its reluctant passenger. "Vincent, I'm going to lie down now."

"Get some rest. Leave everything to me."

After hanging up the phone, Iris remained at the kitchen table. It was the spot where she used to sip wine or vodka and talk over the day with Grace. Now her cupboards were empty of alcohol. Grace had removed everything while she'd been in the hospital. She had, however, overlooked the bottle of Irish Mist in the bottom of Iris's bedroom closet. At fifteen dollars a bottle, Iris couldn't bring herself to throw it out.

Now she imagined pouring some into her coffee. Just a wee bit, enough to warm her insides, to settle her nerves. A small splash would clear her head and allow her to calmly contemplate the upcoming trial.

She was about to rise and fetch the bottle when Patticake leaped onto her lap. Had the cat sensed her intentions? She remembered the warning from the detox unit: "There will be moments when you'll have no defense against that first drink."

Iris stroked the cat's fur. "Thank you," she whispered.

At the end of the week, Iris visited Frank's grave. She carried pink geraniums from the supermarket to complement the rose-colored headstone. Now she could report to Fatima that she'd been tending the grave. Her sister in law had been calling lately, keeping tabs from the West Coast, "I hate to ask you, Iris, but could you visit Aunt Lucy? Janice says she might need gall bladder surgery and I'm not surprised. All summer she's been eating fried clams and ice cream." Fatima sighed into the phone. "Dumb ass."

"Who, Aunt Lucy?"

"No, not Lucy, it's Janice. She's the one who takes Lucy out to eat." Fatima chuckled. "Hey, I shouldn't talk. Alan and I discovered a little restaurant whose chef is an *authentic* German.

Would you believe an Italian gal could fall in love with Weinerschnitzel?"

"I meant to ask," Iris said. "How was your cruise?"

"Fabulous. It was just what we needed. Away from all the depressing memories, Alan learned to live in the moment. One day we had a couples' massage in our stateroom. Alan said he'd never felt so relaxed. His wife's illness took a lot out of him."

"You stayed in the same room?"

"Honey, have you ever been on a cruise ship? It's not like a hotel. Space is scarce. They didn't have two staterooms together, so we got a suite." She snapped her gum. "Worked out perfect."

Now Iris followed the dirt path that meandered through the cemetery. When she reached Frank's grave, she spread a newspaper on the grass. She sat and removed the flower pots and garden tools from a cardboard box. As she dug into the fresh soil of the gravesite, she talked aloud,

"It's me again, Frank. I feel silly talking like this, but if there's a chance you're listening, I'll do it." She whacked the bottom of a plastic pot, dislodging the geranium's root ball. "I want to tell you the news. We're going to court. Frank, I have no choice. You worked hard to pay those insurance premiums so that we'd be taken care of." She stabbed the ground with the trowel, loosening the earth. "It makes me mad to think Lighthouse Insurance would try to cheat us. This trial is for you, Frank. Even though you were bamboozled by that bimbo, I know family came first with you.

"That's why if we win the case I'm using the money to adopt Shannon's baby, our grandchild." She patted the earth around the newly planted flowers with a sense of accomplishment. "I just wanted to come here on this beautiful day to tell you about it. I need that money. I won't let our grandchild be adopted by strangers, no matter how many degrees they have. Family comes first. It's what your mother would have wanted.

"Now I'll have to go it alone, knowing you're with me in spirit." She wiped a tear that rolled down her cheek. "You know what? I can feel your strength surrounding me. Oh, Frank, I've never felt so close to you . . ."

She sank back onto the grass, the autumn sun warming her. She closed her eyes and with a sigh fell into a luxurious sleep.

Fifteen minutes later a harsh sound woke her. A seagull, perched on an overhanging branch, cried shrilly while flapping its wings noisily. It flew to the neighboring tree where it watched her. It was the same gull from the last time Iris visited the cemetery. She recognized the dark swirl over the bird's eye.

Iris struggled to her feet and looked around. Dark clouds had formed behind the distant trees. At the same time, she heard a low rumble of thunder.

She looked up at the bird. "Thank you, seagull, for warning me." The bird stared back. She was about to speak again when a man's voice rang out, "Ma'am, are you feeding that seagull?" She spun around. It was the cemetery caretaker. He lowered his wheelbarrow and scowled at the gull. "I spotted that thing the last time you were here." He fixed his scowl on Iris. "You must be feeding it."

"Of course I'm not feeding it."

"Well somebody is. Seagulls don't hang around cemeteries unless there's food. 'Fore you know it, there'll be a dozen of 'em making a mess of the place."

"Sir, that's no ordinary seagull. Please don't harm him."

The man jerked his thumb at the bird. "Looks ordinary to me. He starts crapping on the stones, I'm gonna poison 'em."

Iris gasped. "Don't do that. This seagull is *special*."

The man gave her a sidelong glance. He clutched the handles of the wheelbarrow and muttered, "Storm's coming." Without looking in her direction, he scurried away.

The afternoon squall had cleared the air. Later, Iris accepted Grace's offer for a cookout. "This could be our last hurrah," Grace said. "You know how it is this time of year. One night you're sleeping on the porch, the next you've got a fire going in the fireplace."

It was growing dark when Iris arrived at Grace's house. A bright Harvest moon shone through the branches of the big oak tree in the backyard. Grace, sipping iced tea, tended the coals while Iris scrubbed the picnic table. After a few minutes she put down the scouring pad and told Grace, "I don't want you abstaining just because I don't drink. In fact, I insist you have a gin and tonic. I need to get used to not drinking in social situations."

Grace sprinkled salt and pepper on the burgers. "That's what I used to tell my friends when I quit smoking, 'Go ahead and light up. I don't care.' When they did, I wanted to rip the cigarette from their mouths."

"But I really don't care."

"I don't want a drink. If I did, I'd have one."

"That's what Tomas said the other night. He used to have beer with his pizza. Now he drinks ginger ale. I insisted he have a beer or I'd order it for him."

"How are things going with Tomas?" Grace asked. "You two madly in love?"

"I was madly in love with Frank and look where that got me. As for Tomas, I like his company. It's very comfortable being with him."

Grace flipped the burgers over. "Sounds dull."

"At this point in my life I welcome dull. Tomas looks out for me."

"And you don't want to jump his bones," Grace said. "Am I right?"

Iris wrinkled her nose. "I can't imagine sex with any man. In any case, it's not an issue. When we go out, his sister is often in the back seat."

"Can't you hint you'd like to be alone?"

Iris shrugged. "Tomas thinks I enjoy her company. Not only that, he's cautious about his reputation. He's the school principal and I'm an employee. That could be a conflict."

"You know what I think?" Grace asked. "Tomas is your security blanket. You feel safe with him."

"It's nice feeling safe for a change."

"That's not why God gave us hormones," Grace said.

Iris eyed the grill. "Keep an eye on the burgers. They look done to me."

After the dishes were cleared away, they brought their coffee outside. The moon had morphed into an oversized disk hanging low in the sky. They gazed at the spectacle. "This is perfect." Grace said, "No mosquitoes and a gorgeous Harvest moon for our entertainment. New England at its finest."

"It's beautiful, yes, but it makes me sad," Iris said. "Summer is over. Soon we'll be huddled indoors."

"Then let's enjoy it now. As the days grow shorter, the moon shrinks. Come Christmas, it'll be a tiny frozen chink in a star-less sky."

"I thought of Christmas the other day," Iris said." I wondered if I'd be celebrating the holiday with my grandchild, or would I be alone?"

"Remember what they told you in rehab," Grace reminded her. "One day at a time." She stood up. "I'm getting more coffee. Want some?"

"Let's go inside," Iris said, shivering. "Suddenly I feel lonely out here."

TWENTY

"All rise."

The lawyers, court officers, spectators, and witnesses filling the courthouse rose. Those who had performed the ritual countless times wearily dragged themselves from their chairs. The newcomers leaped to their feet. Once the assembled were standing, a court officer announced, "The Honorable Raymond Kuszko, presiding."

The judge entered the courtroom from a side door. Head down and black robes flying, he approached the tall desk as if determined to get on with it. Once all were seated, the court officer handed the judge a stack of files.

Iris and Vincent Tosi sat together at a front table. Vincent wore a dark suit and yellow silk tie. He had made liberal use of a cologne smelling of eucalyptus. Periodically, he patted his scalp with a folded white handkerchief. It was a warm Indian summer morning. An overhead fan stirred the heavy air.

Iris glanced around the room. All in all, it wasn't as imposing as she'd imagined. The walls were beige and the ceiling pale blue to match the long drapes. The spectators, many of them retirees, Vincent claimed, filled the wooden seats on either side of a central aisle.

Sitting at the neighboring front table were the insurance company lawyers. The two men were slim and straight-backed, dressed in similar charcoal pinstripe suits. One was silver-haired while the other was younger, late thirties. Models of composure, they never glanced in the direction of the plaintiff's table.

Iris took comfort in knowing her father was in the room, sitting with Grace. At one point she had glanced behind her, hoping to catch a glimpse of them. Instead, she was visibly startled to see Ms. Dutton's beady eyes staring back.

And Shannon's here, Iris thought, albeit upon a court order. Ms. Proctor had waged a losing battle to have the new mother excluded from the proceedings, enlisting the aid of the agency's doctors and lawyers. Nonetheless, Vincent had prevailed; it was agreed that Shannon would not share the plaintiff's table, and would be present for one day only.

Now, as Judge Kuszko examined the file, Vincent whispered to Iris, "The lawyers will present their case and tell the court what they hope to prove."

"Do you know the judge?" she whispered.

"He's okay. Been around forever."

She glanced at the defense table. The older lawyer was speaking quietly to the younger, their faces devoid of expression.

Judge Kuszko broke the silence by rapping his gavel once and nodding at Vincent. "Counsel, will you make your opening remarks."

All eyes turned toward them. Iris sat up straight. She fiddled nervously with the gold buttons on her navy suit. Underneath, she wore a white blouse with ruffles and a bow at the neck. The blouse was Vincent's contribution to her courtroom outfit. She had balked. "Even senior citizens don't dress like this."

"You want to look like what you are, a widowed school teacher."

"I'm a school counselor, not a school teacher."

"Same difference to the jurors."

Now he got to his feet and moved from behind the table. "Thank you, Your Honor." He looked around the courtroom, his glance settling on the jurors. "Ladies and gentlemen, my client, Mrs. Iris Camuso, is the legal beneficiary of her husband's life insurance policy, purchased from Lighthouse Insurance Company in nineteen ninety-eight. On July fifteen, two thousand sixteen, Francis Camuso died at age forty-five, leaving his wife and their eighteen-year-old daughter.

"Immediately prior to his passing, Mr. Camuso had undergone periodontal surgery." He glanced around the room, a wry expression on his face. "Some of you might be familiar with gum surgery?" Several people nodded, chuckling. "In that case you know how uncomfortable the procedure can be. Consequently, Mr. Camuso was prescribed pain medication—strong narcotics.

"On July twelve, a Saturday evening, Mr. Camuso, who was temporarily separated from his wife, sought relief with a few cocktails. I've been informed by experts that alcohol is a poor pain reliever. Likewise, Mr. Camuso augmented the alcohol with prescription pain medication.

"I won't go into the medical details. You'll hear more than you'll care to know from expert witnesses. Needless to say, Mr. Camuso, who hadn't had dinner that night due to his mouth sensitivity, continued drinking. Before retiring, he added prescription sleeping pills to the alcohol and pain meds. No doubt he didn't need the sleeping pill, but at that point we can assume his judgment was seriously impaired."

He turned to gaze at Iris. "Tragically, the combination of alcohol plus pain and sleep medication was enough to put Francis Camuso into a coma. Again, I won't go into the medical details. You'll hear from witnesses how deadly the combination can be.

He put his hands in his suit coat pockets and leaned back. "You will also hear about Frank, the man, who was one of those people we call 'larger than life.' Frank did nothing by half measures. He loved to eat and drink. He loved his family, his friends. A salesman, he sold marine equipment, a job he'd started as a teen and built into a solid company. Mr. Camuso was an excellent provider for his family.

"But like many of us in mid-life, he feared growing old. As a result, Frank sought reassurance outside his marriage. This resulted in a relationship with the woman who was with him the night he slipped into a coma. You will hear her testimony as well."

At this point the room buzzed with whispered conversations. Judge Kuszko banged his gavel. "Silence. Continue, counselor."

Vincent donned a somber expression. "You are not here to judge Francis Camuso, a good but imperfect man. We'll all face our judgment day. Your job is to determine whether his death from an overdose of pills and alcohol was accidental or intentional. I might add that Mr. Camuso was not clinically depressed at this time. Far from it. Those who knew Frank will say he was the last person in the world who'd take his life.

"For these reasons I'm here today on behalf of Frank's widow and young daughter. They've not only suffered the loss of a husband and father, they're being victimized by an insurance company that has tried to sully their loved one's name while denying them their rightful benefits."

He looked around the room. "Ladies and gentlemen, this is wrong. Lighthouse Insurance Company is making a desperate attempt to avoid honoring the policy of a hard-working man who put his trust in them." He shook his head. "Frank Camuso did not commit suicide, *and I intend to prove it.*"

The room was silent as Vincent took his seat. Judge Kuszko said, "We'll hear from the defense."

Iris watched the younger lawyer move to take Vincent's place in front of the room. In earnest tones, he spoke of the "stigma" attached to suicide. "We see it often, the guilt-ridden, bereaved family. It's tragic enough losing a loved one, but losing a loved one to suicide is devastating."

"Pompous twit," Iris muttered.

With the defense's opening remarks finally out of the way, the judge glanced at Vincent. "Are you ready to call your first witness?"

Vincent rose. "I am, Your Honor. I'd like to call Chester Quirk to the stand."

Her dad made his way to the front, moving slower than usual, his cane rapping on the wood floor. As he passed Iris's table, she reached out to clasp his hand. Before moving on, he leaned over to pat Vincent's shoulder. "You're doing good." This caused a tittering among the spectators.

After being sworn in by the court officer, he took his seat and looked around warily. Immediately Vincent approached, moving to the side of the witness chair so the spectators could get a look at the seated man.

"Mr. Quirk, I understand you ran a fish distribution business at the Harborvale wharf."

"That's right. I sold fish for thirty-five years."

"And during that time, before he became your son in law, you knew the deceased, Frank Camuso, is that right? "

"Yes, when you work at the wharf, you get to know everybody."

"Were you friends with the deceased?"

"Friends? Nah, he was a young fella."

"You didn't seek out his company?"

When the old man paused, the spectators leaned forward to hear his answer. "Let's say I wouldn't cross the street to greet him."

"Thank you, Mr. Quirk. Is it true that you tried talking your daughter Iris out of marrying Frank Camuso?"

The young lawyer rose. "Your Honor, I see no point in following this line of questioning. The witness's feelings are wholly subjective."

"That's true," the judge said, "but it helps to create a portrait of the deceased." He nodded to the witness. "You may answer the question."

He shifted in the chair. "I let her know I wasn't crazy about it."

Vincent nodded. "Sir, can you tell the court why you were opposed to your daughter marrying Francis Camuso?"

"Because I knew what would happen."

"And that was?"

He scratched his cheek. "Frank liked the women. Sooner or later he'd break her heart." He glanced at Iris. "I'm sorry."

"Thank you, Mr. Quirk." Vincent turned and took his seat.

A murmur filled the room as the young lawyer approached the witness chair. "Sir, it must be distressing being here today—"

"It beats watching TV," Chester Quirk said.

The laughter was spontaneous. Even the judge couldn't conceal a smile. He leaned over and said, "A simple yes or no will do."

"Thanks, Your Honor. I'll remember that."

The lawyer asked, "Mr. Quirk, isn't it true your late son in law was what you'd call a moody person?"

Vincent got to his feet. "Objection. The witness isn't a psychiatrist. He's not qualified to diagnosis—"

"I'm creating a portrait of the deceased, as counselor claimed earlier," the lawyer said.

"Continue," the judge said. "The witness will answer the question."

Her dad shrugged. "Yeah, he was moody."

"Thank you, Mr. Quirk," the lawyer said. "No further questions."

As the lawyer turned away, Chester added, "Frank was Italian. They're moody people."

When the laughter broke out again, Judge Kuszko rapped his gavel. "That's enough. The witness may step down." The spectators grinned at him as he headed back to his seat.

Vincent called his next witness, Buster Wilder. The man approached the bench with downcast eyes. Despite the heat, Buster wore a brown wool vest over a long sleeve khaki shirt. He was a handsome man if you overlooked the broken blood vessels that gave his nose a purple hue.

After being sworn in, Buster established his credentials. "Owner and operator of Wilder's Boat Yard."

"Mr. Wilder, how long did you know the deceased?" Vincent asked.

"About twenty-five years. Me and Frank were like this," he said, crossing his index and middle fingers.

"I understand you had a working relationship as well. You bought marine supplies from Mr. Camuso, is that right?"

"Sure, everyone bought from Frank."

"Can you tell us what kind of supplies, Mr. Wilder?"

"Oh, lots of stuff. Fishing party boats have to be stocked with everything under the sun. I bought gloves and tackle, oilskins. Last year I ordered a new refrigeration system for one of my boats. Coast Guard says I'll be needing fancy new life vests, too." He paused and looked down at his clasped hands. "Guess I won't be ordering from Frank."

"Is it true that you and Mr. Camuso used to talk business over a drink at the Dirty Dinghy?"

"More than one."

When the spectators chuckled, the judge's retort was sharp, "Answer yes or no."

"Yes sir," Buster said.

"Would you say the deceased spent a lot of time at the Dirty Dinghy?" Vincent asked.

"Compared to a Methodist, I suppose he did. Frank liked a good time—"

The young lawyer half-rose from his seat. "Objection, Your Honor."

"Overruled. Let the witness answer."

"Like I said, Frank liked to have a good time. I'll miss him." He glanced at the judge. "Am I through?"

The judge addressed the defense table. "Do you want to question this witness?"

The young lawyer stared at Buster. After a whispered exchange with his partner, he stood. "I would, Your Honor." He approached slowly. "Mr. Wilder, we're aware of your friendship and loyalty to the deceased. Were you also aware of his marital problems?"

Vincent shot to his feet. "This line of questioning is subjective and irrelevant."

"Your Honor," the young lawyer said, "the question is important to establish Mr. Camuso's state of mind prior to his death."

"I'll allow the question," the judge said.

The lawyer turned to to Buster, who eyed him warily. "Mr. Wilder, we know of your friendship with Frank Camuso. Did you know his wife, Iris Camuso?"

Buster glanced at Iris. "Uh huh."

The clerk called out, "Answer yes or no."

"Yes, I know her."

"And you don't want to embarrass her in court, is that right?"

"Yes, that's right."

"And you were aware that Mr. Camuso, at the time of his death, was not living at home?"

Vincent rose, but before he could speak the judge said, "I'll allow this."

"I'd heard something like that," Buster said, shifting in his chair.

"You're saying that Frank Camuso, your longtime friend, never mentioned his sadness at being separated from his family?"

Buster's face colored. "Frank didn't talk about stuff like that."

The lawyer leaned closer. "Mr. Wilder, are you familiar

with the expression 'No man is an island?'"

He nodded. "I heard that."

"Would you say that Frank Camuso was an island, isolated from his loved ones?"

Buster squirmed in his chair. He hated how the spectators gawked at him like a carnival act. He also hated the fresh-faced lawyer's phony attitude of concern. He stared up at the young man. "Let me put it this way," he said. "If Frank was an island, it was the kind of island with casinos, nightclubs, and girls."

If Buster Wild's testimony had created a buzz, the next witness had the opposite effect. Dr. Kram, the admitting physician the night Frank was brought to the hospital, launched a detailed account of the deceased's vital signs. In nasal tones he spoke of the chemistry of blood. During cross examination when the defense asked whether the patient's drug and alcohol intake was consistent with suicide, Dr. Kram delivered a lecture on the oxygen-starved brain. When he was through, even Judge Kuszko was bleary eyed.

Following that, the defense called its expert witness, Calvin Bigelow, MD. The tall, silver-haired Dr. Bigelow wore a tweed suit and an ascot. As he strode to the witness stand, Vincent whispered to Iris, "I'll bet they paid him a couple grand to be here."

During his swearing in, Dr. Bigelow identified himself as "former Director of Neurology at Harwich University Hospital."

"Dr. Bigelow, do you consider yourself an expert on human consciousness?" the older defense lawyer asked.

He smirked. "I would hope so."

"And you've had a chance to study the late Francis Camuso's medical files, is that correct?"

"Correct."

"In that case, would you agree that the combination of drugs in Mr. Camuso's body—the alcohol, prescription pain killers and sleeping pills—were enough to cause him to lose consciousness and fall into a coma?"

"It doesn't surprise me, yes."

"And does that combination, the sheer amount, suggest something other than a man seeking temporary relief from the pain of gum surgery?" The lawyer's emphasis on gum surgery indicated his disbelief.

Vincent shot to his feet. "Counsel is asking the witness to make assumptions, Your Honor."

Judge Kuszko frowned. "The witness is here to give his specialized opinion. Let him answer."

"It does sound rather excessive," the doctor said, nodding.

The next question slid off his tongue. "Would you say this is consistent with suicide?"

Before Vincent could get to his feet, the doctor answered, "Yes, it is."

At noon, Judge Kuszko announced a lunch break. "Be back here at one o'clock sharp," he said. "No latecomers allowed back in."

People made a beeline for the door. "Want to get a sandwich?" Vincent asked Iris. He mopped at his forehead.

"I'm meeting Grace and my dad at the park. She brought lunch for us. Right now I'm too nervous to eat. I'm worried about Dr. Bigelow's testimony. The guy looks like the Surgeon General."

"He's a paid witness. The jury knows that."

"In any event, they looked impressed."

He patted her arm. "Wait until they hear our star witness."

"Another medical expert?"

He shook his head. "It's Valerie Moles, our ace in the hole. I'm saving her for last."

Outside of an elderly man dozing in the sun, the park was empty. Grace opened a cooler and handed Iris a chicken salad sandwich. "The jury's on your side, kiddo," she said. "They keep giving you sympathetic looks, especially the men."

"I must seem like a nervous wreck," Iris said.

"I wish Shannon would join us," her dad said, unwrapping his sandwich. "I gave her a big hug on the steps. Then she introduced me to her bodyguard." He opened and closed his hand. "That dame's got a handshake like a vise."

"Shannon's only here because Vincent insisted," Iris said.

"I read where men are more sympathetic to woman," Grace said, referring to her earlier remark. "It's a fact, women tend to judge their own sex more harshly. "

"If that's the case, they're not gonna like that bartender, Frank's girlfriend," her dad said. "Did you see her? She looks like she's onstage at the Old Howard."

"What's the Old Howard?" Grace asked.

"A burlesque hall in Boston, back in the forties."

"Vincent said he's saving her testimony for last," Iris added.

"Good," he replied. "It'll keep us awake. She's gotta be more interesting than Dr. Kram. They could use that guy at a sleep clinic. Grace had to nudge me before I started snoring."

Iris wrapped up half of her sandwich and handed it to Grace. "I can't finish this. I keep thinking about Valerie. My stomach's all butterflies."

"She's nothing but a waterfront chippy," her father said.

"Chippy? Old Howard?" Grace smiled at him. "I'm learning so much from you, Mr. Quirk."

He grinned back. "If you'd been around twenty years ago I could have given you the tour."

"Try thirty," Iris said sourly, "or more like forty. I'm glad you're both having such a great time at my trial."

He patted her arm. "Listen to me. You'll get through this the way you get through everything, one step at a time. I'll be right by your side."

"Thanks, Dad." She wiped at her eyes.

Grace got to her feet. "Let's pack up. I want to get there early. I've got a feeling the place will be standing room only." She turned to Iris. "You ready, honey?"

"I'll sit here for a moment and try to compose myself. You two go ahead."

Grace patted her shoulder. "See you in a minute."

After they left, Iris sat back. She felt a rising nausea and looked around, alarmed. She couldn't throw up in a public park. Her stomach growled; at the same time she tasted bile.

She took a deep breath and closed her eyes. Before long the nausea passed. She opened her eyes and gasped. The gull was perched directly opposite her on a bench. Its head was tilted as if studying her.

She leaned forward. "You're my spirit guide, aren't you? Have you come to help me?"

"Iris, who are you talking to?" She spun around. Grace was standing behind her bench. "I didn't hear you," Iris said. "Where's Dad?"

"He's saving my seat at the court house. Vincent told me to get you. He's nervous you'll be late."

Iris held up a warning hand. "Shh, don't scare him away." She indicated the gull sitting calmly opposite her.

"That seagull? Is that who you were talking to?"

Iris nodded. "Someone told me my spirit guide would appear in the form of an animal." She smiled. "I guess that includes birds, right?"

Grace rested a hand on her shoulder. "This trial's taken a toll on you, honey. Hang in there. Vincent thinks it'll be finished today."

But Iris's attention was focused on the gull. "See, Grace? An ordinary seagull would have flown away. Look how it sits there, watching us. Check out the marking over the left eye. Who does it remind you of?"

Grace looked at the bird. "Like a million seagulls at the wharf."

Iris shook her head. "Can't you see how the marking over the left eye resembles a cocked eyebrow? And how the dark swirl of feathers on top of its head looks like hair? Squint your eyes and tell me you don't see Frank."

"You mean Frank, your husband?" When Iris nodded, Grace pulled her to her feet. "Come on. Vincent will be frantic."

Grace led her across the park to the street. As they waited at the crosswalk, she said, "After the trial's over, how about you and me taking a vacation? How does Atlantic City sound?"

TWENTY-ONE

"Ms. Procter will see you now." The gray-haired receptionist lowered her spectacles to peer at Iris. She wore a turtleneck with tiny green whales dotted across her expansive bosom. "The last door on the right," she reminded her.

Iris walked down the hallway, her steps muffled by a worn Oriental runner. The offices of A Women's Issue could best be described as "genteel-shabby." She knocked lightly on the door and heard, "Come in."

Ms. Procter, eyes fixed on a computer screen, said, "Please sit down, Ms. Camuso. I'm afraid I can't spare much time. We're working on next year's budget. I have to submit these figures to the board tomorrow."

"Thank you for seeing me." Iris sat in a straight wooden chair opposite the desk. "I won't take much of your time."

She tore her eyes from the computer and faced Iris across the desk. "By the way, that was quite a picture in *The Barnacle*."

Iris blushed at the mention of the front page photo. Beneath the headline, "Widow Wins Fight Against Lighthouse Insurance," was a picture of she and Vincent on the courthouse steps, giving a thumbs-up. The photographer had descended the moment they stepped outside. "How's it feel to win?" the man had shouted at them.

Yet Ms. Procter's mention of the picture made her feel she'd been caught doing something dirty. "No one likes going to trial," Iris said, "but in this case I had no choice." She added, "I'm grateful Shannon was there."

"I'm afraid she had no choice as well," the woman said

mildly. "What are you planning to do with your winnings?"

"That's actually why I'm here." Iris shifted in her chair. "After my legal expenses, I've got a nice sum." She cleared her throat. "Ms. Proctor, I know we haven't seen eye to eye in the past, and I'd like to put our differences aside. I want you to consider me as a legal adoptive parent for the infant that is my grandchild. I can match whatever sum your agency requires." When Ms. Proctor remained silent, Iris continued. "I'm committed to raising the child here in Harborvale, home of his ancestors. I'm forty-one years old and in good health—"

"Excuse me, but weren't you hospitalized recently?"

"I was, following the trauma of losing my husband—"

"I understand you were hospitalized for chronic alcoholism."

Iris stared into the woman's pale blue eyes. A wave of heat spread up from her chest. She raised a hand. "Please understand the circumstances and issues. My only child had severed relations with her family. Following that, my husband suddenly passed away. It was a heavy burden for anyone. I used alcohol to cope." She sat up straight and returned the woman's flat stare. "The important thing is, I don't drink today. Dr. Laurence Spinney will vouch for me. "

Ms. Proctor sighed wearily. "Ms. Camuso, this agency does an exhaustive search of our adoptive families. In the event we uncover indications of mental illness, that family is disqualified. We're not being heartless. We're simply looking out for the baby's interests. Our standards are rigorous, perhaps too rigorous, but we take no chances."

"But—"

She held up her hand like a traffic cop. "Hear me out. Your hospitalization, however brief, disqualifies you as a potential adopter. Add to that your single-parent status. Lastly, the birth mother has requested that the baby be adopted by a pre-approved family." She shrugged. "I'm afraid it's an irrefutable situation."

"Are you saying you won't consider me, the baby's blood relative?"

"Be assured that this child will be placed with the most outstanding, loving people." Seeing Iris's puzzled expression, she continued. "If I may speak as a therapist here, I'd encourage you to move on with your life as your daughter is doing. The insurance money will allow you to make a fresh start, a new beginning—"

Iris got to her feet. "It just occurred to me that I'm wasting my time talking to a robot who's posing as a woman—"

Ms. Proctor shook her head as if to clear it. She picked up her desk phone and pressed a button on the console. In a business-like voice, she said, "Judy, could you escort Ms. Camuso from my office." Then she got to her feet and looked at Iris. "If you don't leave quietly, I'll call security. The next time you appear at this agency, we'll notify the police. I've run out of patience with you, Ms. Camuso."

At that moment the door swung open. The gray-haired receptionist crossed the room and gripped Iris's arm, saying, "I'll see you out."

"Don't touch me." Iris shook the woman's hand off. She turned to Ms. Proctor. "I thought we could discuss this civilly, but it looks as though I'll be contacting my lawyer. Now the court will decide who has rights to my grandchild."

Ms. Proctor's smile was evil. "A custody battle will eat up your insurance winnings, Ms. Camuso. Our lawyers will make mincemeat of your Mr. Tosi."

"We'll see about that!"

Iris stormed out of the room, the receptionist behind her. The woman followed the length of the corridor and to the exit, continuing down the main staircase. She didn't stop until Iris was safely outside.

Two days later Iris made an appointment with Vincent. She was counting on his optimism and can-do spirit to buoy her. However, after she told him about her custody plan, he frowned.

"I happen to know their lawyers are Fahnstock & Fairchild, the Kennedys' lawyers. The senior partners charge five hundred an hour."

"But Vincent, I'm the baby's grandmother. Surely I have more clout."

"Ms. C., you don't understand custody battles. They're brutal and they go on forever. That kind of custody suit will eat up your money." When she protested, he continued. "Not only that, you'd have to be Mother Theresa to win this case. Look at your record. Let's face it—"

"Vincent, I was briefly hospitalized following my husband's death. It was a voluntary admission. Anyone confronted with that ordeal would do the same."

He sat back in his chair. "Okay, but how do we explain the shoplifting episode at Harborvale Jewelers?"

She stared at him. "How did you know about that? There was no record."

He shrugged. "I've got a cousin, a lieutenant on the police force. You're right, you weren't charged. Yet it's out there, something investigators would uncover."

"Vincent, were you investigating me?"

"I check out all my clients before we go into court. People are selective about their history. By the way, what happened at the jewelry store?"

Iris sighed. "It was a misunderstanding involving a bracelet I forgot I was wearing it when I left the store. Rather than press charges, the manager forced me to go to counseling. She swore she wouldn't contact the police."

"She didn't," he said. "Cops find out those things. And by the way, the manager closed the books as soon as you finished counseling."

"How do you know?"

"As your lawyer, I had to look into it, make sure it wasn't an official shoplifting charge. Before the trial, I went to the jewelry store and had a talk with Ms. Bangs. She's a nut case, but she means well. Said she felt sorry for you, married to Frank."

"I don't want anyone's pity."

He tapped his pen on the desk. "Don't take this personally, Ms. C. You're a nice lady, but your history won't stand up in court. Proctor's lawyers will portray you as an unstable alcoholic and a kleptomaniac. Any other skeletons in the closet, they'll come out. In a custody battle, it's sharks in the water."

"I get the picture." She reached for her purse and stood. "I'm sorry I troubled you with this. "

He got to his feet. "Come on, Ms. C. I'm just laying it out for you, reality. I don't want to take your money for a case that's got no legs."

"I appreciate your honesty, Vincent. The cards are stacked against me."

"What are you gonna do now?"

"I don't know," she said, "but I'm not quitting."

Iris passed very few people as she walked back to her car. Lunchtime was over; the downtown sidewalks were empty. She wondered what to do with the rest of the afternoon. Her life had always been busy and scheduled. Now even her future looked like a wasteland.

When she reached her car in the parking lot, she looked out at the harbor. Everything lay still in the autumn light. A few tourist shops were still open. The striped green and white awnings of the Sacred Cod indicated the deck was open for business.

Iris glanced at her watch. It would be nice to order a salad on the deck, to feel the last rays of the sun on her face. She and Frank used to go there for Sunday brunch until he stopped attending Mass. She remembered their Bloody Marys, tangy with horseradish and lemon. If she had a Bloody Mary, she wouldn't need lunch . . .

She was about to head for the restaurant when a sleek midnight-blue car with tinted windows drove up next to her. The passenger's window rolled down and a voice asked, "How are you, Iris?"

Gloria sat behind the wheel in dark glasses. Her platinum hair was in an upsweep like a fifties movie star.

Iris was startled. She hadn't heard the car arriving. "I'm okay," she said, bending to address Gloria. "How's your replacement hip?"

"I just got permission to drive. I'm managing with the help of a cane, but I do miss Roland's assistance."

"How's he doing at military school?" Iris asked.

Gloria shrugged. "He'll be back for winter break. He's going to help me organize my kitchen." She raised her sunglasses to peer at Iris. "By the way, how have you been doing lately?"

Iris blushed. She had an inexplicable feeling that Gloria knew where she was headed. "As a matter of fact, I've been thinking about what you said about spirit guides. There's a seagull that appears out of nowhere. It's the same gull every time . . ."

Gloria nodded, unfazed. "Pay attention to what it's trying to tell you." With a wave of her hand, she raised the window and drove out of the parking lot. Iris watched her go. When the big car was out of sight, she turned and headed back to her Jetta. If she hurried, she could visit the cemetery before sunset.

The shadows were long when Iris arrived at Shady Rest. Wasting no time, she got a jug of water and clippers from the car's back seat. She tied a sweater around her waist and got to work, trimming the grassy borders and pulling the weeds that had sprung up in her absence. As she worked, she talked.

"Frank, you would have been proud of me at the trial. I maintained my dignity, even while that bimbo was testifying. I never lost my cool, not even when Dad interrupted the proceedings." She winced, recalling the event:

"Your Honor, I call my final witness, Valerie Moles."

With those words a hush fell over the courtroom. The silence, born of pent up anticipation, was electric. Members of the jury sat up straighter. Spectators ceased fanning themselves and eyeglasses were hastily polished.

Valerie Moles, in high-heeled sling backs, sashayed from the back of the courtroom. She wore a tan safari suit, the short jacket open to reveal a low-cut white tank top. Her copper hair was teased and tousled. Gold hoop earrings glinted in the afternoon light. She moved up the center aisle, every part of her in motion. The courtroom was hushed, the only sound the click-click of the ceiling fan and Valerie's heels on the wooden floor. Even Judge Kuszko stared, mesmerized.

The clerk proffered a Bible to the witness and swore her in. Then he said, "State your name and occupation."

"Valerie Louise Moles, bartender at the Dirty Dinghy." She pronounced her Portuguese surname *Moe-lez*. She sat, giving her short skirt a tug and crossing smooth, tanned legs.

Vincent approached, standing to the side, allowing a good view of the witness. "Ms. Moles, you are single, is that correct?"

"I sure am." She smiled up at Vincent.

The spectators, whose numbers had swelled since the morning session, leaned forward. Judge Kuszko leaned far over his desk to say, "A simple yes or no, please."

"Sorry, Your Honor." She gave him a coy smile. "The answer is yes."

"How long have you worked as a bartender at the Dirty Dinghy?" Vincent asked.

"About two years."

"Was the deceased, Francis Camuso, a steady customer?"

"Yes, he was."

"And you two became friends, is that right?"

"You could call it that, yes."

"Ms. Moles, can you tell the court when you and Mr. Camuso became more than friends and became lovers?"

"Objection, Your Honor."

The young attorney was halfway to his feet when the judge said, "Denied."

Val re-crossed her legs. "About a month before he passed away. It was after his wife kicked him out."

"That's a load of bull." Chester Quirk's loud remark, intended for Grace, hung in the air.

"Silence," Judge Kuszko barked. He turned to Vincent. "Counselor, let's not drag this out."

"I'm sorry, Your Honor. I'm trying to establish the bond between the witness and the deceased."

"Fine, but pick up the pace."

Vincent leaned toward Valerie. "Ms. Moles, you and Frank Camuso were lovers."

"Yes, we were."

"Had you made plans for a more permanent union?"

"We were getting married once Frank got his divorce."

At that, Chester Quirk's patience ran out. Grabbing his cane, he stomped down the aisle followed by a red-faced Grace. He stood at Iris's side. "I've heard enough," he announced. "We're going home."

Iris stared at him. "Dad, what are you doing? Sit down."

Judge Kuszko addressed Grace. "Ma'am, is he with you?"

Grace nodded. "He is, Your Honor."

"Please escort him out." When Chester Quirk deliberated, looking from Iris to the judge, the latter said, "One more word and I'll hold you in contempt of court." Perhaps it was the steel in the justice's eyes. In any event, he allowed Grace to lead him out. As they walked up the aisle, spectators reached out to grab his hand.

"I'm sorry, Your Honor," Vincent said when the courtroom doors closed behind the pair. "My client's father is very protective."

"Continue, counselor," the judge rasped. "Let's wrap this up today."

Vincent turned to Valerie, who appeared amused. "Ms. Moles, you obviously were familiar with Frank Camuso's moods. Did you consider him an unhappy man?"

"Not with me, no."

"Was he a generous man?"

She twirled a lock of hair. "He bought me a Boston Whaler."

Vincent returned to the plaintiff's table where he opened a file and extracted a document. "I call your attention to a receipt from Marchetti's Marina in East Boston. It's an initial payment on a seventeen-thousand dollar Boston Whaler." He addressed Valerie, "What were your plans for the boat, Ms. Moles?"

"We were going to tow it to Key West on our honeymoon."

Now Iris watered the parched dahlias. Thanks to the shade trees above, they'd survived the late summer heat. Next year she'd add perennials and maybe a shrub, such as a holly or two. The red berries would provide color in the winter. As she worked, she continued her dialogue.

"I was hurt, Frank, and not for the first time. You bought

that woman a new boat when you wouldn't replace our fifteen year-old dishwasher. Didn't your conscience trouble you?" She brushed dirt from her hands. "If you could reply I know what you'd say, that I'm making 'mountains out of meatballs.' You always said that, as if I were a demanding wife. I believed you because you were so sure of yourself.

"Well, Frank, I found validation in that courtroom. I saw it in the sympathetic eyes of the jury and spectators. When the verdict was read, the room erupted in cheers. Even Judge Kuszko couldn't silence them. Perfect strangers approached to hug me." She wiped a tear with her sleeve and whispered, "It was the finest moment of my life."

It was dusk when Iris collected the gardening tools and carried them to her car. On her way, she spotted the caretaker approaching on the worn path. She turned her back to the man, bending over the trunk. He stopped; she felt his eyes on her.

"You're not still feeding him, are you?"

"Who?" She turned and discovered the man wasn't looking at *her*; he was watching a nearby crabapple tree. The seagull was again perched on a limb. "I didn't even know he was there," she said, slamming the trunk shut.

"Don't get your feathers in a ruff," he said. "I didn't say you're feeding him on purpose. Maybe you had something to eat here and left it behind—"

"I don't consider a cemetery an appropriate place for a picnic." Her tone was frosty.

The caretaker scratched his head. "Then why does that bird only show up when you're here?"

"I don't know what to tell you," she said, getting her car keys from her bag. "You'll have to ask the seagull."

TWENTY-TWO

"Ms. Camuso, come in."

Dr. Spinney beckoned from the door of his waiting room. Iris put down the worn copy of *Parents* magazine, the same issue from her first visit five months earlier. She followed him into the adjoining office and sat in the familiar cracked leather chair.

Dr. Spinney, sitting opposite, crossed his legs to reveal two inches of hairy white shin above striped stockings. He set a clipboard on his knee and said, "I was pleased to get your call. I've wondered how you're doing. How are you feeling?"

"Pretty good, I guess." The psychiatrist raised his bushy white eyebrows, an indication for her to continue. "I don't know what else to tell you. If you questioned half the population of Harborvale, I'm sure that's what people would say—pretty good."

"You've got a point." He glanced at his notes. "Are you back at work?"

"Uh huh."

"How is that going?"

"Do you mean since they learned about my stay at the clinic?"

"Is that an issue?"

"Maybe I'm paranoid, but I think so. I seem to be dealing with the parents a lot more. Some want feedback on my sessions with their kids, as if they doubt my competence. Some insist on being in the room when I'm counseling." She grimaced.

"Oh. How does that affect your work?"

"It's repressive. The kids don't open up with Mom in the

corner. Some mothers interrupt to correct their child's version of events."

He shook his white head. "Can you do anything about it?"

"I've complained to Tomas, the principal. He says as long as the children are minors they can't keep the parents out of counseling sessions."

He brightened. "Is Tomas the man who visited you in the hospital?"

She nodded. "He's been very supportive."

"And have you two been intimate?"

"Dr. Spinney, I'll remind you I'm a recent widow." She felt her face getting warm.

"You've been a widow for more than"— he glanced at his clipboard— "seven months. It's normal for a woman your age to have needs."

"I have needs, I'm just not rushing into anything."

"Has Tomas indicated a desire for an intimate relationship?"

"Right now we're both content to . . . hold each other. We're comfortable with that." She shifted in her chair. "But that's not what I want to talk about. I'm here because my friend Grace insists I discuss something with you."

"Is Grace the person who brought you to the hospital when you were admitted?"

"Yes, and for the record, I was found lying *across* the kitty litter box, not in it. Please correct that in my file."

He nodded. "Continue about your friend."

"Well, she thinks I might have a brain tumor."

"What makes her say that?"

"Um, because Grace stayed at my house recently while Tomas and I took an overnight trip to Rhode Island. She looked after my cat. Anyway, while I was gone, she overheard a phone message, a response from a private investigator I'd contacted—"

"Why was that?" he asked.

"I needed information about my grandchild. I want to know if he's happy and well cared for in his new home."

"Did you learn anything?"

She shook her head. "Even the FBI couldn't infiltrate A

Women's Issue. The investigator said the records are sealed tight. So now that Grace knows I hired a private investigator, she's worried I'll become a stalker, should I discover the baby's whereabouts."

"As a rule, adoption agencies select parents from a different section of the country."

"I'm aware of that. But in this case I believe the baby is nearby and wants me to find him."

"What makes you think that?"

She looked at her folded hands. "Because I hear him. Even before his birth, I heard his cries." She met his eyes. "Actually, that was why I asked Grace to stay at my house. Not to look after the cat. I wanted her to hear."

"Why is it important that she hears?"

"Validation. Proof I'm not crazy."

"Did she hear anything?"

She shook her head. "Now she thinks I might have a brain tumor, or something. That's why I'm here. She wants me to check it out."

"What do you think?" he asked.

"I have no doubt that the baby is reaching out to me. It's blood calling to blood."

Not long after that, Iris and Tomas were lying on the sofa holding each other while watching TV, something they often did on Sunday afternoons. Iris was nearly dozing when the cries began. She sat up and grabbed the remote, clicking off the TV. Looking around the room, she held a finger to her lips. "Listen!"

"Listen to what?" Tomas was surprised by the sudden interruption.

"Shh. Do you hear it?"

"Do I hear what?" He sat up.

"The cries. Don't you hear a baby crying?"

"Upstairs?"

"Just listen. It's faint but . . . can't you hear it?" She watched his eyes scanning the ceiling.

He turned to her. "I don't hear a baby crying. Maybe you have left a radio on upstairs?"

She sighed. "You're probably right."

Now Dr. Spinney said, "You say you're the only one who hears the cries."

"Well, the only human."

"Meaning?"

"My cat has heard them."

"Your cat?"

"Yes, and don't look so worried. I'm not delusional. One morning I woke up hearing the cries. I looked across the bed and saw Patticake, lying nearby. She was looking intently at the closet, the source of the cries. Her ears were pricked and her tail was going back and forth. I know she heard it."

He rubbed his chin. "Hmm, I'll admit that hearing odd sounds is sometimes associated with brain tumors, although in your case I doubt it very much. We'll arrange for testing to ease your fears."

She shook her head. "It would be a waste of time. There's nothing wrong with my head. The reason Grace and Tomas can't hear the cries is because they don't share a psychic bond. Animals, on the other hand, pick up these vibrations because they're attuned."

Dr. Spinney bent over his notes as he wrote. "I want you to make an appointment with the hospital's neurologist—"

"It's like the seagull who's been appearing at significant moments," Iris continued, warming to the subject. "Everyone sees it as an ordinary gull, one of thousands here in Harborvale. Yet I believe it's the spirit of my late husband, sent here to guide me. Now that Frank has crossed over, he's paying off his karmic debt."

Dr. Spinney stared at her for a moment and then flipped through the pages on his clipboard. "We might want to review your medications as well . . ."

As she had promised, Iris called Grace when she returned from her session with Dr. Spinney. "What did he say?" Grace asked.

"That I've got one month left, maybe two."

"It's not funny, kiddo. This could be serious."

She sighed. "He mentioned a neurologist, an audiologist, and a head scan. I told him there's nothing wrong with my head or my hearing." She was tired of the subject. "Do you want to go for an early dinner at Mega Mug?"

"Matter of fact, I bought a couple of steaks I was thinking of cooking outside. It's not too cold tonight. We can wear jackets. It's probably the last time we'll be able to sit out there."

"Only if I can bring something and you promise not to talk about Dr. Spinney."

"Reluctantly, but come over around six."

The sky was streaked with lavender when Iris arrived at Graces A-frame house. She carried her bowl of broccoli salad outside, where Grace was lighting a hurricane lamp.

"I've got ice tea in the pitcher and soda in the fridge," Grace said. "For dessert, I bought an apple pie at Bravissimo, the new gourmet shop near my store."

"Let me pay for that," Iris said. "I don't want you spending all your money."

"No big deal. I had a coupon. Guess who was in front of me, buying a bottle of wine?"

"Don't make me guess. Dr. Spinney?"

"I thought we wouldn't talk about him tonight. No, it was Vincent Tosi. He was all dressed up, looking sharp."

Mention of the lawyer reminded Iris of their less-than-amicable parting. "He was probably heading to a wake. Vincent goes to every wake and funeral in town."

"No, he had a date, with Heidi Masucci. Apparently they're a couple."

"Who in hell is Heidi Masucci?"

"She won the Hot Legs contest at my shop. I took your advice and asked Vincent to be the judge. As a result, he learned that Heidi is a college intern at the Chamber of Commerce. As you know, his office is down the hall from the Chamber."

"An intern?" Iris said, sounding peevish. "Vincent is dating a college student?"

"Heidi is one of those nontraditional students, a single parent returning to school. She's in her late thirties and very attractive."

"With hot legs, too," Iris said sourly. "I'm happy for him."

Grace laughed. "You don't sound happy. Don't hold it against Vincent for being honest with you. Another lawyer might have taken your money and represented you despite his misgivings."

"I was so ready to confront Ms. Proctor in court."

"Forget it. That's an upscale agency that's not accustomed to losing. Vincent spared you a lot of pain while saving you a bundle at the same time." She lifted the cover of the grill to poke at the glowing coals. "Speaking of romance, how's Mr. Tomasillo?"

Iris took a sip of her cherry-vanilla soda. "He's fine. I'm comfortable with Tomas."

"Comfortable? Hmm, that doesn't sound sexy."

"We're taking it slow. I'm a widow who's been through a lot."

"I'll bet you two haven't gotten to second base."

"That's right, and no one says 'second base' anymore. Tomas asked me to go to Puerto Rico with him during Christmas vacation."

Grace turned to stare. "Oh my God, he's getting serious."

"I haven't given him an answer yet. I'm thinking it over."

"I hope so. That sounds like a commitment, meeting the family."

"Tomas has many fine qualities. I came to appreciate them when we went away to Rhode Island—"

"I can't believe you two went away together and nothing happened."

"I told you, we want to feel right about it. Anyway, I had an epiphany Sunday morning at our motel. I looked out the window. Tomas was outside in the parking lot loading up the car. I watched him arranging the suitcases—putting them in, taking them out of the trunk—trying to get a perfect fit. It made me feel cared for."

Grace looked over at her. "Because he knows how to pack a trunk?"

"Because of the attention he pays. It's so different from Frank. He would have crammed the suitcases in. If they didn't fit, he'd swear a blue streak, not caring who heard. Then he'd blame me for packing too much. With Frank, it was always someone else's fault."

"Frank was pretty stubborn," Grace said, lifting the steaks from the grill.

"He thought everyone was out to get him," Iris said. She paused. "To give him his due, he had to be the man of the house at an early age after his father died. His mother and his aunts leaned on him. Frank had to be strong for them." She sighed. "I still can't believe he's gone."

A strong breeze swept into the yard, rattling the dried leaves of the oak tree. "It's getting cool," Grace said. "Maybe we'll have coffee and dessert inside."

December brought shorter and darker days as winter tightened its grip on Harborvale. At the Shady Rest Cemetery, the bare branches of the maple trees were covered with a thin coating of snow. Before the earth had a chance to harden, Iris planted two small holly bushes on opposite sides of Frank's stone. The shrub's red berries would provide color during the iron-gray days of winter.

Once a week she visited her dad, who was spending more time with Betty Ann, his neighbor. Although Iris was happy her father had companionship, she worried that she'd lose him too. It was something she would have discussed with Dr. Spinney, had she been seeing the psychiatrist. She'd stopped therapy when the doctor kept asking why she hadn't consulted the neurologist. "What about the crying?" he asked. "Do you still hear it?"

"Not really."

It was a half-lie. The baby's cries were occurring, although less frequently and for shorter periods. Sometimes the sound was so faint she wasn't sure she heard it at all. She feared the baby was vanishing, pulling away as their link weakened.

"Maybe we should examine the meaning of your phantom baby," Dr. Spinney said. "Have you considered it might be a part of you crying out for attention?"

"It wasn't in my head, Dr. Spinney. I hear the cries." She felt insulted that the shrink gave no credence to her story.

"We all have hidden needs, Ms. Camuso. Sometimes the unconscious employs unorthodox means in order to get our attention."

Later, during a phone conversation with Grace, Iris mentioned the psychiatrist's remark. "He thinks I'm wacky. It's just as well I terminated. Not only that, my health insurance co-pays have doubled. I can't afford therapy."

"Get serious," Grace said. "What about the insurance money?"

"That allows me to work part time until I decide what I'm going to do," Iris explained.

"Are you thinking Shannon might come back?"

"The way she's treated us I wouldn't want her back. There's been too much water under that bridge."

"I meant to tell you," Grace continued, "Shannon's former roommate Amber Spaglione came into the shop a couple of days ago. She bought some sizzling lingerie. When I inquired about Shannon, Amber said she heard she was enrolled in the nursing program at the community college."

"Is that so? I guess mothers are the last to know."

"I only mention it because I want you to realize Shannon's moving on with her life," Grace said. "You should too. Forget about the baby. The kid's been adopted. He's moved on too."

Iris closed her eyes. "Will you stop? Everyone's telling me to move on. Where the hell am I supposed to go?"

Grace laughed. "That sounds like my old buddy. Now promise me you'll return to therapy."

"Of course," Iris said before hanging up. If and when she deemed she needed it.

The following afternoon Iris canceled an appointment with a parent and ducked out of school early. Twenty minutes later she arrived at Harborvale Community College. After parking in the visitors' lot, she went inside and soon located the student bookstore.

There she had no trouble staking out an inconspicuous spot near the shelves piled with caps and sweatshirts bearing the college's logo. After waiting a half hour, she gave up and left, not wanting to draw attention to herself.

She returned the following day, around noon. When she had no sighting of Shannon, she again slipped out. On the third visit, while killing time inside the shop, her perseverance paid off. Shannon walked in the door.

She emerged from a cluster of students congregating near the entrance and moved to stand before a display of greeting cards. Iris, positioned near a rack of sweatpants, peeked out, her heart thumping. She wore a disguise, the gray wig and glasses she'd used at the Ship Ahoy apartments.

From the corner of her eye she watched her daughter browse the holiday cards. Although pale, Shannon looked beautiful. Her dark curly hair fell over the lapels of her navy pea coat. Her cheekbones looked chiseled; all traces of her pregnancy were gone.

As Shannon returned a card to its holder, her eyes flicked over the room. Iris, who'd been staring, abruptly turned to face the shelves of sweatshirts. She squeezed her eyes shut. When she finally looked around, Shannon was striding for the exit, her book bag thumping her back.

Iris was unsure if she's been spotted. If she had, she wished she could assure Shannon that she had nothing to fear. Iris had no intention of returning to the college. She had gotten what she came for—a glimpse of her only child.

The day before Christmas, Iris attended a house party at Janice's. In the past, she often excused herself from Camuso family gatherings. The close-knit clan was friendly enough, yet Iris often felt like an outsider. When she'd voiced her concerns to Frank, he'd dismissed them. "Never mind. You're married to me. They gotta accept you."

This year, however, she felt obligated to attend. For one thing, it was her first Christmas without Frank. She wanted to thank everyone for the many casseroles and pans of lasagna they'd delivered to her door. If that wasn't reason enough, Fatima was arriving from California with Alan, her widowed boyfriend.

"I've been telling him all about the family," Fatima said during a recent phone call. "He's dying to meet everyone, so you better be there."

"Are you two talking marriage?" Iris asked.

Fatima chuckled. "Let me put it this way; I won't be surprised to find a little velvet box under my Christmas tree."

The afternoon party was held at Janice and Artie's split-level ranch set in a subdivision whose meandering roads were dotted with similar looking houses. A helter-skelter line of cars stretched along the Lafata's street.

Iris, in no hurry to join the noisy throng inside, parked at the end of the line. She stood outside her car, looking up at the sky. It was steel-gray, hinting of the snow that was predicted.

The cold finally got her moving and she approached the house. This season the Lafatas had gone overboard in decorating. Multi-colored balls like disco globes hung from a slender cherry tree in the front yard. A giant inflated Santa tethered to an air hose rocked drunkenly back and forth. Two illuminated reindeer with a trio of wise men nearby completed the holiday tableau.

At the front door, Iris heard the cacophony within. Camuso gatherings were always loud. Thus no one heard her knocking so she opened the door. Immediately she was assaulted by the sounds of shrieking children, a blaring TV and raucous adult laughter. All existed against a backdrop of Christmas songs booming from the stereo.

Janice appeared in a green v-neck sweater with a snowman appliqué. She kissed Iris's cheek. "Drinks in the kitchen," she shouted over the noise. "Artie's bartending."

Iris, not wanting to put a damper on the festivities, didn't remind Janice that she no longer drank. She let her hostess take her coat and then followed her to the living room where people were sprawled everywhere. The three aunts sat wedged on a sofa in front of a big picture window. They appeared to be dozing despite the blaring TV in the corner. A football game was on; Camuso males of varying ages followed the action on the screen. Some tore their eyes away long enough to wave to Iris as she navigated the room. She was careful not to step on the paper plates with half-eaten slices of pizza scattered on the floor.

Finally they reached the kitchen. Platters of cheese, crackers, and salami along with bowls of dip vied for counter space. The kitchen table had been moved. Bottles of gin, vodka and scotch along with jugs of wine covered its surface. Janice's husband Artie, wearing a red sweatshirt, presided over the makeshift bar. He leaned against the sink, clutching a red plastic cup to his belly.

"Artie, get Iris a drink," Janice said. She looked around the room. "Where's Fatima?"

He pushed himself away from the sink. "She and Alan went to Sweckler's."

"What for?"

"More cold cuts."

"Why didn't you tell her we had enough food?"

He shrugged. "She wanted to get a platter from Sweckler's. What was I supposed to say?"

"Chrissake, Artie. She's our guest." Janice stormed from the room.

Artie rolled his eyes and reached for the vodka. "Lemme think. Vodka and lime juice, right?" He tossed ice cubes and a slice of lime into a red cup, followed by a liberal splash of alcohol.

She cleared her throat. "Actually, Artie, do you have coffee?"

He raised his eyebrows. "What? Coffee's later, with the cake. Janice bought a huge goddamn cake that'll feed the entire street." He poured a splash of lime juice and seltzer into her drink, gave it a stir and shoved it at her. "Cheers. You look like you could use it."

She stared into the cup, breathing the fresh scent of lime and the bracing tonic of vodka. "What do you mean?"

He leaned back against the sink. "You look a little uptight, but hey, you haven't had it easy, married to Frank."

"I thought you liked him." Iris was aware of the animosity that had existed between Frank and Artie, the latter whom Frank had called an "idiot."

Artie took a long swallow from his cup. "Finest kind, Frank. Yet I couldn't see what he saw in that bartender. With her, everything's fake." His eyes traveled over Iris from head to toe. "You're more natural."

"That's nice of you to say." She gazed into her drink, transfixed by the invigorating scent of alcohol.

Artie laughed. "Go on, drink it. I didn't slip any drugs in if that's what you're worried about."

As she raised the drink to her lips, Fatima's voice boomed from the living room. Seconds later she swept into the kitchen. She was followed by a lanky, gray-haired man in a navy blazer with gold buttons. He carried a large foil-covered platter.

"Oh my God," Fatima shouted, throwing her arms around Iris. Her hair, stiffly sprayed, scratched Iris's cheek. Fatima released her and stood back. "Look at you, you're so pale." With that, she tugged the sleeve of her beaded sweater, holding her tanned forearm against Iris's. "You definitely gotta come visit us."

She turned to look up at her companion. "Alan, this is Iris, my sister-in-law. She was married to my baby brother, Frankie." Her voice broke. "God rest his soul." Alan leaned forward to peck her cheek drily. "Iris is the sister I never had," Fatima continued.

Janice entered the kitchen. "Thanks a lot, Fatima. You said that about me."

Fatima laughed. "You're both special." She moved to the doorway and called into the living room. "Hey, everyone, grab your drink. I'm making a toast."

The men reluctantly pulled themselves away from the TV. They wandered in clutching cans of beer, the kids dragging behind with soda. After everyone crowded into the kitchen, Fatima looked around and said, "Where are the aunties? I gotta have the aunties."

"They're snoozin' on the sofa," Janice said hurriedly. "If you wake them, they'll wanna go to the bathroom and I don't have time to take them. I've gotta put the lasagna in."

"Fine, but they'll be disappointed." Fatima turned to the bar. "Artie, where's our drinks?"

"Coming up." He sprang into action, deftly mixing a Southern Comfort Old Fashion and a gin and tonic. They were handed to Fatima and Alan.

"Everyone grab your drink and gather 'round," Fatima ordered. Holding her glass aloft, she moved to the center of the room. "I want my family to be the first to know because I love you more than anything." She wiped a tear and continued, her voice shaking. "As you know, I've been through a lot this year, but my faith gave me the strength to continue. Now I believe the Holy Mother was looking out for me every step of the way." She paused, fighting for control. "Because next month we'll have a new member in the Camuso family." She turned to Alan. "Please join me in toasting my fiancé, Alan Dennis Kobroski."

The room erupted in raucous cheers as the group toasted the couple. Iris automatically lifted her glass and drank. The alcohol quickly spread its warmth, dissolving the knots in her stomach. She closed her eyes and drank more.

Fatima's voice roused her. "Iris, get over here. I'm gonna tell the girls how Alan popped the question." A group of women immediately clustered around Fatima.

"One minute," Iris said. She wanted to finish her drink but at the same time didn't want Fatima to smell alcohol on her breath.

"Freshen that for you?" Artie, who'd been watching her, held out his hand.

Her head spinning, she automatically handed him her glass. When their hands touched, he gave her a sly wink. She was immediately reminded of an earlier engagement at Artie's house, a birthday party for their daughter Krystal.

Iris, newly widowed and alone, had felt awkward; a few drinks had helped. After most of the guests had gone, she'd stayed behind with the diehards, accepting the cocktails Artie poured. But when it was time to go, Janice refused to let her get in her car. She'd insisted that Artie drive her home.

Through a blur Iris remembered Artie unlocking her front door and helping her into the darkened house. As she fumbled for the light switch, he'd pinned her against the wall and groped her, ignoring her protests.

Now, as Artie poured vodka into her glass, Iris grabbed her pocketbook hanging from a kitchen chair. She rushed from the kitchen and into the living room. In the adjoining sitting room, she found her coat on a love seat piled with other coats. She put it over her arm and hurried back into the living room. The men were still glued to the football game, shouting when the Patriots scored. Nearby, the aunts dozed on the sofa. Over the din, Iris heard Fatima bellowing her name.

She rushed to the front door. In her haste she stepped on a paper plate, her heel puncturing the cardboard. She opened the door. Without a backward glance, Iris stepped outside into the cold.

The sun was sinking as she scurried down the street. At one point she stopped to pull the floppy paper plate from her shoe. Upon reaching her car, she threw herself into the driver's seat. Then she reached for the glove compartment and withdrew her cell phone. With trembling fingers, she punched in Grace's number. Her breath made clouds in the Jetta's interior as she waited. When Grace answered, Iris sighed with relief. "Can I come over?"

"Iris? I thought you were in Puerto Rico with Tomas."

"No. I found out I'd be sharing a room with Aidita. I told Tomas I had to take my dad to his doctor's."

"Where are you now?"

"I was at a Camuso Christmas party. I just left. In a hurry."

"Is that why you sound so frantic?"

Iris exhaled. "I had a drink. If I'd stayed, I'd probably have more. Can I come over?"

"Are you okay to drive?"

"I only had one drink. Honest."

"Come over right now," Grace instructed. "Don't stop any-place."

"I need to run into Mighty Mart for cat food."

"That's a bad idea."

"It's okay. They don't sell alcohol there."

"Fine. Grab the cat food and get over here. I'll make some coffee."

Iris wasted no time at Mighty Mart. After a quick greeting to Sandy, she made a beeline for the pet section. She tossed cans into her basket and scurried back to the counter.

Sandy, wearing a fuzzy red Santa hat, looked amused. "What's the big rush, Ms. C., Christmas shopping?"

"I'm in kind of a hurry."

"You're always in a hurry. You should try tai chi. It mellows you out. Dr. Fung's teaching me."

"Is that so. How's the screenplay coming?"

"Awesome. Dr. Fung showed it to one of his former students who teaches at Emerson College. There's a film club there that wants to make it their senior thesis."

"Sandy, that's great."

"They can't pay me anything, but it'll be entered into a bunch of film competitions, including Sundance."

Iris grinned at her. "Merry Christmas, Sandy. I'm proud of you." She took her bag and hurried for the door.

Outside in the cold night air, she took a deep breath and counted her blessings. She'd had a close call at the party, but that was behind her. Tomorrow she'd call Janice and Fatima and apologize for leaving abruptly. She'd explain how difficult the holidays were without Frank.

Before getting into her car, she looked around the parking lot. Bare tree limbs were silhouetted. High up, the early stars shone brightly.

As she lowered the bag onto the back seat of the Jetta, a baby's cry interrupted the stillness. It was the same cry she'd come to know intimately: blood calling to blood.

She straightened and looked around. A handful of vehicles were scattered around the lot. The cry appeared to emanate from a car parked in the second row.

She closed her door and slowly approached the car whose

motor was running. No one was behind the wheel of the ancient Mercury yet the dashboard's glow revealed keys in the ignition. A Coke can sat in the cup holder. A ribbon of smoke rose from an ashtray overflowing with cigarette butts.

She glanced into the shadowy back seat. A baby, wrapped in a blanket, was strapped into a plastic infant carrier. Although the light was dim, she could make out his blond curls and rosy cheeks. But it was the blanket that caught her eye—crocheted and robin's-egg blue with narrow yellow stripes. It was the same blanket she'd sent to Shannon in the hospital.

Iris rapped lightly on the window. The baby opened its eyes and looked at her. She knew her search was over.

She turned toward the store. A stocky woman in dark jeans stood at the entrance, one hand on the door as she talked to Sandy. A pack of cigarettes bulged from the pocket of her checkered flannel shirt. There was no time to deliberate. Iris opened the Mercury's door and reached into the back seat. Quickly she released the seat belt restraining the carrier. Leaning into the back seat, she gripped the handle and lifted the carrier out. At the same time she spotted a diaper bag on the floor mat. She grabbed the long strap and slipped it over her shoulder. Her arms laden, she nudged the door shut.

Iris raced to her car. She placed the carrier on the back seat. There was no time to secure seat belts now. She hopped behind the wheel and started the car. As she drove out of the parking lot she felt competent, in control.

When she was on the road for a few minutes, she glanced into her rear view mirror. There were no flashing lights, no one pursuing her. She let out a shaky breath and said aloud, "It's just you and me now. We're in this together."

TWENTY-THREE

As if guided by an invisible hand, Iris headed for the shore road. Although the motels at Sandpiper Creek closed after Labor Day, one or two always remained open. They attracted the transients, drifters, and newly divorced. Although the beach was deserted and desolate in winter, its motel rates were reasonable. Not only that, guests could come and go, anonymously.

She would find a place to hide out for the night in the—unlikely—event she'd been seen. As an added precaution, she'd get her car off the road.

But first she needed supplies. Her strategy came instinctively, as if she'd been planning for months. A power greater than herself had taken over, using her as an instrument. As a result, she felt little fear. She'd done the right thing.

When she glanced into the back seat, her heart melted at the sight of the baby, his mouth puckered in sleep. She decided she would call him Chester, after her dad.

Five miles later she approached the Sandpiper Creek bridge and joined the line of cars crawling along. Below the gatehouse, rocking back and forth in the water, was a tall-masted fishing boat waiting to pass. As she inched along in traffic, she examined the contents of the diaper bag. A pack of Marlboros was stuck in an outside pocket. Another held a can of Mountain Dew. She unzipped the insulated compartment and discovered two cans of infant formula, a plastic baby bottle, and a jar of strained cereal. Plastic diapers were crammed into an outside pocket. At least the baby would have enough supplies for the next twenty-four hours.

She glanced ahead anxiously. The traffic had slowed to a crawl. Any minute now the bridge tender would lower the gates to allow the fishing boat to go. Just when she thought she would make it across the bridge, the warning *ding-ding-ding* sounded, followed by flashing red lights.

Her heart beat faster. She could still make it if the beige sedan ahead of her stepped on it. Instead of picking up the pace, the white-haired driver, no doubt frightened by the warning bell, slowed, his brake lights flashing.

Iris groaned. She couldn't risk the exposure of sitting in traffic. She gripped the steering wheel and once again felt a commanding force guiding her on. She yanked the wheel to the right and pressed the accelerator. The Jetta surged, racing past the elderly, startled driver. At the same time, the gates had begun their descent. She pressed her foot on the gas pedal; the Jetta responded by seeming to soar over the bridge.

The bridge tender waved a warning arm. Fortunately, the rising bridge concealed her from his view. Safely on the other side, Iris let out her breath. She picked up speed, passing a line of multinational flags that waved in the wind, as if applauding her courage.

The shore route grew darker, the few street lights reflecting the black surface of the ocean. She drove past one shuttered motel after another: Sea Crest, Tide's Inn, Salty Pines and more. Other summertime establishments, the clam huts, ice cream stands and surfboard shacks, were closed for the season. She continued until she was finally rewarded with a "Vacancy" sign.

The Laughing Gull motel was conveniently situated on a side street off the main road. Iris drove into the parking lot, stopping a distance from the office. Two cars were in the lot, one parked in the rear near a dumpster, the others near the entrance. She surveyed the building, the weathered gray shingles, the small but well-lit office. Lights were on in two of the eight units. Outside, the grounds looked cared for and free of debris. Best of all, The Laughing Gull's rooms were efficiencies, with stoves and refrigerators.

All in all, it looked like a safe place to hide out for a day or two. She turned off the ignition and sat, suddenly reluctant to move. What if the local innkeepers had been warned about a missing baby? They could be suspicious of a woman traveling alone.

She closed her eyes and waited for further guidance. When she opened them, she gasped. Sitting on the roof above the office entrance was a seagull. It flapped its wings as if acknowledging her. In a moment it flew to the chimney where it sat silhouetted against the night sky.

She had gotten her guidance. "Thank you," she whispered and alighted from the car. She moved to the trunk. Luckily the bag containing her disguise was still there. Behind the opened trunk door she slipped on the gray wig and black framed glasses. She wouldn't risk taking the baby inside. He would have to stay in the locked car. She was parked near the office. Once inside, she could keep an eye on the Jetta.

A bell over the office door jingled when she entered. Inside, a thin, elderly man in a maroon cardigan sat behind a counter watching a TV mounted to the wall. He looked up. "Hi. Help you?"

"I'd like an efficiency for tonight."

The man slowly got to his feet. "We got one, no smoking." When she nodded he opened an old-fashioned guest register on the counter. He turned the book to face her. "Sign there, please, and put the make of your car. You pay in advance. Just to let you know, we don't take American Express."

"Oh dear, that's my card," Iris said, grateful for the convenient excuse. "Is cash okay?"

"Cash is fine. The room's forty-nine dollars. How many people?"

"Just me." She took the pen from him and paused. In a round script she wrote, Cheryl Ann Dutton on the signature line. She returned the pen, saying, "You know how it is, visiting family for the holidays. It's best to have your own place to escape to."

He chuckled. "That's why we stay open 'til New Year's."

Iris handed him a fifty-dollar bill. "By the way, is there a convenience store nearby?"

"Follow the shore road another half mile 'til you come to a trailer park set off the road. Look for the sign, Sandpiper Creek Leisure Living. A little store there should be open Friday night." He turned to a wall where several keys hung from hooks inside a frame. He handed her number six. "It ain't been used much this time of year. Leave the window open a bit, air it out some."

"Fine. Thanks." She nodded so vigorously her glasses slipped off, falling to the floor. She bent to pick them up.

"Ice machine's the opposite end of the building," he said. "Don't forget to turn on the refrigerator. We shut 'em off this time of year."

The baby was stirring when she returned. "You've been so good," she cooed. "Let me get a couple of things. Then we'll get settled in our new home."

She got back onto the coastal road. It was narrower this end of the beach. Soon she came to the sign the old man had mentioned. She slowed. In a clearing surrounded by stunted pines sat two rows of trailers, their metal roofs gleaming in the moonlight. Near the entrance was a quasi convenience store, a converted metal trailer with a hand-painted sign.

Iris drove into the gravel parking lot, stopping near the front door. After adjusting her wig and glasses, she got out and again locked the car.

The rusted metal door creaked when she entered the store. A strand of Christmas lights hung from a display of motor oil. A heavyset woman hummed while whisking a feather duster over a row of cans on a shelf. She glanced at Iris and called, "Let me know if you need anything, honey."

Iris grabbed a wooden basket and headed for the refrigerator in the rear. She selected sliced ham and cheese, a loaf of bread and a quart of milk. On impulse, she tossed a pint of mocha fudge ice cream into the basket.

She spotted a shelf of pet food and thought guiltily of Patticake. The cat had water and enough dry food. If she didn't go home tomorrow, she would ask Grace to come to her house. But what excuse could she offer? Her best friend was no doubt worried, wondering why Iris hadn't shown up. She would call Grace later, saying she'd driven "up country," on a whim. Grace would assume she'd been drinking, but at least she wouldn't go to the police.

As the oversized woman rang up Iris's purchases, she maintained a running commentary. "You're visiting at a good time, honey. Come January, the town stops cleaning the beach. They claim no one lives here in the winter. Oh, really? We pay taxes same as everyone else, but they don't care. After a storm, the seaweed's piled on the beach three feet high, a God-awful smell. I says to my husband, 'Next year we're selling and getting out.'"

"Is that so," Iris said, keeping her eyes lowered.

"Yes ma'am. We're going to Arizona. He's got the arthritis and the weather's dry there." The woman handed Iris her bag and asked, "You goin' far?"

Iris stared at the clerk. The blinking Christmas lights were reflected on her cats-eye glasses. Finally she managed to say, "No . . . not far."

"Want a foil bag for the ice cream?" She reached under the counter and produced a bag.

Iris let out her breath. "No thanks."

"Gonna get a little snow tonight. Drive safe and Merry Christmas, honey."

"Same to you."

She moved stiffly to the exit. Walking to her car, she wondered if the woman was calling the police. She set the bag on the passenger seat. The baby stared out the back window as if watching the stars. She would lay low tonight. No more going out. She turned the heater on high and announced, "We're going home, honey."

Later, after the baby had been fed, the bottle heated in the microwave, she made a bed for him. First she removed a drawer from the motel bureau and lined it with a blanket. This she set on the opposite twin bed. The baby, in a blue fleece jumpsuit, clutched her fingers and gazed at her. Iris thought his high cheekbones reflected his Lapland ancestors, although the broad forehead was Frank's.

"I hope you have your grandpa's hair," she said, kissing the tiny fingers.

She'd felt awkward changing him; the new diapers had unfamiliar sticky tabs. After that she propped him in his carrier so he could watch her. In the tiny kitchenette she made a ham and cheese sandwich. She sat on the opposite bed and ate half, storing the rest in the mini refrigerator.

From time to time she got up to peek out the window. The same cars were in the lot, one near the dumpster, one parked in front of unit eight and one outside the office. The latter had a handicapped placard, no doubt the manager's. The car in front of unit eight was long and dark. Although lights showed from behind the room's curtains, no one appeared outside.

Before turning out the lights, she fed the baby the remaining formula. As she did, she rocked him in her arms, her gaze traveling around the room, taking in the faux wood furniture and mustard colored bedspreads. What a dreary place to spend Christmas Eve, she thought. She studied a painting above the dresser. It was a seascape, a desolate winter beach with leaden sky and stormy seas. A driftwood log lay rotting in the foreground. In the background a lone figure, his back to the viewer, contemplated the bleak horizon before him.

She glanced at the clock; it was eight forty-five. She longed to turn on the TV but at the same time was fearful of what she would learn. Tomorrow, when she felt stronger, she would watch the news. She would also call Grace and apologize.

Placing the baby in the makeshift bed, the thought flashed through her mind, What have I done? She had kidnapped a baby.

She wandered to the window and glanced out at the night sky. Where was the assurance she'd felt earlier, the feeling of certainty that she was rescuing her grandchild? Had her spirit guide abandoned her in a shabby off-season motel?

After checking the lock on the door, she kicked off her shoes and got into bed. The mattress was hard and thin, but she was exhausted. Fortunately, the baby was a good sleeper. She turned off the bedside lamp and lay huddled in the dark.

"Help me," she whispered, before falling asleep.

TWENTY-FOUR

Iris dreamed she was back at Sandpiper Beach, racing along the sand. A hurricane was fast approaching and she was desperate to reach the cottage before her family had evacuated. She ran into the wind, the salt spray stinging her eyes. She could barely make out the cottages lining the boulevard. Was she too late? Had everyone gone?

Finally she reached Laughing Water. She raced up the wooden steps and flung open the screen door. Inside was a scene of chaos: curtains billowing in the wind, the floorboards and furniture slick with sea spray. No one answered her call as she ran from room to room and finally up the stairs. The door to the bedroom she shared with Lily was closed. Iris opened it to find clothing and blankets in a tangle on the floor. Rain swept through an open window. As Iris struggled to close it, she spotted a seagull outside on the chimney, huddled against the wind.

"Where's Lily," she yelled. "Where's my family?"

The gull gave her a knowing look and flew off into the storm.

Now Iris sat up in the darkened motel room, her heart pounding. For a moment she thought she was at home until she glanced at the opposite bed. In the dimness she saw the boxy shape of the bureau drawer. She glanced at the lighted face of the clock. It was ten thirty; she'd slept for two hours.

She slid out of the narrow bed and stood over the baby, listening to his soft breathing. He was an excellent sleeper, Iris thought, unlike Shannon, who'd been colicky and fretful the first year of her life. Looking at the sleeping infant, Iris had an image of the woman in the flannel shirt standing at the door at Mighty Mart. She imagined her returning to the car and discovering an empty back seat.

What have I done, she thought, sinking onto the bed. For the first time she realized the enormity of her actions. She'd kidnapped someone's baby, on Christmas Eve no less. Crazy women do things like that, she thought, and wished she could rewind the last five hours of her life. She shouldn't have attended Janice's Christmas party. She'd gone because she felt obligated to Fatima and all the Camusos. After all, who was Iris to refuse their hospitality?

Now she stared at the sleeping infant. The strong kinship she had felt earlier had vanished, along with her bold assurance. Who was that crazy, impulsive woman? She'd heard of people who claimed they weren't in their right minds when they committed acts. Now she knew what they meant. But was it too late to somehow make it right?

I can do it, she thought, getting to her feet. She turned on the bedside lamp. She had a lot to do in the next hour . . .

Iris stopped the Jetta on the hill behind St. Anthony's rectory. She turned off the headlights and glanced at the dashboard clock. It was eleven twenty-five. The early bird parishioners would soon be arriving for midnight Mass. She quietly stepped out of the car and reached into the back for the carrier. It was wrapped in the motel's mustard yellow bedspread. The baby's eyes widened, seeing the flakes of snow tumbling down around them.

"You're safe," she whispered.

Cradling the carrier, she approached the low stone wall that bordered the church property. She sat and swung her legs over the side. From there she moved to stand at the top of a sloping hill. Iris knew it well. She and Lily, along with other neighborhood kids, had spent many afternoons sled-riding behind the church. If he spotted them, the elderly Father Sheehy would chase the kids away while Father Brendan, the young novitiate, would join them.

Phantom Baby

The grass covering the hill was slick with snow. She tentatively started down in a crouch, gripping the carrier. Slipping and sliding, they made it to the bottom. There she huddled behind a tree in the shadow of the rectory. She looked into the bright kitchen, straight ahead. Old Mrs. Duffy, the housekeeper, kneaded dough on a counter. Iris moved to the next tree, hiding in the shadows until she reached the side of the house.

There she stopped under the row of tall pines that separated the rectory from the church. The trees created a dramatic backdrop to show off St. Anthony's pride and joy—a four-foot-tall lighted Nativity. Ever since Iris could remember, the church had displayed this striking Christmas tableau.

After making sure no one was around, she stepped from the darkness under the pines and into the spotlight that illuminated the crèche. She knelt before the manger and gently set the swaddled carrier onto the straw near the wooden cradle. She glanced at the plaster figures of the animals, the lamb, sheep, a cow and a donkey. The expressions on their faces were benevolent, approving.

She leaned forward to kiss the baby. "Goodbye," she whispered. "Don't forget me."

At that moment headlights flashed in the parking lot. Parishioners were arriving. She leapt to her feet and raced back to the safety of the pines. Once inside the sheltering boughs, she waited for the churchgoers to arrive. The baby was front and center of the Nativity, not easy to miss.

She didn't have long to wait. A young couple, holding hands, approached the crèche on their way to the church. "Oh, look," the young woman said, leading her companion to the tableau, "that looks so real."

Seconds later their surprised voices rang out. Iris, who'd been holding her breath, exhaled and slipped away. She ran under the row of pines until she came to the bottom of the hill. She headed up, hand over hand, clutching at clumps of frozen grass with numbed fingers.

At the top, she paused to view the scene below. Snow fell on the small group that gathered around the nativity, their startled voices ringing in the cold air. Soon the side door of the rectory opened. The dark-robed figure of Father Gladioli strode out to join them.

Iris sighed with satisfaction. Wearily she climbed into the Jetta and drove away. When she reached the main road, she turned her headlights on.

Twenty-five minutes later she was back at The Laughing Gull. She decided to play it safe by parking on a side street. She walked the short distance to the motel. Outside of a dim light in the office and one in unit five, the place was in darkness.

She entered her room and slowly unbuttoned her coat. She kicked off the cold, sodden shoes and collapsed onto the bed. A glance at the bedside clock told her it was twelve-thirty, Christmas morning. She fell into a deep sleep.

TWENTY FIVE

The amplified voice blasted her from the depths of slumber: *"This is Lieutenant Boyle with the State Police. Please unlock your door and give up the child. You must cooperate."*

Iris opened her eyes. It wasn't a bad dream. The booming voice was coming from outside the motel door. She struggled out of bed and rushed to the window. A lanky, dark-haired Massachusetts State Trooper in high black boots and wearing the force's blue-gray uniform stood outside holding a bullhorn. Behind him were a half-dozen police cruisers from local towns. If that sight wasn't shocking enough, in the rear of the parking lot were three news vans with satellite dishes perched on their roofs.

She shook the sleep from her head. They think I have the baby, she thought, pressing her hands to her scalp. Don't they know he's been returned? She had witnessed the scene at St. Anthony's, the excited parishioners gathering around the baby. She'd seen Father Gladioli rushing out of the rectory. Hadn't they called the police?

She sat on her bed. Could it be the Harborvale Police had failed to notify the state police the baby was found? And why did they suspect her; she had been careful. Whatever the reason, Iris had to let the lieutenant know there was no baby in her room.

She went to the door and opened it an inch or two, keeping the chain on. "I have no baby," she shouted. "He's safe, at St. Anthony's Church." When there was no response, she opened the door and peeked out.

Lieutenant Boyle had turned to stare, a puzzled look in his blue eyes. Iris realized in that instant that his attention hadn't been on her motel door. No, his attention had been focused on unit eight. She slammed the door and locked it.

"Excuse me, ma'am," he called. "What is your name?"

"Shit," she whispered and quickly opened the door. "Don't mind me," she called out. "I was just dreaming." She gave a brief wave. "I'm going back to sleep now."

Before she could duck inside, the door of unit eight opened and Roland Smedlie emerged, clad in striped pajamas. "I thought that was you, Ms. Camuso," he called to her. "What're you doing here?"

She stared, her mouth open. Finally she said, "I'm escaping the holiday crowds, Roland. What are you doing here?"

"Me and Gloria were driving to Canada. I'm not going back to Standish Academy—"

"Don't say anything more—" Gloria, wearing a long belted robe, pushed past him to stand at the doorway, leaning on a cane.

Seeing her, the media people in the rear of the lot scurried forward, cameras whirring. Lieutenant Boyle motioned to the waiting officers to hold them back.

Gloria smiled ruefully. "I had no choice, Iris. I was afraid Roland would do something desperate. He'd made threats."

"I was gonna hitchhike to North Dakota and live on a reservation," Roland said, his eyes bright.

"I was only trying to protect him," Gloria said, shrugging. "I couldn't live with myself if he did something rash."

"We should have stolen a car," Roland said, producing a banana and peeling it. "The cops had an APB on the Buick."

"I don't regret it," Gloria said, her voice loud enough to reach the crowd gathered outside. "If it means saving a young man's life I'd do it again."

Iris, aware of the cameras aimed at them, shrank back. "I have to go now," she called to the pair. "Good luck."

She ducked inside, locked the door and leaned against it. Once again her impulsivity had gotten her in trouble. She should have kept her mouth shut. She'd assumed the police were outside because of the missing baby. All along it was Gloria and Roland they'd wanted. If she had turned on the TV earlier, perhaps she'd have known this.

Nonetheless, Lieutenant Boyle was not going to let her off easily. He called through the bullhorn. "Ms. Dutton, I need to talk to you. Please open your door."

Ms. Dutton?

Then Iris remembered signing the guest register. At the time it had been spontaneous, a joke. The trooper must have gotten her name from the motel manager. She sat on the bed and hugged herself. She could still emerge intact from this nightmare if she didn't lose her head.

As Iris pondered her next move, sounds of a skirmish were heard outside; shouts and hurried footsteps. She rushed to the window. Gloria and Roland, now in street clothes, were getting into the back of a police car amid an explosion of flash bulbs. Roland grinned, enjoying the attention while Gloria, looking stern in dark glasses, kept her head down. The camera crews chased the car as it drove out of the lot. A convoy of police cars followed, their lights flashing.

She had little time to think before the bullhorn broke the silence. "Ms. Dutton, I suggest you cooperate with the authorities."

Damn. Lieutenant Boyle hadn't gone with the others. Iris rose and opened the door. "I have nothing to say," she called out. "It's Christmas and I've done nothing wrong. Please leave me alone."

She shut the door and stood in the middle of the room. She knew her rights. She didn't have to let them into her room without a warrant. If she voluntarily let them in, they'd find the evidence—the leftover baby food, the diaper bag and its contents. She couldn't flush it all down the toilet.

Yet by not letting them in, she looked guilty. On the other hand, maybe they weren't connecting her to the baby's disappearance. Maybe they thought she was involved with Gloria's attempted escape. After all, she was Ms. Dutton, vice-principal at Roland's former school. What a coincidence; she had taken a room off-season next to the pair.

In any event, she needed to secure her room for her own

peace of mind. She examined the old wooden bureau against the wall. It was heavy, yet she could nudge it along to the door. It would provide a barricade should the cops try to bust in without a search warrant.

Twenty minutes later the bureau was blocking her door. She went to the window and peeked outside. Lieutenant Boyle remained in the parking lot. Most of the police and news people had fled, chasing Roland and Gloria. The one remaining news van, parked in the rear of the lot, was from KLAM, the local cable station. News anchor Myranda Trowt, daughter of the middle-school secretary, stood opposite a cameraman, talking into a microphone.

For the first time since she arrived at the motel, Iris reached for the TV remote. She clicked on channel eleven, local TV. Myranda appeared on the screen wearing furry red earmuffs and a tight red sweater. Behind her was The Laughing Gull motel sign. She said excitedly, "It's Christmas Day, nineteen ninety-nine, in Harborvale, where two local families got the best gift of all, the return of their kidnapped children."

The scene cut away to a clip of Roland and Gloria getting into the cruiser. "Around noon today, fifty-eight year-old Gloria Demaso, Roland Smedlie's alleged abductor, was taken to State Police headquarters. At the same time, the boy's parents, Dr. and Mrs. Smedlie, were reunited with their son." The next scene showed the scowling Smedlies alighting from their Mercedes while surrounded by newspeople. "When asked if they plan to press charges against Demaso, the couple declined to comment."

The camera returned to Myranda's red-cheeked face. "Another happy Harborvale mom is Dolores Fetchko. The Grinch that stole baby Garrett from his babysitter's car at Mighty Mart"—an exterior shot of the convenience store flashed on the screen— "returned him four hours later. He was found unharmed at the crèche on the grounds of St. Anthony's Church."

Now a beaming Father Gladioli stood with Myranda on the church steps. "What can I say on this most blessed day," the priest said into the mike. "God works in mysterious ways."

Myranda spoke into the mike, saying, "Dolores Fetchko's

neighbors have been celebrating baby Garrett's safe return." The screen cut to a low-ceilinged kitchen where a woman, pale and slight, held a sleeping baby in her arms. All around her were people drinking from cups and toasting each other.

Myranda intoned, "When asked if she was bringing charges against her negligent baby-sitter, Ms. Fetchko said she was just grateful for the safe return of her son."

Now Myranda stood in front of the motel. "There you have it, folks, a Harborvale holiday to remember. Who would think this sleepy little town would experience two simultaneous kidnappings?"

She turned to glance up at the sign. "At the moment The Laughing Gull is quiet, although police officials remain behind. Sources say one of the guests is a person of interest. Whether the guest was involved in a kidnapping hasn't been determined. In any case, stay tuned for the latest update on this extraordinary day. I'm Myranda Trowt from KLAM News, reporting from Sandpiper Creek in Harborvale."

Iris clicked off the TV and stared at the screen. She had brought this upon herself by inadvertently tipping off the authorities. Were they going to arrest her? Lieutenant Boyle's presence suggested it. Perhaps he was awaiting a search warrant to enter her room. His voice interrupted her rumination. "Ms. Camuso, you must be hungry by now. We've got an order of crab cakes here for you. Someone said it's your favorite dish."

Iris leaped from the chair. He knew her name, but how did her know about the crab cakes? She shoved the bureau back a couple of inches, enough to open the door. "Who told you that?" she called out.

"Your daughter," he responded. His voice wasn't amplified. "She wants to personally deliver the order."

Iris gnawed on her thumb. It had to be a cop trick. Otherwise, how did Shannon know she was at the motel? She moved to the window and peeked from behind the curtain. In the parking lot, Shannon stood next to the tall trooper. She held a Styrofoam container.

"Good Lord," Iris muttered. She opened the door an inch,

keeping the chain in place. "Is my daughter alone?" she called.

"She's alone. She wants to come in."

"Just a minute." Iris leaned against the bureau and pushed it a foot away from the door. Then she called out, "Tell her she's to come alone."

Minutes later she heard outside the door, "Mom?"

Iris checked to be sure Shannon was alone before releasing the chain and opening the door. "Help me push this back, will you?"

Together they moved the bureau-barricade back in place. Iris sank onto the bed, panting. Shannon handed her the still-warm container. "I told them it's your favorite."

Iris stared at the container, unable to look at Shannon. "How did you know I was here?"

Grace called me," Shannon said. "She recognized you on TV."

"Oh my God. I was on TV?" Then she remembered talking to Gloria while the cameras whirred. "Shannon, if you've come to lecture, you can forget it. I've done nothing wrong."

Shannon sat on the opposite bed. "I came because Grace called me. She thinks you're drinking and in trouble. When that newscaster mentioned the motel guest left behind, Grace thought it was you and you're involved in the kidnapping." When Iris didn't answer, Shannon said, "Grace said he's one of your students."

"He was," Iris said. "It's a coincidence that he and Gloria happened to be staying at the same motel. I was shocked, seeing them. I hadn't been watching TV and didn't know about them running away." A silence fell between them. She gestured to the kitchen. "I've got Diet Coke in the fridge."

"I'm fine," Shannon stood and removed her navy pea coat. Under it she wore jeans and a form-fitting jersey. "Lieutenant Boyle's been awfully patient. If you've got nothing to hide, why don't you talk to him?"

"I see no reason why I should," Iris said. "I've done nothing wrong." She sat up straight and said, "Why are you here, Shannon? You've been avoiding me for months."

She shrugged. "Grace thought you might need a liaison with the police."

"Like I said, I've done nothing wrong. It's a bizarre coincidence with Roland and Gloria. However, I had nothing to do with that."

"Maybe so, but it looks suspicious. You used to be his counselor. You rent a room next door and you were seen talking to them. The police will put two and two together." Shannon's gaze took in the shabby room. "If you wanted to drink, why didn't you do it at home?"

"I wasn't drinking here," Iris said, her voice loud. "It's the first Christmas without your father and I needed a break, a change of scene. Is that a crime?"

Shannon stared at the floor. "You know, when I heard about the baby's kidnapping at Mighty Mart, I thought you were involved. Don't ask me why. I couldn't get the idea out of my head, so I called Grace. She was worried. You were supposed to go to her house last night and you didn't show up." Shannon leaned forward and looked at Iris. "Is it true? Did you take that baby?"

Iris moved to stand in front of the curtained window. "I don't owe you an explanation, not the way you've treated me." When Shannon didn't respond, Iris said quietly, "I thought it was my grandchild. When he looked at me, I knew we belonged together—"

The voice from outside startled them. "Shannon, this is Lieutenant Boyle. Is everything all right in there?"

Shannon moved to the window and pushed back the curtain. She made a thumbs-up gesture and returned to the bed. "Go ahead, finish your story."

"That's all," Iris said, embarrassed by her disclosure. "I saw the baby's picture on TV, you see, and for a moment thought it was my grandchild." She attempted a smile. "I certainly hoped it wasn't. That poor thing was left unattended in a smoke-filled car."

"How do you know?" Shannon asked. "The news reports never mentioned that."

"The babysitter went inside for cigarettes. She's obviously a smoker." Shannon nodded, looking unconvinced. Iris leaned forward. "Shannon, where is our baby? I've felt his presence—"

"The baby is in Ohio, with wonderful people. The father's a pediatrician and the mother's a cardiologist. I met them. You couldn't ask for better parents."

"Ohio," Iris said and sighed. "I was so sure he was nearby." She covered her face and cried.

Shannon watched for a moment. Then she got up and went into the bathroom, returning with a handful of tissues. She sat next to Iris on the bed, pressing the tissues into her hand. After a while, Iris wiped her eyes and asked in a shaky voice, "Why didn't you let me adopt him?"

"Mom, I made the right decision."

"Why not me? You know I'd love him."

She sighed. "I'd be reminded every day that he was mine, and my responsibility. I'd feel guilty for wanting more from life. Eventually I'd resent him. Maybe I'm selfish, but I decided to put myself first."

She paused and continued, "If I stayed at home my life wouldn't change. I'd never have gone to nursing school or lived on my own. The adoption agency gave me a chance for a new beginning. In order to do that, I had to sever all ties."

"But I was there all alone—"

"Mom, you were more alone when Dad was living at home. You just didn't realize it." Shannon rose and put on her coat. "That's all I'll say about the baby. Giving him away was the hardest thing I've ever done." She picked up Iris's coat from a chair and handed it to her. "Lieutenant Boyle and a photographer are waiting outside. It's Christmas. Let's not make them wait any longer."

"Photographer? I can't go out there with a photographer."

"Mom, you're innocent, remember? The cops will probably question you about Gloria. Call your lawyer. He'll straighten it out."

Iris took a deep breath. "I guess I'm ready." She looked around the room. "If you don't mind, I'll leave the crab cakes behind. I don't want to be photographed holding a Styrofoam container."

Together they pushed the bureau back to its original spot against the wall. Shannon stood before the door and looked at her mother. "Are you ready?"

"Do I look okay?" Iris smoothed her hair.

"You're fine." Shannon opened the door.

The photo that appeared in *The Barnacle* showed mother and daughter standing shoulder to shoulder in the motel room doorway. The brief story accompanying the photo told of Iris's alleged involvement in the Smedlie kidnapping and subsequent clearing of her name. "It's an amazing coincidence," lawyer Vincent Tosi was quoted as saying.

TWENTY-SIX

Lucy, the oldest of the three Camuso aunties, had gallbladder surgery at Harborvale Hospital. On her third day home, a visitor filled her in on the latest gossip. Her top story was Iris's involvement—or noninvolvement, depending on one's point of view—in the Roland Smedlie kidnapping. Lucy immediately called Iris, demanding to know what happened.

After giving the woman a bare-bones account, Iris concluded, saying, "Basically, I was at the wrong motel at the wrong time."

Lucy sighed. "None of this would have happened if Francis was still alive. I'm glad his mother isn't here. This would have killed her."

"I was an innocent bystander," Iris reminded her. "My lawyer straightened it all out."

"Is that the Tosi boy?"

"That's right," Iris said.

"I know his mother. She goes to my rosary group. What will happen to that crazy woman?"

"What crazy woman?" Iris said, although knowing whom Lucy was referring to. She and Vincent had been discussing Gloria that morning during a phone call.

"I just wanted to fill you in on the hearing," he said. "You may have to testify as a witness, but it's pretty cut and dried. Gloria lucked out big time. Kidnapping's a federal offense. She was looking at time in the slammer."

"You mean there won't be a trial?"

"The Smedlies aren't pressing charges," he said. "They

know a trial would be a three-ring circus. Without their testimony, the Commonwealth's case against Gloria falls apart."

"Vincent, that's great news. So what will happen at the hearing?"

"Basically, it's a formality. Gloria will be seen as a sympathetic character. She meant well. Probably she'll get probation, providing she has nothing more to do with the kid. The Smedlies are moving to Boston. Roland will be home schooled."

Iris smiled. "That's what he's wanted from the beginning."

"I just hope Gloria respects the Smedlies' restraining order. That ditzy broad tries to contact the kid, she'll find herself in Framingham Women's Prison."

"No contact at all?"

"None, until he turns eighteen. Then he makes his own choices." He paused. "You don't think there was anything *funny* going on?"

"I doubt it. When I first met Roland, I wondered why a young boy would spend so much time with an older person. Until I saw the two of them together. Gloria gave him something he'd never gotten, her unconditional approval. She appreciated Roland the way he was. It's only natural to seek the light."

"Sound screwy to me," Vincent said.

Now Aunt Lucy, determined to set Iris straight asked, "Have you gone back to your job? Idle hands are the devil's workshop, you know."

"I've been volunteering at the women's shelter downtown. I like it. Matter of fact, I'm thinking of going back to school, getting a doctorate in counseling."

"That's a tough crowd at that shelter. Our church group used to help Father Gladioli take Communion over there. Such awful language from those girls."

"I can identify with them," Iris said. "They're adrift on a perilous sea."

"I thought you liked working with children," Lucy said. "Did you lose your job at the school?"

"They didn't fire me, Aunt Lucy. I've done nothing wrong, remember?"

Tomas had informed Iris that he'd fight to save her position. He didn't mention that Ms. Dutton had threatened to file suit against Iris for defamation of character and other charges, should Iris attempt to return. Ms. Dutton had been outraged by Iris's signing her name on the motel's guest registry and the resulting publicity.

"I have told everyone you are innocent of any wrongdoing," Tomas assured her.

Grateful for his support, Iris thanked him. At the same time she said it wasn't necessary; she was going back to school. "I've got the means and the time to get this degree. I want to work with women who've lost their way."

"You will bring them much warmth and kindness," Tomas said.

Iris heard the relief in his voice. "How's Aidita?" she asked.

"My sister has met a man, Mr. Fritz, a widower whose children attend the Tiny Tots school."

"I'm happy for her."

He cleared his throat. "The school frowns on teachers fraternizing with parents. Thus I'm afraid Aidita and Mr. Fritz have been meeting secretly." He paused and added, "Keep this under your hair. I don't approve, but my sister does not listen to her brother."

When they ended their conversation, Tomas didn't mention getting together. Iris wasn't surprised. She had heard he was being considered for the superintendent's post. As a candidate, Tomas's reputation wouldn't benefit from associating with Iris.

Lucy had to end their conversation. The visiting nurse had arrived. "Goodbye, Iris, dear. Have lunch with me at the senior center. We can bring a guest once a month."

"Thanks, Aunt Lucy. Thanks for asking."

After hanging up, Iris stood at the window, looking out. Patticake lay curled on the hood of her car. The afternoon sun was melting the snow that had fallen the night before. Iris listened to the steady drip-drip of the icicles at the window.

She was about to turn away when a dark green Jeep pulled into the driveway. She waited for the driver to back out as they often did, having mistaken her road for the downtown access route. However, the Jeep continued up the drive, stopping behind the Jetta.

A tall, lanky figure dressed in jeans, shoe-boots, and a navy windbreaker got out. Tucked under his arm was a white paper bag. He navigated the slushy path to the side door. Iris opened the door a few inches and peered out. "Lieutenant Boyle, I didn't recognize you out of uniform."

"I take it off now and then," he said, smiling. He handed her the paper bag. "I figured you might need this. The department just released it. They're kind of slow."

She glanced inside. "My makeup case. I guess I left it behind at the motel." She blushed at the reference to the Christmas Day fiasco.

"I was going this way and thought I'd drop it off."

"Actually, I went out and replaced everything." This seemed an ungrateful remark, so she added, "But that's okay. I can always use more." She shielded her eyes and looked up at him. "Thank you for delivering this, and thank you for . . . for being patient with me at the motel." She shrugged. "It wasn't my finest hour."

"I've learned a few things about you from your records. What caught my eye was the fact you'd lost a younger sister in childhood."

She nodded.

"That stayed with me. You see, I had a similar experience. I lost my kid brother."

"How did it happen?"

"We were shooting baskets in our driveway when he collapsed. Matt was small for his age. I was always after him to build up his strength. That afternoon he couldn't keep up. I teased him, called him a wimp." He looked away. "His heart gave out. The doctors claimed he had a defective valve, said he'd probably had it since birth."

She nodded. "It was the same with Lily. We were riding bikes one day, up a big hill. She tried to keep up with me. I didn't slow down for her. I kept on going." She looked at him. "Tell me, do you dream about your brother?"

"All the time."

They stood in silence until she said, "Lieutenant, would you like a cup of coffee?"

"Yes, I'd like that."

"I'm sorry I can't offer beer or wine."

"Coffee's fine, Ms. Camuso."

"It's Iris."

He held out his hand. "I'm Tim."

She stood back and held the door open. "Come in."

Lena Camuso's Haddock Chowder

1 lb Haddock or other mild white fish

1 can evaporated milk

1/2 medium onion, chopped

2 stalks celery, chopped

a few sprigs of parsley, chopped

2 med. potatoes, peeled somewhat (ok to leave some skin)

1 or 2 slices of bacon

1 bay leaf

2 tsp dried thyme (crushed between fingers)

1 chicken bouillon cube

2 tbl cornstarch

generous splash Worcestershire sauce

salt and pepper to taste

Directions:

In a tall pot, cook bacon until crisp. Remove bacon and drain on a paper towel. Save some drippings in pan. Add one tbl olive or vegetable oil Cook the onion and celery until tender. Cut potatoes into bite size pieces and put in pot. Add enough water to cover potatoes. Simmer until tender, about 15 or 20 minutes. Add fish to pot. Add evaporated milk, bouillon cube and l cup of water. Add bay leaf, thyme, salt and pepper and Worcestershire. Let fish come to a gentle boil and simmer until tender, 15 to 20 minutes. Very gently break up fish. Add cornstarch to 1/2 cup of milk (or cream for extra richness) Stir briskly until smooth and slowly add to pot. Add chopped parsley and a pat of butter. Let chowder simmer. You can thicken with more cornstarch if desired and adjust seasoning. As with any soup, chowder will taste better the following day.

Made in the USA
Lexington, KY
10 March 2017